THE DARKLING
CHILD

BY TERRY BROOKS

Shannara
First King of Shannara
The Sword of Shannara
The Elfstones of Shannara
The Wishsong of Shannara

The Heritage of Shannara
The Scions of Shannara
The Druid of Shannara
The Elf Queen of Shannara
The Talismans of Shannara

The Voyage of the Jerle Shannara
Ilse Witch
Antrax
Morgawr

High Druid of Shannara
Jarka Ruus
Tanequil
Straken

Genesis of Shannara
Armageddon's Children
The Elves of Cintra
The Gypsy Morph

Legends of Shannara
Bearers of the Black Staff
The Measure of the Magic

The Magic Kingdom of Landover
Magic Kingdom for Sale—Sold!
The Black Unicorn
Wizard at Large
The Tangle Box
Witches' Brew
A Princess of Landover

The Word and the Void
Running with the Demon
A Knight of the Word
Angel Fire East

The Dark Legacy of Shannara
Vol. 1: Wards of Faerie
Vol. 2: Bloodfire Quest
Vol. 3: Witch Wraith

The Defenders of Shannara
The High Druid's Blade
The Darkling Child

THE DEFENDERS of
SHANNARA

TERRY
BROOKS

THE DARKLING
CHILD

orbit

www.orbitbooks.net

ORBIT

First published in Great Britain in 2015 by Orbit

1 3 5 7 9 10 8 6 4 2

Copyright © 2015 by Terry Brooks

Map copyright © 2012 by Russ Charpentier

The moral right of the author has been asserted.

A CIP catalogue record for this book
is available from the British Library.

HB ISBN 978-0-356-50219-9
C format 978-0-356-50220-5

Printed and bound in Great Britain by
Clays Ltd, St Ives plc

MIX
Paper from
responsible sources
FSC® C104740

Papers used by Orbit are from well-managed forests
and other responsible sources.

Orbit
An imprint of
Little, Brown Book Group
100 Victoria Embankment
London EC4Y 0DY

An Hachette UK Company
www.hachette.co.uk

www.orbitbooks.net

For Anne Groell,
who keeps me honest in all the best ways

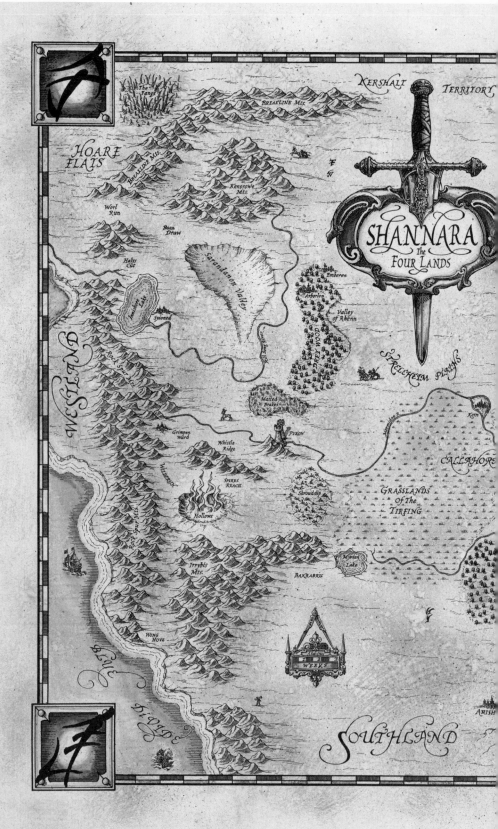

I

PAXON LEAH WAS SITTING ON A BENCH IN THE courtyard gardens of Paranor, paging through documents written more than five hundred years earlier that recorded the events in the life of the Elf King Eventine Elessedil, when Keratrix came for him. He could tell immediately from the scribe's solemn face that something was wrong.

"She's asking for you," the other said without preamble. His eyes seemed tired and haunted. "She says it's time."

Paxon stared. On a beautiful, sunny day like this one? On a day when everything felt right, and it seemed that the world was at peace and life could go on indefinitely? How could this be?

That was what he thought as he measured the scribe's words and let their meaning sink in. He didn't have to ask what Keratrix meant. He knew. He had known this was coming. She had told him so herself.

Aphenglow Elessedil, Ard Rhys of the Fourth Druid Order, was dying.

He rose at once, wordless and shaken, and followed Keratrix from the gardens into the tower that housed her private chambers. The Ard Rhys kept to herself these days, weakened by age and worn down by both the demands of her office and the passage of time. She was housed on the lower floors, no longer able to handle the stairs and the climb that going to her former chambers and to the upper reaches of the main tower required. She had not been in the cold room in over a year. She had not used the scrye waters once in all that time, relying instead on her chosen successor, Isaturin, to carry out her duties. She was in stasis, waiting for the inevitable. If the truth were told, Paxon believed, she was anxious for it to arrive.

And now, apparently, it had.

"Is she sure?" he asked Keratrix as they walked. When he looked at the young Druid, he was reminded of Sebec. Five years earlier, Sebec—then scribe of the Druid order—had been his closest friend at Paranor, and the betrayal of that friendship was a wound that still burned in his memory.

Keratrix—slight and small, scarcely a presence as he wafted ahead of Paxon like a wraith in the shadowed hallways—barely turned. "She insists she is quite sure. I asked this, as well."

Of course he would. Keratrix was efficient and thorough; he would not leave something like this undone.

"I can't believe it," Paxon whispered, almost to himself, though he knew Keratrix must have heard.

And he could not. Five years he had spent as the personal paladin of the Ard Rhys, as the High Druid's Blade. She had brought him to Paranor at a time when he was drifting. She had offered him the position in large part because of his heritage as a bearer of the magical Sword of Leah. She had given him over to training and had kept watch from a distance as he struggled to find his place. When his sister Chrysallin had been taken by the sorcerer Arcannen, Aphenglow was the one who had helped him to get Chrys back and then found a home for her at Paranor—even though Chrysallin had been sent to kill her and had almost succeeded. And all the while, she had been beset by Sebec's betrayal and Arcannen's scheming to gain control of the order.

But perhaps even more important than that, she had taken Chrysallin into the order as a student in training, aware of the importance of the gift she possessed and the need to find a way to manage it. For like her brother, Chrysallin Leah bore a legacy of magic. Paxon's was the ability to unlock the power of the Sword of Leah. Chrysallin's was the presence of the wishsong, which she had inherited as a direct descendant of Railing Ohmsford. However, Chrys remained unaware of her powers. Arcannen had kidnapped her in an attempt to use her as a weapon against the Ard Rhys, but the subsequent trauma of the events that followed had wiped away any memory of those powers. Still, Aphenglow was convinced that her memory would eventually return.

So she had let Chrysallin remain at Paranor, keeping close watch over her and waiting for the moment when her magic would resurface and she could be given over to members of the order who would help her learn to master it—who would train her in its usage and teach her of the importance it held not only in her own life but in the lives of those around her.

So far, that moment had not arrived. To this day, Chrysallin remembered nothing, and no sign of the magic had reappeared. Now, as the Ard Rhys prepared for the end of her life, the task of watching over his sister would fall to Paxon. He was ready to accept this, he believed. More ready than he was for what waited just ahead.

As they neared the entry to Aphenglow Elessedil's room, the door opened and Isaturin appeared. Tall, gaunt, strong-featured, and steady in his gaze, he seemed lessened in all aspects as he approached Paxon. Undoubtedly, he was coming to terms with what the Ard Rhys's passing would mean for him. He was her designated successor, the next Ard Rhys, and the new High Druid of what would continue as the Fourth Druid Order. He had known of his future for many years; she had made certain of it. But it was one thing to know what lay ahead of you and another altogether to have it standing there at your doorstep.

"She is waiting for you, Paxon," Isaturin said, slowing to meet him. "She doesn't have much time, and the journey ahead of us is a long one."

Paxon stared. "Journey? Do you mean her dying?"

Isaturin shook his head. "No, not that. She will explain. Hurry now. No lingering."

He moved away, leaving the Highlander looking after him in confusion.

Keratrix touched his arm. "Go in, Paxon. I'll wait out here."

Paxon went to the door, knocked softly, and heard her voice in response. Though he could not understand her words, he took a deep breath and entered anyway.

"Paxon," she greeted him.

That single word almost undid him. Everything she meant to him, everything she had done for him, all they had shared together seemed caught up in the moment. Memories flooded through him, some sad, some happy, all incredibly vivid—a jumble of connections realized in seconds. He stood where he was, weathering the onslaught, frozen in place.

Then he looked up from the spot on the floor to which his gaze had fastened and saw her. Whatever he had expected to find, it wasn't this. She was sitting up in her favorite chair, a blanket spread across her knees and her hands in her lap, clasped together. She looked old, but not sick; worn, but not broken. Her face radiated strength and certainty, and she had about her an aura of invincibility that caused him to blink in disbelief.

"You thought perhaps to find me abed and failing?" she asked. "You thought I might be breathing my last?"

He nodded, unable to speak.

"It doesn't work that way. High Druids go to their end with some measure of dignity and strength so they can face what awaits. Sit with me."

He took the chair across from her. "You don't look as if you are dying," he admitted. "You look very well, Mistress."

Her face was lined by her years and the stresses and struggles she had endured and survived. She was very thin, and her skin had the look of parchment wrapped about bones. He had seen pictures of her when she was young—portraits and sketches executed by Druids who possessed such skills as would allow them to capture her image accurately. It was said she had been beautiful—tall and strong, a warrior Elf and the descendant of Elven Kings and Queens. He could see traces of that in her even now—small indicators of what she had been years ago.

"Kind words, Paxon. But in spite of what you think you see, my passing is at hand. I must go to my rest in the way of all leaders of the order—and for that, I require your company. I wish you to make the journey with me to the Valley of Shale and the Hadeshorn, where I will be met and taken home. I would like to leave at once. Though I may look strong, I can feel myself failing. It is a scary thing to be strong one moment and know that in the next your life will be over. Will you accompany me?"

"Of course," he said at once. "Should I arrange transport?" He paused. "What happens once we get there?"

She gave him that old, familiar smile. "Best wait and see for yourself. I am not as certain of it as I would like to be. And don't give any further thought to arranging for an airship. Isaturin is taking care of that now. Just sit with me. Keep me company."

Paxon sat back. "Do the others in the Druid order know this is happening?"

She shook her head. "Keratrix will tell them once I am gone. If he tells them now, there will be an unending line of mourners and well-wishers, and I don't think I can bear that. I want to depart this world quietly. When my sister Arling left me all those years ago—when she embraced the fate decreed for her and transformed into the Ellcrys—well, that was quite enough trauma and emotional turmoil for several lifetimes. My departure will be considerably less dramatic."

She gave a deep sigh and leaned back. "Ah, Arling, I wish I could come to you one last time." She closed her eyes, and tears streaked her cheeks. Then she wiped them away unself-consciously and smiled at Paxon. "I have never gotten over losing her. Not even after all these years."

Paxon shifted uneasily, not knowing what to say.

"I have revealed the situation with Chrysallin to Isaturin as the next head of the order," she said. "I have told him of my fears and of my plans for her should her memory of the wishsong resurface. He will act in my place as her mentor and teacher when it becomes necessary. But I rely mostly on you to keep watch over her, Paxon. You are closest to her and likely to notice first if any changes occur. She will be safe at Paranor from everything save herself. You must help her with that."

"I will," he promised.

She straightened, and for a moment he thought she intended to rise. But she remained seated and added, "At some point, Chrysallin will discover the truth. I am convinced of it. I don't know what effect it will have on her, but you need to be there to help her through it. So don't fool yourself into thinking this will never happen. I worry that your decision not to tell her is more an avoidance than a kindness. You hope she will never remember what happened to her, what she had to do to save herself. But she will, Paxon. One day, she will. Don't fail in this. Tell her soon. Chrysallin's power is well documented in the records, and it is a powerful and sometimes unpredictable weapon."

He leaned forward. "I have been considering it. I am aware of the arguments for why I should tell her now. But I cannot get past the danger it poses if I am wrong."

She studied him a moment. "I know you would like this to simply go away, but I don't think you can depend on that. So telling her in advance might be best. Use your good judgment on how to go about it if you decide to do so. She will listen to you. She adores you. Five years ago, it would have been hard to reveal the truth to her. But now she is grown; she is a woman, and her strength and maturity are much greater than when she first came to us."

He found himself amazed that Aphenglow Elessedil would take the time and effort to try to help with his sister when there was so much else she might be doing. But she was still Ard Rhys of the Fourth Druid Order, and she would have her priorities firmly in hand even at the end of her life. She would not deviate from who she had been and what she had done for well over a hundred years. That was her nature, a direct result of the demands of her position. She would want to set her house in order.

"I owe you so much," he said, the words escaping him before he could think better of them. "You've given me this life, and I will never forget that."

"You earned what you have, Paxon," she said quietly. "No need to thank me for that."

He basked in her smile. "Can I bring you something to drink? Or eat? Before we set out?"

She shook her head. "We are not sitting here so that you can do something for me. We are here so that I can do something for you. Part of it is warning you of the risk to your sister. Another is warning you to beware of Arcannen. Do not think him gone for good—no more than Chrysallin's wishsong. He is a dangerous man with a long memory. He will be back for you and for Chrys. He will not tolerate leaving what you cost him unavenged. He will not be able to live with the humiliation and regret. When you least expect it, he will surface again, and he will seek to exact a price for what he has suffered."

"I am not afraid of him," Paxon declared at once.

"You should be. He nearly undid the Druid order before you stopped him. He is capable of great evil. Watch out for him. Be careful of yourself and your sister."

She paused. "One last thing. Isaturin will need time to learn his place as Ard Rhys. No one can prepare for this until they hold the office. It was so for me; it will be so for him. Help him adjust. Give him your support. Keep him safe. You are fully grown into your paladin shoes, a young man with great skill and the good sense to know how to use it. Make use of it for him. Be his right hand and protector in these early months of his service to the order. Now take my arm."

She reached out, and he rose quickly to assist her. Her arm caught hold of his and she levered herself to her feet smoothly, suddenly seeming younger and stronger. She smiled at the look on his face.

"Now we can go," she said.

2

WITH KERATRIX GUIDING THE WAY AND PAXON lending support, Aphenglow Elessedil walked down the corridors and passageways of the Druid's Keep toward the airship platform off the north tower. A few Druids passed them on their way, pausing to offer greetings to which the Ard Rhys dutifully replied before continuing on. A suggestion of haste marked her progress—and in truth haste defined the nature of her leaving, no matter how you looked at it.

She deviated from her path only once. Pausing at the door that opened out onto the landing platform and the waiting airship, she gestured Keratrix away, standing silently with Paxon as she awaited her aide's return. The seconds slipped by in slow procession, the measure of her life steadily shortening. More than once, the Highlander thought to speak with her, but something in her demeanor kept him from doing so. She was alone with her thoughts, and he sensed that, for now, she wanted it that way.

When Keratrix returned, he had Chrysallin in tow.

Paxon's sister rushed ahead of the scribe toward Aphenglow, all protocol and formality abandoned as they embraced. Chrysallin began to cry, her face stricken.

"Don't go, Mistress," she sobbed. "Don't leave us!"

"You've guessed, then," Aphenglow replied, taking her by the shoulders and moving her away so she could look at her. "You are always so quick to know the truth. It will serve you well."

Chrysallin seemed to make a monumental effort to get her tears under control, straightening herself, becoming composed. She was tall and slender, her girlishness gone—a young woman now, strong and steady, her path through the world determined. "Is there nothing that can be done?" she asked the Ard Rhys quietly.

"All that can be done has been. What happens now is preordained. I leave because it is time. My life has been long and full. Do not grieve for me. Celebrate me in your memories."

Paxon's sister glanced at him beseechingly for help, then found the answer in his eyes to her unspoken need and nodded slowly. "I will never forget what you have done for me," she said finally. "I will celebrate you in my memories, but mostly in my heart."

Aphenglow smiled. "That makes me very happy. Now, give heed to me this final time. Should you need counseling at any point, on any matter, speak to Paxon. And listen to your brother. He is there for you if you should need him. He has sworn to me it will be so—though I am certain he would be there for you even without his vow to me. But there may come a time when life becomes so difficult you cannot bear it. If that happens, lean on him."

"I will, Mistress. I promise."

"That's a promise I will hold you to." The older woman leaned forward and kissed her on both cheeks. "Good-bye, Chrysallin."

Once through the door and atop the landing platform, the Ard Rhys and her attendants moved to the fast clipper that Isaturin had prepared and by which he stood waiting. He was to come with Paxon on this journey, and only the two of them would witness Aphenglow's passing from the Four Lands. The Captain of the Druid Guard, Dajoo Rees, and his Troll companions were already aboard and would act as crew. To all who might witness it, this leaving appeared to be just another of many, and not the last. Only the handful gathered at the airship knew the truth.

At the ramp prepared for her boarding, Aphenglow turned to Keratrix and took his hands. "Good-bye to you, young one. You were everything I could have hoped for in a scribe and a confidant in these final years. I hope you will think well of me once I am gone, and that you will remember I tried to be kind to you."

"You were unfailingly kind, Mistress," the scribe managed to say before breaking down.

She took him by his shoulders and hugged him momentarily before turning back to Paxon. "Help me to board," she ordered.

It was done in moments. Standing with the Ard Rhys and Isaturin, Paxon watched the Trolls raise the light sheaths and release the mooring lines. He heard the diapson crystals begin to power up, snugged down in their parse tubes, warm with the flow of energy siphoned down by the radian draws. He watched the sails billow out in the midday breeze, and then they were lifting away, rising into clouds banked overhead, thick and fluffy against a deep blue sky. Below, Paranor's walls and towers grew small against the green of the surrounding forests, and as the airship shifted course south, they faded and were gone.

"The last time," Aphenglow whispered, mostly to herself, though Paxon heard the words clearly.

Isaturin moved away toward the bow, leaving the Ard Rhys with the Highlander. Paxon watched him go. He had noted the other's deep reticence during their boarding, and he believed the High Druid was dealing with these final hours in the best way he knew how—but still he was struggling, his path uncertain. Paxon could not blame him. His own emotions were edgy and raw, his sense of place and time rocked by his own reluctance to accept the inevitable.

The airship flew south toward the Kennon Pass, navigated the narrow fissure that split the Dragon's Teeth, and descended into the borderlands of Callahorn before turning east to follow the wall of the mountains, tracking the blue ribbon of the Mermidon River far below. No one spoke, himself included. There was a surreal aspect to what was happening, a sense of suspension of time as they made their passage. The day eased through the afternoon and on toward sunset, but even knowing their destination did nothing to help dispel the unreality that wrapped the cause of their journey. Paxon kept thinking the same thing, unable to absorb the words fully, incapable of finding a way to accept them.

The Ard Rhys is dying. We are taking her to her final resting place. After today, she will be gone forever.

There had never been a time in the collective memory of living men and women when Aphenglow Elessedil hadn't been a part of their lives. She had been as immutable and enduring as the land itself—a presence unaltered by events or the passing of the years. That she would one day die was inevitable, but it always felt as if it would never be this day, or the next, or any day soon. The constancy of her presence was reassuring and, in some sense, necessary. Her life had been a gift. Her tenure as Ard Rhys had been marked by accomplishment. She had been instrumental in saving the Four Lands from the creatures of the Forbidding when they had broken free. She had reformed the shattered Druid order when all but two were killed and made it stronger and more effective than it had been in years past. She had brokered a peace that had lasted for more than a century between the Federation and the other governments of the Four Lands. She had made the Druids relevant and acceptable again in the eyes of the Races.

Her entire life had been given over to her duties as Ard Rhys. There had been two men in her life, but both had come to her in her early years, and both had been all too quickly lost. It was said that the loss of her sister Arling had been even worse, leaving her so bereft she had never been able to love again, and had supplanted that need with a deeply ingrained dedication to her work. It was said that, with her own family lost, the Druids had become her family.

All this Paxon Leah had gleaned from stories told and writings read—from Druids and common folk alike—and instinctively he knew it to be true. Knowing her confirmed most of it. The rest only added trappings to the legend she had become, wrapped in a mantle of history that would remain long after she was gone, survived by a legacy that would now be passed on to Isaturin. Paxon wondered at what this must feel like to the other man. Everything he did would be measured against what she had done. Everything he was or would become would be compared with her memory.

He would not wish that on himself, he thought. He would not wish that on anyone.

They were seated in front of the pilot box now, watching the sky grow slowly darker ahead of them as the sunset approached—passed now beyond the Runne River, where it turned south to reach the Rainbow Lake; beyond the city of Varfleet, as well; beyond everything of Paranor and the Druids but the airship on which they rode deep along the Dragon's Teeth toward the broad expanse of the Rabb Plains, which could be seen stretching away toward the distant purple wall of the Wolfsktaag.

Then they were shifting north toward a gap in the Dragon's Teeth where Aphenglow had told Paxon a path led upward into the jagged peaks to the Valley of Shale and the Hadeshorn.

"I want you to come with me when I go," the Ard Rhys told him suddenly, leaning close so she could be heard without having to raise her voice over the wind. "Just you and me and Isaturin."

He nodded his agreement, wondering at this, but not willing to question it openly. Why was he being asked to go? Was she worried for her safety? Was the presence of her successor not enough to reassure her?

Then they were down, the mooring lines fastened in place, the light sheaths brought in, and the radian draws unhitched. The hum of the diapson crystals faded as the parse tubes were hooded, and a deep silence descended as everything came to a standstill.

With Paxon's help, the Ard Rhys climbed to her feet and moved over to the railing. Dajoo Rees had already opened the gate and lowered a rope ladder. He tried to help her climb down, his great hands reaching for her, but she brushed him aside and navigated the ladder on her own, beckoning Paxon and Isaturin to follow.

"The rest of you will please remain aboard," she called back. "Thank you all for your service. Please do for Isaturin what you have done so faithfully for me. I will carry my memories of you with me when I am gone and will cherish them always."

The Trolls muttered in response and clasped fists to their chests as a sign of respect. Stone-faced, expressionless, huge, and terrible creatures they could be, yet Paxon could discern a softness in the looks they cast after her.

Once down, the Druids and Paxon set out on the trail that led into the mountains. Isaturin carried torches to help light their way when darkness closed about them. They would be walking for much of the night to reach their destination, and moon and stars alone might not provide enough light to reveal their passage. Paxon worried that the trek might be too much for the Ard Rhys, and he had already accepted that he might have to carry her before it was over.

But it soon became apparent that she would be able to manage on her own, drawing on some reserve of strength she had husbanded deep within, intent on completing the journey to the Hadeshorn under her own power. They walked in single file up the steep trail, setting their feet carefully on the loose rock and uneven earth, allowing Aphenglow, who led the way from start to finish, to set the pace. The sun passed west and disappeared, the twilight deepened into nightfall, and the moon and stars came out in a glorious display across the darkened sky. In the mountains, the silence was deep and pervasive, unbroken even by birdcalls. Nothing moved about them, and only the scrape of their boots and the exhaling of breath marred the utter stillness.

They walked through most of the night—a walk that was more of a slow climb for the first few hours and then a cautious winding among giant monoliths and narrow defiles mingled with sheer drops and broad fissures that required cautious navigation. Only a few times did the Ard Rhys feel the need to reach out for Paxon's strong arm to steady her, and never once did she ask to stop or offer complaint about her weariness. She kept to herself, but stayed steady as she went, and it was Paxon and Isaturin who were at times forced to keep pace with her.

They were still several hours from dawn when they reached the rim of the Valley of Shale. It appeared abruptly before them, the rocks parting to open out on the shallow depression and its acres of smooth, glistening black rock, shards of it spread away on the slopes of the valley and about the lake at its center from rim to shoreline. The lake itself was a dead thing, the waters flat and green and still, not a ripple to mar their smoothness. The travelers stood together for a moment, studying the Hadeshorn, marking its look and feel, casting about for something living where there was clearly nothing to be found. Of living creatures, they had only themselves for company.

"We wait here until just before dawn," Aphenglow said—the first words she had spoken since they had set out from the airship.

So they sat together at the rim of the valley and faced down across the shards of rock to the empty-seeming waters, the moon and stars traveling along their endless course overhead, the earth turning as it had since the beginning of time, the night passing slowly toward dawn. And as they sat, the Ard Rhys began talking, her voice soft and low, but her words clear and measured. She spoke of her love for the Druid order and her hopes for its future. She related stories of her life and her involvement in the events that framed the history of the Four Lands during her years as leader of the order. She told of her sister, whom she had loved more than anyone, and of the Elven Hunter Cymrian, her protector during the quest for the Bloodfire, whom she had loved only slightly less. She told of Bombax, her first love, and of the assault on Paranor by the Federation, which had claimed him. She admitted failures and recounted accomplishments, and there were more of the latter than the former.

Paxon listened without interrupting, entranced. Even dour Isaturin seemed enraptured with her tales, caught up in the drama and humor, in the euphoria and angst. There were so many revelations offered by a life lived long and well.

Eventually she went silent, and for a long time no one spoke, the three of them lost in their separate thoughts as the night advanced and the dawn neared. When the first blush of light appeared on the distant horizon, and the stars began their slow fade back into the growing brightness, the Ard Rhys rose and turned to them.

"It is time for me to leave you. I do so with confidence that both of you will do your best for the Druid order and for the men and women who have embraced its cause. I entrust to you, Isaturin, the future of the order, and to you, Paxon, its protection." She paused, and for an instant her smile was bright and warm. "Shades, but I wish I could stay here with you and help you with your struggles. And there will be struggles, I can assure you."

Then she turned and stared into the bowl of the valley. "Isaturin, I have changed my mind. I would like to go with Paxon alone. Paxon, will you walk me down, please?"

He did so, rising to take her arm and lead her through the loose rock and uncertain footing toward the Hadeshorn. Isaturin remained where he was, looking after them, his expression stoic, his thoughts unreadable.

The Ard Rhys and her Blade made their way to the base of the rock-strewn slopes and moved to within a dozen yards of the water's edge. There, she released herself from the Highlander and turned to him one last time. "Go no farther. Stand where you are until I am gone. Watch and remember what you see this day."

With the darkness still holding back the sunrise, she moved to the very edge of the lake and stood staring out across its waters. She was so still she might have been a statue, back straight, hands clasped before her, and head lifted. Everything froze then, the whole of the valley caught in a moment in which it seemed nothing would ever happen again, and the three who had come there would be left as they were until the end of days.

Then a roiling of the lake waters commenced, slow at first, and then more violent, the surface churning wildly so that waves rose, capped in white foam. The sound of the waves breaking on the shore mingled with the slap and rush of foam, and a sudden hissing that rose out of the depths. It seemed to Paxon in that moment as if the night had closed back down again and no dawn would appear on this day, but only an inexorable darkness. The hissing increased, and abruptly turned to moans. The voices were high-pitched and frantic, as if those who spoke were trapped beneath the waves and desperate to break free. Deeper voices joined in, then all of them turned to shrieks and screams that brought the Highlander to his knees in shock and dismay.

It grew worse when the shades of the dead began to rise from the waters, hundreds of them streaming into the night air, lifting away from the lake in clouds of vapor, their forms small and inconsequential, moths set loose into the world they had lost. They whirled and spun as they circled skyward and then dropped away again, a kaleidoscope of wraiths changing shape and form in a giant disintegrating prism. They came so close to the Ard Rhys that Paxon thought they might touch her, perhaps even bear her away with them. But though they came near, they kept enough distance to ensure that their forms would not interact.

Then the center of the Hadeshorn exploded skyward in a massive geyser, and a huge dark form lifted into view. Cloaked in black robes that were distinctly Druidic, it stood upon the surface of the water as if its size meant nothing and its weight were negligible. It seemed to have no substance, and yet its darkness was more intense than the night around it. All of the tiny shades that had surfaced earlier fled to the edges of the lake and remained there, safely removed, as the waters continued to hiss and steam.

Paxon watched as the form began to move slowly across the waters toward Aphenglow Elessedil. It did not walk as men, but floated, its body and limbs kept still beneath its robes. A cowl was drawn close about its head, and nothing of its face could be seen in the deep shadows that had formed within. When it stopped only feet from where she stood, the Ard Rhys lifted her arms and held them out in greeting.

"Allanon!" she called out boldly. "I am ready!"

Paxon almost went to her then, terrified of what he knew was about to happen, suddenly convinced that it was a mistake, that it was not yet her time, that he must make her see this before it was too late. But he found he could not move, his body frozen as if encased in ice, all chilled and stiff within his clothing. Already the arms of the shade were reaching down. Already the arms of the Ard Rhys were reaching up to receive them.

Then the Shade of Allanon enfolded her like a parent would a child and lifted her away, cradling her as it backed away from the shoreline, not bothering to turn about, not hiding what it intended. It bore her to the center of the Hadeshorn, the smaller shades of the dead now moving to join it, closing about both of them like a retinue meant to shelter and protect—or perhaps to pay homage and celebrate.

Beneath Allanon and Aphenglow, beneath the past and the present, between living and dead, the waters erupted one last time, then drew everything down in a whirlpool that quickly faded back into tranquility.

Seconds later, movement and sound had ceased, and the Hadeshorn had become still and silent once more. On the eastern horizon, above the valley rim, the sunrise erupted in a blaze of golden light, and the new day began.

3

MUCH FARTHER SOUTH, THE DAWN BLED CRIM-
son along the eastern horizon, the color presaging
the blood that would be shed that day. At the bow of
the heavy transport *Argon,* standing at the airship's rail and looking out
over the blasted terrain hundreds of feet below, Dallen Usurient, Federation Commander of the Red Slash, took note. Thirty years in service
to the army, a low-ranking officer risen to high command in record
time, he believed in luck and foretelling only when it suited his purpose. It did so this day, and a hint of a smile creased his weathered face.

We'll end it here, he thought. *Scorched earth and no living creature
left to tell the tale.*

His command surrounded him, stretched out across the transport
decking from port to starboard and bow to stern, five hundred strong,
warriors all—men-at-arms who knew no other way. He had selected
most of them, chosen them from the ranks of other commands from
which they were only too glad to transfer if it meant coming to the
Slash. He knew most by name; frequently, he knew the names of their
wives and husbands and children. He knew their history, their habits,
their strengths, and their weaknesses, although what he knew best
and cared about most was the nature of their fighting capabilities. He
had brought them together over the years, choosing carefully from

among thousands, building his command step by step until he had the five hundred he needed.

Now and then, some would fall by the wayside or leave the service because they could no longer meet his exacting standards. But there were always those waiting to take their place, their names on a list pinned to the barracks bulletin board where all could view them, study them, and offer their opinions. Only a few ever commented, and then only with a deep sense of caution. They revered Usurient, these soldiers, but they feared him, too. Loose tongues and flippant opinions were not well received. Hard fact and steady arguments were what won him over, and everyone wanted to be in his trust.

He had formed the Red Slash ten years earlier, when he had risen to a position in the army where he could do so, and he had formed it for an express purpose. Like First Response—the units that provided the initial defense against any threat to the Federation cities— Usurient wanted a command that would act against threats to the overall safety and stability of the Federation Empire. Not as a defensive unit, but as an attack force preempting the need for any defense. And one not confined to threats against the walls of Federation cities, but against anything or anyone acting in a way that could prove adverse to the Southland as a whole. His was to be a unit that would preempt unwarranted attacks and invasions from any source, no matter how nebulous or remote.

It had invested him with considerable power as a member of the Federation army. But he had used it boldly and successfully, and complaints had been few and largely ignored.

It would be so here today with the coastal fortress of Arbrox, a nest of vipers that had been preying on the Federation for far too long. He had his orders, and they were broad enough to suit his purpose. Scorched earth and bones was the way of the Slash. Complaints were for weaklings and those who hid behind the walls of their houses.

"Just there," Desset whispered in his ear, leaning close and pointing ahead to the bank of fog toward which they were flying.

Arbrox. The first hints of its walls and buildings were just coming into view as the dawn penetrated the marine layer and revealed bits and pieces of the ancient fortress. Thin columns of smoke rose from chimneys and watch fires, and shadows layered the huge stone blocks in dark splashes where the complex sat nestled within the coastal mountains. There were no signs of life, no indication of a presence within those buildings and walls, but Usurient was not deceived. He held up his hand in a prearranged signal, and the huge transport backed off until they were out of sight once more. He would take no chances on being discovered before he was ready.

"Aye, Commander," Desset had told him a dozen times at least before they set sail. "The brigands are in there, like rats in their nests—young and old alike, vermin in need of extermination."

Pirates.

"And the sorcerer?"

"Him, too—though you don't hardly see him much. But that's his hidey-hole, that one. Down in the rocks, deep in the underground. Oh, he's there, all right. A blot upon the earth, a sickness to be burned away!"

He ignored his spy's boisterous words, his suspect characterizations, and his obvious prejudices. He cared only for the accuracy of Desset's insistence on knowing the pirate lair, and in this he was unshakable. The pirates were there. And the sorcerer, as well—the hated Arcannen. After years of trying to track both through hearsay and rumor, through false leads and dead ends, he had them at last.

The pirate raids on Federation shipping had been going on for months, but the bolder, more recent attacks against the diapson crystal transports had been the last straw. The Coalition Council had been in an uproar, the Prime Minister had turned to the Minister of Defense, and the latter had summoned him personally to deal with the matter.

"I want this settled, Usurient," he had announced two minutes after the other's arrival. "I want these raiders found and stamped out. Every last one. No exceptions. The Slash does this sort of work well enough; make sure they remember how to do it. And if the rumors of Arcannen are true, then finish him, as well. The Prime Minister and the Coalition Council have agreed. To the deep pit with all of them; spare the women and children and the sick and old, but no others."

So here he was, a few miles west of Arbrox, his command ready, his orders clear. *Search and destroy.* This was an undertaking that would end in the complete slaughter of those he found—though it was not the mandate the Minister of Defense had given him or one the Prime Minister would countenance. Dallen Usurient was a hard man, and he had lived a hard life. Not for him the pleasures of city life and the comforts of bed and family. His family was the corps and his bedmate was his duty. Whatever comfort he found came from knowing he had never failed either and never would. What satisfaction he enjoyed came from his life as a soldier, from the raw taste of battle and the sweet scent of his enemy's blood. Fighting gave his life purpose and order; fighting was experience and skill and instinct combined to form the heart and soul of a soldier, and in his opinion there was nothing better or more meaningful in the entire world.

The transport was slowing down, and now the warships were moving up alongside. They would wait until the soldiers of the Slash were placed close to the fortress walls, then they would use their big guns to open paths to those who lay sleeping within. A few would be awake even now; a few would be keeping watch on the walls. But no one would be expecting the attack, and no one would be able to stand against it.

Usurient took a deep, steadying breath and exhaled slowly. He would go in first. He always did. You led by example, no matter your rank, no matter the danger. His men took their courage from him. They found their strength in his.

He turned around and faced his men. He was a tall, strong man, standing well over six feet, with a shock of black hair and a scar running crosswise on his face left to right over the bridge of his nose. He made an imposing figure as he lifted his right arm, fist clenched. Five hundred arms lifted in response, mimicking the gesture. Solidarity was everything in the corps. He glanced at Desset, who was looking ahead still, his uneasiness obvious. He was not a part of the corps; he could never be one of them. He was a spy, and his usefulness would end after today. His narrow frame, all bones and angles, his strange eyes with their cat-like slits, and his narrow chin did nothing to flatter him. He was a necessary evil, and he would not be missed by any of them.

"Be calm," Usurient whispered to him.

"You're not the one the survivors will come looking for when this is over," the other hissed.

Usurient shrugged. "There will be no survivors."

"Just make sure."

"Stay aboard, and stay out of sight. Wait for us here."

The cat's eyes flicked in his direction. "Not much else I can do, is there?"

The transport began to descend onto a flat that appeared between a swarm of gullies and ridges fronting the mountains ahead. When they were close enough to set the mooring lines, Usurient ordered the ladders thrown out, and the entire command began to climb down. Their progress was quick and efficient. It took less than ten minutes for all five hundred to disembark and form up below, organized by squads—scouts at the fore, heavy weapons at the rear. The squads consisted of bowmen, swordsmen, and spearmen, each with a specific task and all with a single command—to seize the fortress and kill everyone within.

Usurient had thought earlier to amend that order on the chance that useful information might be gleaned from those kept alive. But in the end it was simpler just to kill them all. What information they had was likely of little use, and there was less risk to his people with a kill order than with a capture-and-detain proviso.

He glanced around, standing now at the forefront of his corps. Ahead, the terrain was a barren mass of rocks and fissures. No vegetation, no sign of life. Not even a bird took flight at their arrival. Such a squalid, pointless bit of earth, he thought. How could there ever be anything here worth keeping?

His squad leaders crowded close as he repeated one last time the instructions he had given them twice already. Wait for the assault from the warships. Once it ceased, move forward into the gaps in the walls—swordsmen in the lead, spearmen following, bowmen in reserve, and heavy weapons as backup. Find those still alive and kill them. All of them. Ferret them out, if they were in hiding. Leave no one behind.

Then he moved them forward, taking up a point just behind the scouts as he led the way toward the peaks and the fortress they warded, the entire command spreading like a huge, silent stain across the landscape. They fanned out in two directions, forming a vise to imprison and contain those within the walls ahead, their lines staggered to prevent any escape. The roar of the ocean crashing on the rocks and the constant wail of the wind hid their approach, muffling the clank and rattle of metal and scrape of boots.

When they were in position, Usurient sent up the agreed-upon flare, and the warships eased forward to begin their assault. Turning broadside, the big flash rips mounted on the decking released the power fueled by the diapson crystals, and waves of explosive fire hammered at the now fully visible fortress. Entire sections of the walls disintegrated in minutes, and the main gates went down in splinters of wood and iron. Cries of alarm rose from those within, and men surged onto what remained of the walls to fight back. They stood no chance. The warships attacked relentlessly, sweeping the men away, disabling their inferior weapons, and knocking out the ramparts and towers on which they stood.

When the airship weapons ceased, Usurient howled out to his five hundred, and the whole of his command surged toward the walls, flooded through the ragged gaps in the stone, and charged inside.

What happened next was predictably horrific. The killing was rampant and unceasing as swordsmen and spearmen took out what few remained of the defenders and then went after everyone else. Men, women, and children, old and young, whole or damaged, were cut to pieces. They died screaming and begging. They died fighting and running away. They died where they were hiding or as they were seeking escape. But they died all the same. None was spared and none escaped. Blood and flesh lay everywhere, a lifeless mass of what had once been a human population, decimated in less than an hour's time. The entire assault was executed flawlessly. Less than a handful of the Red Slash soldiers were killed in the process, and less than two handfuls injured in even the most minor ways.

Even so, there were those who stood stunned in the aftermath, looking down at their handiwork, amazed at how terrible it was. The reaction was decidedly mixed. There were tears shed. There were muttered oaths and soft prayers asking forgiveness. There were wild excuses and insistences on the necessity of it all. There were boasts and sneers. A mixed pack, but a pack, all the same.

Usurient walked through the carnage wordlessly, his hard face expressionless, taking it all in. He was pleased at how well it had gone, but irritated that his troops did not seem to have found the sorcerer. Desset had seemed so certain he was there, yet there was no sign of him. A canvas of his squad leaders did not reveal Arcannen's fate, and that meant, in all likelihood, that the sorcerer had managed to escape.

"Bring the men out," he ordered. "We're done here. A fine day's work by all of you. The men get an extra ration tonight of any libation they desire, spirits or otherwise. Let them know."

He stood outside the walls as his men filed out, noting the mix of expressions on their faces, noting those who would not look at him and those who stared boldly; noting how they behaved with the battle behind them and the killing done. All sorts of responses, yet every soldier had done his or her duty and that was what mattered. The horror of the moment would fade; the memory of the dying would soften. In the not so distant future, no one would even think on it.

When the heavy armor appeared, he sent them back in with portable flash rips to burn everything that was left, bodies included. "Leave no trace of any of it," he ordered.

He waited until he saw the fires spring up and smelled the stench of burning flesh permeating the sea air before turning and starting back with the others. The remains of this day's work would disappear with the first strong storm off the Tiderace. After that, only blackened stones and shattered walls would mark the ruins of what had once been Arbrox.

. . .

The sun rose from behind the Tiderace in a haze of gray and silver, chasing the marine layer and brightening the blackened ruins of Arbrox. Trails of smoke rose from those ruins in slender threads that were quickly snatched away and dispersed by the sea winds. Gulls and cormorants and other seabirds began to wing their way in from distant haunts, settling down to feast on the remains of the dead, uncaring of the loss represented, caught up in the appeal of easy food and an uninterrupted meal.

West, the Federation warships and transport were just disappearing into what remained of the fading night, winging their way toward the city of Sterne.

The man in the black robes stood outside what remained of Arbrox and its dead, watching. His gaze shifted between the fortress and the warships, dead and living, thinking thoughts so dark that if it were possible to touch them it would be as touching shards of fire.

A single question dominated his thoughts.

How could they do this?

Yes, Arbrox was a pirate fortress, and its people were pirates and the families of pirates. Yes, they had raided Federation shipping as a means of subsistence even though they knew that retaliation was likely and that it would put their lives at risk each time they set out on a hunt. Yes, they lived on the edge of the sword and point of the spear.

But to kill off every last man, woman, and child? To destroy an entire population and raze a village back into the earth as if it had never existed? His fury was all-consuming. This was a mark of such darkness that it must be avenged. Though the hunt had not been for him—or at least not exclusively for him—it felt personal in the extreme. The people of Arbrox had taken him in when everyone in the rest of the Four Lands had been intent on hunting him down. These people had fed and cared for him, they had treated him as one of their own. They had given him back his life, and they had asked nothing in return.

They did not deserve to die as they had. They did not deserve to be wiped out like vermin.

He would have died with them if he had not chosen this night to sleep apart in the coastal shore watchtower he favored when his darkness most consumed him. He would not be seeing this sunrise if he did not know when it was time to step away and remain apart until the blackness passed and his good humor returned.

Pure chance that he was still alive. And fate, perhaps?

He pulled his cloak closer about his shoulders and looked down one final time on Arbrox and his friends. Someone had betrayed them. Someone had known of their lair and given them away to the Federation. The Slash could not have found them otherwise.

Time enough to settle that score—to settle with betrayer and killers both. But a way must be found that would catch them all up at once and feed them into a chamber of horrors equal to that which had consumed the people of Arbrox.

And who better than himself to find such a way?

Who better than Arcannen Rai?

4

SIX WEEKS LATER, ON A RAINY NIGHT MADE CONSID-
erably less pleasant by a sudden drop in the temperature
just before dusk, Reyn Frosch walked into the Boar's Head
Tavern in the village of Portlow shortly before performance time.
Shivering with the damp and cold in spite of his heavy all-weather
cloak, he stood in the tavern doorway and brushed himself off, shed-
ding raindrops and discomfort while he scanned the faces of the patrons gathered in the great room.

More than a hundred, he guessed. Many more, in fact. They were
three-deep at the serving bar, and the tables were filled. Well, almost
filled. He noticed one at the back of the room where a man in a black
cloak and hood hunkered down over his drink in splendid solitude,
the rest of the room choosing to give him a wide berth. No one had
mustered the courage to ask for the two chairs that sat empty in front
of him, even though other patrons were standing everywhere about
the room, most of them finding places to help hold up the walls.

He let his gaze drift until he found the Fortren brothers and felt a
sudden weight settle on his shoulders. He had hoped they would not
be here. He had hoped they would find another tavern and another
musician to taunt. But apparently they either lacked the initiative or
had decided it would be more fun to continue tormenting him. Yan-

cel glanced up unexpectedly, saw him looking, and grinned. Borry turned and offered a tip of his battered hat. Both waited for a response, but he ignored them. What else could you do with people like these?

Shrugging the strap of the case that protected his elleryn higher onto his shoulder, he moved over to the serving counter and stepped around its end to reach the kitchen. He gave Gammon a wave as he passed through the door, not bothering to slow. The room beyond was filled with casks of ale, dry foodstuffs, packages of meats and bins of vegetables, table settings and implements, candles and lamps, a pair of stoves, and a cook standing over a griddle working diligently on preparing food for customers.

"Reyn, lad," the old grease-dog offered, one hand lifting in an attempt at a jaunty salute.

Smoke rose and steam spat from the griddle and food smells filled the room, the mix venting poorly through screened openings in the walls. In spite of the vents, the room was stifling. Reyn waved back and walked over to the coatrack to shrug off his instrument and cloak and hang both over the wooden pegs.

Gammon came through the door. "Big crowd for you tonight, Reyn. Hope you've got your nimble fingers and angelic voice finely tuned and strongly flavored!"

He always said that, but Reyn grinned anyway. "Maybe you could keep an eye on the Fortren brothers for me?"

Gammon laughed. "Them? No need. I talked to them already. Told them one more incident, one more bit of trouble, and they were out of here for good. I don't care who fathered them or how many more of them are out plowing fields and mucking pigsties. I told them that, I did."

Reyn was less than convinced by what Gammon might or might not have told them. He would have been happier if the barkeep had just thrown the Fortrens out in the first place. But he knew he couldn't do anything about it except what he always did, which was to keep an eye out for trouble because trouble had a way of finding him. It had a strong attraction to him, one he understood all too well because it had charted much of the course of his life.

Still, he was able enough that even the Fortrens didn't frighten him. He was a boy technically—just past his sixteenth birthday, no whiskers showing on his face in spite of his size, which was considerable. Already, he stood six feet tall, and his broad shoulders and strong arms suggested he could look after himself well enough if he had to. He had been on his own since he was eight, no mean feat in the outland villages of the eastern Southland, orphaned and set adrift—well, set to flight, actually—with no idea how to care for himself and no clue where to go to find out. But luck and providence and common sense had seen him through, and now here he was, supporting himself nicely, a member of a community that for the most part liked him well enough to welcome him into its fold.

He brushed drops of water from his shaggy blond hair and snatched a roll from a pan cooling on the stovetop. The cook gestured threateningly with his spatula but without enough emphasis to be convincing, then motioned to the platter of meat sitting next to him. Reyn helped himself, building a sandwich and devouring the results. Gammon found him a glass of ale to wash down his food and brought it over to him.

The barkeep paused, watching him, then headed for the door. "Soon as you're done, come on out and do some songs. They're getting restless out there. If you can soothe them a bit, maybe they'll fuss less."

"Voice of an angel, is it?" the grease-dog purred and grinned broadly.

Reyn knew better than to say anything back and simply nodded as if it were a compliment rather than a taunt. One thing he could say for certain—there wasn't an insult he hadn't heard or a name he hadn't endured. It came with the territory, and he'd learned long ago to absorb the blows.

His voice—that was the spark to the fire. His fortune and his misfortune. Hard to know which, sometimes. Both, he supposed. Right now, it was paying for his way in the world and his place in Portlow, so he was feeling good about it. Other times, it had been a different story. That was the way life worked, though. He'd learned that much along the way.

He finished his sandwich and drained his glass of ale. Moving over to the coatrack, he took down the elleryn, removed it carefully from its case, and slung the strap over his shoulder. Standing in the kitchen amid the smells of the cooking and the rise of the heat from the stove and griddle, he tuned it carefully, turning the pegs that tightened the eight strings one after another while plucking experimentally to bring them all into sync. Then he fastened the metal slide in place at the apex of the instrument's narrowing neck and fretted multiple chords to check for tuning.

When he was satisfied with the results, he took a deep breath, exhaled, gave a cheery call to the grease-dog, and headed for the tavern door.

It was pandemonium beyond. Shouts and jokes and raucous laughter, voices seeking to be heard over the roar of other voices, empty tankards of this and that libation slammed on the bar in search of a refill, feet stamping and backs being slapped, the room jammed with patrons locked elbow-to-elbow and shoulder-to-shoulder, heads bent close, bodies radiating heat and sweat. There was barely room for him to get to the small platform where he performed, set back against the wall at the far end of the room. The tables and chairs closest were pushed right up against the edge of his four-by-four space. As he neared, shouts and whistles rose from listeners familiar with his playing, sounds of encouragement and approval that caused him to flush with pleasure. He knew he was good. He knew he could make them feel things they didn't even know they were capable of feeling. He had the gift.

He stepped onto the platform and settled himself on the stool placed there for his use. The room began to quiet immediately. He tested the strings of the elleryn once more, strumming chords, ear held close so he could hear accurately. By the time he was finished, voices had quieted almost to silence, and all eyes were on him.

Without preamble, he began to play. He chose a crowd favorite, a tale about a highwayman and the woman he loved—who betrayed him to the authorities so that he was trapped and died calling out her name. It was sweet and poignant, its refrain instantly memorable after one hearing:

Call, he did for Ellen Jean
She who was his sweetest dream
Call for her in spite of cost
For Ellen Jean, his life was lost.

When he was finished and the highwayman was dispatched and Ellen Jean was revealed for the faithless woman they all knew she was, you could have heard a pin drop. Then the clapping and pounding began, and the room was on its feet, calling for more. He went back to it immediately, another crowd favorite, a drinking song featuring an old woodsman and his dog.

He played with almost no pause for the better part of an hour, his music and his voice ensnaring them like wondering children, mesmerizing them as they listened. He wove their emotions into each song, making it live and breathe for them in ways a mere tune never could. All felt the emotional ache his music aroused within, rejoicing in the happy songs, mourning with the sad. All were caught up in a transformative experience that for a few minutes at least changed everything about them.

It was his gift that captured them, that wove through their hearts and minds and made them smile or cry. It was not the playing, which was only an accompaniment. It was in his voice where the real magic could be found, in the way he worked a song through changes in modulation, pauses, slides up and down the scale, emphasis added and withdrawn. With his voice, he could make them *believe*. No one was immune. Wherever he went, whomever he played for, they were his for as long as he sang.

The problem was that it didn't end there and the result wasn't always pleasant. His voice could provide a healing balm, but it could be a weapon, too. And in the heat of a moment's careless lapse or an ill-considered emotional surge, it could shift from the former to the latter.

And even that wasn't the worst of it. What it did to him was even more terrifying. When he used the magic in the wrong way, in an ill-advised response to anger or fear, it whisked him away and dropped him into a deep, dark nothingness, into a place where everything disappeared and time stopped. It happened all at once and without warning. It was as if he had been yanked outside himself. This had happened only a scattering of times—but they were times that were among the blackest of his life. To lose all sense of what was happening, to be stripped of control and become a helpless prisoner in a timeless nothingness was something he could barely stand to think about.

He did not want it to happen to him ever again. He would do anything to prevent it.

He sang his last song for the hour and stood up to receive the resultant applause before departing the tiny stage and moving back behind the bar to gain some space. Calls for drinks for the player, the singer, the music man rang through the great room, but he declined them all. Drink fogged his mind, and a fogged mind was dangerous for someone with his condition. As marvelous as his gift could be, it could also be unpredictable. No matter the urges he felt, he couldn't let his guard down. With a moment's carelessness, the darker emotions could take control and his singing could turn lethal.

It had happened only that handful of times, but he remembered the consequences of each one vividly. He didn't want any more memories to add to that bin.

He stood behind the bar and drank from a glass of water, smiling and waving at his listeners. Off to one side, the Fortren brothers stood talking, heads bent close. Scheming, he corrected himself, not talking. Like weasels. The music never seemed to affect them in the way it affected others. They weren't immune to the magic; they couldn't be. They seemed mostly enraged by it, as if it awakened something in them that they would have preferred to leave sleeping. They had threatened him on more than one occasion because of it, never saying exactly why they were so troubled.

At the back of the room, the stranger in the black cloak was staring at him, his narrow features revealed, bladed and flat. His eyes glittered, but there was no malice or ill intent reflected.

Odd, Reyn thought. Then the head lowered, and the face disappeared into shadow.

The boy studied him a moment longer, then he turned and went back into the kitchen for something more to eat. The singing, the turning of his audience from doubters into believers, the giving what they didn't even know they wanted—it was all hard work and it made him hungry. Standing at the griddle, he made himself another sandwich, casting occasional glances at the old grease-dog as he cooked food, prepared plates, and called off the orders to Sorsi and Phenel, the two serving girls.

His gaze shifted to a tiny window and the darkness outside. He wished he knew more about the source of his power. He didn't question that it was a form of magic; he had accepted that a long time back. If you could use your voice to do the things that he had done— good and bad—you commanded magic. But where had it come from? Why did he have it? His parents hadn't told him, assuming they had even known. They were dead before he was even old enough to ask the questions that plagued him now. He could still see them in his mind, dragged from their home by the townspeople to be stoned until they were dead.

Because of him. Because of his voice. Because of what he was suspected of being by frightened, superstitious fools.

He shut his eyes against the thoughts and memories. He hadn't seen them die, though he knew they had. He had been gone by then. He had done what they had told him to do and hidden in the old man's cart so he could be spirited away from what was coming. He hated himself for having allowed it. He could have helped them. He could have stopped what had happened.

Or he could have died with them. Or the old man who took him could have left him and gone his way.

But none of that had happened. That was how life worked.

At the back of the great room, Arcannen sat pondering the contents of the tankard of ale in front of him. He was not drinking from it; he was using it as a prop to suggest that he was just another customer, albeit one who valued his privacy. He had just finished exchanging a long, searching look with the boy, and now he was considering, still wanting to make certain that what he believed to be true actually was. But having witnessed an hour of his singing and having watched the effect it produced on the raucous crowd, he felt there could be no mistake.

The boy was an Ohmsford scion, and had inherited the use of the wishsong from his ancestors.

But what to do about it?

That he would do something was a given. That boy would give him the means to alter the history of the Four Lands in dramatic fashion. He knew the legends of the wishsong. He knew what it was capable of doing—what it had done for various Ohmsfords over the years. That there was one member of the family still alive was no small surprise, even after the rumors had reached him of this boy's gift. He had suspected the truth then, but had not been convinced until now. What this boy could offer him, what he could provide in the way of support, was immeasurable. Paxon Leah had held promise as a bearer of the Sword of Leah, but a user of the wishsong could offer much, much more.

He struggled to contain his excitement as he sat staring down at the tabletop, thinking. He didn't show it, his face impassive and his body still, but his insides were roiling. With this boy as an ally, anything was possible. With this boy's power . . .

A chair scraped, and when he looked up the boy was sitting across from him. "Did you like my singing?"

Arcannen steadied himself, then smiled and nodded. "You have great talent."

"I saw you staring at me."

"I admit, I was staring. I apologize. But I was surprised by how good you were. Much better than any singer I have ever heard. Who taught you?"

The boy drank from a glass of water. "I taught myself."

"How did you end up here?"

"I just did. Let's back up. I think you were staring at me because you know me from somewhere. Am I right?"

Arcannen hesitated. "I know *of* you. I know something of the magic you possess."

The boy said nothing. He just stared. He was very self-possessed and calm where others would have kept their distance. Arcannen admired that.

"Who says it's magic?" the boy challenged him at last.

"I know it is magic because I have the use of magic myself. Tell me more about it. How long have you had it? How well can you control it?"

The boy rose, his face tight. "Right now, I have to sing."

Then he turned abruptly and walked away.

5

REYN FROSCH WASN'T SURE HOW MUCH OF WHAT the black-cloaked man had told him he believed, but of one thing he was very certain—the man knew entirely too much about him. And that frightened him—badly. He had spent his life hiding what he was, and to be revealed now was deeply troubling.

Reyn crossed the great room to the kitchen door, noting as he did so that the Boar's Head was even busier now than it had been earlier. There were no longer any seats or tables to be found, and what little space was left to stand in was down to almost nothing. He was forced to maneuver his way using shoulders and elbows to get through the raucous, hard-drinking crowd, and it occurred to him that if any sort of fight broke out at this point it would be difficult for Gammon to get out from behind the serving counter to put a stop to it.

He made a mental note of that as he reached the bar and worked his way around one end toward the kitchen door.

"You in a hurry, boy?" a familiar voice spat at him, one hand clamping on his shoulder.

Borry Fortren. Reyn stopped and turned, facing the bully. The face that leaned into his was big, battered, and ugly. Nothing new there. Huge shoulders, massive arms, lots of muscle on display. "I've got a job to do," he said evenly.

"Singing that sissy music for these cow heads? Making everyone go all soft and squishy inside with your pretty words? What do you do to them, anyway, to make them all into chicken guts?"

Reyn smiled. "I take their minds off faces like yours. Now get away from me or I'll show you something really bad."

Borry hesitated. As he did, the boy turned away and continued on, forcing himself not to look back. Stupid oaf. He wouldn't give this up until the two fought—something Reyn did not intend to do. Borry's reputation suggested that he won fights however he needed to. He always carried an extra blade or two tucked into his clothing. One man he fought had him beaten, but Borry had used the knife and left the man with one good eye and one good ear. People were frightened of Borry and his brothers for a reason.

Reyn passed through the kitchen door and went over to the coat-rack to retrieve the elleryn. Strapping it across his shoulder, he drank another glass of water and went back out into the crowd and their immediate applause.

He played for another hour after that, trying to calm his fears about the black-cloaked stranger. He worked his way through his repertoire of songs, using his voice and the elleryn to maximum effect, swaying the crowd's responses by using the skills with which he had become so adept. Only once did he catch sight of the Fortrens, standing at the bar, heads bent close once more, backs turned. The only backs in the room that were, he noted.

And he found the black-cloaked stranger, as well, still seated at the same table, still nursing the same glass of ale, his head lifted now, watching him, a noticeable gleam in his eyes as he listened. But looking at him made Reyn's mind wander and his concentration on the music slide. He regrouped quickly, looked away from the stranger, and refocused on what he was being paid to do.

When he finished and was standing in the midst of the crowd's applause, he took a moment to look around once more but couldn't find the stranger or the Fortrens. The table at the back of the room sat empty, and the brothers were nowhere to be seen. He took a short bow and walked off the stage for the kitchen. He had just passed through the door when Gammon followed him in, clapping him on the back.

"Aye now, that was your best, Reyn! Just wondrous singing and playing. Everyone loved it. They're all staying put for the last set, so you get whatever you need to eat and drink before you go back out. Really, you were amazing, lad!"

The boy nodded and smiled, thinking that if Gammon knew what else he could do with his music he might not be quite so complimentary. That if he realized Reyn's parents were dead because of him, he might feel differently. But the boy accepted the tavern owner's accolades wordlessly, and the other beamed with satisfaction and disappeared back out into the great room.

Reyn started to hang the elleryn on its peg with his cloak, but changed his mind and decided to keep it with him. He walked over to the counter and poured himself another glass of water, drank it down without stopping, then did the same with a second. He would need to relieve himself before he went back out to play, but he felt dried out and empty inside, and the cold well water helped with both. He lingered for a few minutes, trying to decide if he needed food. But food didn't seem necessary just then, so he set down his glass and went out the back door into the night.

It was cool and overcast, but the rain had stopped. He fingered the strings of his instrument for a few minutes, taking advantage of the silence to adjust the sound of each as he plucked them one by one. Satisfied, he stood staring into the darkness and found himself remembering another night like this one. He had been eight years old, the only child of a baker and a home-keeper living in a Southland village below the Duln—a small community that in most ways was very much like every other. It seemed a long time ago now, though it was only a little more than seven years. He still remembered his parents' faces and a few of their expressions and mannerisms. He remembered them as kind and good and caring. He used to fish with his father in the streams that ran through the woods surrounding the village. He used to take walks to the market with his mother to purchase goods.

Then, one night, for reasons he never found out, he was attacked by a group of boys. They came at him in a swarm, and they overpowered his feeble and ineffective efforts to defend himself. They beat him until he was unconscious. They broke bones and cracked ribs. They nearly blinded him. He begged them to stop, pleaded with them to tell him why they were doing this, but they ignored him and continued pummeling him until he lost consciousness.

His parents and the village healers nursed him back to health. No one could identify the boys responsible or say why they had chosen to make an example of him. No one seemed to know anything about what had happened. His father went door-to-door and spoke to everyone who would listen. He did this for days. One man told him he'd heard it was a mistake, that the boys thought he was someone else. Another man said he thought it was something Reyn had said or done. Nothing came of any of it.

Months went by. He recovered from his injuries, and the details of the incident dimmed in his memory. Life returned to normal.

But all too soon the boys came again. They caught him coming home after an afternoon of fishing. It was night, and he was alone. They came at him in a clutch, whispering what they were going to do to him. Terrified, he screamed. And something happened. His voice slipped out of register, the level of intensity shifting dramatically. He lost control of what he was doing. All at once his scream had an impact to it, a punch that struck his attackers like a physical blow and sent them sprawling. Many were left unconscious. The others picked themselves up and ran. The boy stood staring after them. He had no idea what he had done.

Several days later, a couple of them found him again. But this time one of them had brought his father. The man was big and mean and drunk, and he was carrying a knife.

"Gonna carve you a new face, boy!" he hissed. "Gonna cut that wailing witch tongue right out of you!"

Reyn Frosch never hesitated. He screamed again, but this time with dark intent and terrible purpose. The big man slowed, dropping to his knees, hands over his ears. He screamed back at the boy, then scrambled to his feet and lurched toward him anew.

And then he simply disintegrated. His body blew apart; separating at the joints, bones breaking, blood emptying out, he turned into a lump of raw, shredded meat.

In that moment Reyn seemed to lose consciousness. He didn't fall, didn't collapse; he simply lost track of what was happening. He stood there in a daze, his mind gone somewhere else, and it was several long minutes later before he even realized where he was.

By then, the boys who had brought the man had fled. Reyn stared at what was left of his attacker, appalled by what he had done. Even to save his life, he shouldn't have done this. But the power of his voice was new to him, and he had been frightened so badly by the size of the man and the presence of the knife that he had simply reacted. He ran home to tell his parents.

The boys who had attacked him had run home, too. But they still weren't finished with him. Over the next few days they revealed themselves, telling everyone what he had done. A black haunt, they called him. A wraith of darkness and destruction. He'd killed a man for no reason. He was possessed and should be stopped before he could hurt others. No mention of their intentions toward him; no mention of the knife.

Eventually, they stirred up a response from the already superstitious townspeople. They came for him then, dozens of them, men and women from the taverns and ale shops, intoxicated and angry, their courage emboldened by numbers, a mob made wild at the thought of a creature in their midst that was inhuman and capable of doing great harm. The family of the dead man was among them, fueling the flames of fear and rage, knowing only one way to deal with things they didn't understand.

A miller from the next town over, a friend of Reyn's father's who did business with the bakery and had stopped in one of the taverns for a drink before heading back, rushed to tell the family. Reyn's father persuaded the miller to hide the boy in his wagon and spirit him to safety until matters settled down. The miller, an older man with grown children and better sense than those who were hunting for the boy, agreed to help.

So Reyn was hiding in the miller's wagon beneath an old canvas covering, rolling down the road leading out of town when the mob surged past, heading for his home. He never saw what happened after that, but he heard. Just hearing was enough to imprint on his mind the scenes that followed. The mob breaking into his home and dragging his parents out. The destruction that followed as his home was torn apart by those searching for him. The deaths of his parents, whom the mob decided quickly enough were likely the same as he was, creatures of the netherworld who spawned this demon that had escaped them, and so should be stoned.

Soon enough, the miller and his wife had decided Reyn could no longer stay with them. The townspeople who had killed his parents were still hunting for him, obsessed with their task and consumed by their fears. Already, the search was widening to the surrounding communities. The boy would have to go. The miller would take him to one of the cities, far enough away and sufficiently populous that he would not be found.

Thus, at the age of eleven, he found himself making his own way in the world and discovering just how badly equipped he was to do so.

And all this had happened because of his voice, because of a magic that caused him to do terrible things. There was no escaping the truth of the matter, though he tried for years to deny it, arguing in the privacy of his mind that he had only done what instinct and fear had driven him to do. Had he known the truth about the sort of power he possessed, he might have been able to change the way things turned out. Had he known, he might have been able to save his parents' lives.

So he believed, and the belief hardened into certainty and became a weight around his neck that would not release itself. He carried it everywhere, and after another few incidents in which he reacted spontaneously and foolishly with similar results, he needed no further convincing that it would always be there. If not for adopting a regimen of strict control over his life that mostly separated him from encountering the extreme emotional moments that would cause the dark side of his voice to resurface, he would have remained cursed every waking moment for the rest of his life.

But it was the singing that saved him, too. The discovery that he could infuse listeners with whatever emotions he chose to stir, just by modulating the sound of his voice, provided him not only with a way to make a living but also with the realization that he could control his own fate. Now his voice became a gift as well as a curse, and he employed it to good advantage. A sense of self-confidence followed, his growing skill and experience in using his voice providing reassurance that he needn't go through life afraid that he was without hope.

Of course, there were still lapses. And there was that odd and troubling disconnect he experienced each time one happened, a going away from himself that left him empty and vulnerable . . .

"Well, well, look what we have here."

His thoughts and memories scattered, and the night closed in about him, its silence suddenly oppressive. He glanced over to find Borry Fortren standing only a few feet away.

"He looks a little surprised, don't he?" Yancel, moving up beside him, laughed. "Guess he thought he could slip out the back door, and we wouldn't know."

"That what you doing, chicken-boy?" Borry Fortren pressed, his smile an ugly sneer. He made a rude gesture and spat. "You trying to get away from us?"

Reyn shrugged, fighting to remain calm. "Staying away from you two is a lifelong ambition."

"Oh, listen to him!" Yancel clapped his brother on the shoulder. "Clever with words, ain't he? Does all that singing, and now it turns out he thinks he can be clever, too!"

"He ain't so clever." Borry was cracking his knuckles and moving to cut off any attempt at escape, which Reyn could already tell was not going to happen in any case. "Else he wouldn't have let himself be caught out alone like this. You want to try us now, boy? Or do you just want to take what's coming to you and be done with it?"

"Yeah, maybe that. Just take your punishment for that smart mouth. We won't break too many bones."

"'Course, you won't be playing those pretty songs for a while. Or maybe never, once we're done with you."

"Singing, Yance. He won't be doing much of that, either, I don't expect."

"Well, I'm sick of his singing in any case. Best if we don't be hearing him at all after this. You know what he's gonna sound like? Like a chicken head after it's been twisted off, throttled good and proper, all croaking and slobbering. No one gonna understand him anymore. Not a word."

So there was no avoiding this, no way to keep it from happening. Reyn thought momentarily of trying to dash back inside fast enough that they couldn't catch him. But if he did that, he would be a marked man and they would call him a coward. There would be no end to their mockery. Better to try to stop it here and now. He was strong enough to take either one alone. He might have a chance against both if he kept his wits.

And if they didn't use knives.

Then he saw the iron bar that Borry was holding down against his leg. So much for that.

"You really don't have much confidence in yourself, do you?" he said, taking a step toward them. "If you need that iron bar, you must think you're in trouble."

Borry laughed. "Don't need it, chicken-boy. I just like the idea of it. I don't want to hurt myself more than I have to on pig slop like you. Come on, step a little closer."

Reyn unslung the elleryn and leaned it back against the wall of the building, searching as he did so for something he could use as a weapon. He saw a washtub and a clothesline. Useless. Some wood was stacked against the back wall. He moved over quickly and snatched up a four-foot length. Better than nothing.

"You sure about this?" he asked them, advancing a few steps.

The brothers exchanged a quick glance, and then both grinned. "Sure enough," Yancel spat at him.

"Gonna hurt you bad," Borry added. "Real bad."

They came toward him, separating slightly so they had room to maneuver. Reyn kept his eye on Borry and the iron pipe, letting Yancel think he was free to act. As he expected, Yancel came at him first, charging in a sudden rush that surprised his brother and caused him to shout out a warning.

The big man paid no attention, however, and threw himself at

Reyn in an attempt to overpower him using his superior size and strength. But the boy dropped into a crouch, braced himself, and jammed one end of the piece of wood deep into his attacker's stomach. Yancel gasped, retching uncontrollably as he dropped to his knees. Reyn was already leaping up to meet Borry's attack but to his surprise found the other Fortren just standing there, staring at him.

"You're so tricky, ain't you? Just think you can make us look like fools, but I ain't stupid, chicken-boy. I ain't my brother. I got something else in mind for you."

Borry backed toward the tavern wall. "See, hurting you ain't just about breaking bones. It's about breaking your heart. By doing this."

With inexorable purpose he moved to where the elleryn rested. Several violent swings of the iron pipe smashed it to pieces. Reyn stared in shock as his instrument was reduced to broken bits of wood and severed strings, ruined beyond any hope of repair.

Borry turned back to him. "How do you like that, you pissant? How do you like your pretty plaything now? Why don't you play something for me? Why don't you make your pretty music?"

Reyn felt the rage building in a slow, steady boiling that worked through him like a fire given life by kindling and air. He started toward Borry, gripping his piece of wood.

But Borry was ready for him. He had discarded the iron pipe and now held a long knife in its place, the blade glinting in the moonlight. "Oh, you think you're ready for this, do you? Come get it!"

Fighting down the urge to run, Reyn braced himself, ready to block the other's knife. But suddenly arms wrapped about him from behind as Yancel, having finally regained his feet, came to his brother's aid. Reyn thrashed and twisted, but Yancel was strong and his grip solid and unyielding.

Borry howled with glee, then lifted his knife and charged.

Reyn, all chance of escape or defense gone, howled back at him in response.

Instantly the air seemed to change color, even in the darkness, and the faint silvery light of moon and stars seeping through the departing rain clouds took on a crimson blush. Borry Fortren felt the impact of the magic as he slammed into its invisible wall, not two feet away. The knife blade shattered. Reyn screamed louder, any attempt at control lost. Yancel's arms released their grip on him, and he tumbled away.

Borry, still fighting to get close enough to grip the boy with his bare hands, simply exploded. It happened spontaneously, with a shocking and terrible suddenness, pieces of the big man flying everywhere. Reyn stumbled back, shielding his eyes, trying to stay upright. But Yancel snatched at his legs from where he lay on the ground in an effort to topple him. The boy reacted instinctively, all hope of ending this any other way gone. His scream came from somewhere deep inside. It felt as if it came from somewhere else entirely, the intrusion in his own body harsh and raw. Yancel was flung backward, his arms torn from his shoulders, his blood flooding out of his body as he lay gasping out the last of his life.

Then Reyn Frosch felt the familiar disconnect, and he was tumbling into that familiar dark hole in which there was no light or sound and from which he could not extricate himself.

Everything around him disappeared, and his thoughts ceased.

6

WHEN REYN WOKE AGAIN, IT WAS MORNING. Bright light streamed through the gap in the curtains of his room, though the light was gray and hazy rather than sunny. He lay in his bed in the loft room over the back half of the tavern, listening to the sound of voices coming from below. He remembered right away what had happened, and he took an extra few moments to check himself over, searching for injuries.

There were none.

Not to him, anyway. But two of the Fortren brothers had suffered the sort of injuries from which you did not recover. And he was the cause. Reyn closed his eyes against the visions that suddenly thrust themselves to the forefront of his mind—Borry, torn into pieces of bone and slivers of flesh; Yancel, armless and bleeding out; his elleryn, its broken remains lying scattered on the ground; himself, falling out of the world, tumbling down into the pit of non-being, everything he had brought to pass left behind.

He closed his eyes. So it had happened again, just as he had feared in those last moments when he faced the brothers. Just as it had happened all those other times. He had been provoked, had lost his temper and composure, had given way to his emotions, and had vented through deadly use of his voice. In an instant's time he had ruined everything.

Conflicting questions rose in a rush. Why couldn't he have prevented it from happening? Why couldn't he have found a way to stop it? If he could control the modulation of his singing, why couldn't he do the same when he screamed? A light and a dark side to his voice—shouldn't he be able to manipulate both instead of only one?

He reached for the glass of water by his bedside and drank it down. He felt bereft. Two dead; two more ghosts that would haunt him forever. It didn't matter that they had hated him and that he cared nothing for them. It didn't matter that they had provoked him in a way that had effectively removed every other option if he wanted to stay alive. Nothing mattered to ghosts save that they haunted until they found peace, and there was no peace to be found for Borry and Yancel Fortren.

Nor any for him.

He was finished in Portlow. He would have to leave now. There were Fortrens everywhere, and they would be hunting him. And even if they weren't, the townspeople would be appalled by what he had done. It didn't matter how much they loved his music or admired his singing. Doing what he had done, killing two men in the manner he had—even if they didn't know exactly how he had done it—would be beyond their understanding. In truth, it was beyond his. He couldn't explain it any better than they could. He could barely accept it as a part of who and what he was.

He had risen and was dressing when Gammon came through the door. He saw the wariness in the other's eyes immediately and felt ashamed.

"Feeling better now?" the tavern owner asked, closing the door behind him. "You don't seem hurt."

He shook his head. "No, I wasn't hurt. I killed them before they could do anything."

"Self-defense, though. Found Borry's knife. Everyone knows it. So no question about what happened. But the knife was shattered all to pieces. How did you do that?"

"Rock."

"You used a rock on him and his brother? Looked like they'd been sent through a shredder."

"They were. In a manner of speaking. Look, Gammon, I won't talk about it. I just won't. I know I have to leave, and I'm sorry about what happened. I didn't like those two, but I didn't want it to come to this. I liked being here. I liked singing in the tavern. I wish I could take it all back." Reyn sighed. "You've been good to me, and I appreciate it."

Gammon came over to him. "Look, Reyn, your business is your own. Even with this. You were attacked, and you defended yourself. They smashed your instrument, tried to take your life. Everyone knows it. No one likes the Fortrens, so losing Borry and Yancel won't cause much loss of sleep." He paused. "But it's the way it was done, don't you see? If you could just offer something . . . explain it a little . . ."

The boy smiled. "I can't do that. I can barely explain it to myself, and trying to explain it to anyone else won't help. I have to leave. It's best for everyone. The rest of the Fortrens will be coming for me. That's a given. If I'm not here, there can't be more of what happened last night. And there will be more, Gammon, if I stay and try to explain."

The tavern owner nodded, a resigned look on his face. "Your mind's made up, I see. But you might not find leaving so easy. There are Fortrens already watching the roads. They know what you intend, and they will try to stop you. So don't do them any favors. Stay a bit longer. Give this a little time. You can keep your room here. Some of us like you enough that we've agreed to watch over you until we find a way to sneak you out. What do you say?"

Reyn finished dressing, then picked up the remainder of his clothes and stuffed them in a travel sack. "I say you are a good friend, and I've found a home in Portlow that I hate to leave. But I won't risk you and those others you've persuaded to help you. I'll have something to eat and be on my way. Come now, tell me who found me last night. Was it you?"

"The old grease-dog. He heard the howling outside his door and opened it just in time to find the Fortrens—or what was left of them—on the ground and you standing there staring into space like you'd lost your mind. He couldn't get you to talk or respond in any way, so he brought you inside and walked you up to your room and left you there. I came up later and checked you for injuries. You didn't have any, but you still kept staring at nothing. So I tucked you in and left you. Guess you came out of it at some point and fell asleep."

The boy shrugged. "I couldn't say. I don't remember any of it. I was fighting to stay alive, and then I woke up in my bed. Everything between then and now is a black hole in my memory. Can we go down and get something to eat? I want to leave right away."

They left the room and descended the stairs together. The steps ended at the back entrance, and they turned into the kitchen through a second door that bypassed the great room. There wouldn't be many patrons there at this hour, but even one would be enough to sound the alarm. Gammon motioned him over to the cook's table and went to pour him some of last night's beef stew, which was simmering in the kettle set over the stove flame at a low heat.

"You really ought to give it another day," he said, but Reyn didn't respond. He was finishing the last of his stew when there was a knock at the kitchen door leading in from the great room. He looked up expectantly. He couldn't remember the last time anyone had knocked on that door. Staff used it mostly, and there was no reason for them to knock.

Gammon walked over and pulled the door open. The black-cloaked stranger from the night before was standing there.

His eyes settled on the boy. "Would you be willing to spare me a few moments of your time?" When Reyn hesitated, he added, "I can sit with you right there. You won't have to move. Just a few moments."

Reyn wanted to say no. In fact, he was all prepared to say no, but something stopped him. Maybe it was the way the stranger was looking at him or maybe it was simply his own curiosity. The stranger had known he had magic. Could he possibly teach Reyn more about it, how to manage it so he wouldn't have to keep living in fear of losing control? He nodded and beckoned the other over.

The stranger took the chair across from him. "You certainly are full of surprises. Everyone's talking about you."

"What do you want?" Reyn asked, anxious to get on with things.

"You're planning to leave?"

How did he know that? Reyn shrugged. "It seems like a good idea."

"I'd like you to stay another couple of days. I have business that needs my immediate attention, but I don't want to lose track of you. I can be back quickly enough when it's finished."

"I don't think I have two days. I doubt that I have two hours."

"The Fortrens?"

"You seem well informed about my situation."

"I am well informed about most things, your singing included."

Reyn paused. "You know what I can do?"

"I not only know what, I know why. I meant what I said last night. There is a history to your talent, and I can tell you all about it. I can offer you a better understanding of what it means and perhaps give you a way to control it."

"But not now?"

"My business is pressing, and the need to address it is urgent. I must go at once. But I will be back, and we can talk then. At length, if you choose."

"Well, perhaps you can tell me a way to reach you?"

"Or perhaps not. You intend to disappear somewhere the Fortrens and their ilk can never find you. One of the Southland cities, perhaps? Well, I need to be able to disappear, as well. So I need you to wait right here."

He paused, his bladed features taking on a strangely feral look. "What if I guarantee you that the Fortrens will leave you alone until I get back? What if I can make certain they will not try to harm you? Or even come into the village?"

Reyn gave him a dubious look. "I think you offer more than you can deliver. The Fortrens aren't the sort to listen to reason."

The stranger stood up. "I'll speak to them immediately. I'll make the time. You won't have to worry. Look for me in two days. You will be glad you waited. I will make it worth your while in more ways than one."

And like that, without waiting for a further response from the boy, or even giving him another glance, he was out of his chair and gone.

• • •

Arcannen left the Boar's Head quickly, anxious to wrap things up in Portlow so he could make his appointment in Sterne. He was already thinking ahead to what he would do once he got there, his plans taking shape as he mulled over his options. But now there needed to be some revisions. The boy was intrigued enough by Arcannen's promise to reveal more about the nature of his magic that he would stay where he was for two days. Although once back again, Arcannen knew he would need more than a few promises to persuade the other to his cause.

What he would need was something the boy didn't have but would want, even if the boy didn't know what it was.

Fortunately, his sorcerer's talents allowed him to divine the needs and desires of others. He had been able to do so here, and now all he needed to do was to produce what was required. The trouble this would require would be worth it in the end. Ten times worth it, if he could make the boy his ally.

But first, the Fortrens must be dealt with.

He had gleaned a little of their family history from talking to a few of the townspeople in a discreet and seemingly conversational way, so as not to cause suspicion. There was nothing very complicated about them. Their patriarch was Costa Fortren, a man nobody seemed to like and everybody feared. He was the one who could exercise control over the others, and there were plenty of others if you counted all the shirttails and hangers-on. Well over a hundred.

But Arcannen had been confronted by situations like this before, so he wasn't at a loss to decide what needed doing.

He took his Sprint from where he had left it concealed in the surrounding forests—a modified two-man vessel that was sleek and fast. It was all that remained of his once-powerful fleet of airships, but then almost everything else was pretty much gone by now, as well. His failed attempt to subvert the Leah siblings and kill Aphenglow Elessedil had cost him everything, and he was still trying to figure out how to get it all back. The irony, of course, was that if he had just waited five years, the woman would have died anyway. Dealing with Isaturin as Ard Rhys would have been less of a challenge than dealing with Aphenglow, but the chance of gaining immediate control over the Druid order had been too tempting. Well, it was all water under the bridge now, and he did his best not to dwell on how things had turned out.

Save for the matter of Arbrox. That was too recent, and the emotional damage he had suffered as a result felt as fresh and raw as it had on the day the atrocity had been committed. That could not be forgotten.

He flew only a short distance before reaching the Fortren compound, a sprawling complex of houses and outbuildings—some barns, some storage bins for food and what he guessed were stolen goods—sitting out in a meadow with good sight lines in all directions. He crisscrossed the area several times so that everyone could get a look at him, then he brought the Sprint down close to the main house and climbed out.

Men converged on him from all sides, many carrying portable flash rips and spring guns, others crossbows and blades. They approached cautiously but showed no signs of being intimidated. He stood where he was as they closed in, wrapping himself in protective magic in case one or more got a little careless with their weapons. He hadn't come out here to end up the victim of some fool's overzealous behavior.

"Costa Fortren!" he called out boldly, scanning the faces around him. "Are you willing to speak with me?"

There was momentary silence; then the front door of the main house crashed open and a huge bear of a man lumbered into view. He was wearing furs and leather, and there were blades hanging from belts and sheaths all about his body. He glared at Arcannen, then stomped down the steps of the building and came over. When he was a dozen feet away, he stopped. A handheld flash rip appeared in one great hand.

"Who are you?" he roared.

"My name is Arcannen."

The big man shook his head. "Never heard of you. What are you doing here?"

The sorcerer ignored him. He gestured at the other's weapon. "You seem well supplied with illegal goods. Those flash rips are meant as army issue only."

Costa Fortren laughed, his belly shaking, his thick beard billowing out. "The army won't miss them. You come here to try to take them back from us? You a Federation official?"

The sorcerer shook his head. "Hardly. They want me dead. They probably want you dead, too. So we have something in common."

"We have nothing in common. You look like a Druid to me."

"It might look that way, but I'm no Druid—though I do have the use of magic. I was passing through Portlow when I stumbled across someone I've been hoping to find for a very long time. Trouble is, you want to kill him."

The other man's eyebrows beetled together as he scowled. "You mean that boy? The one that killed Yancel and Borry? Would you be his friend, maybe? Come to beg for his life?"

Arcannen shook his head. He didn't like all the dark looks he was getting from the rest of the assemblage. "I want to point out something before we continue. If any member of your family decides to use a weapon against me, it will end badly for them. I'm only here to talk."

Costa Fortren glanced at the men and women surrounding them and shook his head. "Weapons down!" he roared. The response was immediate, as everyone took a step back. The big man looked at Arcannen. "No one does anything unless I tell them to. Say what you have to say. But don't waste my time."

"I have a request to make." Arcannen kept the protective magic in place. "I need the boy alive because I have a use for him. My intention is to take him away with me. When I do, you will never see him again. But I need you to promise you will do nothing to him until then. Two days, maybe three from now."

The Fortren patriarch stared at him. "He killed two of my sons. I don't care what you want him for or why. He has to pay for what he did. I'll never allow him to walk free."

"I thought you might feel that way, but I have to warn you," Arcannen continued. "He is not exactly what he appears. He is much more dangerous than you are. You or your whole family. He didn't just kill your boys by accident. He has the use of powerful magic, and if you go after him, bad things will happen to you, too."

"It doesn't matter. He dies all the same."

"There is every reason to believe that if I take him with me, he dies anyway. So why not wait and see? That way we both get what we want. If he lives through what I've got planned for him, you can always come after him later."

"You talk nonsense, sorcerer! You talk like a fool."

It wasn't Costa Fortren who spoke this time. It was a young man who had stepped forward from the others, a flash rip lifted and pointed. The boy was young but his mean face and hard eyes suggested that he was old in other ways.

"Antriss!" Fortren snapped at him. "Did I not say to lower all weapons? Who leads this family?"

"I'll not listen to any more of this man's talk, Pap!" Antriss snarled. "He's not taking that cow-dung music boy anywhere!"

He was working himself up to using the flash rip, and Arcannen was concerned that if he did so, it would set off all the others. His magic was significant, but it was not all-powerful. He had assumed something like this would happen, however, so he was prepared. He had known he would have to make an example of someone.

"Hold!" he snapped at the boy, one hand lifting, palm extended.

Instantly Antriss was frozen in place as the sorcerer's magic wrapped him about. He fought to free himself, but the bonds were too strong. Arcannen left him that way and turned back to his father.

"How many sons do you have?" he asked, keeping his hand extended toward Antriss.

The big man hesitated. "Three, with Borry and Yancel gone. Let him go."

"Is he your youngest, then?"

"He is. Now let him go or you'll regret it."

Arcannen smiled. "Not half so much as you will if you cross me.

Will you grant me my request? Or would you prefer to lose another son? Or . . . would you like to see exactly what I can do?"

He twisted his outstretched hand slightly. Slowly, painfully, unable to keep himself from doing so, Antriss lifted the flash rip and pointed its barrel toward his own throat. "Father!" he croaked.

"Stop this!" Costa Fortren roared at Arcannen. "Let him go!"

Arcannen didn't move, holding the boy and the weapon fast, watching the big man, waiting for a further response. "Do we have an understanding?" he pressed.

The Fortren patriarch fumed, barely able to contain himself. Then he nodded. "We do. Let him go!"

"Your word, please? Promise that neither you nor any of your family will harm the boy before I take him away. Promise that not one of you will even go into Portlow until then. Say it."

Shouts and cries had risen from the remaining members of the family, some anguished, some furious, all directed at him. Arcannen paid no attention, his gaze locked on their leader.

"All right!" the big man howled, his face gone red, his body taut with rage and frustration. "I give you my word! On everything you just said!"

Arcannen gestured again, and Antriss lowered the flash rip. He stood there in silence, a stunned look on his face.

"A promise made under duress is not a binding promise!" Costa Fortren spat out the words venomously. His weapon lifted. "You realize that, don't you?"

Arcannen did not respond. Instead, he gestured once more at Antriss, who raised the flash rip a second time, turned it toward the family members standing right behind him, and shot a man standing not six feet away. The charge from the weapon burned a hole through the man's midsection and dropped him where he stood.

"Are you sure about that?" the sorcerer asked. A second motion of his hand had Antriss pointing the weapon at his own throat anew. "Very sure?"

"Enough!" The big man had gone pale. "I take your point. You have my word. I will keep it. The boy will be kept safe. Now get off my land!"

Arcannen nodded. "Just remember. If anything happens to that boy—anything at all—I will come looking for you. If I do that, your family will cease to exist. Every man, woman, and child. Don't doubt me on this. I am a bad enemy to make, Costa Fortren. Much worse than you know."

Keeping the protective magic wrapped close, the sorcerer eased toward his Sprint, eyes sweeping the faces of those surrounding him, watching for any sort of treachery. But everyone seemed thoroughly shocked by what he had just said, and no one was doing anything but watching him.

He reached the Sprint without difficulty and climbed back aboard. He felt reasonably certain he had convinced the Fortrens to do what he wanted. The boy would be safe until his return. There was nothing like an object lesson to make a point. Actions really did speak louder than words.

If not, it would be the worst mistake they had ever made.

He powered up the diapson crystals, and moments later he was winging his way toward Sterne.

7

PAXON LEAH WAS WORKING OUT IN THE PRACTICE yard with Oost Mondara, his prickly Gnome sword master and close friend, his black-bladed sword flashing in the sunlight as he progressed through a series of feints and strikes, thrusts and parries, incorporating everything into positions of defense and attack. It had been five years since these lessons had begun, and another man might have decided long ago that he had learned all there was to learn of swordsmanship and there was no point in continuing to study. But Paxon wasn't just another man, and he took nothing for granted when it came to improving his skills. That he had discovered the power of the ancient Sword of Leah was a gift to be honored. That he had been given the chance to serve as the Ard Rhys's Blade and had been given a home and life in the Druid order was not something he would ever take for granted or fail to view as a challenge.

So every day he came down to the yard to practice with his blade, and every day he learned a little more and progressed a step further. Oost continued to instruct him, doing it now more out of the satisfaction he derived from viewing Paxon's enthusiasm and steady development than he did out of a sense of obligation. In Paxon, the Gnome had found a kindred spirit—a fellow believer in the importance of hard work and dedication to a talent that clearly set him apart from almost everyone. Paxon was good with a blade, maybe the best the gnarled trainer had ever encountered, and if there was a way to make him even better then there was no reason not to employ it.

But Paxon was bored with practice and anxious for a chance to do something of a more practical nature, so he was excited and relieved when Keratrix arrived to tell him that Isaturin wished to see him when his practice time was finished. Paxon tried not to rush through what remained of his session, but failed miserably. Finally, Oost broke it off, throwing up his hands.

"That's enough. You are sleepwalking through your disciplines! I've lost you completely." His voice was gruff and accusatory. "Go find out what the Ard Rhys wants of you. Might as well do *something* useful."

With muttered apologies thrown back over his shoulder, Paxon hurried off to do as the other had suggested, a sense of anticipation making him light-headed and happy. He was certain a mission awaited him, a chance to travel to another part of the world, an opportunity to use his skills to help someone. It was the reason he had accepted this position in the first place, the end result of the effort Aphenglow Elessedil had expended to convince him to abandon his old life hauling airfreight and to bring him to Paranor.

He thought momentarily of his mentor and benefactor, dead six weeks now, gone down into the netherworld and the company of Druids past. She had done much more for many others than she had for him, but he treasured the gift of the life she had given him every day. He would never forget what she had meant to him. He could still see her face in his mind as clearly as he had on the last day he had been with her, accompanying her to the Hadeshorn to bear witness as the Shade of Allanon bore her away. He could still hear her voice, encouraging him to believe in himself, telling him there would always be a home for him and for Chrysallin at Paranor.

His sister, he believed, owed Aphenglow even more than he did. It was Aphenglow who had saved her, who had taken her in and helped her to heal. But this reminded him that the Ard Rhys had wanted him to tell Chrys about her magic—something he still had not done. He had not found the right moment or even a way to act on her warning. So he prevaricated, still uncertain. But he did not think he could put it off much longer. Sooner or later, something would happen to cause the wishsong to surface again. The consequences of that happening were unknowable. The Ard Rhys had believed it would help Chrys if she understood what was happening and could find a way to better deal with it. But Paxon continued to worry that telling her would have the opposite effect and send her back into a state of catatonia similar to the one she had been placed in after her first use of the magic.

Since he could not reconcile his fears with hers the debate continued, unresolved.

These were his thoughts as he changed out of his practice clothes, washed himself down, dressed anew, and climbed the stairs to the Ard Rhys's quarters. It still seemed odd that Isaturin now occupied those rooms and that Aphenglow was really gone. He liked Isaturin well enough, although he would never think about him in the same way he thought about his predecessor. For Paxon, Aphenglow Elessedil would always be the real Ard Rhys of the Druids.

Still, on this occasion he was more than anxious to meet with the new Ard Rhys and find out if there was finally something for him to do besides practice with his sword and sit around waiting.

"Come in, Paxon," Isaturin said at his knock, looking up from behind a desk as the Highlander entered. "Come sit."

Paxon did so, noting that Isaturin seemed as consumed by record keeping and paperwork as Aphenglow had, his work space littered with documents and books. Keratrix stood to one side, organizing files, handing things over and taking them away, all without a word being spoken, apparently knowing exactly what it was the Ard Rhys required.

"We've registered a disturbance of some significance in the scrye waters." Isaturin leaned back, locking his fingers behind his head. "It happened late last night and was reported to me this morning. This is of particular interest because the nature of the disturbance closely resembled the one we recorded when Chrysallin used the wishsong."

Paxon was surprised. "Someone else has use of it?"

"Possibly. The reading of the waters isn't an exact science. We can tell the general nature of a disturbance. We can tell the extent of the power expended to create it. And we can tell where it came from. The rest we have to guess at, using whatever information we have at our disposal. In this case, the Druid monitoring the waters was the same Druid who was monitoring when your sister used her powers."

"So we have a solid comparison. Who was the Druid?"

"Avelene."

An image of her face came immediately to mind—small, slender, dark skin, lavender eyes, sharp features that seemed perfectly suited to her look and temperament. He hadn't seen much of her in the past few years, busy with his own pursuits, caught up in caring for Chrysallin. But he remembered hearing about her in snatches of conversation. Fiercely intelligent and independent-minded. Always ready to challenge authority if she didn't agree. A student of magic, her own and others' no matter the nature.

"Can I speak with her?"

Isaturin cocked an eyebrow. "All you want. She will be your companion for the next few days. I'm sending you both south into Federation territory to try to sort this out. I want the source of the magic found and its nature determined. If you think it advisable, I want it recovered and brought here. Avelene will be in command of the expedition; you will act as her protector."

Paxon started to rise, anxious to begin preparations. "Wait a minute." Isaturin held up his hand. "We haven't finished here yet."

Paxon sat back down. "There's more?"

"There is. Tell me about your sister. Have you spoken with her about her condition?"

It was a reasonable question, but Paxon felt himself become irritated anyway. "Aphenglow must have told you she recommended that I tell Chrys. But I'm still not certain that's the right thing to do."

"I find myself wondering if there is a right thing, Paxon. This is a difficult situation with no clear path forward. But maybe you should consider the relative risks. If you tell her now, you can be there to talk to her about it. You can make use of the Druid Healers to help her come to terms with it. But if you wait and she discovers it on her own—perhaps in a life-and-death confrontation of the sort she faced before—you will have to hope she isn't so severely impacted by the unexpectedness of the surfacing of the magic that she is flung into an even deeper catatonia than she was the last time."

"I *am* doing what I can!" Paxon snapped back. "A day doesn't pass when I don't think about it."

Isaturin nodded. "Indecision is the enemy. I think you should tell her. I know I am meddling, but I have an obligation to persuade you to what I think is the right course of action. Please give it some thought."

Paxon forced himself not to say something he would regret later. "I will. I promise."

Isaturin was already turning back to his paperwork. "Now go find Avelene and make your plans. I have assigned you one of the clippers and a crew of three members of the Druid Guard. You leave at first light."

Paxon went out the door, still angry about the Ard Rhys's interference, stomping down the hallway toward his quarters, paying no attention to those he passed on the way. What angered him most, he realized by the time he had reached his room and closed the door behind him, was that he knew Isaturin was right. Just as Aphenglow had been right. He should tell Chrys. He shouldn't leave it to chance.

The real problem was that he was afraid to tell her. He was afraid of what it would do to her. She had been so good since her recovery. She had become a familiar face in Paranor's halls and a friend to many who lived there. She had done well with her studies, and she had regained her footing in a way that encouraged him to believe she could find a home here—just as Aphenglow had promised.

He didn't want to risk all that. He didn't want to disrupt her life by revealing a truth so startling and immense that it might leave her crippled all over again.

He stood where he was in the middle of the room for a long time, pondering the matter, thinking he should put it behind him by going to her now, telling her the truth, getting it over with, and letting them face the consequences together.

He turned back toward the door and went out again into the hallway. But instead of going to look for his sister, he began searching for Avelene.

He found her a short time later in a quiet corner of the garden, sitting on a bench with her feet up, bent over an open book with several more sitting on the ground next to her. She looked up at his approach, and he was reminded again of how supportive she had been of him on his arrival five years earlier.

"So we're off on an adventure together," she said, arching an eyebrow at him. She set down the book. "Do you think we're up to it?"

He grinned. "I think you are. I hear you might be the best in all Paranor when it comes to magic."

"I hear you might be the best swordsman in the Four Lands. If Oost Mondara can be believed."

Paxon stared. "Oost really said that? Was he sober?"

"Apparently you impressed him considerably with your work ethic. Impressed me, too, I might add. I've had my eye on you, even if you didn't see me. You work hard. You've dedicated yourself to becoming the Ard Rhys's Blade. No one gave you anything. You worked for all of it."

"You, too. Can I sit?"

She moved her legs to give him room, drawing them up to her chest and wrapping her arms around them. "Seems like a long time ago that we first met," she said. "You were kind of uncertain back then. I don't see any of that now."

"Oh, I'm still pretty uncertain about most things. I've gotten comfortable with using a sword, but you can't cut your way through uncertainty. I still struggle with the moral issues surrounding the uses of magic."

"Well, mostly, it's not your concern, is it? It's a Druid issue."

"That might be, but I'm acting as their representative. I like to be sure about what it is I'm representing."

She laughed. "That's fair. But remember, we all struggle with what's right and wrong, Paxon. That's the nature of our lives. We have to figure out what we can live with, and hope that what we do to bring it about doesn't exact a cost that's too high. We have to decide where to draw the line. Are you thinking of Sebec?"

He shook his head. "Not so much. I was thinking more of Chrysallin. I haven't figured out if she's where she belongs, being here. I don't know if studying to join the Druid order is what's right for her."

He was hedging with his response. His real concern was not his sister's presence at Paranor but his reluctance to be honest with her about why she was there. But he couldn't tell Avelene that.

"She's fine here. She's got you to watch out for her. She's got people who care about her. Lots of them, in case you hadn't noticed. She's made friends, Paxon. She belongs as much as you do."

She brushed at her dark hair and studied him. "But that's not what you're talking about, is it?"

Too perceptive by far, he thought. "Can I ask you about your readings of the scrye waters? Isaturin said you were on duty with this latest disturbance, but you were on duty, too, when Arcannen was trying to take over the order. Isaturin said you believed the magic used might be the same?"

"I said the *properties* evidenced by each were similar."

"Can you explain that to me?"

"Magic of different types causes different sorts of disturbances to the scrye waters. Not in the strength of the disturbance, which is really a result of the power expended, but in the look of the ripples and shimmers. Rapidity, length, closeness, even color—these all say something about the magic. We keep records on this, as you know, and over time we have been able to determine after the fact where the similarities lie."

"So the records told you something about these two?"

"No. In this case, we don't seem to have any records. We never found out the exact nature of the magic that erupted five years ago, and it's up to you and me to try to determine it in this latest instance. What I do know, since I was on duty both times and had a chance to observe personally, was that they were almost exactly the same. That's not a coincidence."

"But shouldn't there be something in the records?"

"We only started keeping those records since Aphenglow Elessedil decided to track down and recover the magic that was being used by those not of the Druid order. So we have barely more than a hundred and fifty years of records to date. This magic, whatever it is, might have been around awhile. It might have been used countless times over the centuries. We just don't have anything that would tell us that."

Which would explain why no one in the Druid order but Aphenglow and now Isaturin knew it was the wishsong. Both must have decided it was better to keep it quiet.

Then he wondered suddenly how much Avelene knew. Could Isaturin have decided not to tell her about the wishsong? Had he kept that to himself? Or if she knew about it, why was she hiding it from him? Was it because he wasn't a Druid?

"I have to go," he said. "I just wanted to tell you how much I'm looking forward to going with you. I wish it could have happened sooner."

She gave him a look. "You do?"

"I said so, didn't I?"

She studied him a moment. "See you bright and early then." She picked up her book and went back to reading. "You do have something of a silver tongue, don't you? You just make my little heart beat with excitement."

She was angry. Or, at the very least, irritated. He started to say something in response, but gave it up. Whatever retort he made, she would have another poised on the tip of her tongue.

"I meant what I said," he threw back anyway.

She didn't look up—just gave him a dismissive wave of her hand.

He was a dozen steps removed when something occurred to him. An Ard Rhys would never dispatch members of the Druid order on a mission like the one they were embarking on without telling them exactly what they were up against. Not if he knew, and Isaturin did. It would be putting Druids at risk unnecessarily. And there was no good reason for him to do so here.

He slowed, and then turned around. Avelene was still reading her book. Slowly, he walked back over to her and waited until she looked up at him.

"Forget something?" she asked.

"Common sense," he answered. "The magic we're looking for is the wishsong."

Her smile was brilliant. "Now, that wasn't so hard, was it?"

"You already knew?"

"Of course."

"And you didn't think you should tell me that?"

"Well, you've apparently known for some time, right? Shouldn't you have been the one to tell me?"

He took a deep breath and exhaled. "That was what I just decided. If we're traveling together to find what might be a wild magic, we need to trust each other."

She nodded. "And now we do. I do, at least."

"I do, too."

"Then all is right with the world." She resumed reading. "See you in the morning, Paxon."

This time she sounded happy about it.

8

ARCANNEN FLEW WEST THROUGH THE REMAINDER of the day, losing himself in the piloting of his Sprint, enjoying the passing countryside below and the sweet smells of the summer day. He did not spend time thinking about what lay ahead; he had done enough of that already. Instead, he gave himself over to clearing his mind and letting his thoughts drift wherever they cared to go. Rest came with difficulty these days; the long comforting sleep of his time in Wayford had devolved into catnaps and guarded dozing. Being hunted did that to you. Being prey instead of predator required that you always have one eye open.

Unbidden, his thoughts jumped to Leofur. He wondered how his daughter was, how her life was going. He had not had contact with her in five years—not since Paxon Leah had given him his freedom in exchange for the medication that would cure his sister of her hallucinations and nightmares and give her back her life. Leofur had no idea where he was, of course. Like the rest of the world, she had been left behind. Not that they had been close before; not that leaving her caused him any particular pain. It certainly couldn't have mattered to her when he disappeared; she had been trying to kill him. Or at least trying to help the Highlander do the job. She had forsaken him a long time ago.

Wasn't it odd then that he was wondering about her now, that he found himself thinking about her when there was so little reason? But there it was, an inescapable fact. He supposed he wondered about her in a generic sort of way and not with any real hopes or aspirations. He did wonder how she had ended up with Paxon Leah and what had become of that relationship. He had sensed at the end that it might have been more than casual, that they might have cared about each other in a more serious way. But he couldn't say why he felt this was so; he couldn't explain it with reasoning or logic.

Eventually, his thoughts drifted on to other things. To the boy, waiting for him back in Portlow. He didn't even know his name. Wasn't that odd? He had such plans for him, such possibilities in mind, and he didn't know who he was. It was his nature not to get too close to people, of course. People were there to be used, instruments to be applied to a task. The boy was no different. Not in that way. In the way in which he might serve, he was decidedly different. In the nature of his power and his legacy, he was perhaps one of a kind.

But at the end of the day, the boy was there to be set on a course of action and made to follow through. He was just another weapon to be used against Arcannen's enemies.

He wished suddenly that he still had someone inside the Federation government to whom he could turn. It was helpful having a highly placed collaborator working to help you realize your plans or aid you in obtaining special favors. He had no one like that these days. Sebec had been purged from the Druid order, and he himself had eliminated Fashton Caeil, the Federation Minister of Security Against Magic.

Still, if you were on your own, you depended on no one to accomplish what needed doing, and the chances of mistakes were considerably lessened. He had learned that lesson a while back, and even though it placed a larger burden on him, it also assured that what was required would be done right.

Like now, when he was on his way to visit an old friend in the Southland city of Sterne in an effort to repay a debt.

He left his Sprint at the edge of the city airship field and walked

several hundred yards to the field manager's office to arrange for payment and a promise to watch over it. If he lost his airship, he would
be in deep trouble. So a few extra credits paid to make sure that didn't
happen were credits well spent. The field manager was open to an
arrangement—the pay he received from the city being less than what
he believed he deserved—and a bargain was quickly struck. The
Sprint would be carefully watched with an understanding that its
owner would be back to claim it before dawn.

His escape route assured, Arcannen set out for the Federation
barracks at the west end of the city.

He took a carriage to a place less than a quarter mile away—a
shop that specialized in opiates and other mind-altering potions and
plants—and stood outside until the shop had emptied of customers,
checking a final time through the small glass windows to either side
of the door to make certain before going in. The shop was small and
cramped with shelves and bins backed up against all the available
wall space and then stacked so high that a ladder was needed to reach
the two top levels. A counter no more than four feet long sat well
back in the shadows, its top clear of everything but a single cup and
saucer and a smoking pipe resting in a bowl.

An old man sat behind the counter, eyes fixed on Arcannen. He
might have been a hundred years old or a thousand. He was bent and
withered, and until you looked closely you might have assumed that
he had died and no one had noticed. He wore tattered gray clothes and
a skullcap. Arcannen had never seen him wear anything else. His
beard and hair were so wispy and thinned out, you could count the
strands.

"Eld Loy," the sorcerer greeted him, giving the old man a small
bow. "All is well? Nothing has changed?"

The old man nodded.

"My friend still occupies the same quarters?"

Another nod.

"He sleeps alone?"

A shrug. A nod.

"The Red Slash do not ward him, I mean? I don't care about the
women."

Still another nod.

Arcannen reached into his robes and withdrew a pouch filled with credits. "Yours, for your services—unless they prove inaccurate. In which case, they will pay for your burial."

The old man didn't blink. Arcannen bowed again and went back out the door.

He waited until close to midnight before making his way to his destination. It was a tavern set close to the barracks and frequented by the soldiers and their companions. It was the property of a retired squad leader and a few of his mates, and it catered almost exclusively to those who shared their worldview—which is to say, other soldiers. Even with midnight approaching, the tavern's interior was well lit and filled with boisterous men and women, shouting and laughing and singing songs of army life. A few of those with too much drink and a vague notion that it was time to get home had made it as far as the front stoop before falling by the wayside.

Arcannen stepped around the bodies carefully. Because Eld Loy had given him a diagram of the tavern's layout, he knew to go to the back door, step quickly inside, take three steps left to the rear stairwell, and climb to the small bedroom on the third floor. No one saw him enter the building; no one heard him ascend the stairs. This was not surprising, given the amount of noise and drunkenness in the tavern below. Arcannen had counted heavily on the distraction to keep from being noticed.

He paused at the door to listen. There were no sounds coming from inside. He tried the knob; it turned easily. He opened the door and peered in. Pale light from a streetlamp seeped through curtains hung over a solitary window to reveal that the room was unoccupied. Arcannen stepped in. The room was dismal—a squalid box with a bed, an old dresser, a table with a basin, and a wicker chair. There were some clothes on the floor and a few odds and ends of personal effects.

He glanced up. A heavy lamp was suspended from a hook screwed into one of the ceiling beams, but it was unlit.

Arcannen took another look around, moved the chair into the shadows to one side, and sat down to wait.

· · ·

Miles away, in the village of Portlow, Gammon was confronting Reyn Frosch. It was after midnight, and the tavern patrons were finally beginning to make their way home, the great room quieting down. Even in the absence of the boy's music, the people of the village had come to spend the evening, perhaps in the hope that he would resume playing. But Reyn had not found a way to replace his elleryn, and in spite of the assurances of the stranger that the Fortrens would leave him alone, he was not convinced.

This was being reinforced by Gammon as they spoke in the privacy of the boy's room.

"You can't trust a man like that," Gammon was insisting. "Did you see his eyes? Of course you did. How could you not? Wicked. Dangerous! He may well be the man to convince the Fortrens to let you be, but what do you want with a man like that?"

"He knows something about my singing." Reyn rubbed his temples. His head ached. "Maybe he can explain what happened."

"Maybe. But maybe he wants something more from you. Why would he help you otherwise? I think you should go. Get away from here. Find a new town and a new tavern that needs a singer with your talent."

"I told him I would wait."

"You owe him nothing! Think about what you are doing!"

Reyn sighed. This discussion was going nowhere. He could not make Gammon understand. The tavern owner was fixated on the stranger's darkness, as if it were a portent of impending doom. The boy didn't sense that at all. He was less concerned with the way people dressed and looked. What determined a man's character was how he behaved. The stranger had done nothing to him but show interest.

"I have to sleep now," he said finally.

"Fine," Gammon declared, rising. "But before you do, I have something for you. Wait here for me."

He went out and was gone for perhaps five minutes. When he returned, he was carrying a package wrapped in cloth and bound with string. The size and shape caused the boy's heart to quicken. He took the package from the tavern owner and swiftly unwrapped it.

A new elleryn, its burnished wood gleaming brightly, lay in his hands.

"She's beautiful," the boy whispered. He looked up at Gammon. "But I can't afford her."

"You don't have to pay anything. It's a gift."

"But I'm not playing for you anymore. I can't take this."

Gammon laughed. "You made me enough money over the last two years to pay for this ten times over. I owe you this. You take it. Keep it." He shrugged. "If you would agree to leave here tonight, I would pay you something extra to help you on your way. But I can see your mind is made up."

Reyn smiled. "I won't ever forget this."

"I should hope not." Gammon stuck out his hand. "Luck to you, Reyn. Whatever you decide to do. Luck always."

The handshake was warm and firm. Reyn wished once more that things could have worked out differently. Then Gammon released his grip and was out the door.

It was several hours later when Arcannen heard footsteps on the back stairs leading up to the bedroom in which he waited. The footsteps were clumsy and uncertain. There were frequent stumbles. He could tell that the man coming up was drunk and unsteady, anxious to reach his room and tumble into bed. It would make his task just that much easier, if not quite so satisfying. He would have preferred the other sober and fully aware of what was about to happen. He would rather the fear reflected in his eyes and voice not be dulled by drink.

But you couldn't always have things the way you wanted them. If you could, the events that created the reason for his being here would never have come to pass.

The footsteps reached the top of the stairway. Soundlessly, Arcannen rose and moved to stand just behind the door. The man without fumbled with the handle, and the door swung inward. When the man was inside the room, Arcannen quietly closed the door behind him.

The man turned back unsteadily, peering at the dark shape behind him, unable to focus.

"Who is it?" He slurred his words, swayed unsteadily. "What do you want?"

"I want you, Desset," Arcannen answered.

Desset tried to scream, but Arcannen grabbed him, muffling his cries with one hand, bearing him backward onto his rumpled bed, pushing him down until he was pinned, his eyes wide with fear, his body quaking in the sorcerer's strong grip.

"Shhh, shhhh," Arcannen whispered. "There's no point in trying to scream. I took your voice so we wouldn't be disturbed. Do you know what's going to happen to you, Desset? Of course you do. It's what happens to all traitors sooner or later. I hope the last few weeks of your life were worth what you did."

Climbing atop the other man, he pinned his arms and took his head gently in both hands, lifting it so that they could see into each other's eyes clearly. Desset was thrashing feebly beneath him, and tiny whimpers were coming from his throat as he fought to scream for help.

Arcannen smiled down at him as he cradled his head. "You knew the price you would pay for betraying me, didn't you? Or was it just bad luck that it worked out this way? Were you only interested in destroying Arbrox? No, they wouldn't pay you well enough for that. Something, for certain, but much more for me. You couldn't pass up the chance to get your hands on that kind of money. All you had to do was make certain I died along with all of the others. Those people were my friends, Desset. They sheltered and protected me. They helped me when no one else would. And now, because of you, they are all dead."

Arcannen paused. "And now you can join them."

Tightening his hands on Desset's head, he wrenched it sharply to one side and then quickly the other way. He could feel the neck bones giving way; he could hear them cracking and snapping. Desset shuddered and clenched and finally went still.

Arcannen released the dead man's head and stood up. That wasn't nearly as satisfying as he would have liked, but killing seldom was. It was a task performed out of necessity, and while the act itself could be fulfilling, the aftermath seldom induced any sort of euphoria. It was so here. The sorcerer was already thinking beyond what he had just done to what still needed doing.

He pulled a length of cord from a pouch at his waist, tied one end tightly around Desset's neck, and formed a loop at the other end. Then he shouldered the dead man, climbed atop the chair to gain the necessary height, and, after removing the lamp, slung the open loop over the ceiling hook and left Desset hanging.

Then he seated himself, printed a few words on a piece of paper, and attached them to Desset's body. He studied his handiwork for a few moments more, watching the dead man swing gently from the ceiling hook as a breeze through the window caught his body in a twisting motion.

Now we will see, he thought.

Then he went out the door, down the stairs, and into the night.

It was shortly after dawn the following morning when Dallen Usurient, Commander of the Red Slash division of the Federation army, climbed those same stairs behind the officer who had summoned him and entered Desset's quarters. Desset's body still hung from the ceiling hook, lifeless and beginning to smell as the day's heat reached it. Usurient saw the note pinned to the body right away and walked over for a look.

He read the note carefully and stepped back again, his face dark with anger.

"Do you know what it means, sir?" the officer who had summoned him asked quietly.

Usurient nodded. He knew exactly what it meant.

WE ARE COMING FOR YOU.
ARBROX.

He looked at the officer. "It means Arcannen is still alive."

9

ARCANNEN, IN THE MEANWHILE, STOOD OUTSIDE a large residential building that was colorful and ornate, its wooden siding and trim painted in soft pinks and greens. It sat on the outskirts of the village of Hennish, which was not far from the much larger city of Wayford, where Arcannen had made his home until the Druids had driven him out. It was several hours after sunrise, and he had flown all night to get here. He'd had no sleep and he was tired, but his visit couldn't wait.

He could see the girls moving about inside the pink-and-green building and hear their chatter and laughter. Some of them, at least, were up early. Perhaps they had chores. Perhaps suitors. Business would commence whenever a customer came calling, and assigned chores must be completed before then.

Yet this was not a pleasure house and these girls were not here to be used. This was the House of Rare Flowers. The sign over the veranda boldly declared it, and everyone who knew of its existence knew its purpose.

He watched awhile longer, readying himself for his encounter with Corussin, who was the proprietor of this establishment. They had done business before, and they knew each other well. They were friends, after a fashion. But both possessed strong personalities and harbored grand ambitions, and each wanted to feel in these business transactions that he had gotten the better of the other.

Arcannen could not see the guards, but he knew they were everywhere. Corussin was not the sort of man who took chances. It was easy enough to walk into the House of Rare Flowers, but if you broke the rules or did anything inappropriate while you were there, it wasn't always so easy to walk out again.

Finally, Corussin stepped through the doorway onto the veranda and stood looking at him for a moment, hands on hips. The proprietor was a small, slender man, well groomed and finely dressed. His long black hair was an affectation he had embraced years ago, his tresses falling in waves to his waist. For a time, he had worn a beard, as well, but he appeared to have abandoned that.

After a moment, he beckoned Arcannen forward. Arcannen nodded and approached.

"Were you going to stand out here all day waiting for an invitation?" Corussin growled. "How long would you have lasted if I hadn't seen you?"

The deepness of his voice always surprised the sorcerer. "I don't like to arrive unannounced and give the impression that I simply assume you have time for me," he answered.

"Oh, I always have time for you, Arcannen. Though of late, you've been mostly absent. About five years now?"

"My fortunes took a downturn, as you've undoubtedly heard. But I have reason to think they might be on the upswing. Can we talk?"

Corussin took him through the front door of Rare Flowers and down a hallway to a quiet reception room at the back of the house. On the way, they passed several of the girls who lived there in the process of preparing for the day. Some were doing their assigned chores; some were dressing for suitors. Their purpose in coming to Rare Flowers and Corussin was simple. Each of them was looking to improve her situation through a display of beauty, intelligence, and marketable skills. Each gave herself over to the proprietor for the time it took to refine all three attributes, and then an employer/mate/sponsor was found who would take her to live with him under whatever arrangements the two of them had arrived at. The man lucky enough to win over one of these girls—and win her over he must, just as surely as she must work hard to present herself favorably—paid Corussin richly for the privilege of meeting the right girl. The money was paid up front, and it was nonrefundable. If things didn't work out, that was just too bad. This was a business transaction, first and foremost. Let the buyer beware.

But the buyer was given ample opportunity to decide if this was the right match, and the girl was given an equal amount of time to determine the same. It worked out more often than not.

Arcannen always thought it odd that all this couldn't be achieved in a less complex and formalized fashion. But it was clear that, for many men, an arrangement of this sort was more attractive and reliable than simple courting. And for most of these girls, who came from dubious circumstances and less-fortunate backgrounds, it offered a better-than-decent chance for living in a safe and sheltering environment.

The sorcerer and the proprietor sat in facing chairs by floor-to-ceiling windows that opened onto an extensive garden. Several of the girls were walking the pathways with the groundskeeper, who was imparting his knowledge of his craft. Beyond, the high walls surrounding the garden kept curious sightseers at bay.

Anonymity was a large part of the advantage of placement and resettling at Rare Flowers. No one besides Corussin knew the identities of all the girls or the men. There were no open houses or visiting hours. No one who didn't live here or come on business was allowed in. It was a tightly run operation, and it was this reputation that largely contributed to its success.

A stunning young woman with olive skin and ink-black hair hanging straight and long below her shoulders entered the room and bowed to Corussin.

"Evelin Emiko," he greeted her, bowing back. "Something cold for my guest and myself. You remember Arcannen?"

Emiko bowed to him, and he returned the gesture of respect. Emiko had come to Rare Flowers almost ten years ago, and had decided she should stay on as the proprietor's business partner and consort. Efficient and capable, she was the perfect companion for a man whose reputation and livelihood relied on discretion and satisfaction for all clients.

It didn't hurt that the proprietor and Emiko were in love. And they were, desperately.

She left the room, her footfalls silent. "What is it you're looking for, Arcannen?" Corussin asked, watching his life partner go.

The sorcerer smiled. He liked it that the other man never wasted time when business was involved. He always got right to the heart of the matter and didn't pretend he didn't know what the client had come for.

"I am looking for a girl," he answered. "Not a young woman, but a girl. I need her to be no more than twenty years of age. She must be . . ." He paused, thinking. "Different looking. Unusual. She must be strong-minded and intelligent. More so than average. It would help if she had an innate sense of the appropriate and reasonable. She will be dealing with a very strong, very determined young man."

Corussin smiled. "I don't see this young man sitting next to you. You are not referring to yourself, are you?"

Arcannen laughed. "No. The young man in question doesn't know anything about this."

"Well, then. You know the policy, Arcannen. Your young man must undergo an interview to allow the girl to determine his suitability."

"Perhaps that won't be necessary here. Their relationship will be short-term, and it will not involve any sort of permanent commitment. The temporary appearance of the possibility will be sufficient. I will pay you double your usual price, and I will pay her the same amount for her trouble."

The proprietor sighed. "What are you up to? Because you have a plan in mind, clearly. Tell me something that will make me want to consider your offer more seriously."

"The young man in question has the use of a very powerful form of magic. I want him to put himself in my hands. In order to make that happen, I need to give him a reason to do so. I intend to offer him something he wants. A girl. He may not know it, but he wants someone to love him. He wants someone to care about, to ground him, to give him a purpose in life. Any girl might suffice, but why settle for anything but the very best? So I have come to you."

Emiko reappeared carrying a tray containing a pair of silver tankards. She offered the first to Arcannen and then moved over to Corussin with the second. As soon as the tray was empty, she left the room, closing the door behind her.

"So you intend to manipulate this nameless young man." The proprietor steepled his fingers in front of him. "Which means you intend for the young girl you select to act on your behalf. Because she must, mustn't she? So she must be clever and intuitive. As well as possessing the other attributes you listed. I imagine she needs to have a high opinion of herself, as well. She must be the sort of girl who will always put herself first so that her manipulation of this young man won't trouble her."

"But she must not put herself before me," Arcannen added quickly. "Her interests must not come before mine. She must be prepared to do whatever I ask of her."

"Well, she will have to determine if your interests conflict with her own, don't you think? You can't have her strong-willed and at the same time subservient, no matter how badly you might wish it."

Arcannen nodded. "I can let her know up front what I expect. I can give her assurances of what I will not do that would cause her discomfort. That might help ease her concerns. But once I have set her the task I am employing her for, she cannot deviate from what is required to achieve it."

Now it was Corussin's turn to laugh. "You don't ask for much, do you, Arcannen? Where do you think I am to find such a girl? Excuse me—young woman. Girls usually don't have that sort of experience and maturity. Girls are manipulative, and it usually shows."

Arcannen shrugged. "You are the purveyor of quality partners of the fair sex in business and life. You must have someone you can show me."

"Yes. But I am already partnered with her, and she is too old for what you seek. A woman and not a girl. Let me think. Why don't you take a walk in the garden while I consider?"

Arcannen rose and walked out through the garden door as his host held it open for him. He sensed that Corussin had someone in mind already, but for one reason or another was not ready to reveal his choice. He would make Arcannen wait a bit first, perhaps allow him to think that finding what he wanted was much more difficult than expected and therefore deserving of a greater payment.

Arcannen moved over to a nearby bench and sat down. Off to one side, young women enraptured by the teachings of the grounds-keeper were bending over a cluster of particularly beautiful bushes with bright crimson leaves and tiny purple berries. The voices of the young women were audible, but too soft to understand. He watched and listened to them until finally they moved on and disappeared from his view.

His gaze shifted to the majestic trees that grew along the far wall of the garden and just inside its barrier. White oaks, he decided, perhaps two hundred years old. They were canopied over the extensive grounds beyond. Guards would be on patrol there, chasing off would-be tree and wall climbers, keeping the affairs of the residents of Rare Flowers private.

He allowed himself a moment to recall Arbrox, wishing that none of this was necessary, that the Red Slash and Usurient and Desset had found something else on which to focus their bloodthirsty urges. It would have made things so much easier if he could have remained in the village, a guest of the pirate community, until he was better prepared for a return to the larger world.

The day was sunny and bright, and the air sweet with the smells of flowers and grasses. A light breeze ruffled the plants and the leaves of the trees, and the sorcerer took a moment to close his eyes and breathe it all in.

When he opened them again, a young woman was standing a few yards away, looking at him. She did not attempt to shift her gaze when she realized he was looking back. She kept her eyes fixed on him as if he were the most interesting man she had ever seen. What struck him, besides the fact that she could make him feel that way, was how different she looked. Her hair was a strange toffee color streaked with gold so richly toned that it seemed to flow through her tresses like liquid. She had small, perfect features—the face of a child's doll. She was tiny, but she had a presence to her even so. A deep green velvet dress, trimmed with silver thread on the cuffs, neckline, and hem, clung to her body, suggesting that she might be something ethereal.

Immediately he was struck by her.

Now, there is what I was talking about . . .

He left the thought unfinished. She was walking toward him, approaching with clear intent and a strong sense of self-confidence.

She came to a stop in front of him and smiled. "Hello."

"Hello, young lady," he answered.

"May I sit?"

He nodded and slid sideways a few inches. She moved to the bench and seated herself carefully, very close to but not touching him. He realized suddenly that his new companion was not a young woman after all, but exactly what her appearance had suggested—a young girl.

"I'm looking for a match," the girl said, her eyes fixed on his face. "Not a match that would satisfy most women, but one that will satisfy me. I think you might be it."

He smiled back. "What makes you say that? You know nothing about me at all. I might be here for any reason."

"Let me test myself. Tell me if I am wrong in what I surmise. You are a sorcerer. You possess great power, but you use it sparingly. You are very smart, but not reckless. You are not happy with your life at the moment, but you think you might be able to change that soon."

"Very good," he admitted. "I congratulate you on your perceptiveness. But I am not looking to make a match."

Her smile did not waver. "Perhaps you are and you don't realize it. Most men don't know what they need. Most men don't even realize the depth of their need. They think of satisfying basic instincts that are shallow and temporary, and that is enough for them. But we don't believe that at Rare Flowers. We are taught otherwise. Men need a companion who is their equal, and a match in the true sense of the word. They require someone who can offer strength where they are weakest and support where they most miss it."

"And what do young girls like yourself require?"

"Security and hope. Kindness and honesty. For young girls like myself, as you put it, a true match is never achieved in hours or days or even years; it is achieved over the course of a lifetime. Commitment is the means by which we attain it. Commitment is a journey that works best when each step taken is carefully measured."

"Pretty words. How is it that one so young has reached these complex conclusions? You seem very insightful."

"I am pleased you think so. Would you like to hear my story?"

He was enjoying this. He hoped Corussin wouldn't resurface right away. "Please. Tell it to me."

"I am the child of Rovers, a chieftain's daughter. Not a firstborn child, but one younger. When you are not firstborn, you have little worth in our culture. Mostly, in the eyes of our parents, we serve as marriage material. My father sought to match me with a rug seller in exchange for a few of his wares and some gold. I decided not to agree, so he threw me out. I took my leave of him and of my people and set out for the Southland. I quickly discovered how difficult it is for a girl of fifteen to make her way in the world. A few hard lessons and a few narrow escapes followed, and six months ago I found myself on the doorstep of Rare Flowers, asking Corussin for a place. I was taken in. I learned the things I needed to know fairly quickly. Now I search for a match. But the men with whom I have interviewed have failed to measure up to my requirements."

She was bold to tell him this, making her offer of a match more like a challenge than a request. But he had already decided she knew more than she was letting on. No one this young could be anywhere near as prescient as she seemed to be. She was Corussin's choice; the proprietor of Rare Flowers must have had her in mind all along. Now he had dispatched her to him, wanting her to demonstrate how clever and manipulative she could be. He would have told her about him first, of course, giving her just enough information to act on when she found him. But it was no coincidence that she was here.

Still, he admired her greatly and thought she might do.

"What if I were to offer you a temporary match with someone besides myself?" he asked. "I would take you with me and pay you very well for your time and trouble."

She shook her head. "I am not interested in anyone else. I am interested in you."

"But I told you I am not looking for a match."

"And I told you that sometimes men don't know what they are looking for. I suggest that you reconsider."

He was perplexed. He had expected her to jump at his offer. She was staring at him with frank but unyielding determination. She was not going to back down, he realized.

"You are too young for me," he tried. "I am more than twice your age. I would be old and useless before you reached your prime. You require a younger man."

"I require what is suitable for me. Age has nothing to do with it. I am searching for the man who will complement me as I intend to complement him. You are that man."

His patience slipped. "Corussin put you up to this, didn't he? This is meant to demonstrate your talents. Very well. You have done that. I accept that you have demonstrated your capabilities. You are exactly who I am looking for. But stop pretending you want me."

The girl's face darkened. "I have no idea what you are talking about. Corussin has nothing to do with my coming to you. I saw you earlier, standing in front of the building. I watched you meet with him and then come into Rare Flowers and retire to the back rooms. I took your measure all the while, making up my mind. When I saw you come out into the garden, I decide to approach you with my offer."

Arcannen was stunned. Could she be telling the truth? Did she really know nothing of his purpose in coming to Rare Flowers? Had Corussin not spoken to her?

"How do you see our time together?" he asked impulsively. "What would you and I do?"

She hesitated for the first time. "I wish to study magic with you. I wish you to be my mentor. In exchange for this, I would be your companion. In time, if we both agree that it feels right, I would become your bedmate. But this is not what I am seeking at present. Nor are you, unless I have misjudged you."

"You have not," he assured her. "And if our arrangement begins to feel wrong?"

"Then we would part company. If you feel you have been misled or misused, I would return half the money you have given me. I do not ask for anything I have not earned."

He studied her anew. She was very young, but she had an old soul. "I might end up using you badly in this bargain."

"I will take that chance." The girl leaned in a bit. "I know my confronting you like this is unusual. The rules are clear. You are not to be approached by the girls who come here. But I am tired of waiting on Corussin to provide me with suitable choices. I am bored and eager to get on with my life. I know what I want when I see it, and I know the direction I wish my life to go. Take me with you. You won't regret it."

Across the way, a door opened onto the garden and Corussin appeared. For the first time, the girl looked unsettled. "Please decide quickly," she whispered, rising and stepping back.

Her haste reinforced his growing conviction that the proprietor had indeed not sent her as a prospect. It was clear that she did not think he would be happy to find her with him.

"Here is my bargain," he said. "I will take you with me and make you my student and teach you magic if you will agree to the following. There is no time to explain all the details, but it involves a boy about your age. I require his special talents. I need you to help me persuade him. I need you to make him fall in love with you and then manipulate him to act on my behalf. It must be done without him knowing the truth. It is only for a month or perhaps two. Not a long time in a young girl's life. After that, I will take you away. Do you agree to my offer?"

She nodded at once. "I do. Unless you intend to ask me to harm him. Then I must refuse."

"I promise not to ask that of you. But I may ask other things that you will not find agreeable. Nothing that will harm either you or him, but that you will still find distasteful. Do you still agree?"

She nodded quickly. "I do. Now help me."

"Lariana!" Corussin shouted at the girl, coming up swiftly. "What do you think you are doing?"

She turned to face him, but she did not reply. Arcannen rose to stand with her. "Any luck?" he asked the proprietor.

"A little," the other answered, but his attention was all on the girl. "You know the rules. You do not approach the gentlemen who come to call at Rare Flowers without an appointment and my express permission."

"I only came over to ask if he required anything," she responded.

"Yes, that is so," the sorcerer agreed.

"It doesn't matter what you thought you were doing. It is forbidden to approach anyone with whom you do not have a prearranged meeting. You will go to your room until I am finished here. You might want to consider packing your bags."

"Yes, why don't you do that," Arcannen agreed. He turned to Corussin. "I have decided to take her with me. She is the girl I want. She will provide exactly the services I am seeking. How much do I owe you?"

The proprietor was stunned. Then he wheeled on Lariana. "Why are you still here? Do as I have told you."

The girl nodded and left at once. Corussin watched her cross through the garden and disappear back inside the building before he turned again to Arcannen. "You do not want this girl," he said.

The sorcerer was surprised. "I think maybe I do. I spoke to her at length. Quizzed her, really. Her answers were impressive. What is the problem?"

"I don't know. Not exactly. But there is something not quite right about her. She is beautiful, intelligent, and well-spoken. She is extremely strong-minded. But she is ambitious, too. And there is something more. I sense it in the way she keeps herself apart from everyone. She considers herself superior to all of us. She dismisses her suitors in the most abrupt and unflattering ways. She is never satisfied. I have kept her this long only because I keep hoping the right match will appear."

"Perhaps it has. Let me have the use of her for a short time. If she becomes a problem, I will dispose of her and not ask for a single credit back. If she turns out as I hope, I will keep her with me."

Corussin shook his head. "This is a mistake, Arcannen. I have never before tried to talk a customer out of making an arrangement with one of my girls, but I am doing so now. Let me find someone else. There are dozens of girls here, many of them persuasive in the ways you have already mentioned. Talk to a few of them. See if one of them won't do."

Arcannen shook his head. "Time slips away. The chances were small when I came to you that I would be able to find the girl I needed. Unexpectedly, I did. But the chances that I will find her again are minuscule. I choose her. Name your price."

"As an old friend and business partner, I urge you to—"

"Name your price!" Arcannen snapped, cutting him short.

It was three times what he had expected he would end up paying, an attempt by the establishment's proprietor to punish Arcannen for his boldness, but a bargain if Lariana proved to be as resourceful as the sorcerer believed. Corussin was right. There was something about this girl, and whatever it was, it might prove to be the difference in winning or losing the boy. Life was a gamble. There was no point in wishing things would change now.

Besides, he had always relied on his instincts, and his instincts told him she was the one.

10

WHILE ARCANNEN AND LARIANA WERE DE-
parting Rare Flowers in preparation for the return to
Portlow, Paxon Leah and Avelene were flying toward
the same destination. As planned, they had left at dawn, passengers on a
clipper piloted and crewed by three members of the Druid Guard—huge
Rock Trolls with flying skills and no-nonsense attitudes. The trip would
take most of the day, so the Druid and the Highlander had settled down
on padding built into the front of the pilot box where they could speak in
private or read the books they had brought with them detailing portions
of the history of the wishsong copied down from the Druid Histories.

Paxon already knew a little of this history because of his heritage.
The intermarriage of the Leah and Ohmsford families had brought
their recent pasts together through shared memories and writings
that had been in Paxon's family since before he was born. This history
was neither deep nor complete, but it provided a clear look at how the
magic had influenced various members of the two lineages from the
time of Grianne Ohmsford forward. So he was well versed in the voyage of the *Jerle Shannara* to Parkasia, where Grianne and Bek had
been revealed to be not only members of the Ohmsford family, but
also sister and brother. He also knew of Pen Ohmsford's subsequent
involvement in putting a stop to the attempt by Shadea a'Ru to over-
throw the Druid order and reform it under her leadership.

But it was Avelene who knew the details of the older history of the wishsong better—of its origins, of the beginning of the magic as it became integrated into the Ohmsford bloodline in the years following Wil Ohmsford's terrible quest to aid Amberle Elessedil in finding the source of the Bloodfire to renew the Ellcrys and repair the walls of the Forbidding that imprisoned the demons.

"It's fascinating to read how the wishsong has evolved over the centuries," she told him. Her dark eyes looked introspective, fixing on his face as she spoke. "Wil Ohmsford didn't realize what was happening when he used the Elfstones to save Amberle. He was not even half Elf, and no one whose blood wasn't pure Elf was ever supposed to use Elven magic. But he did it anyway because it was his only choice. And maybe because he loved her. But it infused his blood with a deviant form of its magic, and that form in turn underwent a change when it was passed from him to his children."

"To Brin and Jair Ohmsford," Paxon interjected. "A familiar story in my family. Rone Leah went with Brin on her quest to find the Ildatch. Allanon led them, but it was Brin's use of the wishsong that was key to their success. Although, I believe, her brother's lesser magic turned out to be just as important."

"It did. Neither could have succeeded without the other. She had the real magic; he had the illusion of real magic. But in the end, she needed him to save her. Here's what's interesting, though. His illusory magic changed as he grew older and eventually became the real thing. He became her equal in use of the wishsong. There were stories of what happened to them later on in life, when both had use of the wishsong magic."

"And that was only the beginning of its presence in the Ohmsford line, wasn't it?" he asked. "Didn't it reappear in the time of Morgan Leah?"

She nodded, tapping the notes she was reading. "Says so right here. Keratrix has done a thorough job of detailing what happened. Par Ohmsford inherited it several hundred years later, at a time when magic was outlawed throughout most of the Four Lands. His experience was similar to Brin's, though the effect and the extent of its presence differed. But Par found a way to use it to help defeat the

Shadowen, who were seeking to drain all the elemental magic that lies within the earth and use it for their own purposes. Hard to imagine anyone being able to do such a thing, but apparently the Shadowen had found a way. Walker Boh played a central role in the effort to stop them. He was Allanon's successor, and each was the only Druid of his time."

"It must have been incredibly difficult for a single Druid to stand alone against all the terrible creatures of dark magic that tried to destroy the Four Lands." Paxon shook his head. "How much it must have cost them."

Avelene gave him a look. "It cost them everything. It cost them their lives. Walker Boh died on the journey to Parkasia. Allanon died on the journey to find the Ildatch. Since then, we've always had more than one Druid in the order."

"Still, even now, with Aphenglow gone forever from Paranor," Paxon said, "the order feels fragile. Arcannen is still out there, and I don't expect he's forgotten what the Druids did to him. He's not finished with us. I wish we had Aphenglow back."

"Don't be too quick to write off Isaturin," Avelene said quickly, her eyes narrowing. "He might just surprise you."

Paxon blushed. "I didn't mean to imply that he is the lesser person. I don't have that right. But I knew her so well, and I don't really know him. She gave me my chance as Blade. She helped me find something that mattered. When my sister was threatened, she brought her to Paranor and helped her heal. She was the one who recognized that Chrys had use of the wishsong. I guess I am in debt to her so deeply that I see her as superior."

Avelene grinned, her smile making her suddenly look beautiful. "Listen to you, opening up at last about your sister. I was wondering how long it would take. When you admitted you knew we were going in search of someone who apparently has used the wishsong, I waited for you to mention her. It was Aphenglow who told me, months before she left us. Did you know that?"

He shook his head. "I assumed she told only Isaturin."

"She told me, as well. Do you know why?"

"I don't. She must have trusted you."

Avelene laughed. "I suppose, but I think she had no choice. She knew the end was approaching, and she had to pass along the things she knew that would otherwise be lost. Most of these, she imparted to Isaturin because she had selected him as her successor. But when it came to your sister, she found herself in a bind. Isaturin knew, but what if something happened to him? That left you. You hadn't shown any inclination to tell Chrysallin what might happen to her. She didn't approve of your decision, but she also wanted to give you time to come to terms with the problem."

"So she told you?"

"Yes, but there's more to the story. Two years ago, she selected me for a special task. She wanted someone to research the evolution of the wishsong magic in the Four Lands, beginning with Wil Ohmsford's transformation as a result of using the Elfstones improperly. She chose me to do this. She didn't tell me why exactly; she didn't say anything about your sister. She was more circumspect than that. But the wishsong was the most powerful Elven magic in the Four Lands, and it was essentially a wild magic. It could not be contained; its appearance could never be determined in advance. It resided in the Ohmsford bloodline, but it didn't manifest itself in every generation, and no one had ever been able to determine in which members of the family it would surface. It's been gone since the time of Redden and Railing Ohmsford, so far as anyone knows. But she believed that at some point the wishsong would reappear, and when it did she wanted someone in the order to be prepared to deal with it. She wanted one of us to be an authoritative source. I became that person."

"Then, six months ago, she told you about Chrys," he finished.

"Right before she died. I wasn't to do anything to persuade you. I was to monitor your sister and observe. Obviously, I would have counseled you if she had agreed to let me. But she didn't."

"Yet you choose to tell me all this now?"

"It's past time I did, Paxon. Like you with Chrys, I wasn't sure if I should say anything, or when I should say it. But this journey has given me a reason to decide. Besides, you're not a boy. You're a grown man. You need to hear how other people think about the things you're not sure about. Not in a critical way, but constructively. So I'm telling you everything. Maybe it will help. Maybe I can offer insight. But it is pointless for me not to be honest with you about what I know and how I know it." Her sharp features softened. "I know you've struggled with this."

"More deeply than you can imagine. I juggle my choices like live coals and burn all the while. I live with the possibility that Chrys will become catatonic again. I wish I had a better sense of what to do." He paused. "Maybe what happens on this search will help me decide. Maybe when we discover what this magic we're looking for really is and who is using it, the solution to my own situation will become clearer."

"Maybe," she agreed. Then, with an ironic smile, she added, "Or more complicated."

They didn't talk much after that. Avelene began reading through her notes again, pursing her lips and wrinkling her forehead as she did so. It gave her an odd look, but Paxon understood. She was intense and fully engaged in what she was doing. That look pretty much defined her; that was how she had seemed to him every time he had encountered her since his arrival at Paranor. She didn't do things in a casual manner; she gave herself over to her efforts entirely. Like him, she had found her life here. Perhaps not so dramatically, but she had found it all the same.

He leaned back against the wall of the pilot box and stared out into the blue of the morning sky. He remembered another journey like this one on a similar quest, and he started thinking about Leofur, the woman he had met—Arcannen's estranged daughter.

She was smart and resourceful and accomplished, and she had dazzled him at the time. He had felt so intensely about her, but somewhere along the way he had lost that. She had given him the time and space to consider his feelings. She had told him to think about whether or not she was one of the things in his life he needed to leave behind.

It hadn't helped that he had devoted so much of his time to serving the needs of the Druids and looking after his sister. Free time barely existed for him, and when he found a chunk of it here and there, he chose to use it doing things that didn't require him to fly all day to another city.

The one time he threw caution to the winds—months after he knew he should have gone to see her—she wasn't there when he arrived. Her little house was locked and no one within responded when he pounded on the door. He asked a few people who lived nearby if they knew where she was, but they only shook their heads or shrugged.

He left without finding her and hadn't been back since.

Five years.

Now he found himself uncertain about how he felt. Did he still care for her as much as he had before? Perhaps his infatuation was peculiar to that time and place and the events surrounding both, and couldn't sustain itself. He still thought of her, but it seemed impossible now that he could go back and find things between them the same. Or even find her waiting. She would have found someone else by now. She was independent-minded and practical. She would have decided long ago that he wasn't coming back.

Perhaps she had seen things more clearly than he had.

Besides, here he was stealing glances at Avelene, finding her attractive and interesting, thinking of what it would be like to be with her. If he was thinking such thoughts, how could he expect to begin a fresh relationship with Leofur?

He was lonely; he could admit it to himself if not to anyone else. He wanted to share his life with someone, wanted to be in love, wanted to have more than what he had gained by becoming the Ard Rhys's Blade. Perhaps that was selfish and greedy. Wasn't being a part of the Druid order what he had worked so hard to attain? Did he really need to have someone to love, too? If so, wasn't it easier to find someone already close to him, someone who could share his life's work?

He was still mulling this over when his eyes grew heavy from the fresh air and sun, and he fell asleep.

· · ·

When they reached the village of Portlow it was late afternoon, and the sun was already slipping toward the horizon. The village was small, barely filling a wide space between the forests surrounding it. A single road wound through its center; the businesses on either side—many of them taverns—stood shoulder-to-shoulder for perhaps four hundred yards. Several clusters of residences bracketed the town north and south. There were fenced pastures with horses and cows and a scattering of crop fields that looked small and unproductive and more on the order of private gardens. There were a few sheds and isolated barns, and not much of anything else. This was a poor community, and neither Paxon nor Avelene could understand exactly why it was even here.

It struck the Highlander that if you wanted to disappear off the face of the earth, this would be a good place to do it. Because anyone who had use of magic in the Southland, where it had been outlawed for decades, would not want to make it public knowledge, and he imagined that very little attention was paid to whatever happened here.

The village was too small for a regular airfield, so they had the Trolls land the clipper at the edge of a plowed field near the north end of the village. While the crew unhooked the radian draws and pulled down the light sheaths, Paxon turned to Avelene.

"You need to take off your robes," he said.

She gave him a look. "I do?"

"If you go into a Southland village as a Druid, no one will talk to you. No one will have anything to do with you. We need to look like other travelers passing through. Starks taught me that. So take off your robes."

She went belowdecks and changed, appearing again wearing pants and a tunic with a long knife belted at her waist. She touched the hilt of the knife. "This is just for appearances. I don't know anything about using blades."

"You don't have to know anything," he said. He reached for the Sword of Leah and strapped it across his back. "That's why I'm here."

After giving brief instructions to the Druid Guards, they climbed down from the airship and began walking toward the village.

"I've never done this sort of thing before," Avelene admitted as they neared the first of the residences. "I've never been on a search. All my work has been at Paranor. Can you tell me what to expect?"

"It's not complicated," he assured her. "We'll go into the village and find a tavern that serves food. It's almost dinnertime, so we should eat. We'll listen; maybe we'll exchange a few words with the residents. Perhaps we can learn something about the magic. The use was recent. You said yourself it was noticeable. Someone must have seen something."

She nodded. "All right. What do we tell people if they ask about us?"

He thought about it a moment. "These are rural people. They won't be open to anything that seems out of the ordinary. So we tell them we are newlyweds traveling to visit your aunt and uncle in Sterne. We'll have to spend the night here unless we get very lucky, so we'll take a room. I don't want you sleeping alone—in a separate room, I mean—where I can't protect you if you need it."

"Is this the story you usually use on these outings?" she asked, one eyebrow arched.

"Usually I don't have the pleasure of a woman's company." He grinned. "Especially not one with your talents."

She rolled her eyes and looked away. "I was right. You really are a silver-tongued fellow."

They reached what was clearly a popular inn, with tables and chairs set outside along the front wall as well as inside. They went into the building, found the innkeeper, asked for a room, and went up to drop what little gear they had brought. The room had a single large bed, a chair, a table, a closet, and that was it. Without comment, they left their belongings and went back down to the tavern. Sitting in a corner near the bar, they ordered food and ale, and sat quietly eating and drinking as they listened to the conversations taking place around them.

For a long time, no one said anything about unusual occurrences or the presence of an unexpected magic. But after the first hour, Avelene reached across the table and said quietly, "Table to my left."

Two men were sitting there, workingmen and friends by the look of them, nursing tankards of ale as they leaned forward and spoke in hushed tones. Paxon listened carefully, but he only caught snatches of what they were saying.

". . . no sign of any of them!" the first insisted, shaking his head.

"I thought sure . . . come in to make the boy . . . disappear . . . like he did Borry."

"Not enough left . . . that he was human. Explosion . . . earth burned all around. Torn apart, Rab! Did you . . . mess . . . ?"

" . . . just pieces, all's I saw." The man drank deeply, shuddered. "How could . . . happen? What creature . . ."

"What I been saying! Fortrens got to come for him! You know . . . will sooner or later."

"Gammon . . . won't allow . . . so there's no one who . . . you wait, something . . ."

They went silent then, brooding over their drink, eyes lowered to the tabletop.

Paxon leaned across the table. "Stay here."

She grabbed him by the wrist and held him fast. Her grip was surprisingly strong. "No, let me do this. You get up first and walk up to the bar and order us two more tankards. Stay there until I signal you.

He hesitated a moment, then nodded. He had misgivings, but she seemed confident. Besides, as a Druid, she was in charge. He rose, walked to the serving counter, and stood there until he got the barkeeper's attention. After giving his order, he glanced back to see Avelene seated at the table with the two men, deep in conversation.

"You never know," he muttered to himself.

He waited patiently. The fresh tankards were delivered and he paid. Avelene was still talking to the men. He waited some more. Finally, she stood up, spoke a few final words, and returned to the table, glancing over at him as she did. He picked up the ale and went back to join her, sitting down and scooting his chair close.

"What did . . . ?"

"Not here," she said quickly. She pushed his tankard at him. "Drink some of this. Look happy. You've just been given good news. I am your new wife, and you love me."

He went through the motions, and they played their parts for a while longer before she reached over playfully, took him by his arm, and led him from the room and up the stairs to the sleeping chambers. In the darkness of the hallway at the top, she moved him back against the wall, her hands fastening on his arms to hold him there.

"Two nights ago, when the disturbance to the scrye waters was recorded, there was an incident at a tavern several doors down called the Boar's Head. There is a family that lives here called Fortren. No one likes them. They bully everyone, intimidate and steal, pretty much cause all sorts of trouble. A couple of them have been harassing a boy who works at the tavern as a musician. He sings and plays the elleryn. They say he is very good. They cornered him out back of the tavern and attacked him with an iron bar. Smashed his instrument."

She paused, her grip on his arms tightening. "He must have retaliated as a result, they say. He tore them apart. No weapon, no indication of how he did this. But by the time he was done, they were barely recognizable as human. Gammon is the tavern owner. They say he looks after the boy. But no one has seen the boy again since the incident. These men I was talking to think he is in hiding because sooner or later the Fortren family will try to come after him. They take care of their own, and pay back whatever debts they think are owed harshly."

Paxon grinned at her. "How did you manage to learn all that?"

"Easily," she said. "I told them I overheard snatches of their conversation, and I was frightened. You and I are traveling on, but not for a few days. We're newly married, and I didn't want anything to happen to us if it wasn't safe here. Maybe other travelers ought to be warned. They couldn't tell me fast enough how safe things were in spite of what I might have assumed."

Now it was her turn to grin at him. "A lady in distress always brings out the protective side in men. Didn't you know that?" She released her grip and stepped back. "Let's go find this boy."

They slipped down the back stairs and continued down Portlow's only road, walking on until they saw a sign for the Boar's Head. It was a big, sprawling building with dozens of windows that allowed the light from inside to spill out onto the surrounding grounds. Shouts and laughter came from inside, their intensity a clear indicator of the tavern's popularity.

"Wait here," Paxon told her, slowing as they neared the front door. "Let me see if I can find this fellow Gammon and persuade him to come outside to talk so we can hear each other."

When she didn't object, he moved quickly to the door and stepped inside. The tavern was crammed wall-to-wall with people and thick with smoke. The sound was deafening. He waited a moment until a serving girl came by and caught her arm. She gave him an annoyed look, but didn't pull away.

He leaned close. "Gammon?"

She nodded toward a man working behind the service counter, took her arm back, and moved on.

Paxon squeezed his way over to the counter, waited until he caught the man's eye, and beckoned him over. Gammon was burly and bluff; his face reflected an enthusiasm for his work. Or perhaps it was just the credits it generated. "Help you?"

Paxon smiled and bent close. "There's someone waiting outside who needs to talk to you about the boy. She knows quite a bit about his history and is here to help him. Can you come talk to her?"

Gammon studied him. "Who are you?"

"A man in her service. Please. We mean no harm. We just need a few minutes of your time."

Gammon studied him some more, and then he shrugged. "Why not? I've talked to everyone else under the sun."

He came out from behind the bar, and together they made their way to the front door and outside where Avelene was waiting for them. She offered her hand to Gammon and introduced herself. All around them, patrons of the Boar's Head were coming and going, some of them singing loudly and shouting, so Avelene took Gammon by the arm and led him all the way across the roadway to a quiet space between two shuttered buildings.

"How do you know Reyn?" he asked her.

"I don't know him personally," she answered. "Is that his name? Reyn?"

Gammon bristled, glaring at Paxon. "You tricked me into coming out here. You aren't friends. You have some other—"

"We might be his best friends," Avelene interrupted him. "I'm a member of the Druid order, and I've been sent by the Ard Rhys to find this boy and warn him about what's happening. His magic is an old one that has been in his family for centuries. I'm not sure he knows this, but he needs to, because using magic as he does is dangerous. I don't want anything from him; I just want to warn him."

Gammon looked suspicious. "His family, you say? He doesn't know who his family is. He told me so. A couple took him in when he was young and raised him. How can you be sure about what you're telling me?"

"We can track the use of magic from Paranor. We can identify it. This magic matches one we already know, one that is linked to singing. And the match tells us he comes from a particular family that has had the use of that magic for a very long time. We need to speak with him."

Gammon shook his head. "You and a few others. But no one can speak to him anymore. He's gone. Set out this morning. Said he couldn't stay around here any longer with the Fortrens looking for him. Didn't matter what he promised that stranger."

"Do you know where he went?"

"He wouldn't tell me. Just said he had to find a new place, far away from here. Those Fortrens don't ever quit coming for you if you hurt one of them. He knew that."

"Wait a minute," Paxon said. "You said there was a stranger?"

"Wanted the boy to wait here for him. Wanted to talk to him about his singing. Was he another Druid?"

"No." Paxon didn't bother to hide his consternation. "Can you describe him?"

Gammon did so. "I didn't much like him."

"Your instincts aren't lying to you. He's very dangerous. If he comes back here, keep away from him. His name is Arcannen. He is not a good man. The Federation and the Druid order have both been hunting him for years."

"Well, then, maybe it's a good thing the boy is gone." Gammon turned away. "Anyway, that's all I know. I have to get back to work."

"Do you know which way he went when he left?" Avelene called after him.

Gammon made a dismissive gesture and disappeared back through the tavern entry.

"He's lying," she said. "Or, at best, shading the truth."

Paxon nodded slowly. "Should we go back in there and confront him?"

She thought about it a moment. "No," she said finally, "let's wait and see what happens. Why don't you go around and watch the back door? I'll remain here. I have a feeling about this."

She moved farther back into the shadows and followed Paxon's progress as he made his way back across the roadway and around the tavern. Intent on what she had decided to do, she missed noticing the black-cloaked form coming up behind her.

Reyn Frosch was sleeping when Gammon knocked on the door.

"Open up! Hurry! Something's happened!"

Still sleepy-eyed and muddle-headed, the boy climbed from the bed and walked over to the door. "Gammon?"

"Yes, it's Gammon! Open the door!"

It sounded urgent enough that Reyn did so, stepping back quickly as the innkeeper pushed his way in and closed the door behind him. "You've got to leave now! Right now!"

The boy found himself waking up more quickly. "What's wrong? What's happened?"

"There's two people downstairs asking for you. They say they are Druids. Or at least the young woman does. Don't know about the other. They lured me out to talk to them by saying they knew you, then said they didn't know you personally, but knew about your singing. Said it was a magic that ran in your family. They said that black-cloaked stranger you're waiting for is a sorcerer and too dangerous for you to be getting involved with. I don't know if I believe them or not, but I think you should get as far away from here as you can. Are you listening to me?"

Reyn nodded. "Of course I'm listening. You're shouting right in my ear! If all they want to do is talk . . ."

"That's what they say, but how can you know? I can't even be sure if they're Druids! They could be anyone. I don't like it. You should get away. Besides, the Fortrens are back, hanging around at the edge of town, watching. They know you're still here. It's too risky for you to stay any longer. Go away for a while. Get to someplace safe. But go!"

He was intense and frantic enough that Reyn decided maybe he should pay attention. He gathered up his clothing and personal items, stuffed them in a pack, and slung it over his shoulder along with the new elleryn.

Gammon clasped his hand. "Get a message to me when you're settled. Let me know how to find you. If I have any news, I'll pass it on. I'm sorry about this, Reyn. I wish you could stay."

The boy shrugged. "I'm used to quick departures. Good-bye, Gammon. Thank you for the elleryn. And for everything else."

He shook hands with the tavern owner and went out of the room and down the back stairs to the rear door, where he spent a long time peering out into the darkness.

Just like that, he was cutting ties again, leaving for a new home.

He closed his eyes against the despair that filled him.

Finally, satisfied no one was watching, he went out the door and hurried toward the woods behind the tavern.

I I

PAXON WAS STANDING DEEP IN THE SHADOWS CAST by the trees at the rear of the Boar's Head when the back door eased open and a figure emerged into the light. It was hard to be certain who it was—even if it was a man or woman—but a rucksack and a leather case shaped like a musical instrument were strapped to its back. Paxon stayed where he was, watching the figure cross the open space almost directly toward him, moving quickly.

When the figure was less than a dozen yards away, he stepped out of the trees. "Reyn?" he called.

The boy stopped, his face lifting into the misty moonlight, clearly revealed now, surprise and consternation imprinted on his young features. For a moment, he looked poised to run. But then he seemed to think better of it and held his ground.

"Who are you?" he called back.

"My name is Paxon Leah. I came here from Paranor with a Druid companion. We need to warn you about the magic you are using."

"How do you know I use magic?"

"If I am mistaken, just say so."

The boy hesitated. "I'm just leaving. Please let me go."

"I'm not here to cause you trouble," Paxon said, pressing ahead quickly. "I just want to explain what sort of . . ."

In the next instant a rope of fire burst from between the buildings behind the boy, barely missing his head. He threw himself aside, trying to protect his belongings as a second explosion flashed past him, this one even closer.

"Stay down!" Paxon yelled, rushing to his aid, his black sword drawn and held protectively before him.

But Reyn was up and running, bolting away from Paxon and the source of the fire both, sprinting along the rear walls of the buildings left of the Boar's Head until a gap appeared between them and he disappeared from view. Paxon kept advancing toward the source of the fire, but no further bursts appeared. Whoever had attacked them was gone.

"Reyn!" he called after the boy. "Wait! Come back!"

But he wouldn't, of course. He would run and keep running. He would believe it was the Druids who had attacked him. He would think Paxon lured him out so he could be disabled or killed. But unless for some unknown reason it was Avelene who . . .

He caught himself and stopped short.

Avelene. Where is she?

He gave up on the boy. If they were going to find him, they would have to track him down in daylight and try to explain to him why he was mistaken. Assuming he was. *Would* Avelene have attacked him? No, there was no reason for her to do so. He began running hard, passing between the Boar's Head and the building next door to the roadway and then crossing the street to where he had left her.

There was no sign of her. It was so shadowy in the narrow opening between the darkened buildings that he could barely see. He rushed back across the street, took down a torch from one of a matching set bracketing the front door to the Boar's Head, and raced back across. Using the light it cast, he held it close to the ground and began to search. Like most Highlanders who hunted extensively, he could read sign. He found Avelene's footprints right away, and then a second pair close behind where she had stood. A man's, from the size of them. She had been facing away from whoever had come up on her. There were no signs of a struggle, just the prints coming up behind her and then moving away again.

Only they were deeper than before where they turned back. As if whoever made them had been carrying something heavy.

Someone had caught her off guard, rendered her helpless, and borne her off. He followed the prints to a door behind the building to his right. The door had been locked, but the lock was broken—burned loose from its hinges. His torch held out before him, Paxon slipped into the room.

Boxes, crates, and barrels were stacked everywhere. He held up the torch and looked around. He saw no one moving, sensed no one waiting. But he remained cautious anyway as he pushed farther in. The silence suggested nothing was amiss, yet something felt curiously out of place. He studied the stacks of supplies cautiously as he moved through the room, tying to decide what it was.

Then he noticed a patch of deep blackness. It was nothing more than what appeared to be empty space back between the crates, but his torchlight would not penetrate it. Tightening his grip on the Sword of Leah, he took a few steps forward, trying to make out what it was.

Even when he got close, though, it still didn't seem to be anything more than an especially dark place. He reached out to touch it and discovered he was wrong. The blackness surrounded a hard shell, a sort of cylinder propped upright against the wall. He sheathed his sword and ran his free hand over the surface, gauging its size and strength. If there was something within, he couldn't tell from looking; even when standing right on top of it he could not see inside.

After a moment, he stepped back again. Whatever this was, it didn't belong here. It did not remind him of anything he knew or had ever seen, and he was pretty sure it did not contain supplies.

He felt a chill sweep through him. Magic? Could magic be involved? Didn't it have to be? The fire thrown at the boy from the darkness between the buildings was clearly generated by magic. A magic wielder could have conjured this black cylinder.

Right away he thought of Arcannen.

Wedging the torch between stacks of boxes nearby so that he still had the use of its light, he unsheathed his sword once more and placed its edge against the surface of the black container, testing its response.

Instantly the familiar green snakes began to crawl through the weapon's blade, writhing and twisting, and Paxon felt a familiar jolt as the sword's magic awoke in response. A second later the opaque surface of the cylinder turned transparent, and he could see Avelene's body suspended inside. She was held in place by invisible bonds, hands at her sides, body still. But her eyes were open, and she was looking at him.

Her eyes told him she was terrified.

He lifted his blade away from the cylinder and watched it go dark again. For a moment, he considered simply smashing his way into the young woman's prison, but he resisted the urge. If whoever captured her wanted her dead, why hadn't they simply killed her and been done with it? If they wanted her to be found, why bother with all this elaborate imprisoning?

Unless his suspicions were right, and it was Arcannen who was responsible. Especially if he knew Paxon was there. Wouldn't he find it fitting if Paxon bulled his way recklessly into the black cylinder using his precious sword and thereby caused the death of the person he was supposed to be rescuing?

What he needed was someone who knew more about magic than he did. Someone who knew what they were doing. Someone who could tell him if by opening the container he was putting Avelene in worse danger still.

He sheathed his sword. The boy would have to wait. His first obligation was to the Druids he was sworn to protect. Avelene would have to be transported—cylinder and all—back to Paranor. He could only hope a way to release her could be found when he got her there.

Frustration at feeling so helpless gnawed at him as he made his decision. He was almost certain by now that imprisoning Avelene was Arcannen's work. This whole business had a personal feel to it, and his suspicions suggested strongly that it was the sorcerer who was behind it.

He expected he would know soon enough.

Retrieving his torch from where he had wedged it between the supply boxes, he went back out into the night to find help.

Not until he had arrived at the outskirts of Portlow, following the road that led east toward the coast, did Reyn Frosch stop running long enough to pause and look back. No one seemed to be following. He thought the man who had approached him behind the tavern might have given chase, but apparently he had decided against it. Perhaps his cohort, the one using the magic, had held him back. Or perhaps they would try to track him after it got light. Anger and determination flooded through him. They would never catch up to him now. They had lost their best chance when the fire had missed and he had managed to escape. Now he would be watching out for them.

All that talk about warning him and wanting to help was nothing more than a ruse to delay him. He wondered what they were really after. Whatever they wanted, it must be connected to his use of magic. All magic was outlawed in the Southland, and there were rumors that the Druids were seeking to acquire any magic not already under their control.

Which suggested they might be trying to acquire his. His battle against the Fortrens might have drawn them to him. He had heard stories about the Druids and their machinations. He had heard how they hunted down and destroyed those who used magic.

It was beginning to rain. Hunching his shoulders, he tightened his travel cloak and pulled up its hood. He had lost the rucksack that contained his clothing and possessions. All he had managed to salvage was the elleryn Gammon had given to him. He had no food or water. A handful of Federation credits were stuffed down in his pants. It was a poor start to a new life, but he would have to make do.

He began walking, moving away from the lights of the town. If he could reach Sterne, he could disappear into the larger population. He couldn't sing or play anymore—not in public, at least. Word would get around. It would draw attention. The Druids would hear of it and come for him once more.

His best bet was to work at a job that would give him enough money to buy passage on an air transport west into Elven country, where use of magic was not outlawed and therefore less noticeable, and a man could change his identity with ease. He could find a place in a Rover village, perhaps. He could use his voice again to make a living working at a tavern. He could start over.

Thoughts of what he could and couldn't do ran through his head as he pushed ahead through the rain. The roadway quickly turned sodden and muddy, and he moved off to the side in the tall grasses where the ground was more solid. After a time, he deliberately angled toward the fringe of the forest trees. Standing out in the open seemed like a poor idea.

He tried to prepare himself mentally for what might happen. He could protect himself if his pursuers continued to come after him; he was not helpless against them. The magic would keep them at bay. But they had been so quick to attack him back in Portlow. Why would they do that when they didn't even know him? The man who had approached him had seemed willing to talk. Why hadn't they given him a chance to explain himself?

Something streaked past his head and struck the trunk of a tree to one side. A crossbow bolt. He darted into the trees at once, seeking shelter. Another bolt followed, this one nicking his shoulder as it sped past him into the darkness and disappeared. He dropped into a crouch, looking around frantically, fixing on the direction from which this new attack had come.

"Pap!" a voice shouted. "He's over here! I've got him trapped!"

At once he was up and running, weaving through the darkness, angling away from the voice and the attack. He ran deeper into the woods, the elleryn clutched to his chest. He had forgotten about the Fortrens watching the roads leading out of Portlow, of Gammon's warning that they were waiting for him to try to escape. He was so caught up in the mystery behind the Druid attack that they had slipped his mind completely.

Still, whatever his assailant might think, he was far from trapped. He tore through the rain and the dark, fighting down the fear build-

ing within him. The road branched just ahead, one path running on
to Sterne, the other to Wayford. Along the way were dozens of small
villages. He needed only to reach one of them to find a place to hide.
Someone would take him in.

But when a fresh crossbow bolt whizzed past to one side, he was
reminded that the Fortrens were woods people and more at home in
these surroundings than he was. He ducked instinctively and took a
new direction back toward the road. The trees and the heavy scrub of
the woods hindered his efforts, and he might make better time in the
open. He wasn't as skilled at wilderness survival as the Fortrens, but
he was strong and quick. He might be able to outrun them.

A tree trunk exploded in a shower of bark nearby, seconds before
the explosive discharge of a handheld flash rip. Others followed,
bracketing him as he twisted and dodged, fighting to keep his feet in
the slick grasses. There were more than one of them now, the pursuit
growing. If he couldn't find a way to lose them, he would have to turn
and fight. The thought chilled him. Use of his magic would likely lead
to someone dying. Worse, it would alert the Druids to his presence
and bring them down on him.

But what choice did he have?

He was breathing heavily now, the ache in his leg muscles slowing
him. He was running out of space and time; his strength was failing.
He pushed himself harder, clearing the fringe of the trees just where
the road ahead branched toward Sterne and Wayford. He felt a surge
of hope. Which should he take? What if he took neither, but went
between them, angling toward the former but keeping off the road
entirely? It might confuse them enough to make them decide to wait
until daylight, giving him extra . . .

The thought died before he could finish it. Ahead, a grouping of
figures emerged from the darkness to block the split, closing off all
choices of where he might flee. He slowed automatically, knowing
that he could not go forward, that he must turn back. But that would
mean returning to Portlow, and there was no hope for him if he did.

Figures emerged from the trees behind him, his pursuit having
caught up. He stood frozen in place for several long moments, watch-

ing the figures close in from all sides. He must run, but he no longer believed that running would be enough. He would have to stand and fight. He would have to use his magic if he was to get out of this alive.

He set down the elleryn. He was about to step away from it, still hoping to protect the one possession he had left, when he was struck a blow to the head that knocked him sprawling. The blow had been sharp and painful, and he knew a sling stone had struck him. They were disabling him before he could do anything. He tried to rise, but he was dizzy and slow, and those closest were on top of him too quickly, bearing him to the ground. Screams and shouts of wild elation filled the air.

"Got him, Pap!" one yelled, whooping and laughing. "All mine, he is. You watch what I do to him! Just let me have 'firsts.'"

Reyn tried to see what was happening, but there was blood in his eyes. When he tried to use his voice, he found his throat constricted by an arm locked about it. He was helpless.

"You do nothing, boy!" a rough voice snapped. He recognized it at once. Costa Fortren. The family patriarch's shadowy form loomed through a haze of blood and raindrops. "He's mine. His life belongs to me, and I am the one who shall take it from him. You can have him back when the light begins to leave his eyes."

Reyn tried to blurt out a final plea, but all that emerged was a strangled gasp. Dark figures were clustered all around. Voices filled with hate and bloodlust traded laughter and jokes. He heard his new elleryn being smashed beneath boot heels.

He closed his eyes. It was over for him.

Then someone gasped—a sound filled with fear and loathing. Bodies shifted, and from out of the darkness a figure emerged, blacker than the night, robes billowing in the wind, a wraith exuding terror.

"I warned you not to harm him."

The voice was a crackle that rose above the sounds of the storm. Everyone went silent. For an instant the entire world seemed frozen in time. Costa Fortren turned. "We have no need to do as you—"

"You have every need," the wraith replied. "But now it is too late."

In the next instant the entire area lit up in sudden explosions of fire as huge torches burst into flame and screams filled the air. But the torches were neither of wood nor pitch, but of human flesh as the Fortrens and their allies caught fire, one after the other. Burning alive, unable to extinguish the flames, they ran screaming this way and that, rolling on the ground, flinging themselves into puddles of mud and water, beating at their flaming bodies helplessly. Their efforts failed. The fire was relentless. One by one, they were consumed, collapsing in charred heaps, their lives extinguished until all that remained were Reyn Frosch and the dark figure striding toward him.

"I told you to wait!"

The boy still couldn't talk, his voice little more than a ragged croak. He pushed himself into a sitting position, trying to avoid looking at the bodies heaped all around him.

Strong arms pulled him to his feet. The black-cloaked stranger from the Boar's Head leaned close, his features bladed and hard. "We'll talk about this later. For now, hold tight to me."

Aching and worn, the boy held on for dear life.

12

REYN REMEMBERED LITTLE OF WHAT HAPPENED next. The strong arms guided him through the dark and the rain to where an airship waited and then helped him aboard. His body was battered and bloody from the pummeling he had taken at the hands of the Fortrens, and exhaustion and weakness combined to cloud his thinking. He stumbled several times and almost fell off the ladder once, but eventually he was settled in a corner of the vessel beneath a canopy and wrapped in blankets with his head pillowed. Drowsiness overcame him, and he was asleep almost instantly.

But just before consciousness faded, he was aware of someone else moving over to sit next to him. Soft hands loosened his clothing, and wet cloths were applied to his injuries. A voice whispered, soothing and low, and he was infused with a sense of peace.

He remembered, too, the sound of the airship powering up and lifting away, of the rush of the wind and the whisper of the rain continuing to fall, and finally of terrifying images of men turned into human torches.

After that, he slept. In his sleep he dreamed, and his dreams were dark and haunting. He was fleeing once more, pursued by a nameless terror, a black wraith cloaked and hooded that appeared each time he thought he had left it behind, thwarting his every attempt at escape.

It neither spoke nor acted against him, yet he knew it was evil and intended him great harm. He fought hard to evade it, to place obstacles in its path and hide from its coming. But nothing worked. It was an inexorable force intent on crushing the life out of him.

At one point, men tried to stand against it. And as it was with the Fortrens, they were set afire and turned to ash, their lives extinguished in the blink of an eye.

When he woke again, it was dawn. The first of the new day's light was just a faint glow on the horizon. The airship had landed, and the diapson crystals were silent within their hooded parse tubes. The light sheaths rippled and flapped softly in a gentle breeze. The rain had moved on. Overhead, the sky was clear and offered the promise of a sunny day.

He lay where he was for a few moments, not wanting to disturb the feeling of comfort that cocooned him. Hints of his injuries surfaced when he tried to move, so he chose not to. Not right away. He began thinking of what had happened the previous night, the horrific images resurfacing as his memories returned. He had been chased and hunted and nearly killed before the black-cloaked stranger had rescued him and the Fortrens had all burned . . .

A shadow fell over him, a pair of slender arms reached out, and soft hands began to stroke his face. "Wake up, Reyn," a voice urged. "It's morning."

The girl eased down next to him, moving into his field of vision. Her smile was radiant, filling him with such wonder and happiness he could barely keep the tears from his eyes. She was beautiful in an exotic, almost otherworldly sort of way. Her skin was white and flawless. Her hair was a rich toffee color, streaked with gold that suggested threads woven within. She was tiny, and her features hinted at the presence of Elven blood, although it was clear to him that she was not the product of a single Race, but of mixed heritage. Her green eyes held him mesmerized as he fought to say something.

"That was you next to me last night?"

She nodded.

"You dressed my wounds, took care of me?"

"I did. How are you feeling?"

"I'm all right. But I wouldn't have been if not for . . ." He paused. "Well, I guess I don't know his name."

"Arcannen," she said. "He thinks very highly of you. He believes you have great promise. He also believes your magic places you in serious danger."

"I suppose it does. Are you his daughter?"

She laughed. "I am his assistant. If I serve him well in this capacity and demonstrate promise, he will teach me his skills. He is a great sorcerer."

Reyn took a deep breath and exhaled slowly. "He told me he understood. He knew about my singing. He said he could explain it to me. He could tell me its origins."

"If he said he could do so, then he can."

She adjusted his blankets and eased him into a more comfortable position. He liked the feel of her hands on him. She made him feel safe.

"Where is he?"

She smoothed his hair back from his forehead. "He's gone into the city to find supplies for us. He will be back soon."

"Where are we? What city?"

"Sterne. On the outskirts at the edge of the public airfield. He has enemies here, so he must be very cautious. As soon as he returns, we will leave again."

"Leave for where?"

She smiled and reached over to stroke his cheek. "I believe that depends upon you."

She rose and left him then. He wanted to call her back, to tell her to stay with him so they could continue to talk, so that he could feel her hands on him. But she was gone too quickly for that, whispering as she left that he needed to rest and she would be back later.

Surprisingly, he was asleep in minutes. This time there were no dreams, and he slept undisturbed.

When his eyes opened again, the sun was overhead and he could hear birdsong and the rustle of leaves. A breeze cooled his face, and the air smelled of woods and grasses.

The girl was sitting next to him, looking down, smiling. "Much better, are you?"

He nodded. "Much." He tested his arms and legs. There was some achiness, but the pain was minimal. "Can you help me sit up?"

She reached down for him, put her arms around his body, lifting him as he scooted back into a sitting position. She was strong for all her delicacy. She seemed to know exactly how to lift and position him, as if she understood how his body felt.

"Who are you?" he asked when she was done.

"I've already told you."

"No. What's your name?"

"Lariana," she answered.

"I've never heard of another with that name. It's beautiful. How long have you been with Arcannen?"

"Not long. I had to talk him into taking me with him. He was re-sistant at first. He didn't believe I could be of service to him. I think he is used to being alone." She smiled. "Are you like that?"

He shrugged. "Probably. I never thought much about it."

"But your magic sets you apart, doesn't it? It makes it easier if you keep to yourself. Then you can avoid questions and the need for ex-planations you don't want to give."

"I suppose it does. Mostly, I've spent my time trying to feed my-self. I've been alone since I was eleven."

And just like that, he was telling her the story behind the deaths of his parents and his subsequent flight from his home and efforts to make his own way in the world afterward. She listened without inter-ruption, her expression shifting with each new revelation, her inter-est complete. He found it easy to talk to her, and he never once thought to ask himself if revealing so much would in any way prove detrimental.

"You've had an interesting life," she said.

"Tell me of yours."

She shrugged. "There's not much to tell. Like you, I was alone early. I came to the Southland and lived right here in Sterne for sev-eral years while I tried to find a way to make a living. It wasn't easy. A young girl on her own doesn't have many choices. But I found a way. Eventually, Arcannen met me and I asked if I could come with him. We agreed on the bargain I already spoke about."

"Can you do any magic?"

She gave him a sly look. "Not so you would notice. I'm pretty good at healing injuries, though."

He laughed. "I guess I'm proof of that. How did you learn healing?"

"Just another skill I picked up along the way. Are you hungry? Would you like something to eat?"

He decided he would, so she reached down inside the small storage compartment of the Sprint and brought out cheese, bread, and ale for them to eat. They sat together in the midday sun, enjoying their food and continuing their conversation. Reyn told her about Gammon, and how he had been almost like a father to him during his stay in Portlow. She told him, in turn, about a year she had spent with an elderly man in Sterne, looking after his affairs, caring for him as his life leaked away but his good humor and kindness never wavered.

"I was lucky to find someone like that," she said. "There were others who treated me much differently. There were times when I didn't have any choice but to let them."

He studied her face, thinking that he would never treat her badly. She spoke of it almost matter-of-factly, with no bitterness or anger, without any hint of self-pity or weakness. It did not seem as if she expected anything else from life than what she had encountered. She appeared to have no illusions about how difficult it could be or how demanding. He understood that. He had seen and experienced enough to have developed a thick skin and a cautious sense of trust.

But he believed Lariana was more mature and better equipped to face life's hardships than he had ever thought of being.

They finished their meal, and she cleared away what was left. Sitting next to him, she sipped at her ale contemplatively, pressed close.

"When did you first discover you had this magic Arcannen talks about?" she asked him finally.

He thought about it a moment. "I was almost eight. It was an accident. I became angry with this other boy and yelled at him. My voice changed register; it grew more intense. I could feel it when it happened. Suddenly this boy was picked up and thrown backward. I never touched him. He was so scared he got up and ran away. Nothing came of it. I didn't tell my parents, and he didn't tell his. But when it happened again, there were other people around. You know the rest."

"You get so angry you can't control it?" she asked. "But you must have some control."

"I do. It's just not always reliable. I have to make myself stay calm. I can't allow myself to get angry. I just keep it inside, bottle it up. I can use it on purpose, though. But mostly it's better if I don't. Better if I don't let anyone know I have it."

"But you sing for a living. You're a musician. You have to use it then. You have to let people know about it."

"Except they don't know what it is I'm doing. Mostly. They just like my singing and playing and don't pay attention to anything but how good it makes them feel or how sad or whatever other emotion it arouses in them."

"But Arcannen knew."

The boy nodded. "He's a sorcerer, right? So he must have sensed what it was." He paused. "What does he want with me? Why did he bring me with him?"

She gave him one of her dazzling smiles. "I imagine he will reveal that to you when he returns. But he didn't tell me."

Then she leaned in suddenly and kissed him—a soft, lingering pressure of her mouth on his before pulling back.

"But you'll tell me when he does, won't you?"

He nodded solemnly. In truth, he would have promised her anything.

When Arcannen finally returned, arriving in a cart laden with supplies and driven by an old man, he climbed down and walked over to where the boy and the girl sat together in the shade of the canopy at the rear of the aircraft. Lariana rose immediately and went to him, and he directed her down off the vessel to help the old man unload the supplies from the cart.

Reyn started to rise to help her, but the sorcerer reached out quickly and held him back. "Not yet, Reyn. You need to rest a bit longer, recover a little more of your strength. Lariana can manage the supplies."

The boy leaned back again, glancing past him momentarily to where Lariana was disappearing down the ladder. "I'm well enough already."

"She's quite remarkable, isn't she?" the other asked, arching one eyebrow. "Did you have a nice talk?"

"She says she is your assistant. Is that so?"

The sorcerer nodded. "She applied for the job, even though I wasn't offering it to her. She is quite persuasive. I agreed to take her on because I like her determination and confidence. How did she do with caring for your injuries?"

"She did well."

"Did she tell you who I am?"

"Arcannen. You're a sorcerer."

"I am a practitioner of magic. Which is why I wish to speak with you. It's very important that I do. I thought I made it clear that you should remain at the tavern until I returned. Apparently, you lost faith in me."

Reyn shook his head. "A pair of Druids came to find me. Gammon told them I had already left, but he thought I should get away before they could find out the truth. So I tried to sneak out the back door, but they were waiting. One of them attacked me. What was I supposed to do? I ran; I tried to get away from them. But the Fortrens found me." He paused. "Why did you set them on fire?"

Arcannen gave him a look. "I warned them to leave you alone." He shrugged. "They were trash, anyway. And trash should be burned."

Reyn almost said something critical in response, but decided against it. He didn't know Arcannen well enough to question him too closely, and he couldn't ignore the fact that the man had saved his life. How he had managed it wasn't something Reyn cared to look into too deeply.

"Did you tell Lariana about yourself?" the sorcerer asked.

"We talked about a lot of things."

"Why don't you tell me a little of what you told her? When did you first find out about your magic? About what your singing could do? Tell me that, and I'll tell you what you don't know about both."

So Reyn told him of his past, relating pretty much the same details he had revealed to Lariana. He wanted to discover what Arcannen knew about his magic, thinking that this might be his one chance to learn something useful about its origins. He took his time, pausing now and then to see if the other had questions. But the sorcerer said nothing, letting him do the talking.

"Have you tried using this magic in other ways?" he asked when Reyn finished. "Besides singing? Have you attempted to do other things with it? Experimented with it?"

Reyn was confused. "No. What sorts of other things?"

The sorcerer ignored him. "Has anyone ever instructed you on how to use your magic? Have you been taught by anyone?"

"Is that what you want to do? Teach me to use my magic? Is that why you've been after me?"

Arcannen looked at him as if he were an idiot. "I would be interested in teaching you to use magic, yes. But I am much more interested in finding a way to help you stay alive. Or did you miss that part?"

Reyn flushed. "I know what you did for me. I'm just trying to understand what's happening."

"All right." Arcannen gave him a long look. "Let me keep my part of the bargain and tell you what I know about your magic. Then you can decide for yourself what you want to do about it. But first we need to leave this airfield. I've been here too long already."

He signaled to Lariana, who was just finishing up with loading their supplies, and she moved immediately to begin the process of attaching the radian draws and raising the light sheaths. Because the Sprint was small, the work went quickly, and within short minutes they were lifting off, turning east from Sterne. Arcannen was at the helm and Lariana was sitting aft with Reyn. Sprints were small; the three of them pretty much filled up the cockpit.

Reyn, left to his own devices for the moment, began conversing with the girl once more. "Do you know where we are going?"

She shook her head. "He didn't say. Why don't you ask him?"

But Reyn didn't want to do that. He didn't care where they were going; he just wanted an excuse to talk to her. "I can wait," he said.

The wind swept back her caramel hair, and the streaks of gold that ran through it flashed brightly in the sun. She lifted her head and closed her eyes, reveling in the feel of it. She was, in that moment, the most beautiful girl he had ever seen.

"I love flying," she whispered, her eyes still closed.

He smiled. "I'll tell you a secret, if you want."

She opened her eyes again and looked over. "Of course I want. Tell me."

"Until last night and now, I had never flown in an airship. Not once."

She held his gaze. "Aren't you glad your first time was with me?"

Finding the right words to answer her proved impossible.

Farther north, within the ragged cradle of the Dragon's Teeth, Paxon and the Rock Trolls who had accompanied him to Portlow in search of the bearer of the wishsong bore the black cylinder in which Avelene was imprisoned down off the clipper and into the recesses of Paranor. There were other members of the Druid Guard there to meet them, and within minutes Isaturin had come down from his tower quarters for a look.

It was nearing midday by now, the journey home again having taken the travelers the remainder of the night and most of the following morning. Paxon had managed a few hours sleep aboard ship, but had spent most of his time keeping watch over Avelene. It wasn't as if he could do anything further to help her, but with the edge of the Sword of Leah placed against the hard side of her prison, he could banish the darkness long enough to look inside and let her look out at him and know that he was there.

In truth, she seemed calmed by his presence, aware that he was taking her somewhere, trying to do something to help. They could not hear each other—though they had both tried speaking through the cylinder walls—but they could find reassurance in knowing that there was a link between them and both were handling the situation in the best way they could.

Isaturin examined the cylinder, spent a few minutes touching it and bending close to listen, then used his own magic to turn the enclosure clear enough to see the Druid inside and to give her a few quick signs with his fingers that she seemed to understand.

When the cylinder went dark again, he had it picked up and carried to one of the workrooms. "It's magic-generated," he told Paxon as they followed in the cylinder's wake. "Likely this is Arcannen's work. It is sophisticated and, as you had assumed, a trap. Any forcible effort to free Avelene would cause the walls imprisoning her to collapse, crushing and suffocating her."

"He would have been counting on that," Paxon said angrily. "He would see tricking me into killing one of the Druids I am sworn to protect as a fitting punishment for what I did to him five years ago."

Isaturin smiled. "But his plan didn't work. You've grown less impulsive over the years. Now let's see about getting Avelene free without harming her."

The big man moved ahead, speaking now to another pair of Druids he had summoned, presumably to help with the unlocking of the cylinder. Paxon hung back, content to let them take the lead. Isaturin appeared to know what he was doing, and since Paxon's fears about using his sword were confirmed, it was best to let the Ard Rhys find a way through Arcannen's magic.

Once within the work area, the door was closed and barred by Druid Guards. Isaturin had the cylinder placed on a workbench. Stationing the two Druids who had accompanied him on the far side of the bench, he stood across from them. Together, the three began to weave separate spells, using fingers and voices, each deep in concentration. Paxon stood back, watching carefully. The air began to thicken, turning misty and dark, taking on a substantive appearance. Streaks of color emerged and then vanished again. Smells were emitted—some like burning, some like oiled metal. The cylinder began to pulse softly, its opaque appearance lessening, Avelene's frightened face coming into sharper focus within.

It took them a long time to accomplish what they were attempting, and at more than one point Paxon began to worry that they couldn't manage it. But finally the surface of the cylinder began to split apart, a jagged seam opening vertically down its middle. A rush of foul air exploded from within, turning black as it did so, morphing into dozens of insects. Isaturin sprang backward, warding his face and gesturing heatedly. One of the other Druids collapsed into the arms of the second. For a few moments, everything was in chaos.

Then Isaturin's countermagic took hold of Arcannen's, scooping it up and shrinking it down to nothing. The insects disappeared, the air cleared, and the black cylinder melted away, leaving Avelene lying wide-eyed and shaking atop the workbench.

Without being asked, Paxon rushed forward and covered her with his cloak. He lifted her off the bench, cradling her in his arms. He could feel her trembling.

"I thought I was dead," she whispered, clutching him to her. "I was certain of it."

"Paxon," Isaturin said, coming up beside him. "Carry her to her room and put her to bed. She needs rest. Give her as much liquid as she can hold before you leave her. Just water, nothing stronger— nothing to stimulate her system. Wrap her in blankets. She's shaking as much from the cold she's feeling as from what she's been through. Hurry now."

Without a word, Paxon carried the young woman from the room and down the hallways of the keep to where she slept. He had to ask her how to get there because he had never been to her chambers, but she managed to direct him without once looking up from where she nestled her face against his shoulder.

"He caught me by surprise, Paxon." He could hear the bitterness in her voice. "That never should have happened. I was so intent on watching you cross the roadway and then disappear behind the tavern—so certain you would call for my help . . ."

She trailed off, her voice breaking. "You aren't the first to have that happen," he said quietly. "I'm just grateful you're alive. I was scared to death for you."

"What happened to the boy?"

Paxon grimaced. "He got away in the confusion. We'll find him later. First, we have to get you well again."

She was silent for a long time. "I don't know if that's possible," she whispered. "You can't imagine what it was like inside that container, everything dark and no way to get free. If you hadn't—"

"But I did," he said, interrupting her with a hushing sound. "Just try to forget about it. Just think about sleeping now."

When they were inside her room, he laid her on the bed and poured water from a pitcher on the dresser into a glass, holding it for her while she drank it down. He stayed with her while she finished it, then brought her a second glass and held her while she drank that one, too.

"So thirsty," she mumbled.

He put the glass on the bedside table, took off her boots, and pulled back the bedding, easing her beneath the covers. He rose and walked toward the door. "Go to sleep now. I'll see you when you wake."

"Paxon!" She called his name with some urgency, bringing him back around. "Don't go. Don't leave me just yet. Please."

He came back over and sat down beside her. He could see the fear in her eyes. "I'll stay if you want."

"I just don't want to be alone right now. I'm sorry."

"It's all right."

"Would you lie down beside me? Would you just hold me for a little while? Until I stop shaking?"

He did as she asked, snuggling close to her and putting his arm across her so that she could feel his warmth. She scooted back against him, burrowing close. "Thanks," she said so softly he almost missed it.

She was asleep before long, and the shaking stopped. He stayed with her anyway, wanting to make sure. But he also stayed because he liked holding her, liked being close. And for the first time since Leofur, he found that he needed the comfort of another body.

13

"THE MAGIC YOU POSSESS IS VERY OLD," ARCANnen explained. "Centuries old. And only members of a single family inherit it. When it first surfaced, it was called a wishsong, and the name has stuck."

Reyn was sitting with the sorcerer in the stern of the Sprint, shoulder-to-shoulder in the small space, both of them looking ahead at where Lariana stood behind the controls of the two-man, guiding the airship east. She had taken over at Arcannen's request a short while ago, and he had given her a heading and a set of landmarks by which to navigate. Now she watched the land ahead as they flew, but Reyn noticed her intense expression. She was clearly listening to every word.

This did not seem to bother Arcannen, who continued his explanation. "Your family surname is Ohmsford. Frosch is either a given name or perhaps a name taken in marriage and passed down to you. But the name that matters where the wishsong is concerned is Ohmsford. The magic surfaced three generations after Shea Ohmsford used the Sword of Shannara to destroy the Warlock Lord. It was passed down from his grandson Wil to Wil's two children, Brin and Jair. Wil Ohmsford had gone with the Chosen Amberle to save the Forbidding when it failed, and in the process had used Elfstones once given to his grandfather by the Druid Allanon. Shea was a Halfling, but Wil was less an Elf than a human. Use of Elfstone magic is dangerous if you are not a full-blooded Elf, the more so if you are not even a Halfling. So Wil risked much in using the Stones, but he did so to save the Chosen's life. As a result, his body was changed by the magic, which infused his blood. This infected blood, in turn, was passed to his children.

"But it was a different sort of magic that emerged. Singing generated the magic of the wishsong, creating a fresh reality, changing and enhancing or diminishing in the process. The girl, Brin, had the stronger magic at first. Whenever she wanted to impact the world around her in a physical way, she needed only to imagine it and sing it into being. She was an extremely powerful magic wielder, and she nearly lost her life to her own magic. Her brother, Jair, had the use of the wishsong, too, but for him, it wasn't real. He could only create the impression of something happening, not the reality. Smoke and mirrors were his stock-in-trade—although that changed for him later in life—but it proved to be enough to save his sister."

Arcannen paused. "Do you recognize the similarities with your own magic? By singing songs, you affect your listeners. They see in their own minds what they wish to see. You sing lyrics and music that create impressions or recall memories or simply stir emotions that make them want more of what you are giving them. I don't think you do this consciously. I don't sense a singular purpose in your singing. I think you just offer it for them to sample. Am I right?"

Reyn nodded. "I guess so. I know I can make them feel things, but I don't necessarily set out to make them feel anything in particular. I just want the music to reach them." He hesitated. "But stirring up emotions and recalling memories is only part of it. The magic kills people, too."

"Yes, but that's not peculiar to you. All of the Ohmsfords who inherited use of the wishsong had that power. And almost all of them killed someone, intentionally or not. They were all faced with life-and-death situations in which either they fought back using their magic or they died. Hasn't it been like that for you?"

Reyn glanced at Lariana, not wanting her to hear this part. But even though she was not looking right at him, he knew she was waiting to hear his answer. There was nothing he could do to avoid it unless he refused to continue.

"I haven't tried to kill anyone. But when I defend myself, I can't seem to control it. I become so emotionally distraught that the magic gets away from me. It lashes out with such power I can't seem to stop it. Then people die. That's what happened with the Fortrens when they attacked me. It's happened in other places, too."

For just an instant, he thought about explaining how he would become temporarily catatonic afterward. But he did not feel comfortable revealing that he suffered from such a debilitating and dangerous weakness.

Instead, he kept his gaze steady and said, "Can you teach me how to stop this? Can you help me do better about controlling the magic of this wishsong?"

Arcannen smiled. "I can do that and much more. I can teach you to use it in dozens of new ways. I can show you how it can be applied to do things you haven't even thought about. The wishsong is a powerful and dangerous magic, Reyn, but it is a versatile magic, as well. Give me the chance, and I will open the door to its secrets. I will give you the knowledge you need to stay safe."

Reyn glanced at Lariana, but she was looking out onto the horizon again. He waited a moment, hoping her gaze would shift, but she remained steadily focused on the way forward, as if no longer listening. "What do I have to do for you in return?" he asked Arcannen absently.

"Nothing! I *want* to do this. I want to help you. Do you think I haven't been subject to the same misgivings and fears that have haunted you? Do you think that mastering my magic was any less traumatizing or difficult? No, Reyn. It is like this for all of us who possess such gifts. And you do possess a gift of great worth. You will come to see."

The boy nodded and found himself suddenly eager to start with his lessons. "When can we begin?"

"Very soon, but I have a prior obligation I must satisfy first. We travel now to make that happen. I am hopeful you will come with me. Perhaps you can even help. It would be your choice, of course. But, in fact, I can set you down and leave you wherever you like and come back to find you another time."

"No!" Reyn was shocked at the vehemence of his response. The thought of becoming separated from Arcannen now, when he was so close to finding out secrets that would change his life, was unthinkable. He steadied himself. "I think it would be better if I stayed with you."

"Then stay with me you shall." Arcannen rose, clapping the boy on his back and giving his shoulder a squeeze. "Now rest yourself. We have much to do in the days ahead. I have more to tell you, but it can wait. You know the gist of things, and that's what matters. Lariana! Come sit with our young friend and keep him company. Let me have the helm back for a time. I feel rested enough to manage."

The girl waited until her mentor reached her, then stepped away as he whispered something and came back to sit once more with Reyn.

"What did he say to you?" the boy asked.

She grinned. "He said I should think about considering a future with you. He apparently thinks you and I would make a good match."

Reyn blushed. "We haven't known each other that long."

"Well, I don't know that there's a timetable on these things. It seems to me you just have to let them happen. Look at me."

He did, and she leaned in to kiss him on the lips. He kissed her back without thinking about it, wanting it to last longer than it did.

There was mischief in her eyes as she backed away. "See what I mean?"

Arcannen stood at the airship's controls, awash in a welcome sense of satisfaction. Manipulating the boy had proved far easier than he could have imagined. The boy had no inkling who had attacked him back in Portlow; he still believed it was the Druids. He did not suspect the sorcerer, whom he now trusted and was convinced intended to help him.

Well, in a way, Arcannen did intend to help him, but only in order
to help himself.

He could not yet be certain how useful Reyn would be, but the
possibilities were intriguing. The potential was there; the wishsong
magic was incredibly powerful. He needed to find a way to unleash it,
though. The boy was frightened and reluctant to make use of it in the
way Arcannen needed. He was hampered by his own insecurities and
lack of confidence. Arcannen would have to change all that. He would
have to reveal just enough to persuade the boy to do what was needed
without hesitating or thinking too long about it. But manipulation
was his specialty, and he would find a way.

He glanced down at the boy and Lariana. Perhaps the girl would
do it for him. She had already enchanted Reyn; the boy could not take
his eyes off her. His sorcerer's instincts had not failed him; she had
been the right choice after all. She was the perfect combination of ap-
proachable and unattainable. She was exotic, but at the same time she
could draw you in. More important, though, she was willing to do
whatever was necessary to further her own interests. His promise to
teach her magic was a lure she could not resist. She wanted to better
herself, and she knew that she needed help doing that.

She would be given her chance. If he still liked her well enough at
the end of things, he would keep her on to serve him in whatever way
he deemed best.

And if not, she would be left behind.

That was how life worked.

They flew on through the remainder of the day, continuing east-
ward toward the coast, speeding over increasingly rugged and barren
terrain as farmland and inhabited country were left behind. There
were no longer any towns or small settlements this far out. There was
nothing much to sustain life this far into the badlands, and aside
from small rodents and insects no evidence of life. Even the birds
avoided this part of the Southland. Sparse grasses and scrub dotted
the rocky countryside, but these were brownish and sunburned.
Nothing green was in evidence; no water sparkled in the sun. It would
be like this until they reached the coastal villages, which were still
several hours farther on.

Arcannen's passengers were sleeping, slumped against each other, the girl's arm about the boy's shoulders. It was a touching sight, but he did not respond emotionally. How they felt about each other was how he had told the girl they must, and she was working hard to make it happen. The boy would let her manipulate him; he wanted her badly enough that he could not help himself. He might question her motives—although Arcannen doubted it—but he would respond nevertheless. She would gain his confidence and help shape his thinking. In the end, it would be enough to place him firmly in Arcannen's experienced hands.

He thought momentarily of the Druids, and especially of Paxon Leah and his sister. It was Paxon, back in Portlow, who had attempted to intercept the boy. He had known he would run across the Highlander sooner or later; there was a connection between them that made it inevitable. Perhaps it would be a while before it happened again, especially if Paxon had tried to save the female Druid by smashing his way into the cylinder that imprisoned her. He felt a momentary pang of regret that he hadn't been able to stay around and watch it happen. It would have eased his unhappiness about driving Leofur farther away and losing Chrysallin Leah's services.

By nightfall, their destination appeared ahead, misted and darkening, the last of the daylight fleeing west at their backs. Overhead, the moon and stars were visible in a clear, cloudless sky. He could smell the ocean—the vast waters of the Tiderace—wafting on the evening air, strong and familiar. He could just begin to hear the booming crash of the waves against the rocks.

The boy and Lariana were awake, peering ahead through the gathering haze. "Look ahead!" Arcannen shouted over the rush of the wind. "See the buildings?"

In truth, the buildings were toppled and crumbling, their walls blackened and their roofs mostly collapsed. Ruins awaited them, the devastation left by the men and women of the Red Slash.

"What is it?" Reyn called back.

Arcannen smiled and made a sweeping gesture. "Arbrox! Your new home!"

. . .

When they had landed and climbed from the Sprint, Reyn said to Arcannen, "*This* is our new home?"

Lariana, too, usually stoic and unruffled, was looking around doubtfully. "What is this place?"

Arcannen gave them a moment. They were standing at the perimeter of what had once been the fortress of the raider village. The walls were broken and collapsed from the attack of the Red Slash six weeks earlier. Charred and blackened stone marked the remains of the fires that had been set to burn out the inhabitants who were still in hiding after the Federation soldiers had killed the rest. Bodies picked down to bones by carrion birds and four-legged scavengers littered the landscape both inside and outside the shattered walls, dull pieces of white in the fading daylight.

"This way," he ordered without explanation, moving toward a breach in the crumbling stone.

Inside, the collapsed buildings echoed with their footsteps in the deep silence as they picked their way through bones and debris. Nothing moved in the ruins, not even the birds that had fed on the dead after the carnage was complete. Arcannen remembered it all as if it were yesterday. He had never spoken of what happened here—not to anyone. Not until now. But today he would talk of it. These people had been his family—or the closest he had known in the five years of exile he had suffered after his flight from Wayford. They had taken him in, sheltered and fed him, made him one of them, and never asked a thing in return. Old Croy, who mended his shoes and clothing and told stories of his past. Melinhone, who cooked for him every day and kept him warm at night. The boy Phinn and the girl Derinda, brother and sister, who played in the yard of the home next door to his own, still children when they died.

The list went on and on, and every face on it was etched into his memory. All had died in the attack, and there had been no effort to spare them. It was understandable that the authorities would come after the raiders who had risked their lives from the moment they had chosen to prey on Federation shipping, but to make no distinction between those who were guilty and those who were innocent—those who were instigators and those who were no more than bystanders— was unforgivable. It was an affront to Arcannen and a blatant disregard of the laws of civility, and he could not abide it.

He explained all this now as he walked them through the remains of Arbrox from end to end, pointing out this and that space where a memory recalled itself, offering brief stories of those dead and gone, relating bits and pieces of the life he had enjoyed during the time he had lived here. The pain he felt in doing so was immense, but it was cleansing, as well. By telling of what hurt, he found fresh fuel for his determination to see it avenged.

"Do you not see the injustice of it?" he asked the boy as they walked on across the darkening landscape, glimpses of moon and stars now providing light for them to find their way forward. "A handful of these people broke the laws of a powerful government, but all who lived here were made to suffer for their violation. There was no effort to determine the guilty. The soldiers of the Red Slash were told that everyone was to be killed. The attack—which I witnessed— was meant to eradicate an entire people. It was an abomination against humanity."

"But why do you still consider this your home?" the boy pressed him. "It isn't really your home anymore."

"Come," Arcannen ordered, turning away.

He took them a short distance to an open doorway and then inside rooms where the ceiling was collapsed and the floor strewn with rubble. Without pausing, he continued on to an opening in the cliff wall behind and through to a darkened hallway. With a snap of his fingers, he produced a flame that danced on his fingertips. In the glow of its light, they made their way back into the darkness until he reached a shuttered door, heavy and metal-bound, the lock that secured it new.

Digging into his black robes with his free hand, Arcannen produced an iron key that released the lock. Without a word, he opened the door and stepped inside. The boy and the girl followed. Reaching out with the flame he had conjured, he lit a series of torches fixed in wall brackets until the room in which they stood was flooded with light.

"As you can see," he said, indicating what lay within with a sweeping gesture of his hand, "it is indeed still my home."

The room was furnished sumptuously and decorated with ornate wall tapestries and silks, colorfully woven rugs, and bright paintings. Fixtures of gold and silver glittered in the torchlight, and colorful glass bowls shone from where they sat on tables and pedestals. Through other doorways and openings, the faint outlines of furnishings revealed bedrooms and a kitchen, and showed the length of a long hallway that tunneled back into a deeper darkness.

"I returned when it was safe to do so and found these rooms empty and untouched. I brought in the things I required to make it comfortable, and I resolved that Arbrox would rise from the ashes. I could not save her people, my friends and protectors, but I could save their home. I could make it mine again, and I could live here as once I had intended I might. No one would come to bother me here—not in this dead and ruined place—so I did not need to worry about discovery. In its destruction, it came to serve me as the perfect hiding place while I considered what I would do to the Red Slash in retaliation for their acts against these people."

"You are all alone here?" Lariana asked him, her face solemn.

"Until now. I am not the sort of man who requires a great deal of company. I can manage on my own, even though I would have preferred things to remain as they were before the attack."

"But you intend to avenge what happened here?" Reyn hesitated. "How will you do that?"

"First things first," the sorcerer declared, squaring up before the boy. "Gaining revenge on the Red Slash on behalf of the dead of Arbrox is the prior obligation I mentioned. I seek your help in completing it. Will you consider doing so? Will you provide me with the assistance I need?"

The boy looked uncertain. "Wait. Are you asking me to use the wishsong to kill these soldiers you blame for what happened here? These men and women of the Red Slash?"

Lariana stepped close to him and took hold of his arm. "I don't think so, Reyn. I think he has something else in mind."

She said it in a way that warned the sorcerer he would be making a serious mistake in giving Reyn any other answer. He smiled inwardly at her perceptive recognition of what would amount to crossing a forbidden line, and was reassured anew that she had been the right choice for aiding him in his efforts to win over the boy.

"No, Reyn," he said. "I am not asking you to kill anyone. I would never ask that of you. I know how you feel. Killing others is exactly what you are seeking to avoid! You have asked me to help bring your magic under control, and I will do so. What I need to know is whether you are willing to help me in another way. Exacting revenge is my business, but you could help me with the details. Please consider doing so. You can see what has happened here. Do you not think, as I do, that it was an injustice and a travesty?"

The boy nodded slowly. "I do." But the uncertainty had not left his eyes.

Arcannen seated himself, fixing his face with a troubled look. "We are both victims of a world in which magic is mistrusted and disdained. Here, in the Southland, under the auspices of the Federation government, it is even outlawed. Druids hunt down those who possess it in order to take it away. A movement is afoot to stamp it out completely where it is not under the control of those who judge that they, and they alone, should make use of it. Look what happened to you in Portlow. There was no effort to talk to you; you were attacked. Your magic is considered dangerous, just as mine is. We are outlaws and exiles by the very nature of who we are and what we are capable of doing. No thought is given to intent or character. We are hunted and in most cases we are exterminated. Surely, you cannot believe this is right?"

The boy shook his head slowly. "I don't. But if I can bring my magic under control . . ."

"No!" Arcannen slammed his hand down on the tabletop next to him with such force that both the boy and the girl jumped. "You miss the point. We have to look beyond specific instances. We have to consider the larger picture. Bodies of men and women as powerful and ruthless as the Federation government or the Druid order will not be deterred until they are confronted and forced to stand aside. An example must be made that will convince them that it is better if they do, that any other choice will be more costly and damaging than what they are prepared to accept. So it is here. If I can show that they are helpless in the face of the magic I possess, I can demonstrate why leaving people like you and me alone is their best option."

He paused. "Yes, I intend to avenge my friends who died at Arbrox. But by doing so, I also intend to provide the Federation with an example of what will happen if they continue to pursue magic users like ourselves. I will give them a reason to think twice before they do so again. How they treated Arbrox is just another indication of how the powerful treat the powerless; it is a clear indication of their arrogance and disregard for others. Such behavior must be punished, Reyn. Such atrocities must be brought to an end!"

His voice had risen steadily as he talked, and by now he was practically shouting. But the boy was still listening and did not seem appalled. If anything, he looked to be deep in thought, caught up in what the sorcerer was saying, weighing his words, considering his advice.

Arcannen leaned back in his chair and smiled disarmingly. "I apologize. I was carried away with my passion for my beliefs. But at least I have voiced them so that you can consider."

He rose. "Enough for today. It is late. We will sleep here tonight. Take that time to think about what I have said. We will talk about it in the morning. Sleep where you like. Choose a room and a bed that suits you. Whatever is mine is also yours."

And he rose, went into the nearest bedroom, and closed the door behind him.

In the wake of Arcannen's departure, Reyn moved over to take the chair he had vacated. The sorcerer's words still echoed in his mind as he looked up at Lariana, standing across from him. "What do you think?" he asked.

She fixed her green eyes on him. "Why do you ask? What matters is what you think. You are the one he is asking for help. He already has mine."

"I was just asking your opinion."

"Well, don't. It isn't helpful. I don't have magic like you do. I can't tell you what to do. You have to make up your own mind."

He compressed his lips in a gesture of frustration. "I cannot use this wishsong, as he calls it, to hurt people. I've hurt too many already. It does something bad to me each time. It leaves me a little less whole, a little more diminished."

"Then don't use it."

"Is it that easy? He says he isn't asking me to hurt anyone. He says just the opposite, in fact. But he intends to make an example of the Red Slash. I don't think for one minute that he doesn't plan to kill some of them. Maybe the whole bunch. He hates them for what they did to this village. If I agree to help him, what am I risking?"

She said nothing, waiting.

He looked away. "I guess I know the answer."

"Let's go to bed," she said wearily. "I'll keep you company while you puzzle things through." When he hesitated, flushing with the heat that rose from his neck to his face, she laughed aloud. "I didn't mean it like that. I'm just coming in to sit with you. Maybe talk a bit more, if you want."

She walked over and pulled him to his feet. Her smile was unsettling. "What's the matter, Reyn? Are you frightened of me?"

Maybe, he thought.

But he went with her anyway.

14

MIDWAY BETWEEN DUSK AND MIDNIGHT, DAL-
len Usurient departed his quarters in the Red Slash
barracks on the edge of Sterne and walked north. The
Shadow Quarter was the one place in the city where there were no laws
enforced against people who dabbled in questionable trades as either
purveyors or customers. It was the part of the city where you went to find
entertainment of the sort that would not be allowed anywhere else, but
for which there was a strong demand among a certain percentage of the
population. If you wished to patronize a pleasure house or gambling par-
lor or engage in any otherwise forbidden activity, this was where you
went. Whatever you desired that was normally outside the restrictions
enforced in other parts of the city, you could find here.

Usurient went for the drask fights, where he knew that, on this day
of the week, he would find Mallich.

He had changed out of his uniform into ordinary clothing,
wrapped himself in a heavy travel cloak, and donned a slouch hat to
keep his features shaded. It did not matter much that he might be
recognized, but he saw no need to advertise who he was. As a member of the Federation army—and particularly of the Red Slash—he
was not all that popular with those men and women who might once
have served under him before going on to things even worse after-

ward. Nor did he think it expedient or wise to advertise his presence when what he was seeking to accomplish was every bit as illegal and reprehensible as anything those who spied him out might be engaged in.

Usurient was a practical man. He understood that sometimes you had to step outside the boundaries of sanctioned conduct and approved behavioral codes to achieve a righteous end. Sometimes you had to embrace the very thing you sought to put an end to in order to bring it close enough. So it was now. Arcannen had crossed a line by disposing of Desset in such a blatant and confrontational manner. If it had been done quietly and without any attempt to draw attention to it, if it had not been meant as an obvious challenge, he might not have given it a second thought. He had cared nothing for Desset, after all. But it was obvious that the spy's death was a lure meant to draw him back to Arbrox and into a confrontation with the sorcerer.

It troubled him that Arcannen was being so open about it. The man was fortunate to have escaped him the last time, yet he seemed untroubled by how close he had come to dying along with the rest of the ruined city's population. He was taunting Usurient, daring him to make a second attempt. His arrogance was startling, even slightly mad. But Usurient could not afford to let it be known that he had failed to respond. He kept command of the Red Slash by ensuring that no challenge to his authority or to the reputation of his Federation command would be allowed to go unanswered. A response was needed. A quick and certain resolution of the matter would have to be implemented—one no one could mistake. He had been given no orders to that effect, but sometimes the situation demanded that you act without them.

Yet there was nothing to say all this could not be achieved in a more unexpected and less conventional way than what the sorcerer might be expecting or his authority allowed.

Wrapped in his cloak, he slipped from the barracks and started down the road that would take him to the Shadow Quarter and the arena where the drasks engaged in combat. Mallich participated regularly; his animals were among the most fearsome in the city. He fought them once a week, every week, on this night only, pitting them against whatever challengers were brought in from other cities to vie for the fat purses offered by the organizers to the winners. Few in Sterne gave any thought to challenging Mallich these days. The odds were too great and the outcome too predictable.

And yet outsiders still thought his reputation inflated. They came from all over, from every walk and persuasion of life, professional breeders from as far away as the deep Southland cities and the distant mountainous regions of the Eastland. Some were newcomers, unwilling to believe the stories, convinced they would be the ones to prove them wrong. A man couldn't always win, they told themselves. No animal was unbeatable.

Except for Mallich's.

Usurient had no idea what Mallich did to create such monsters, and it seemed better to him to leave it that way.

In any case, it wasn't his breeding techniques that compelled the Red Slash commander to go searching for him. It was his hunter's skills, and his unerring ability to seek out prey and corner it, frequently with little more than a hunch and his instincts. Mallich understood fear and anger and frustration better than any man or woman alive. For more than twenty years, he had used that understanding to track down and subdue the enemies of those who hired him. For much of that time he had served the Red Slash. Then, nearly four years ago, he had quit. He had never offered an explanation, but Usurient knew the truth of it.

Likewise he knew a thing or two about the human condition, and he believed that even after you had left there was always a way to bring you back. Quitting was not forever; it was simply until the right impetus or the necessary compulsion changed your mind. All that was needed was to discover the nature of the lure.

In the case of Mallich and the sorcerer, Usurient thought he knew the answer.

When he reached the cavernous building that housed the fighting pits, he found it already packed to overflowing with customers and participants. Large crowds were gathered at all the entry doors, men

and women fighting to get inside, yelling and screaming at the door-
keepers, holding up credits and in some instances pieces of gold. One
man even thrust out a diapson crystal, his certainty in his betting
prowess evidenced by his willingness to part with something far more
valuable than anything he could hope to win inside the ring.

Ignoring the clamor and the bodies that pressed close, Usurient
worked his way around to the back of the building, where the gates to
the walled area reserved for participants stood closed and under
guard. But nothing was off limits to him, so he walked up to the
guards, identified himself, and was promptly admitted. Only once
had he been refused—more than ten years ago now. In retaliation, he
had brought two squads of soldiers in the next day, confiscated all the
drasks, money, and equipment, and sold it all off in Wayford.

After that, no one had ever questioned his right to be there.

Inside the yard, the drasks were straining against their chains and
bindings from within the cages where their keepers housed them.
They were strange beasts at first glance—a mix of dog, wolf, ape, and
something more that Usurient had never been able to define. Or perhaps he had chosen not to try to explain, because it reminded him
too much of some of the men he had known. It was only after you
considered the drask's purpose that you understood why it was perfectly constructed. Deep chest, massive shoulders, short, powerful
legs—the front slightly longer than the rear—square head that was all
bone and gristle, massive jaws, eyes that were restless and hungry.
Fighting animals, drinkers of blood, takers of life. They were covered
in bristling hair sharp enough to prick the skin, and the air was filled
with low growls and the warning snap of teeth.

Usurient cast about, searching for Mallich. Drasks weren't the
only animals he raised and trained. He also favored oketar—trackers
that, once they were on your scent, were almost impossible to throw
off. And then there were cretex—huge, lumbering beasts strong
enough to carry a dozen men and pull sleds piled high with stones.

And the crince, of course. Mallich was one of only a handful of
men who bred those. The less said about them the better, although he
imagined Mallich would want to use one against Arcannen.

After a few minutes of shifting his position in the courtyard to gain a better view and scanning through the large number of participants in a night's action that would continue until dawn, Usurient found his man. Mallich was seated on a stool over by the back wall, dressed in his familiar loose-fitting gray work clothes and ancient scuffed-up boots. His beard and frizzy hair were as gray as old ashes and his skin as gray as his hair, giving him the appearance of the walking dead. He was smoking a short pipe and gesturing at a scrawny boy who was serving as his assistant for the evening. Mallich kept a handful of them around—off-leash street kids with no home, no parents, and no life beyond what he provided for them and what they could find on the streets. Everyone else in the drask business used full-grown experienced men and women; not Mallich, though, who seldom did anything like anyone else.

He glanced up as Usurient approached, a glimmer of interest surfacing momentarily on his weary features before quickly fading. He nodded in greeting as the Red Slash commander took a seat next to him.

"Looking for a little excitement, Dallen?"

"Looking for you."

"Ah." The other shrugged. "I'm retired. No more hunts."

"Just drask fights and breeding these days."

"Oh, I wouldn't put it that way. I still find time for other forms of entertainment. Pretty much like you. I just prefer sticking close to home."

"You're entered tonight?"

"Two bouts. Want to place a bet?"

"Only if it's on you."

"Of course it's on me. But I wasn't talking about the drasks. I was talking about the odds of my not agreeing to whatever proposal you've come here to offer."

"You're telling me to save my money."

"And your breath. But you're going to make the offer anyway, aren't you?"

"What sort of man would I be to back away every time someone tells me to? Should I never take risks again? Should I stay only with the safe and known?"

Mallich considered him a moment and then rose. "I have to go. My first bout is coming up. My animal is favored to win at five to one. You should place a bet you can be sure about."

Usurient rose with him. "Let's see how it goes."

Usurient went inside the building through the participants' door and found a seat high up on the arena's back wall. The building was cavernous and filled with bodies and raucous yells. There were no empty seats farther down; there was barely standing room. Torches lit the darkness at the rear of the structure in a smoky haze, but at the arena level smokeless lamps cast a clear, sharp light. Usurient watched expressionlessly while Mallich's black-as-coal drask tore the opposing animal to shreds in under a minute. It was brutal and final, an overwhelming victory meant as both an object lesson and an arrogant challenge. Fight Mallich's drasks and you took your chances. Go up against his animals at your peril.

When the bout ended, Usurient kept his seat. He studied the crowd, picking out men and women he knew. Several were from the Red Slash, come for an evening's entertainment. None of them approached him. Even if they recognized him, they would keep their distance.

The second bout took a little longer than the first. The drask challenger was a sturdy, low-slung creature, its body scarred and ridged with muscle, its head not much more than eyes and jaws. Huge paws and thick legs supported its odd, piggish frame. It was durable and vicious, trained to go for the eyes and legs, and seemingly impervious to pain. What saved Mallich's reputation was most likely the homework he had done on the animal ahead of time—something he did as a matter of course in order to select the proper opponent from among his own stock. In contrast with the challenger, his drask was lean and lanky and cat-quick—the kind of gray ghost that was there one minute and gone the next, so quick you could barely follow its movements. It dodged the other animal with practiced ease, snapping and tearing in a flurry of strikes while keeping carefully clear of the arena sides and corners where it might become trapped. If the attacker had been able to pin it down, the fight would have ended quickly. But Mallich's drask was too quick. The minutes dragged on. Though the attacker kept coming in spite of the injuries being inflicted on it, the damage began to tell.

When finally it tired and went down, helpless to rise and defend itself, Mallich's animal carefully circled behind it, seized its neck, and bit down with an audible crunch that signaled an end to the battle.

Usurient waited until Mallich had led his blood-smeared drask from the ring and the process of mopping up the remains of the loser had commenced, then left his seat at last and went back down into the participants' yard.

"Very impressive," he acknowledged, coming up to the other and handing over a purse of gold coins. "I shouldn't have bet against you."

The gray man studied him a moment while he hefted the purse and then handed it back. "If I take your money, I will owe you. This is just a way to get me to consider your offer."

Usurient smiled, accepting the purse back. "Why don't we do this? You take care of your drasks and then come to the Broken Soldier for a drink. We'll celebrate your victory. I will make my offer; you will listen and decide its merit." He shrugged. "However it goes is how it goes."

Mallich spat. "Waste of my time. Besides, I'm tired and I don't need a drink. You'd best be on your way, Dallen."

The Commander of the Red Slash shrugged. "Have it your way." He turned to go, and then stopped. "By the way. Did I mention that my offer concerns Arcannen?" He waited a beat. "So if you know of somebody who might be his equal, perhaps you could send word to me?"

Mallich did not stop what he was doing. He did nothing to indicate that he had heard anything the other had said. But Usurient knew he had heard every word. He smiled. "I'll be at the tavern, if you change your mind about that drink."

Then he turned away once more, and this time he kept going.

. . .

He never once worried that Mallich wouldn't follow him to the tavern. Any mention of Arcannen would be enough to draw Mallich's attention. Any suggestion that there was an opportunity to track down his most hated enemy would win his active support.

Because Mallich did indeed hate the sorcerer worse than anyone.

And for a very good reason.

Five years earlier, Arcannen had murdered a minister of the Federation's Coalition Council in the guise of a member of the Fourth Druid order. It had taken the personal intervention of the Prime Minister and an agreement with the Ard Rhys of the Druid order to unmask the deception, but it had been discovered and Arcannen had been forced to flee his home in Wayford, leaving everything behind. For a time, he had disappeared completely. Both the Druids and the Federation had searched for him, but rumors of sightings and efforts to bait him into showing himself had yielded nothing. After nearly a year of searching, any active hunt had been abandoned.

Then, shortly afterward, a report surfaced that the sorcerer was living in a small village south and east of Wayford called Dorrat. A member of the Federation army, while visiting his wife's family, had seen the sorcerer engaged in a discussion with the village blacksmith. Aware of the stalled hunt for Arcannen, he had reported his discovery immediately upon his return to his company in Sterne, and word had eventually filtered back to Arishaig and the senior commander of the Federation army.

The commander, in turn, had given the job of following up this latest rumor—one that he believed worth examining more closely—to Usurient and the Red Slash. Find out the truth of things and report back.

But Usurient—choosing to reinterpret his orders—decided that men other than regular soldiers should handle the matter. He called in Mallich at once, told him of the assignment, and asked if he would undertake it. If the sorcerer was found, he was to be killed at once. No consideration was to be given to any other course of action. Arcannen was extremely dangerous; killing him swiftly and without hesitation was the proper resolution to the task. Mallich could accomplish this any way he chose; he could take with him any others he felt would aid him. He could use whatever methods he felt necessary. Whatever the nature of any damage or condemnation that resulted, Usurient would make certain there were no repercussions.

Because of the sorcerer's reputation and the challenge offered in hunting him down, Mallich accepted the assignment. He did not do so without a full awareness of the danger he would face, but his confidence in his own considerable skills and experience persuaded him that he was more than equal to the task.

For support, he took with him two of his oketar trackers, a drask to protect them, and a handful of the men who had assisted on hunts like this in the past—all of them familiar with what was required and willing to do whatever was demanded of them to achieve the result Usurient desired.

He also took with him his only son, a sharp-eyed, hulking boy of twenty years named Mauerlin.

Taking the boy was a bad idea, Usurient believed, because while fully grown and otherwise entirely capable, Mauerlin lacked experience. But he said nothing to Mallich because it wasn't his place to do so. As one of many, perhaps the boy would be in no special danger. Surely the father would recognize the need to keep a close eye on his son.

But he misjudged Mallich's determination to give his son an opportunity to prove himself. Arriving at the village of Dorrat, the company split in two. Mallich took command of the first unit and gave the second over to his son. Each of them would take one of the oketar, and Mauerlin would be given the drask, as well. Their quarry's scent was provided through a piece of clothing retrieved from among the clothes Arcannen had abandoned in Wayford when he had fled the city. A quick sniff was provided to the animals, and the two expeditions were off.

They approached their search methodically, coming toward each other from opposite ends of the village. They held off until after nightfall, biding their time until they knew most of the villagers would be in bed. They searched quietly and efficiently, allowing the oketar to set the pace. Mallich had already determined, through a surreptitious investigation by one of his most trusted scouts, that Arcannen was still in the village. It was troubling to him that no one seemed to know exactly where the sorcerer kept his quarters, but overall that seemed an inconsequential obstacle.

In fact, it was their undoing.

However he managed it—whether through some mistake made by Mallich or some warning system he had set in place previously—Arcannen quickly discovered that he was being hunted. Rather than waiting around to be found, he went down into the streets and began to track the hunters coming at him from the north.

Mauerlin's unit.

What happened afterward was never entirely clear to anyone, in part because there was no one left to describe it. Arcannen took out the drask and oketar first, and when the hunters were left blind and in disarray, he took them out as well. One by one, he picked them off until all lay dead save their leader.

Then he set out to make an example of Mallich's son before fleeing into the night and disappearing once more.

When the father found his son, Mauerlin was hanging inside the blacksmith's by his arms. A weight was tied to his legs, which in turn were connected by a length of rope that was fastened about the boy's neck in a noose. So long as Mauerlin kept his legs raised, he was safe. But when he tired and the weight pulled his legs down, the noose about his neck tightened.

Usurient, who had seen men die in every way conceivable, knew what that must have been like for the boy as he fought to keep from strangling and for the father when he found him afterward.

They had never talked about it, Mallich and he. But Usurient, who knew men and understood their passions, never doubted what the boy's death had done to the father or how badly the father hungered for retribution. He might act as if the matter were over and done with and he had gotten past it. He might pretend that he didn't spend every waking hour waiting for a chance to do to the sorcerer what he had done to Mauerlin. But Usurient knew better.

You never got over the death of a child and the guilt that somehow attached to it.

It was not more than thirty minutes after he arrived when the tavern door swung open and Mallich appeared. Usurient had chosen a table near the back of the room that allowed him a clear view of those who entered but forced the latter to search a bit in order to find him. Mallich was quick, however, finding him almost at once and moving over to the table to sit.

Usurient signaled for a tankard and leaned back again in his chair. "I can order you something to eat, if you wish."

Mallich glowered. "You can stop being clever. If I weren't persuaded to listen to your offer, I wouldn't be here. So let's get on with it. Say what you have to say."

So Usurient did, detailing the destruction of Arbrox, the failure to find and finish Arcannen, the subsequent killing and hanging of Desset, and his own determination to ferret out and put an end to the sorcerer. He covered it all quickly and sat back to measure the other's reaction.

"Desset." Mallich scowled. "No great loss there. He wasn't worth his weight in pig spit. So you don't see this as revenge for someone as worthless as Desset. Perhaps you think revenge might suit me better?"

Usurient shrugged. "That isn't for me to say. But this is a rather obvious chance to bring Arcannen to bay, isn't it? And who deserves such a chance more than you?"

"But you are the one he threatens. You are the one at risk. You see this as a preemptive strike. Get to him before he gets to you."

"He won't get to me so easily. But he's a nuisance, and I want him gone. Same rules as before. Find him; kill him. No restrictions on how you do it. Anything you need, I will get it for you."

Mallich regarded him for several long, uncomfortable moments. The tankard of ale arrived and the hunter drank from it, sat back, and regarded him some more.

Finally, he said, "I don't like being used."

"You are a hunter, aren't you? You do work for hire. You are argu-
ably the best there is. I would certainly say as much, if asked. So of
course you are being used. That is the nature of our arrangement; it
always has been."

Mallich drained his tankard, leaned back. "All right. I'll take your
offer. This is my price."

He named it. Usurient wondered where he would find such a sum,
but decided he would worry about that later. "Done," he said. "What
else do you need?"

"A visit to the prisons, with you as company. I will find the men I
need to help me there."

Usurient felt a faint shudder slide through him. "You don't mean
to take Bael Etris, do you? I can't allow that."

Mallich rose, stretched, and looked down at him. "If you want this
done, you do what I tell you to get it done. Meet me at midday at the
prisons. If you're not there, we forget the whole thing. If you choose
to object to the decisions I make, we forget the whole thing." He
leaned down. "I know how to use men, too, Dallen."

Then he turned away and was gone out the tavern door.

15

IDDAY OF THE FOLLOWING DAY WAS CLOUDY, gray, and oppressive, and it mirrored Dallen Usurient's mood as he waited for Mallich just inside the entrance to the prisons at Sterne. The building was a two-story stoneblock monolith with barred windows and watchtowers, and it looked just exactly like what it was intended to be. The guards were members of the City Watch, men and women trained for and assigned to this particular duty, and they all wore matching blue uniforms with prison insignia. Guards staffed all entrances and passageways and the watchtowers at the corners of the building. The smells that permeated and the gloom that shrouded every part of the building reflected the grim and hopeless nature of the prisoners lodged within.

Usurient was engaged in reviewing his decision to send Mallich in search of Arcannen, wondering anew if he had made a mistake. He had not counted on the other man turning to prisoners to accompany him on his hunt, believing he would settle for his animals and one or two men from the old days. One or two men not locked away. But the more he thought about it, the more sense it made that the other would come here. Mallich did not intend to risk losing anyone else he cared about to this endeavor—not after what had happened to Mauerlin. Instead, he would take men who had no future and about whom he cared absolutely nothing. Their loss would not impact him, and it might even be that he expected to lose them and they were meant to serve as little more than a distraction for his quarry.

But Bael Etris? Usurient shivered at just the mention of the man.

He leaned back against the wall, forcing his nerves to steady. Etris had once been a member of Mallich's cadre of hunters, a proficient tracker and a ruthless killer, useful in certain situations, but sometimes unmanageable and always unpredictable. He overreached himself when, two years back, while serving Mallich—but under Red Slash auspices nevertheless—he killed an entire family of Southlanders who were rumored to be magic users. It wasn't so much that he killed them as that he did so without making sure he had the right family—which he didn't. And it wasn't even so much that as what he did to them. When he was finished, there was barely enough left to identify them as human and nothing to say which parts belonged to which person. What was clear from the carnage was that the man had enjoyed his work to a degree that verged on madness.

It was brutal and unnecessary, and the Federation High Command had tried Etris for murder and mayhem and sentenced him to life in the prisons. There the man had found a new calling, a fresh challenge to his twisted worldview. Within the first three months, he had killed three other prisoners. Within the first six, he had killed four guards, as well. After that, he was confined to solitary indefinitely and not allowed out save for one hour a day so that he could exercise by walking around the perimeter of a twelve-by-twelve-foot open pen. Even then he was kept under heavy guard.

Etris had been left to rot, and there wasn't anyone Usurient knew who thought this wasn't as it should be. Men like Bael Etris did not belong in the larger world. They barely belonged in cells where they could be caged like the animals they were.

And now Mallich wanted to let this creature out.

Usurient had racked his brain all night trying to find an excuse for not doing so, a reason that the other man would accept, any alternative that would appeal. But Mallich was not the sort to adjust his thinking without good reason, and in this case he had made up his mind when he had accepted the job of tracking down Arcannen that he would take Etris with him.

Who else did he intend to take?

"You don't seem happy, Dallen."

Mallich was standing right in front of him. He had been so absorbed in thinking about Etris that he hadn't heard the other come up. He straightened, making an effort to appear casual. "I was just wondering how you plan to keep yourself alive if you have Bael Etris sleeping next to you."

Mallich gave him a crooked grin. "You needn't worry. I can manage him. It's you who should worry if I fail to come back from this. He genuinely hates you."

This was true. Usurient had instigated the court action that had resulted in Etris's imprisonment. For all intents and purposes, he was responsible for what had been done to the man. Not that he regretted it. But he would have preferred that Etris remain where he was rather than be set loose again.

"He might kill you just to get to me," he pointed out.

Mallich shook his head. "I will treat him like one of my oketar, only with less patience and a very short leash. He won't be able to get near me. Now, are we through discussing this? Because it really isn't your concern, is it? So can we go to his cell and speak with him?"

Usurient nodded reluctantly. "Wouldn't it be better if you went alone?"

"Why? Don't you want to come with me? Does he frighten you so?"

Angered by the other's impudence and recognizing a challenge when he saw one, Usurient stalked over to the guard station where visitors were required to sign in. From there, they went through a steel door, down a hallway, up a set of stairs, down another hallway, and finally through another steel door into a short corridor that was so quiet, it seemed to Usurient you could hear the walls breathing.

At the far end, the guard released a lock on a floor-to-ceiling sliding steel panel and then rolled the barrier back to reveal a set of bars separating them from Bael Etris.

The prisoner sat on a hinged bed frame staring at them. He was unusually small, barely more than five feet, his prison clothes hanging on his slender frame as they might on a scarecrow. His limbs and body, however, were ridged with muscle and ritual scars, and you could feel the power radiating off him. His face was oddly beatific—smooth, calm, devoid of expression—almost child-like until you looked into the strange green eyes and saw the madness reflected there.

"Usssurrrient," he whispered in what came out as a slow, drawn-out hiss. "Have you come to beg my forgiveness?"

He rose and came to stand a few feet away as he looked up at them, his gaze shifting from one face to the other. Then he spat on Usurient through the bars.

The Commander of the Red Slash flinched in spite of himself. But Mallich stepped forward to block an effort at retaliation. "Your fate rests with me, Bael. So perhaps you ought to stop acting like a child and listen to what I have to say before you do something you'll regret."

The other cocked his head. "I never do anything I regret. Only what I fail to do in a timely manner."

"Are you finished pissing around?"

"Oh, I've no quarrel with you, Mallich. None at all. I've never had one with you. You weren't the one who had me locked away. You weren't the one who betrayed me. I have no wish to anger you. Say what you came to say. I will pay close attention."

His voice was soft and appealing, a clever and practiced tone. Usurient wiped the spit off his face and clothes, thinking of ways he could make the man's life so unbearable he would beg to be killed. But that wasn't an option. Not yet, at least.

"I am going to track a man into the far eastern shores of the Tiderace. I require someone with your skills to join me in my hunt. If you agree to come, you will earn your freedom by doing so. Are you interested?"

Etris cocked his head, his arms folding close about his small body. "Who is it you track?"

"The sorcerer Arcannen."

Etris smiled. "Rumor has it he is already dead. Would you kill him a second time just to make sure?"

Mallich smiled back. "He is not dead; he is alive. And I would kill him as many times as I could for what he did to Mauerlin. But neither of us will speak of that again, will we?"

Etris shrugged. "What of your companion? Does he travel with us?"

"So that you might find an opportunity to kill him? No. He remains here in Sterne. This sort of work is best left to men like you and me."

Bael Etris pursed his lips, then shifted his gaze to Usurient. "Understand something, Commander. If I am released, I will do whatever Mallich tells me to do to hunt down and kill the sorcerer. But when that work is finished, I will come looking for you. If I find you, do not expect me to show you any mercy."

Usurient laughed aloud. "You tell me this and still expect me to set you free? Why in the world would I even consider doing so after such a bold statement?"

The little man's grin was wicked and sly. "You wouldn't have come here in the first place if you had any other choice. Whatever I say or do at this point, you will free me. You want Arcannen dead as much as Mallich does, that much is clear. Now let me out."

"Tomorrow, at sunrise," Mallich interrupted. "I will bring you all the weapons and gear you need. We leave for the coast from here." He paused. "But let this be a warning. No tricks while we're out there alone. I'll have you tied to a crince, Bael. You even look the wrong way and it will rip out your throat." He smiled. "Just in case you were thinking of trying to rip out mine."

Then he reached for the sliding steel door and slammed it shut.

In the underground refuge of Arcannen, beneath the ruins of Arbrox, Reyn Frosch stumbled muddle-headed and sleepy-eyed from his bedroom into the central living quarters of Arcannen to find Lariana already busy preparing breakfast. Or was it lunch? He wondered suddenly what time it was. How long he had slept?

"Good morning," the girl greeted him from the kitchen area. Her strange, exotic features brightened as she caught sight of him.

"Is it morning?" he asked, his voice rough and oddly strange to him.

"You are asking the wrong question. You should be asking what day it is. You've been asleep for two days."

He stopped where he was. "Two days? How could I have slept that long?"

She walked away from what she was doing to bring him a cup of steaming tea. "I gave you a little something to help you sleep. You were in need of rest. Are you hungry?"

He nodded, still in a daze. She took his arm, led him to a small table, and sat him down. A moment later he was eating fry bread, smoked meat, dried fruit, and cheese. He had never been so hungry.

She sat down across from him, watching. He was aware of the whiteness of her skin, its flawless surface radiant. Her green eyes stayed on him as he looked at her, locking with his own. He remembered she had slept with him that first night, but he could not remember her leaving. In fact, he could not remember anything after falling asleep save the warmth of her body pressed close against his.

When he was finished, he cleared his throat in the ensuing silence. "I guess whatever you gave me worked. I didn't wake once. Two days?" He shook his head and smiled. "Best sleep I ever had."

"Most snoring, too, probably," she added. "I had to leave you to it pretty soon after you drifted off.

"Sorry about that."

"Don't be. It's worth it to see you looking so much better."

She cleared his dishes, and he wondered again at how much he had come to like her in the short time they had been together. He had found her intriguing from the first, but most of that was because of her unusual looks. By now, what he was feeling ran much deeper. He felt happier and more settled than he could remember ever being before.

She came back to the table, walked to his side, and bent down to kiss him on the cheek. "I liked sleeping next to you. Being with you made me feel happy."

Reyn grinned. "I felt like that, too."

"Do you want to go outside, take a short walk?"

"Through the bones of the dead? Charming."

"No, there's another choice. Wash and dress, and I'll show you."

When he was ready, she took him through the sorcerer's quarters down the back hall to a second door. This door was ironbound and heavily warded by locks, but she opened it easily and took him out into a stone passageway, up several sets of stairs, and outside into the open air. The day was overcast and windy, the clouds scudding along from south to north, and the taste and smell of the sea filled Reyn's nostrils.

They were standing on a promontory above the ruins, looking down on the crumbling walls and collapsed roofs, the bones of the dead clearly visible in gray patches within the courtyards and open chambers. Seaward, waves crashed below them against the rocks, and to the west the land spread away in a rocky, barren terrain that ended far distant where mountains rose against the horizon.

Lariana put her arms around Reyn and pulled him close to her, leaning her head against his chest. He reciprocated, and they remained like that for a time, neither of them saying anything as they stared out at the landscape and breathed the salt air.

"This way," she said finally.

She released him and led him down a path that ran along the ridgeline south, picking her way while she held his hand as she might a child's, her honey-streaked hair flying out behind her in the wind. They walked for more than a mile, pausing now and then to look out at the sea, to study rock formations, to watch the flights of birds winging their way through the damp haze.

"Where's Arcannen?" Reyn asked her.

She shrugged. "He took the Sprint to one of the coastal towns yesterday and hasn't been back. He said he had some business to take care of. Do you miss him?"

He smiled in spite of himself. "Not much." He paused. "Tell me something more about yourself. You've barely said anything."

She neither demurred nor hesitated. She simply responded, telling him about her life as the child of a Rover chieftain, of her parting with her family when she was barely thirteen and was told she was to be given to a rug merchant as his bride in exchange for certain valuable wares, of her flight east to the Southland cities of the Federation, and of her subsequent education at the hands of various wealthy and influential men who sought to keep her for their own, but could never hold on to her. He was more than a little surprised by her candor, her admission of the harshness and subjugation she had endured and somehow put behind her. She seemed untroubled by what she had weathered to reach this point in her life, and she avoided saying much at all about her arrangement with Arcannen beyond declaring that she intended that the sorcerer should one day mentor her in the use of magic.

"But you," she said. "You were born with magic. It's always been a part of you. What must that be like?"

They were sitting on a rock bench, looking out at the ocean, feeling the spray on their faces one minute, the wind the next. He looked at her in wonder, the question so strange he had trouble finding anything to say.

"I don't know how to answer that. I think it's wonderful and terrible both. It can be good and bad. Magic is unpredictable. It does things to you, even when you don't want it to."

She stared at him. "Are you saying you wish you didn't have it?"

"Sometimes I feel that way."

"But it makes you special, Reyn!" There was an unmistakable urgency in her voice. "No one else is like you. Everyone wants what you have. I want it!"

"Maybe you should be careful what you wish for."

There was disbelief mirrored in her eyes. "Maybe so. But I don't feel that way. I don't know that you should either."

He sighed, bending his head close to hers. "Right now, I'm struggling with it. I'm haunted by what the magic does to me. There's more to this than what I've told you. I just can't talk about it right now."

She cupped his face in her hands and kissed him. "Then you don't have to. You never have to with me."

And she kissed him again and again.

. . .

"We're not finished here yet, are we?" Usurient asked as they navigated various fresh corridors and passed through several more steel doors, realizing suddenly they were not moving in the direction of the entry. "Is there someone else you want?"

"One more," Mallich acknowledged. "Then we can go." He glanced over. "Stop worrying about who it might be. This isn't someone you know."

Usurient couldn't decide whether to feel relieved or concerned. On balance, he thought, it was better just to wait and see.

They moved from the wing of the building in which Etris was caged to a different section, descending a stairway to the ground floor. But soon they were going down another set of stairs and then another, and Usurient realized they were moving into a cellar level, an area of the prisons to which he had never been and about which he knew nothing at all. How Mallich, who was no longer affiliated with the Red Slash and lacked the requisite standing to enter these prisons without a member of the Federation in tow, knew his way around so well was a mystery.

Eventually, they were deep underground in a warren of tunnels and passageways with steel doors inset on both sides, all of them closed and locked. Although Usurient listened for sounds coming from behind those doors, he heard nothing.

"Never been down here before, have you?" Mallich asked suddenly.

"Never. What is this place?"

"This is where they put the prisoners no one ever wants to see alive again—either because they are already dying or because someone in power in the Federation wants them dead. The prisoners down here are refuse, garbage. Nothing is ever said about them. Their names are never spoken once they've been sentenced."

"But Etris isn't here?" Usurient asked. "Why not?"

Mallich smiled. "I thought he should be kept where he is—that I might have need of him again someday. A bribe to the right person can buy you anything."

They walked on, the echo of their footfalls in the corridor the only sound that broke the silence. Smokeless lamps lit their way.

"How many are down here?" Usurient was unable to keep himself from asking.

"Not many. Most of these cells are empty. Men don't last long down here."

"Are there women?"

"Now and then. You don't want to know."

What he was hearing about the prisons was unsettling, but what he was seeing in Mallich was even worse. Until now, he had thought him a hunter and a trainer of fighting animals. But he was clearly something more. There was a side to him revealed by this visit that was beyond disturbing, and Usurient was catching glimpses of darkness in the man that he didn't want to get too close to. Again, he wondered if he had made the right choice in deciding to send him after Arcannen—not because he thought he was incapable of succeeding, but because there was clearly more to the man than he had realized and not knowing the men with whom you surrounded yourself was dangerous.

"You've chosen to take someone out of these cells?" he asked finally. "Why would you do that?"

Mallich shook his head. "We aren't taking any of these men out. These men aren't all that useful. Not like Etris. It's their keeper I'm interested in."

Usurient frowned. *Their keeper?*

They reached a bend in the corridor and found themselves standing before a desk tucked into an alcove in the wall. A solitary individual sat behind the desk, bent over pieces of metal rod that he was twisting together to build something. He was using his bare hands. He made it look easy. As it should have been, given his unusual size. He was easily seven feet and three hundred pounds, but none of it looked as if it had been acquired by accident or neglect.

The man remained hunched over the rods as they stopped before him and didn't bother to look up. "What?" he rumbled.

"I need you to come with me," Mallich answered.

Piggish eyes shifted momentarily. "Mallich? Where this time?"

"The Tiderace. Somewhere around what used to be Arbrox."

The big man lifted out of his hunched position and regarded him. "Who is this?" He pointed at Usurient.

"The man who is going to pay you a lot of money for your services. Will you come with me?"

The other man shrugged. "Why not? I have time coming. I need to get away. Just you and me?"

"And Bael Etris."

A smile now. "Must be blood involved if he's going. Whose blood?"

"Arcannen."

"The sorcerer. Well, now." He rose, towering over both Mallich and Usurient. "That's blood that won't be shed easily. Arcannen has more lives than a dozen cats." He paused. "I don't trust Etris, even if you think you can."

"I don't trust him, either," Mallich said. "But he can be useful even so."

"Maybe. Maybe not."

"I'll pick you up here tomorrow at sunrise. Upstairs."

The other shifted his gaze to Usurient, then back to Mallich. "I'll be there. The money had better be good."

This last was spoken sideways to Usurient, who nodded almost without thinking about it.

Then he and Mallich were retracing their steps down the hallway toward the cellar stairs. Usurient realized suddenly that he had been holding his breath back there, unsure of what might happen.

"Who is that?" he asked finally.

"Don't know his real name. Everyone calls him The Hammer. He rules the basement level of the prisons and those given over to his tender care. He decides who lives and who dies. How he does this is anyone's guess. No one asks that question. Look at him; you can see his value."

"You've used him before? But not asked me?"

Mallich glanced over. "Not everything I do concerns you and your Red Slash. Some things I do are for other people and different reasons. The Hammer has been useful in a few of those."

He stopped suddenly when they reached the basement stairs and turned to face Usurient. "Don't question me further on this or I will let you find someone else to handle it. You've done your part, all but the payment. I make the decisions on how we get to Arcannen and how we dispose of him. You stay out of it."

He turned away and started up the stairs with a dismissive gesture. After a moment's hesitation, inwardly seething at the other's treatment of him, Dallen Usurient followed.

16

I T WAS JUST AFTER MIDDAY WHEN ARCANNEN PILOTED his Sprint over the last of the coastal landscape separating him from the ruins of Arbrox and made a cautious landing in the sheltered area he had chosen earlier for his craft's concealment. On the coast, vessels were in constant danger from high winds and sudden storms, but he faced an equally daunting prospect from the risk of discovery. If anyone found his vessel and commandeered it, he would be trapped in his lair. Escape without a flying vessel was out of the question. Between the miles of barren terrain surrounding his hiding place on three sides and the churning maelstrom of the ocean on the fourth, the only way a man could flee with any hope of success was through the air.

So hiding his Sprint was a necessary effort each time he returned. His current choice was a deep depression in the rocks inland from the coast proper about a mile from Arbrox, tucked back in a mass of boulders and broken rock that no one could successfully navigate on foot without knowing how to do so beforehand. Using rock walls and cliff overhangs, he was able to place his airship almost completely out of sight. Finding it on foot would require an extraordinary stroke of luck. A careful air search in the right weather and with sufficient sunlight might reveal it, but the persistent marine layer and frequent rains reduced the chances of that happening considerably.

Besides, he lived in the ruins of a village to which no one came.

Or hadn't before now. But come they would, and very soon. He had made sure of that—all part of his plan to provide Dallen Usurient with an irresistible opportunity to bring the Red Slash back to the coast to find him. Not that he expected Usurient himself would do so. No, Usurient would take a different approach, one less obvious to those watching for it. He would send someone other than himself, reluctant to make a return trip if it wasn't necessary, believing that hunting down and killing off Arcannen could be achieved without his personal involvement. He would send men skilled at the sort of undertaking with which he would task them, their orders clear and their destination determined through the rumors and reports with which he had provided them.

And they would journey to their doom.

But that was all part of the game, and Arcannen loved nothing better than contests of wit and machinations and, ultimately, surprises.

He covered the Sprint with a canvas that was the exact same mottled gray and brown as the rocks within which it nestled and began the walk back to the remains of the village. All about him, the damp and the gray bore down in a heavy shroud. The wind whipped about him fiercely, constantly changing direction and force, a wild thing that nothing could contain. Ahead, the crashing of waves against the rocks was a steady booming that drowned out the rest of the world's sounds.

By now, he was thinking, Usurient would have begun the process of choosing the men he would send and providing the equipment and supplies they would need. By now an expedition would have been mounted, and if it had not already been dispatched it soon would be.

He must prepare for them. He must anticipate their arrival and their intentions in ways that would allow him to dispose of them quickly.

The seeds were planted, he assured himself. He had planted them himself. It would be interesting to discover what sort of crop they would yield.

Arcannen was, at heart, a fatalist. He believed that most of what happened was predestined and that his own involvement was preordained. Life offered opportunities, and you made the choices that were demanded of you. To some extent, you influenced the results of what happened—but never completely and not always in the ways you anticipated. You had to accept that much of life was chance and luck, and so you rode that sea of the unexpected and unanticipated from the moment you were born until the moment you died. Sometimes the ride was smooth and easy, but often it was rough. The intangibles always dictated the outcome in ways you could not entirely predict or alter.

So it was that his plans for Usurient and the Red Slash were fluid. He would arrive where he needed to be, but the journey would not go entirely according to his wishes.

He wondered suddenly how things were proceeding with the boy and Lariana. She was clever, that one. She had already won the boy's heart; he was so in love—even if he did not realize it—that his choices hereafter would begin and end with her. She was every bit as clever and manipulative as Arcannen had believed she would be. He was pleased enough with how she had handled herself that he decided he would give her instruction in the use of magic and perhaps even agree to take her on as his apprentice. He would have given that honor to Leofur had she not spurned him, but that was all water under the bridge now. And Lariana might prove the better choice in any case.

As he closed on the ruins, he saw nothing of the happy couple. Nestled inside, he imagined, perhaps sharing secrets in ways that he had given up on long ago. Young love—such a tender, wonderful thing. Such an attractive nuisance. It stole away your reason; it ensnared your common sense in euphoric dreams. Useful here, however. In the end, it would net him what he needed to fulfill his plans for revenge against his enemies.

When he reached the sealed door and released the locks, there was still no sign of them. Down the hallway and into his quarters he proceeded, listening for the sound of their voices. When he heard them, he slowed automatically to listen. But their words were low and indistinct.

On entering his quarters, he found them sitting at the kitchen table sipping tea and smiling at each other. *Good enough,* he thought. "Well met, young friends," he said cheerfully. "Reyn, are you rested and fed?"

The boy nodded, sharing a look with the girl. *Oh, rested and fed, indeed,* the sorcerer thought.

"Is your business concluded?" Lariana asked. "Did things go well?"

He moved over to stand next to them. "Unfortunately, not all went as well as I had expected. Word has gotten out that I am living in these ruins or somewhere close by. I had hoped that a tighter lock might be kept on loose lips, but it hasn't worked out that way. I expect I am compromised."

Lariana gave him a direct look. "What does that mean exactly?"

"It means that Usurient and the Red Slash will soon know—if they don't already—where I am."

"They will come here?" the boy demanded.

"Not right away. And not Usurient. He will send someone else."

"He will send assassins," Lariana said.

He was pleased at how quickly she caught on. "I imagine so. He will choose a handful of killers to hunt me down, keeping at a distance so that no blame will attach to him. If that fails, *then* he will come himself."

"Maybe we should leave," Reyn suggested. "There are other places we could hide."

"And other places we could be found. No, Reyn. Running away isn't the answer. The hunting won't stop unless we make it stop." He was purposeful in using *we* rather than *I*. "We will make our stand here."

The boy exchanged a look with Lariana. "How do we do that?"

Arcannen smiled reassuringly. "Well, in the first place, I'm not going to ask you to use the wishsong to help protect us. Not in a way that requires you to hurt anyone, at least. So you needn't worry about that. Mostly, you need to keep your eyes open for the men Usurient will send. When they come, I will deal with them myself."

"But if we are threatened," Lariana interrupted quickly, turning now to the boy, "we may have to defend ourselves. So there is no guarantee you won't have to use your magic that way. Does that frighten you?"

Arcannen could hear the challenge in her voice. She wasn't leaving anything to chance. This was what made her so valuable to him. She anticipated everything so well.

"I will do what I have to," the boy said at once. "But I would not like it if I had to hurt anyone."

Lariana nodded. "I would not like that, either. But it seems we are fated to be hunted by these people." She turned to Arcannen. "These are the same people who massacred the population of Arbrox, aren't they? They will treat us the same way."

Arcannen nodded. "And there are others we need to fear, as well. The Druids hate us, too. They fear my use of magic will somehow compromise them. They wish to stop me completely from using it. Understand. Not only do we need to protect ourselves now, but we also need to find a way to prevent this harassment—this persecution—from continuing. We need to persuade all of these people to leave us alone. Because once they find out the truth about you, Reyn, they will come after you, too. Just as they did in Portlow. You can't allow that to continue."

"I know." The boy nodded slowly. He had already begun to come around to the mind-set Arcannen wished him to assume. "But how do we do that?"

"Can you tell us?" Lariana asked quickly, anticipating once again what was needed.

Arcannen stepped away from the table. "I can do better than that. I can show you. Come with me."

Paxon Leah was exercising alone in the training yard, working his way through a series of complex defensive maneuvers, when Keratrix found him. He was stripped to the waist, sweating in the hot sun, enjoying the strain on his body as he whipped the Sword of Leah from left counter to right thrust, blocking and counterattacking, twisting and turning his shoulders and arms in a mock battle against an invisible enemy. Most of the moves he was employing had been taught to him by Oost Mondara over the past five years, skills he had studied, practiced, and finally mastered in his continuing efforts to make himself more deserving of his designation as the High Druid's Blade. He was so deeply enmeshed in his efforts that it was some time before he noticed that the scribe was standing off to one side watching him.

When he stopped and looked over, the other shook his head and smiled ruefully. "You make it look so easy. But I know it isn't."

Paxon rolled his shoulders and stretched. "It helps if you do it about a million times. Besides, I'm still learning."

"You don't look like you need to learn anything more." Keratrix paused. He brushed at his mop of dark hair. "Sorry to bother you, but the Ard Rhys would like to see you. When you're finished here."

Isaturin. Paxon walked over to the battered old scabbard that had protected his sword's blade for so many generations and sheathed the weapon carefully. "I'm finished," he said. "Let me wash up and I'll come up right away."

He went inside the building to his quarters and bathed and changed his clothing. He was wondering what Isaturin might want of him. He had not been asked to undertake anything since his return from Portlow. No further missions had been assigned, and no reports had come in on Arcannen or the boy with the wishsong. Avelene had recovered from the trauma she had suffered at the sorcerer's hands and had gone back to her studies. Since the night she had asked Paxon to stay with her, she had barely spoken to him. He thought she might be embarrassed at what she perceived to be a display of weakness, or perhaps she simply didn't want him to get the wrong idea. He had not pressed her about any of it, leaving her alone except to exchange pleasantries when they encountered each other, letting her work her way through her feelings, not presuming anything from what had happened and how she had reacted.

In truth, he didn't know quite what to make of her. She had shown no interest in him before they had set out in search of the source of the magic that approximated the wishsong. Even then, her feelings had appeared mixed. And her response to him after being freed from the black cylinder appeared to have been generated mostly out of fear and desperation. He was reluctant to read anything more into it.

When he reached the Ard Rhys's quarters, Isaturin was waiting in the doorway. "I got tired of reading documents and decided to give my eyes a rest," he offered, leading the way back inside. "I needed to look at something besides symbols on paper. Are you well?"

Paxon nodded. "As well as ever. Is there any news?"

They sat on opposite sides of Isaturin's desk—the one that had belonged earlier to Aphenglow Elessedil and which, to Paxon's way of thinking, always would. But he forced himself to shove the image of her still sitting at it out of his mind.

"A rumor has reached us of Arcannen's whereabouts," Isaturin said. "He was spotted somewhere near the ruins of Arbrox, a coastal town that was a haven for pirates and their families until it was completely destroyed by Federation forces about six weeks ago."

Paxon was confused. "What would he be doing there?"

Isaturin shrugged. "With Arcannen, you can never be sure about anything. Even the rumor is suspect. There is no clear reason for it. Arbrox is miles up the coast from the nearest inhabited village. All that remains are its ruins. How is it that not only has the sorcerer decided to inhabit these ruins but also foolishly allowed himself to be seen? Word got back to the Federation, so they are sending a contingent of soldiers to find out if it's true. But the Prime Minister wants us to look into this, as well."

"That's odd, isn't it? Why would he want us involved if the Federation army already is?"

"I'm not sure. But the Prime Minister was fond of Aphenglow. They were friends, so I don't want to dismiss his request out of hand. He works hard to maintain a delicate balance with the various ministerial offices within the Coalition Council, and even with Aphenglow gone he has managed to maintain a close relationship with the Druids."

Isaturin pursed his lips. "I think he is curious about the Federation army's reasons for undertaking this investigation. There were rumors of a massacre when the Red Slash went into Arbrox six weeks ago. In any case, I have decided to respond to his request. You are to go to Arishaig to speak with him directly and determine the real reason for our involvement."

Paxon was caught by surprise. "You're sending me?"

"He asked for you specifically. He has something he wants to say to you. It seems he believes your previous encounters with Arcannen might prove valuable. If what he tells you persuades you to go on to Arbrox for a closer look, then I want you to do so."

Paxon shook his head. "I hope he's not putting too much faith in what I know about Arcannen."

"Don't worry. You won't be alone in deciding what needs doing. Avelene will be going, too. I want you to act as her escort and protector."

"Avelene?" The Highlander hesitated. "I don't know if that's such a good idea. Is she . . . well enough?"

"If you are asking me if she is physically well enough, I am assured by our healers that she is. If you mean emotionally, we'll have to wait and find out. Are you worried?"

"For her I am, yes. She underwent a great deal of trauma. I don't know if she can handle any more just yet."

"I don't, either, so I want you to find out. If she is to serve in the field—as I think she should—we have to test her at some point. This seems as good a time as any. But she will be in command, Paxon. As a member of the Druid order, she will lead."

"I wouldn't expect it to be any other way." Paxon hesitated again. "Do you mind if I speak to her about this before we leave?"

Isaturin rose, and Paxon stood with him. "Speak to her all you like. But you should know before you do that I didn't ask *her* if she wanted to go. She asked *me* if she could."

The men stared at each other until Isaturin gave Paxon an amused smile. "You never know, do you?"

Then he gestured him out the door.

. . .

Arcannen took his young charges from his living quarters, down the hallway, and out into the open air. He led them past the debris and the remains of the dead to a section of the fallen village that featured neither. There, in a mostly sheltered courtyard, away from the sudden spats of rain, standing beneath a sky of perpetual gloom and clouds, he faced them.

"When you respond to threats like the ones you faced from the Fortrens, do you consciously think about what you are going to do?" he asked Reyn, standing close enough to be heard about the howl of the wind. "Or do you just react spontaneously without thinking at all?"

The boy shook his head. "I just act. If I get pushed too far, everything just breaks free."

"When this happens, you are enraged and maybe afraid, too, aren't you?"

Reyn nodded, exchanging a quick glance with Lariana. The wind was whipping strands of hair about her alabaster skin, giving her face a veiled look. She smiled encouragingly and nodded an unspoken understanding.

"What are you asking me to do?" he demanded of Arcannen, suddenly frightened.

"What you need to do! To learn to think before you act. To not be so easily pushed into reacting in ways you don't want to. Don't you understand what is happening? Don't you see what is being done to you?"

He seemed angry now, almost threatening. Reyn took a step back in spite of himself. But Arcannen seemed to realize he had overstepped himself and held up his hands in a placating gesture.

"I'm just trying to make myself clear. I want to help you. If you take time now to learn how to master your magic—when it doesn't matter and there is no danger—you will be able to exercise more control when you need it. That's the task I've set you. Practice using your magic in specific ways. Think it through first. Here."

He came over to Reyn, turned him toward what remained of one wall, and bent close, standing behind the boy, his mouth at Reyn's ear. "To control magic, you have to imagine what it is you want it to do. You have to visualize it happening. You have to form the image in your mind and do so in a clear, concise way. Don't think about anything else. Don't let your mind wander. Keep the image at the forefront of your thoughts. Then sing it to life."

Reyn hesitated. "Is that how you do it?"

"I don't have your kind of magic. Only you do. Now do as I say!"

"Then how do you know . . . ?"

"Just do what I say!" The sorcerer cut him short, impatient and irritated all over again. "All magic works on the same principles. You either layer on its use or you wield it like a hammer. You want the first; the second is what got you into trouble in the first place. Try it. Visualize, then sing to make it real."

Reyn started and stopped. He tried again, stopped. "I don't know what I should try to make real."

Arcannen's hands tightened on his shoulders. "Picture one of the Fortrens. They caused you enough trouble; think about one of them. Imagine him coming at you, wanting to hurt you. See his face in your mind!"

The boy reacted, barely hesitating this time. His memory of Borry and Yancel Fortren was so strong that their faces came to mind instantly. He didn't try to choose one, but fixed on images of both— seeing them just as he had that last night he had faced them in Portlow behind the Boar's Head Tavern. The images formed, and then he began to hum softly to bring them to life. He wasn't sure what he was doing, but his instincts took command of his voice. Slowly, the images began to gain substance and color and finally a real presence.

And suddenly, just like that, they were there, Borry and Yancel Fortren, standing in front of him, advancing with their familiar looks of cruelty and disdain, weapons held ready for use.

In the next instant the image was gone, shattered as if by a hammer taken to glass. Reyn gasped and staggered back into the immediate support offered by Arcannen's strong arms. "What happened?" the boy demanded. "I had it and then it went away!"

"You lost control," the sorcerer answered, straightening him up.

"You lost focus. It only takes a second. This is new to you. It won't happen all at once. You need to spend time working on it. You have to practice using it. I want you to begin this afternoon, right now. Work with Lariana. Remember, she can see what you visualize into being. She can tell you what you are doing. She can suggest things to you. Try as much of this as you can. Work hard at it. It's important."

"Won't you be here to help?" the boy asked at once.

"Later. After you've experimented on your own. I have something else I need to do first. We're in some danger here. I need to change that. I won't be long."

Arcannen moved away, heading out into the wilderness surrounding the village ruins, satisfied that the boy and Lariana would do fine without him. He would be more comfortable with her, more willing to try things. She would exert no pressure on him; she would suggest and encourage. He had already spoken to her at length about what would be needed for the boy to be won over. He had explained how the magic worked and what was needed for the boy to develop it sufficiently to help him with his plans.

He walked several hundred yards away from the ruins, looking out over the barren rugged terrain surrounding him, wondering how long he had to prepare. Not long, he thought. Usurient wouldn't waste time. Whoever he was sending was likely already on their way. He could only hope, against all odds, that the Commander of the Red Slash had decided to come himself, wanting to make sure.

But it didn't matter. At the end of this business, Arbrox and her people would be avenged, and he would have made it clear to the Federation and the Druids and everyone else that he and those like him were to be left alone. He would make them so afraid of him, so unwilling to come near him, that by the time he had found a way to subvert the Druid order it would be too late for any of them to do much about it, and he would have gained control of all the magic that mattered.

Most especially the magic wielded by that boy.

Turning back to the task at hand, he began the slow, tedious process of laying down the wards that would alert him to the presence of the men who were coming for him.

17

STANDING AT THE BOW OF THE DRUID CLIPPER, PAXON glanced around doubtfully. Clouds layered the skies north to south, east to west, the whole world blanketed for as far as the eye could see. There was a dreary, sullen cast to the day that presaged rain by nightfall. If there was a sun above those clouds, it was keeping its presence hidden, the absence of any source of light a clear indication that any appearance it made would be momentary. The air was awash in grayness at a thousand feet, and with clouds above and trailers of mist below and the light muted and diffuse, the landscape was leached of color.

It was depressing really, but Paxon tried not to feel that way. Instead, he told himself that today marked the beginning of a journey that would at last lead him to the ever-elusive Arcannen and perhaps to a confrontation that would at last put an end to that chapter of his life.

He almost glanced over his shoulder to where Avelene sat writing in front of the pilot box, but in the end managed to refrain from doing so. It would be nice if he could find in her face what he was feeling, but he knew that was asking too much. Yesterday she had come to him to tell him how much she was looking forward to another trip with him, but within moments her demeanor had changed and she had departed abruptly with no explanation. This morning she had boarded with a closed-off attitude that suggested she was in no mood to discuss much of anything, and he had left it that way. He was himself conflicted about her presence. In spite of Isaturin's reassurances, he was not persuaded that she was as ready for another encounter with Arcannen as he was. There was a reticence to her, a tightening down, that suggested she was still haunted by memories of how Arcannen had locked her in that black cylinder and left her to die. Her behavior suggested that the trauma she had endured—presumably banished with her release—might return, given provocation. This worried him. He needed her to be strong and steady if they were to deal successfully with Arcannen. The sorcerer would exploit any weakness he found in either of them. Doubts and fears could not be allowed.

He wished she was more willing to talk so he could take her measure and decide how badly damaged she was, but she had shown no interest in conversation. Instead, she had gone straight to the spot she occupied now, opened the packet she was carrying, and begun writing. All around her, preparations for lifting off had been under way, the Druid Guard working the lines and sails, the big Trolls tightening down radian draws and light sheaths, yet she had acted as if none of it had anything to do with her.

She had offered him a perfunctory greeting and then dismissed him with a shifting of her gaze to her work.

It irritated him no end, and suddenly he decided enough was enough. She would speak with him whether she liked it or not.

He walked back to where she was sitting in front of the pilot box and sat down beside her, watching the smooth movement of her quill across the paper mounted on the writing board as the shaved tip dipped into the inkwell, transported its gathered contents to the white parchment, began to form fresh words and symbols, and then repeated the process time and again.

Finally, she looked up. "What is it?"

"Perhaps we should talk."

She studied him a moment, then set aside her writing materials, capped the inkwell, and looked back at him. "What would you like to talk about, Paxon?"

"About what we are doing. What we are going to do. How we are going to do it. Do you have a plan?"

"Of course I have a plan. I am leader of this expedition, am I not? I am the one who will speak to the Federation Prime Minister. I am the one who will ascertain why it is he asked for us to come—for you to come, in particular."

"Is that what you are writing out? What you intend to say?"

A wash of heavy mist coasted across the decking, and for a moment she disappeared into it as if a ghost. It was so unexpected that it caused Paxon's nerves to jangle. "Avelene?"

She reappeared as the mist cleared. "What you want to know is whether or not I can handle another meeting with Arcannen. Why don't you just come right out and ask me instead of going to all the trouble of working up to it?"

She sounded calm enough as she confronted him, but he could sense an undertone of anger and frustration nevertheless. "All right, I'm asking."

She gave him a bitter smile. "Sorry. You don't have the right to ask. Isaturin selected me for this mission. You are my protector, not my equal. You have no standing to question me."

He saw that she was not going to make this easy. "Where we are both at risk if either of us fails, I have every right to make certain you are well. You suffered a horrendous experience, one that might easily have unhinged another person. I was impressed by how you handled it. I do not seek to question your selection as lead in this business. You are clearly the better choice to make a presentation to the Prime Minister. Nor do I suggest that I am your equal in standing or that I am in any way a full member of the Druid order."

"But still you doubt me," she said slowly. "Among my other skills as a student and practitioner of magic is the ability to sense other people's hidden feelings. Not always, but now and then. Yours were so strong last night when I came to see you that there was no mistaking how you felt about me. You think it possible I am unable to carry out this mission. You worry I am weak and vulnerable. If you had your way, you would not let me come. Do you deny it?"

He stared at her. "No. Although the way you characterize my feelings is not entirely accurate. My fears are for you, not for myself. I worry that you have not had time to heal properly. I worry that if confronted by a sorcerer with the experience and power of Arcannen, you will be overmatched. I worry that *I* will be overmatched, for that matter. I cannot help it; it is in the nature of who I am. Would you not worry if our positions were reversed?"

She glared at him. "I have something to prove here. To myself, but to Isaturin and to you, as well. I accept that. I don't intend to be cowed by one experience, no matter how nasty it was. I was caught by surprise, but that won't happen again. I am confident in my training and my skills. Arcannen will not overmatch me when I confront him. And I *will* confront him. I want it to happen as badly as you do. And don't try to tell me that's not how you feel. You do. It radiates off you."

"So what do you want to do?"

She paused. "Let's just start over. I am sufficiently healed now. I am able to do whatever is needed. Just like you. So let's not speak of it again."

He nodded slowly. "All right. Let's not."

Her disposition improved then, although it did not quite reach the level of warmth. But she did relate how she intended to approach their interview with the Federation Prime Minister and what she believed he might be seeking. Given the ongoing threat from within the Southland government structure to any existing Prime Minister—not to mention most lesser Ministers of the Coalition Council, as well—they could suppose that Arcannen might have become a threat in a way that the Druids did not yet understand. Since the Druid search for the sorcerer was still active, it made sense for the Prime Minister to use the order in any way that would benefit him.

"He was close friends with Aphenglow Elessedil during her last years as Ard Rhys, but he does not enjoy the same closeness with Isaturin who, quite frankly, distrusts him," she said. "So he will keep to himself as much as possible of what he knows and intends. Our job will be to worm it out of him any way we can while we have the chance."

Paxon nodded. "I imagine you can manage that."

"Not just me. You, as well. You are not to sit idly by if you see a chance to push him a little. I want you to engage him in conversation, argumentative or not, when and if it feels right to do so. I trust your judgment. Don't be afraid to exercise it. Don't ignore opportunities that present themselves."

So they talked about it further, and then she went back to her writing and he returned to the bow to watch the land ahead as it passed beneath them. They would reach Arishaig by nightfall in this fast clipper, and after a good night's sleep they would be given an audience with the Prime Minister in the morning. Paxon had never met the man, although he had heard Aphenglow speak of him. A good man, by all accounts. But a cautious man, as well—one who did not trust easily and who understood the value of subterfuge and duplicity in politics. If you were his friend, he would not betray you. All others were subject to the whims of his assessment in any given situation.

All of which meant they would have to be careful.

By the time nightfall came and the lights of the Capital City crested the horizon, he was fast asleep. It was Avelene who woke him, shaking him gently and whispering, "Sorry I was so hard on you," as he pulled himself to his feet.

Although afterward, when he thought back on it, he wasn't at all sure that was what she said.

He slept poorly that night, in part perhaps because he had slept earlier while still aboard ship, but in part, too, because he was anticipating the events of the coming day. He went to sleep thinking of them and woke without any resolution. He was troubled by the role Avelene had assigned him—as instigator or investigator where comments merited intrusion. He had no idea how he would manage this or what he would say. He imagined it was not possible to know until the moment was at hand. He could anticipate, but probably not by more than a sentence or two. It was like lying in ambush without knowing who might be coming.

After washing and dressing, he met Avelene for breakfast in a dining hall that served members of the Coalition Council and their staff as well as visitors housed in the complex that comprised the Federation government offices. He saw a few faces he thought he recognized, but no one spoke to him. He was dressed in loose-fitting hunter's clothes overlaid by his well-worn black cloak, which bore the emblem of the Druid order. Avelene wore similar clothing, although her cloak was the more distinct and recognizable garb that marked her clearly as a Druid. They ate alone and with little conversation, absorbed in thoughts of the meeting ahead, focused on thinking through what they imagined the Prime Minister might have to say to them and how they might respond.

When breakfast was finished, they walked from the dining hall to a tiny garden off to one side and sat on a bench while waiting for the appointed time for their meeting to arrive.

"Have you met him?" Paxon asked finally.

Avelene shook her head. "Everyone says he is a good man."

"Aphenglow Elessedil thought so. She had a high opinion of him. She said he could be trusted."

"Be careful anyway." She caught his eye. "We are babes in the woods in this business. Don't forget it. Tread lightly."

When the time for their appointment arrived, they rose from the bench, walked over to the building that housed the offices of the Prime Minister, and climbed three flights of stairs to where his staff greeted them. With no waiting at all, they were ushered into his empty offices and seated in chairs in front of a massive wooden desk polished to such a high sheen that the glare of the diffuse daylight off its surface caused them to squint.

There they sat, waiting. They neither spoke nor looked at each other. Paxon felt his nerves grow taut and his expectations heighten. He had removed the Sword of Leah from where it had been strapped across his back and had laid it on the floor next to his chair. He felt oddly naked without it, and wondered how quickly he could reach it and draw it free of its sheath if the need should arise. It was foolish thinking, given where he was, but it was the kind of thinking he had grown used to as a protector of the Druid order.

When the Prime Minister finally arrived, he was smiling broadly and anxious to reassure them that his tardiness was the result of another meeting and in no way intended to suggest that this meeting was any less important.

"No one wants to feel as if they are being dismissed prematurely," he added, reaching down to shake their hands warmly. "So I had to exercise some caution in ending the previous meeting. How are you? Did you sleep well? Were your quarters comfortable?"

He was a slight man, taller than average and rather spindly in appearance. He was probably in his late sixties or early seventies, and there was a somewhat worn look to his expressive face. His grip was strong, though, and he seemed to have abundant energy in spite of his age and the toll his position as leader of the Federation might have taken on him. Glancing at the glare off his desk, he asked them to sit with him off to one side where there was a small grouping of couches and easy chairs, all padded and pillowed and comfortably drawn in for private conversation.

Before joining them, he stuck his head back out the door and asked that tea and ale be brought. While waiting for that, he kept the conversation limited to small talk—how were things in Paranor, was Isaturin settling in as Ard Rhys, was the order continuing to add new members to its roster?—all of it accomplished with a smoothness and openness that attested to a lifetime spent mastering the fine art of engaging in easy communication with others.

When the beverages arrived, he asked the bearer to advise the staff not to disturb him until he was finished with his visitors.

"Now then," he began, as the other departed, pulling the door closed tightly behind him, "where to begin."

He rocked back slightly, considering. "I am faced with a difficult and potentially embarrassing situation. It all revolves around Arcannen Rai, but he is not the instigator of the problem. You may have already heard some of what has happened. Almost two years ago, a band of airship pirates operating out of a coastal village called Arbrox began raiding Southland freighters and transports. The thefts were annoying at first, but grew steadily more troublesome until they became intolerable. So to try to discourage further raids, I asked the Federation Army High Command to put an end to it one way or the other. Unfortunately, the command assigned the job to the Red Slash division out of Sterne, which pretty much determined how things would go. The commander of the Red Slash, a man named Dallen Usurient, has little patience and less tact. He quickly decided a scorched-earth approach was warranted. He conveyed his soldiers to Arbrox, attacked the village, and killed everyone—men, women, and children. He did this without anyone's authorization and without any measurable consideration for the consequences. Then he tried to cover it up, insisting that only men—the pirates in question—had been killed. I found out soon enough that this was not the case. But I let the matter slide because the disciplining of soldiers in these situations is a tricky matter. How clear were their orders? How much leeway did they have? If Usurient overstepped himself, should punishment be visited on his men? What sort of resistance do I encounter if I intervene and ask that he be removed as Red Slash Commander and another be appointed to fill his shoes?"

He sipped his tea. "All questions I could only answer as Prime Minister and not as philosopher to my conscience. In any case, a new wrinkle developed shortly afterward. Unfortunately for the Federation, the pirates were sheltering Arcannen at the time of the attack, and although the Red Slash were quite thorough in killing everyone else in sight, they somehow missed him. Arcannen took the attack personally and decided to avenge the deaths of his protectors. He sent word to Usurient that—and I quote—'Arbrox is coming.'"

"Odd that he used the name of the village and not his own," Avelene noted.

"Arcannen is nothing if not enigmatic. When I learned of this— something not reported to me by Usurient, but by another who values loyalty over self-interest—I waited to see what my commander would do. What I expected was that he would not wait for Arcannen to come to him but would go after Arcannen first—most likely taking a large contingent of the Red Slash with him. He has authority to do that, although only in situations in which he views Federation interests to be in immediate and substantial peril. But Usurient has his own measuring stick for these things. Do you like the tea?"

Both Avelene and Paxon nodded. "Herbal," the Highlander said. "A mix of mulkeet, basil brew, and lavender."

The Prime Minister raised an eyebrow. "Very good."

"My mother used to make it. She gathered the ingredients and mixed them in proportions I have forgotten. But I remember their taste."

They all sipped silently for a moment before the Prime Minister continued.

"So. Defying my expectations, Usurient decided on a different approach to the problem of Arcannen. Instead of sending the Red Slash, he dispatched a small band of hunters and cutthroats who have served him in various ways in the past. Their leader, Mallich, is well known; he raises fighting animals called drasks. Ugly creatures, very dangerous. He also raises others, including crince. Even more dangerous than drasks, those crince. You might have heard of them. In any case, none of them is safe to be around, even if you were the one who raised and trained it. But Mallich is more dangerous still."

He paused. "And the men he took with him on this outing were released from the Federation prisons in Sterne. One is a killer who was supposedly locked away for life; the other is one of the keepers. I do not deceive myself. Either is capable of committing unconscionable acts without the burden of thinking on it afterward. All three will present a test even for someone as versatile and creative as Arcannen."

"So they have been sent to kill Arcannen?" Avelene asked. "But why is this a problem? What do you care what happens to the sorcerer?"

The Prime Minister nodded, as if wondering himself. "I care nothing for Arcannen. Do not mistake me. But I would prefer it if he came to an end at the hands of proper authorities and not through a rogue enterprise sanctioned by one of my commanders acting outside his authority. I would prefer it not result in collateral damage of the sort that occurred during the massacre at Arbrox. I alerted Isaturin and the Druid order when I discovered what was afoot because your own interests in Arcannen are at least equal to those of the Federation. We all want the same thing—Arcannen brought to justice. If an opportunity exists to make this happen, we should work together."

"But you asked for us specifically," Paxon pointed out.

"Yes, what is it exactly that you want us to do about all this?" Avelene added quickly.

"Nothing that you wouldn't do anyway." The Prime Minister finished his tea and set the cup down carefully. "Go to Arbrox, assess the situation, and do whatever you feel is appropriate. If Usurient's creatures are successful, then Arcannen is no longer our problem. If they fail, perhaps an opportunity for you to succeed will present itself. I would, of course, appreciate being advised as to how this turns out by someone I can rely upon to tell me the truth."

"Which you do not think Usurient will do?"

"Which I do not think Usurient will do."

"Again," Paxon said quietly, "why did you ask for us specifically?"

"For *you*, in point of fact, young man. So that I might speak to you directly. You know Arcannen better than anyone. You've fought against him, and by all accounts you are the only one to survive such an encounter—and not once, I might add, but several times. I know you serve as the High Druid's Blade. It is logical you would be designated as both companion to and protector of whichever Druid or Druids Isaturin sent to Arbrox once you got word that Arcannen was there. I felt it important to advise Isaturin that your inclusion in this effort was important."

He leaned back in his chair and steepled his fingers. "Now listen carefully. The Federation is supposed to be allied with the Druids in this matter. We are supposed to be working together. I seriously doubt that Usurient's men will see it that way. I am admittedly anxious to avoid an incident where Druids and Federation are suddenly engaged in a life-and-death struggle with each other."

"So this is a warning to be careful."

"That, yes, but something more. I am offering up, here in the privacy of my office, the bitter admission that for the moment I seem to have lost control over a small faction of my army. It isn't the first time and, quite possibly, it won't be the last. Even more galling is the realization that there is a limit to the amount of interference the Federation Army Command will tolerate from its Prime Minister. I must tread lightly in this matter. But you need to be aware that those members of the Federation you might run across on your search for Arcannen do not represent the government's interests. More to the point, you need to understand how dangerous they are. I do not wish you placed in needless peril, so I am telling you how things stand. If by some circumstance these creatures come to a bad end at your hands, no blame will attach to you because of it. Whatever becomes of them, I give you my word that the Federation will not hold you or anyone connected with the Druid order responsible."

Paxon knew at once that there was more to this disclaimer than what the other was telling him, but he couldn't decipher at that moment what the Prime Minister was keeping hidden.

"So you are saying we are free to do whatever is needed to protect ourselves," Avelene finished. "We need not concern ourselves with what happens to Mallich or his men or their fighting animals. Or with what happens to Usurient, as well?"

The Prime Minister nodded slowly. "If it comes to that. Usurient has overstepped himself, and a reckoning is inevitable. Your safety and your assessment of what that requires take precedent over concerns for Usurient's fate. I thought it important for you to understand how matters stand. I have sent word to recall these men and their animals, but I expect it will not reach them in time. I don't even know if Usurient has gone with them. I don't know if you will encounter him. I do know that if there is any reason for them to act against you, they will not hesitate to do so. Any of them."

He paused meaningfully. "Just so you know that Arcannen is not your only concern."

The silence that followed was ominous and heavy with unspoken thoughts. Then abruptly the Prime Minister rose and extended his hands. "I must leave you now. I have another meeting to attend. Endless meetings are the pattern of my life. I sometimes wonder if there is any other point to my service as Prime Minister."

Avelene stood with him. "Thank you for taking time to warn us about your commander and the others," she said, taking his hands and holding them momentarily. "We will be careful."

"I do hope so," the old man said softly.

Then he turned from them and was gone.

When they were clear of his offices and safely out of earshot, departing the building for the airfield where their fast clipper waited, Avelene turned to Paxon. "You know something, don't you?"

Paxon nodded. "I *suspect* something, anyway. He told us what he wants us to know about these rogue soldiers who act against his interests. He says he wants us to be prepared so that we can act freely against them. I think he wants them dead. If we manage to kill them, that would save him the trouble of having to dispose of them later."

"But you also think he will throw us to the wolves afterward?"

Paxon shrugged. "I think he might. If he finds it convenient to do so. But he wants the Druid order to continue to support him, so that would likely be a last resort. Blaming us for anything that happens won't help him maintain a good relationship with the Ard Rhys."

She smiled. "You are very good at this. I am impressed. But here's something you missed. What drives the Prime Minister is something more primal than what he suggested in his analysis of the situation."

"He's angry?"

"No, Paxon. He's afraid."

18

"CONCENTRATE," LARIANA URGED HIM, STANDING off to one side, safely clear of any blowback from losing control of the magic.

Reyn tried hard not to look at her, although looking at her was what he wanted most to do. Instead, he stared out into the bleak emptiness of the rocky terrain that spread away from the ruins, poised atop what remained of one wall. Arbrox was behind him—or at least what remained of it was, its cluster of shattered buildings with walls and roofs collapsed in rain-dampened heaps barely recognizable for what it once had been. There was nothing here for him to look at save her, but he knew that doing so in the midst of a summoning was dangerous for them both.

"Concentrate," she repeated patiently.

They had been working at this exercise for two days—today for almost six hours, the sun by now gone so far west it had disappeared into the mountains, the light dimming as the clouds lowered and the rain increased. He was cold and miserable, but there was no help for that. He must keep practicing. He must try and try again until he found the key that would allow him to master the magic. But it was hard. And monotonous and discouraging. And now, after so many hours with no success, it was beginning to seem pointless.

If he could just look at her once, he thought. Just once. Then he would feel encouraged enough to continue. He had been staring at nothing for so long that both his stamina and his focus were beginning to waver. His efforts at imagining something coming alive and taking form were losing strength. Six hours, and he had almost nothing to show for it but weariness and despair.

How could he ever hope to aid Arcannen against whatever was coming for them if he could not do what was expected of him? How could he hope to protect her—she, for whom by now he would give his life if it were required?

"Close your eyes," she told him.

He did so, happy to close out the cold and the gray, the rain and the dark—happy to be somewhere else, if only in his mind. Anywhere else.

"Now picture it. Find it and hold it in place. Then use your voice. Make the image come alive."

Her words so calm and steady, her voice so determined. She seemed to know what to tell him, almost as if Arcannen had trained her to do so. Was that possible? He had not thought so before this afternoon, yet now he was beginning to wonder. She seemed so certain of what was required of him and of how to go about securing it. Yet Arcannen had not once appeared to witness her efforts. He was inside, away from everything that was happening—or not happening—so that they were left alone to carry on.

Reyn did as he was told, humming softly, making the man become real enough to move about in his mind, turning him this way and that, an image of what he would create. But the process felt cumbersome and awkward, and he could not quite get comfortable with it.

"Relax, Reyn. I can feel you straining. You can't make it happen that way. You have to let it come naturally. Just breathe in and out slowly and steadily and let go of your tension. Just see what it is you seek. Envision it as real."

Lariana, I would do anything for you.

He settled deep into himself and began to form the image he was seeking, the tonal vibration of his voice building it piece by piece. A man. No one he knew—a figure identifiable only as any of a hundred anonymous men. He shaped him slowly, building his body and then his clothing and finally his features so that he was real and measurable and present. He turned him about, examining him from several angles, making sure he was perfect.

Then he put a weapon in his hands, a long knife, slender and deadly, and poised him for an attack.

Ready?

Crouching.

Now!

But when he opened his eyes to brace himself against the attack, the man was gone. Just as before. Just as it had happened every time. There was no one there. The image had died inside his mind. Whatever was real or might become real had been left there.

"I can't do it!" he screamed in frustration.

Instantly Lariana was standing beside him, arms about his shoulders as she pulled his face close to hers and kissed him hard on the mouth. "Yes, you can, Reyn. You can." She spoke the words with her mouth pressed against his, still kissing him, still holding him tightly. "Look at me."

She backed away and waited until he met her eyes. "I saw him that time. I did. But he wasn't where you thought he was. He wasn't in front of you. He was behind you. He was real. As real as you or I. He was there, and he was whole and complete. You did it, Reyn."

"No." He shook his head emphatically. "I didn't do anything. I couldn't make it work. I would have known. I didn't feel anything. You're mistaken. There was no one there."

"No one coming at you? Even now, behind you, where I can see him and you can't? No one, you think? A man with a long knife, ready to plunge it into your back? Creeping closer?"

She took a slow breath and let it out slowly. "Better turn around, Reyn. He's getting closer." He didn't move, staring at her as he might a crazy person, wondering what in the world she was talking about. "Reyn, turn around. Right now."

"Why are you doing this?" he asked in disbelief.

"Reyn!" she screamed. "Turn around!"

A slash of fear ripped through him, and he whirled about in spite of himself—just in time to see his attacker coming for him in a rush, a big man carrying a long knife, all fury and brute force, his face crushed in on itself with unspoken rage. Reyn knew—and at the same time wasn't sure—that he had done this. And while it wasn't real, somehow it was, and he lashed out with his voice in defense, ripping into the man and exploding him so that nothing remained but a darkened swatch of air.

Gone, just like that. As if it was never there.

Which, in fact, was true. Yet he had seemed as real and certain as the rubble in which Reyn stood.

Lariana was holding him again, arms wrapped tightly about him. "You see?" she whispered. "You thought you couldn't control your magic, but you did!"

"But it wasn't . . . ," he started to protest, wanting to be sure she understood that his control over the creation wasn't complete, but seriously lacking.

"Do it again," she said quickly, not letting him finish. "Right now, while you remember. Don't think about it. Just let it happen."

So he did. He wasn't sure how he had managed it the first time, what he had done to make it possible, and he wasn't sure how to do it now. What he remembered at the end of it all was how when he opened his eyes nothing of what he thought he had envisioned was there and he just sort of let go of everything in his despair. So he approached it that way again, humming softly, making the man come alive in his mind until he was fully formed and then just opening his eyes.

Sure enough. Nothing. The image he had created wasn't there. At least, not where he was looking. But when he turned upon hearing Lariana's excited gasp, there his invented adversary was, behind him once more, coming for him again, a re-creation of the last one. He exploded this one, too, filled with euphoria and satisfaction at the result.

"Reyn!" Lariana screamed with glee.

Without waiting for her to say anything more, he closed his eyes and did it again, changing the look and feel of this new image, giving it a more animal-like appearance, a creature crooked and feral and hunched over. He let it wander through his mind for a moment until he had a feel for its movements, for its smell and taste—pungent and foul—all the while using his wishsong's magic to animate and build on it. He could hear Lariana trying to speak to him, shouting something, dancing at the edges of his vision, but he blocked her out, concentrating on his creation.

Opening his eyes, he found it shambling toward him from just off to one side, jaws wide and slavering, claws digging into the earth. Lariana actually screamed in shock, and suddenly he felt her pressing up against him, seeking shelter. He wrapped her in his arms protectively, fully in control now, and exploded his creature, turning it into darkness and air.

He stopped then, panting for breath. All of a sudden he was weak from his efforts, the strength sufficiently drained from him that he felt he might collapse. He staggered, and abruptly it was Lariana who was holding him up and not the other way around. Dizziness swept through him, a rush of blackness enveloping him in the process.

"Too much," he managed to gasp. "Too fast."

Then he disappeared into the darkness.

When he came awake again, he was still exactly where he had been before. Lariana was right in front of him, holding tightly to his arms, making sounds, none of them intelligible.

Until suddenly they were.

"Reyn, look at me. Are you all right? What happened to you? Can you hear me at all?"

His gaze shifted to find her emerald eyes, and he nodded slowly. "I can hear you. I'm all right." He blinked rapidly, trying to focus, to steady himself. "How long have I been standing here?"

"A couple of minutes, no more. You've been staring into space, seeing nothing, not speaking or anything. What happened?"

Her features tightened with concern, and he reached out and

pulled her against him, cradling her head to his chest. What should he tell her? What *could* he tell her? The catatonia—he had forgotten all about it since he had stopped having to use the magic on impulse. He had thought maybe it was a thing of the past, an occurrence that would not result from his more controlled use of magic. But he should have known better. It was what always happened—what always would happen—no matter how the magic was used.

She backed him off abruptly. "Say something, please. Was it the magic that did this?"

He decided on a half-truth. "I think so. I think I got overexcited and used too much all at once. It felt like it overwhelmed me. The power is so great, Lariana. I couldn't manage it there at the end. It made me black out."

She studied him doubtfully. "You were conscious, but you were not able to respond to me at all. This is something more than blacking out. What's going on?"

He experienced a sinking feeling in the pit of his stomach. If he told her, she would feel obligated to tell Arcannen. That would be the end. Arcannen would send him away. If he knew Reyn couldn't ever manage the magic adequately, he would lose interest.

"Can we not talk about it just now?" he begged.

She took his arm, led him over to a place where they could sit, and pulled him down next to her. He went docilely, his strength still sapped, his willingness to resist gone with it.

"You're afraid of what Arcannen will do, aren't you?"

Droplets of dampness glistened in her gold-streaked hair, and her deep green eyes glinted brightly. She stared at him directly, studying his face, her own mirroring such anguish and sadness that he could hardly bear to look at it. She seemed to want to help him, but he did not think she could. He felt her hands squeeze his arms as she continued to hold him in place, and there was a reassurance to their grip.

"He might not want to spend any more time helping me."

There, it was out. He lowered his gaze, ashamed of himself. What was it about her that eroded his resolve so easily?

"Listen to me," she said softly. "I will reveal nothing to him that will hurt you. That is my promise, and I will keep it. Now tell me the truth."

Oddly, he believed her. Perhaps it was because he was so enamored of her, so deeply under her spell that he could not make himself believe otherwise. But her words convinced him, and he knew at once that he would tell her. Which he did, completely and without subterfuge. He told her how the magic generated a catatonic effect in him every time he used it in a stressful situation. He explained how it stole away his control over himself and left him in a black space from which it sometimes took up to several hours to extricate himself. When that happened, he was left completely without defenses and had to rely on others to steer him to safety and to care for him.

"It has always been like that," he finished. "And each time I fail to contain the magic, the catatonia gets a little worse. I thought that being able to direct it to accomplish specific tasks might put an end to all that. But it doesn't seem that's possible."

He waited in the ensuing silence. "First of all," she told him carefully, "you haven't mastered control of the magic. You said so yourself. You are just beginning to learn how. It's probably too soon to be able to stop what's happening to you. You need to give yourself more time. But eventually Arcannen is going to discover what you're hiding. Sooner or later, the magic will break free in his presence, and he will realize the truth. What are you going to do then?"

He shook his head. "I know you are right about Arcannen. But maybe he won't find out right away. If I am careful, maybe I can keep from being overstressed while learning how to keep control. Maybe I can avoid having to use magic for real. I should be able to tell the difference between what's real and imagined. I just need to work at it a little more."

"All right," she said, nodding slowly. "Let's find out if that's so. I won't say anything to him about what happened. We can just tell him you managed to create images that took on a presence and leave it at that. But, Reyn, this is a dangerous game you are playing. Arcannen is not someone you want to anger. He says he wants to help you and maybe he does, but he could turn on you in a moment. I've seen that in him. He is unpredictable. It might be better to admit what is going on and take your chances. I will stand by you if you do."

"It would be foolish of you to do that. You're his apprentice."

She gave him a look. "I am my own person before I am anyone's anything. I have learned to look after myself, and I will not be made to give that up."

"I don't want you involved."

She laughed softly. "Really? You don't? But I'm already involved." Then she leaned forward and kissed him softly. "Haven't you noticed?"

It was fully dark by now, the last of the sunlight faded, the skies gone black and only slivers of moonlight seeping through gaps in the heavily layered clouds to illuminate the coastline of the Tiderace. The air was cold and damp, a fine mist settling over the ruins of Arbrox. Somewhere nearby seagulls were crying mournfully, and the crashing of the waves against the rocks was a cacophony of thunderous booms.

Lariana and the boy appeared through the doorway of Arcannen's refuge looking slightly bedraggled and thoroughly worn out. The sorcerer looked up from the tide tables and charts he had spread out across the work space he kept for himself to one side of the room, taking note of their condition.

"Success?" he asked them, raising one eyebrow.

Lariana nodded. "It took all day, but in the end he managed it."

She went on to describe what the boy had created—the men first and then the four-legged beast. She gave an accurate description, concluding with her personal belief that in another day or so Reyn Frosch would master much, much more.

When she had finished, Arcannen leaned back and contemplated her words. There was something wrong with what she was telling him, but he was not sure what. He didn't think she was lying exactly, but he suspected she was leaving something out. He couldn't say what made him think this—the words, her tone of voice, the smoothness of her recitation, the look on her face—but there was a gap that troubled him. His instincts were good at warning him of such deceptions, and he had learned to trust them.

But why would Lariana be deceiving him? Why would she not be entirely honest? She had been until now. Hadn't she? He pursed his lips. He was troubled enough that he had to scratch this particular itch.

"Does she speak for you on this?" he asked the boy.

He nodded quickly. "She does."

"And you were able to bring these images to life, to give them the appearance of flesh and blood, to move them like living creatures?"

"Until I grew tired. But I will try again in the morning, after I've slept and rested a bit. I was starting to make mistakes at the end, small lapses that let the image fail. My control was slipping."

Arcannen got to his feet. "I don't think we should wait that long. I think we should test your control now, while the experience is fresh. I might be able to help you with any difficulties. Sort out the small things that might trouble you later."

The boy and the girl did not look at each other, their eyes fixed on him. "It's awfully dark out there," Lariana said finally.

"We can light things up," the sorcerer told them. He smiled. "Come along."

They departed the room, went down the hallway to the entry leading out into the ruins, threw on cloaks against the weather, and went outside. The darkness was complete, the clouds having closed away every last vestige of moonlight, the rain falling in heavy sheets, and the wind howling mournfully across the barren rocks. They could just make out the sheen of slick dampness that layered the rubble beyond their doorstep in the faint light cast by the opening of the door to the outside. Lariana and the boy, leading the way, stood in the opening uncertainly.

"A good challenge for your talents, Reyn!" Arcannen shouted at him in order to be heard over the wind. "We might see more of this weather before it has blown itself out."

He watched the boy closely. No reaction. Just a blank stare. The girl was the same. But he sensed an uneasiness between them nevertheless. Not everything was as it appeared on the surface.

"Let's cast a little light on the situation," he said to them.

A quick flick of his fingers brought fire to his fingertips, and a series of quick snaps of his wrists sent sparks out into the rain and the dark. Wellsprings of flames erupted suddenly on the damp rocks and burned as if fueled by dry wood. Sheets of rain formed hazy curtains in front of these magically generated sources, but there was light now where there had been none before.

"All right, step outside. Let's see what you can do."

He gestured for Reyn to proceed, and after a moment's hesitation the boy did as he was told. Rain pummeled him as he advanced into the open space between the fires. Lariana started to follow him, but Arcannen grabbed her arm and pulled her back.

"Let's see what he can do without our interference," he told her, bending close.

She gave him an irritated look, but stepped back. "You're putting an awful lot on him, don't you think?"

Her willingness to challenge him caught him by surprise. "I think it is my business to make that decision and not yours."

Together, they watched the boy move out into the center of the circle of flaming stones, standing alone in the rain and the near darkness, shoulders hunched beneath the all-weather cloak, head lowered inside the shadowed hood. For a long time, he stood motionless, a vague figure within the sheeting rain. He appeared to be doing nothing, but Arcannen assumed he was concentrating.

Nothing happened.

Then, abruptly, a singular figure appeared to one side—a huge misshapen creature covered in hair and spikes, a nightmare come alive, rising up out of the broken carpet of stones as if born of them, all size and bulk. It heaved itself upward to its full height of well over eight feet and turned toward the boy. The boy, in response, turned to face it, standing his ground as he did so, watching as the creature advanced in a shambling lurch. He waited until the creature was within a dozen feet, then he swung his gaze toward Arcannen. The creature, as if responding to this movement, changed direction abruptly and started toward the sorcerer.

"Isn't that something," Arcannen said softly, aware of the girl moving away from him, distancing herself.

He kept his eyes on the creature. He hadn't heard even the faintest sound of the wishsong over the wind and rain, hadn't caught even a shadow of movement from the boy. He peered through the rain and the gloom, picking out the creature's blunted, twisted features, noting the threatening glint in its eyes, measuring the nature of the threat it offered. He smelled its stench, raw and pungent; he could hear its shambling movements through the rain. It was only an image, he told himself. Yet it felt like something more. It moved as if it had substance. For all intents and purposes, it felt as if it could crush him with its massive arms if it got hold of him. He could hear it breathing now, could see puffs of breath on the cold air as it drew closer.

"That's enough, Reyn," he called out, eyes riveted on the creature.

But the boy did not respond. The creature continued to advance, close enough now that it was blocking out several of the fires behind it. Its clawed hands flexed and its maw widened to reveal huge canines.

"Reyn!" Arcannen snapped, angry now. "Dispatch it or I will!"

In the next instant the creature fragmented in a cluster of darkness and became bits and pieces floating in the wind. A moment later it was gone entirely. Arcannen found himself exhaling in relief.

The boy turned to him. "Good enough?" he asked.

It wasn't a challenge exactly, wasn't meant as an angry response, so the sorcerer didn't take it that way. What it felt like instead was a sigh of relief, a sort of expression of satisfaction at having done what was expected and without giving way to anything that might have caused matters to go awry. But sending the creature directly toward him was a statement, too—a demonstration of the extent the boy could control the magic of his gift. Arcannen had ordered him to find a way to take charge of the wishsong rather than the other way around, and the boy had felt the need to show exactly how far he had come in managing to do that.

Lariana was at his elbow again. "What do you say to that?" she asked softly.

He smiled in spite of himself. "I say you have done your job well."

But something still felt wrong, and he was determined to find out what it was.

19

MIDNIGHT HAD COME AND GONE BY THE TIME the heavily armed dual-masted flare cruiser had crossed out of the coastal range and begun the slow sweep downward toward the shores of the Tiderace and the ruins of Arbrox. Mallich stood at the helm, maintaining a slow, steady pace through storm winds and heavy rains, his vision considerably lessened since leaving behind the clear skies on the western expanses they had flown through earlier. He wore his all-weather cloak with the hood raised to keep off as much of the rain as was possible, although after several hours of an unceasing downpour he was already soaked through. He peered ahead through the gloom and the emptiness toward the shores of the ocean, hoping his compass had kept him on track to find their destination.

Below him, seated on opposite sides of the ship's main deck, were Bael Etris and The Hammer, huddled within their cloaks to ward off the damp and chill as best they could. The former, small and malleable, was barely visible, not much more than a motionless shadow pressed against the railing. The latter, huge and thick, was difficult to miss. They didn't care much for each other, these two, and neither had done anything to try to change that since they had set sail. They were not airmen and of no help at all in the flying of the ship. They could fetch and carry, but tried their best to avoid doing so. Mallich took some comfort in knowing that their real use would come later, when the search for Arcannen began. He had given thought to enlisting crewmen, which would have eased his workload, but in the end had decided that keeping this venture quiet was more important. He found himself questioning that decision now.

Still, he had gained unexpected support from another quarter.

On that very morning, only an hour before their departure, he had come to an emotional crossroads and gone to confront Dallen Usurient, warning him that unless he came with them, the search was off. The threat was simple enough to understand. Usurient had at least as much invested in finding the sorcerer as Mallich did, and ultimately the consequences were his to bear, for better or worse. Since that was so, shouldn't he be a part of this quest? Shouldn't he be involved to the same extent as Mallich? Shouldn't he be there to lend a practiced hand should the need arise?

In spite of what he had claimed earlier, Mallich was uneasy with the idea of traveling alone with Etris and The Hammer at his back and only the oketar and the crince for protection. Usurient's presence would even the odds, should things start to fall apart. It would help maintain a balance between those who possessed a semblance of a moral code and those who did not. Looking back on it, Mallich believed he would have ended up going anyway, even if Usurient had turned him down flat. But he wasn't sure, and now he didn't need to be. Because after suggesting that being present personally was the only way to guarantee that there would be no further sleepless nights worrying over Arcannen, imagine his surprise when Usurient not only agreed but did so almost as if he had already made up his mind.

"I think you have it right," the other said. "This seems to me to be one of those times when direct involvement is necessary. I wouldn't want to spend my days wondering how this turned out if the news did not get back to me."

"My thoughts exactly," Mallich had said.

"Besides, I will take a certain pleasure being there when the life goes out of Arcannen's eyes and I can see he knows who brought it about."

There might be something else at work here, Mallich knew. Usurient was nothing if not devious. But he had resolved that the other should take the same risks and, however this turned out, should share the same fate. Besides, the two of them together would have a better chance against the sorcerer than either one of them acting alone.

Now, skimming the jagged surface of the flats running down to the coastline from the mountains, passing through mist and soaking rain, he watched Usurient leave his post at the bow and start back for the pilot box. When he reached it, the Commander of the Red Slash swung up the ladder and climbed inside to stand next to him.

"Where do you think to land?" he asked, raising his voice to carry over the howling of the wind.

"Just ahead. Another mile at most, well back of the ruins. I would leave the airship there and walk in to see if Arcannen is in residence."

"How will you know if he's there or not with this going on?" Usurient gestured at the weather, the rain running down his dark face as he bent close.

"The animals," Mallich answered him. "They'll sniff him out. Even if he's hiding belowground within the ruins—which I think is likely—they'll catch his scent. We can ferret him out after that anytime we choose. In fact, better we do our scouting in this weather, when he will not be expecting us, than when it's clear and he can see us coming."

Usurient shook his head. "It might seem so, but he will detect us anyway if we do what you suggest."

Mallich scowled. "What do you mean?"

"I mean he is smarter than you give him credit for. He is a sorcerer, Mallich. He won't rely on his senses alone to keep watch. He will have set wards in place to alert him to our arrival. He will have strung them all across the flats leading to his safehold. They will tell him we are there the moment we pass through them."

"What do you suggest then? We need to get close enough for the animals to do their work!"

"Indeed. But we need not come at him in the way he expects. Think on it a moment. Why did I choose this vessel for our journey?

Why did I insist on leaving now when there was a storm approaching the coast and I knew we would have to fly right into its teeth?"

Mallich was irritated at the questioning and with the other's self-satisfied attitude, so smug he could barely contain himself. "Why don't you just tell me? That way I won't have to wait a moment longer to appreciate how clever you are."

The shadow of a smile twisted Usurient's thin lips. "This airship is built to fly in heavy weather, and this weather is perfect for conceal-ment. Our approach is all that matters. We'll fly past Arbrox and out over the sea. We won't land where he will expect us. And make no mistake—he will be expecting us. His wards are of no use if we don't cross through them. We will land on a promontory I am familiar with farther north of Arbrox and then follow the coastline, skirting his wards. That way, none will be broken; no warning will be given. Your animals can sniff to their hearts' content from the coast side of the ruins and tell you all you need to know, and he won't suspect a thing."

Mallich thought it over for a few moments and found no flaws in the other's reasoning. He gave a curt nod and went back to working the controls.

They had flown another few miles at slow speed through the storm when Usurient had him change course, pointing the bow farther north from their current course to bring them to the promontory he was seeking for their landing. Flying almost blind, Mallich wondered how the other could be so certain of where they were. But rather than argue the matter, he decided to wait and see. The airship edged ahead, plowing the deep haze and sheets of rain, navigating the darkness. The wind had picked up and was blowing harder, and instead of clearing the air it was causing the mist and rain to swirl in sudden gusts that obscured things even further.

But finally they broke free and found themselves moving out over the Tiderace, and immediately Usurient had Mallich swing the air-ship back toward land, peering intently ahead, sighting whatever landmarks he could see that were apparently hidden from the hunter. He must have found them because within minutes he had them de-scending onto a plateau within a cluster of jagged rocks and scrub, settling carefully in place so that the ship could be anchored by The Hammer, who had at last deigned to do something.

When the airship was made fast, Mallich turned to Usurient, the other two still out of hearing while he spoke. "I will take the oketar now and find the sorcerer's lair. You can come with me or stay here with them. It makes no difference to me."

Usurient gave a quick glance at the giant, where he was still tightening the anchor ropes, and at Bael Etris, who slouched against the railing, watching. "You trust them here alone?" he asked.

Mallich snorted, his weathered face wrinkling. "I don't trust them anywhere. But the crince will be watching them."

"Then I'll come with you."

Much farther west, a disgusted Paxon and Avelene stood hunched against the advancing rain on the public airfield in the city of Wayford, staring at their grounded clipper.

"What's happened is the contacts between the parse tubes and the draws have frayed sufficiently that the power directed by the light sheaths into the draws is not reaching the diapson crystals. This happens over time, which is why the contacts are usually changed out after, oh, maybe ten thousand flying miles or so. The exchange of energy just wears them down in the natural course of usage. Unless, of course, they are weakened deliberately. From no small amount of experience, I would have to say, after looking at yours, that they were tampered with."

Grehling Cara paused, his explanation complete, and waited for a response. Paxon was struggling with the fact that the tall, limber young man standing before him was the same boy he had encountered while in pursuit of Arcannen five years earlier. Not yet fully grown, but well beyond his boyhood, he looked like someone else entirely.

"You're sure about this?" Avelene pressed, tight-lipped.

The young man nodded. "Just on the left rear tube, though. The others seem fine. But if you lose that one, your ship doesn't fly right and your power drops by thirty percent, which creates drag and swerve due to loss of power and uneven response from the thrusters."

"But you can repair this, can't you?"

Grehling nodded. "By morning."

"No sooner?"

He shook his head. "Replacing contacts is a delicate operation. Everything has to be set precisely and tested to be sure the transfer is solid. Otherwise, it's like you never did anything in the first place." He paused. "I can get to work on it right away, once I haul her into the hangar."

Avelene sighed. "Go ahead."

"Good to see you again, Grehling," Paxon added, giving the other a smile. "Even under these circumstances."

The young man smiled back. "I thought I would see you before now, Paxon. I thought you would come back to visit Leofur, if not me."

"She still lives here, then?"

Grehling shrugged. "Right where you left her."

He turned away and directed the men standing in the background to help him float the moored bulk of the clipper inside the waiting hangar so he could begin work. It was odd to see him in charge of the airfield now, succeeding his father as manager, still as bright and quick as ever, and still as knowledgeable. Paxon knew airships because he flew them, and he had known what the problem was from the moment she shuddered and began to lose power ten miles out. It was nice to see that Grehling had picked up on it immediately, having become every bit as skilled in the art of airship repair as he had demonstrated he one day would be five years earlier.

"I don't understand," Avelene said, taking hold of Paxon's arm and guiding him toward the manager's office so they could be out of the rain. "How could anyone sabotage our airship? It was under guard at Arishaig the entire time we were there. We were ambassadors, not some casual visitors. No one would have been allowed close to that ship."

"A better question might be why," Paxon added, settling into one of the hard-backed chairs where they would wait out their time on the ground. They could have chosen to find an inn, but it seemed too much trouble for the few hours that remained until morning, when the clipper supposedly would be fixed.

Avelene shook her head. "One explains the other, I imagine. Maybe the damage was done in Paranor before we even set out. It wouldn't be the first time we harbored an enemy in our midst. Especially if it's one working for Arcannen."

Paxon nodded, but he didn't think this was the case. It would be too much of a coincidence to have that happen again so soon. Besides, Arcannen's network of allies and conspirators had been broken when he had fled Wayford for parts unknown. He had been in hiding for five years, several of those spent in the wilds of the Tiderace's coastal regions. It didn't feel right.

"We're missing something," he offered quietly. He paused. "Maybe someone else has a stake in this game, someone we're overlooking."

She gave him a look, pulling back the hood of her travel cloak to reveal her dark hair damp against her face. Looking off into the darkness, he missed the shift of expression on her face. "Who's Leofur?"

He shrugged quickly. "Just someone I used to know."

She kept looking at him, and he kept his gaze averted. Mention of her brought a wave of fresh guilt, especially coming from Grehling, who had been friends with both of them. Leofur, with whom he had once thought he was in love. Had been in love, he admitted. It seemed impossible. He could hardly explain it, considering it in objective terms, realizing how little it had taken to change the direction of his life. Had he gone to her in the beginning, as he had promised he would, everything might have been different. But he hadn't wanted it that way. He had wanted to be the High Druid's Blade. He had wanted his life at Paranor more than he had wanted her, so there was no room now for regrets.

Even so, he thought momentarily about seeing her. He could do so and be back in plenty of time to continue his journey. Just go to her house and wake her. Just tell her he still loved her and was sorry for not coming sooner. Just admit he had made a mistake.

But had he? He wasn't sure that starting up with her again was what he wanted. He couldn't quite make himself believe that it was the right thing to do. If he came back into her life, it would create expectations for both of them that had to be acted on. After so much time had passed, how would that feel?

Avelene looked away. "Just someone you used to know, huh?" she repeated.

He slouched down in his seat, stretching his legs. "You told me back in Arishaig that you sensed the Prime Minister was afraid of something. You never said what."

She sighed and looked around the cramped room as if searching for the answer. "Didn't you see it in him, too?"

"Not as clearly as you did, I guess."

She smirked. "I don't think you see much of anything as clearly as I do, Paxon." She left this enigmatic observation hanging. "I'm guessing now, but I would say from what I know about his history as Prime Minister that he's caught between a rock and a hard place. Remember how he was thinking of stepping down at one point? The rumor was he'd had enough. Ex-military and weapons-centric men and women had come to dominate the Coalition Council, and he was no friend to any of them. So he wanted out; he wanted to quit. But then he decided not to. Maybe because he couldn't stomach what that might mean for the Federation. Aphenglow always said he was a good man."

"So now he is afraid he might be at risk because of staying on as Prime Minister?" Paxon sighed. "It's true that there is a history of termination with prejudice in that office. Maybe he feels threatened by this Usurient fellow and he brought us in to help him eliminate that threat."

"That would be my guess." She shook her head. "Politics makes my head hurt. Too many mind games and too much deception and trickery."

"At least we don't have that problem at Paranor," Paxon said.

She looked at him. "Is that what you think?"

After that, they were silent for a long time.

Usurient made his way over the jagged terrain of the coastal cliffs, following a narrow pathway that cut through the rocks like a snake, tracking the dark shape of Mallich, who was just ahead, and the oketar, who were no longer even visible. Rain sheeted down, the storm continuing unabated. The wind was much stronger out here on the cliffs, exposed as they were to the open seas, and therefore much more dangerous. He had to keep pressing back against the cliff face or, when on higher stretches where there was no protection at all, bend low to the ground to avoid being swept off his feet. He had been relatively dry when they had set out, but by now he was soaked through.

Usurient was thinking hard about what might happen once this matter came to a head. If they found the ruins of Arbrox inhabited tonight, he was certain Mallich would want them to go in tomorrow when the weather cleared. They would take Bael Etris and The Hammer with them, and they would attack and keep attacking until Arcannen was dead. How this might happen—and who might survive it—was open to debate. But he had already determined that his own involvement would be minimal. In spite of what he had told Mallich, he had not decided to come on this expedition so that he could make certain everything went as it should or even to have the pleasure of watching Arcannen take his last breath.

He was there because, when it was all over and done with, he intended to kill everyone left alive.

There could be no witnesses to any of this, after all. This operation was outside the purview of his authority and would certainly not be sanctioned by the High Command, let alone the Prime Minister. No evidence of it could ever be allowed to surface. Once Arcannen was dead, he would eliminate the men with him, as well.

What he wished at the moment, however, was that he had not been so hasty about coming out with Mallich. Staying aboard the airship, he might have remained somewhat dry and warm. Out here, he was merely miserable and irritated by the slowness of their progress. How long had they been walking, anyway?

Ahead, Mallich slowed and looked back at him, motioning him forward and leaning close, his voice a whisper. "What remains of Arbrox is just around that cliff face. When we get there, I will send the oketar ahead to sniff around. They will keep to the ruins, so they shouldn't trip the wards. Those will have been laid farther out along the inland perimeter. When they've found what we're looking for, they will come back to me."

He started to turn away, but Usurient grabbed his arm. "Wait. How will we know what they have or haven't found? They can't talk, can they?"

Mallich gave him a look. "They can to me. Have some faith, Dallen."

A few dozen yards farther on, they reached the bend in the cliff face and came to a second stop. Peering into the gloom ahead, Usurient could just make out what remained of the walls and roofs of Arbrox.

Moments after that, Mallich dispatched the oketar and they disappeared into the ruins.

Arcannen was sitting at the little kitchen table reading from ancient books he had brought down from a set of shelves nearby, paying no attention to Reyn and Lariana as they sat next to each other in the adjoining room, heads together, whispering.

"You risked too much out there!" the girl hissed at him, her face dark with anger and misgiving.

"I risked what I had to," he answered.

"What if you had gone catatonic?"

"But I didn't! My control is getting better."

She shook her head. "One time. That's all it was. You can't be sure."

"You have to start somewhere. Besides, what other choice did I have?"

Arcannen looked over suddenly. "Can you please take your conversation into the bedroom?" he asked irritably. "You are disrupting my concentration."

Lariana stood up abruptly and pulled Reyn up with her. "Fine. We'll leave you to it."

The sorcerer went back to his reading. Lariana led Reyn into the bedroom and closed the door before turning to him again. "I don't like how this is going," she said so softly he almost couldn't hear. "Why is he making you do this . . . this creating of people out of images? No, don't say it's to help you learn to control your magic. This can't be the best way for you to learn to do that. By having you bring imaginary people to life?"

They both paused, casting quick glances at the door. "I don't know," Reyn said finally. "How can anyone know what's best?"

"I know this much," she answered. "It's causing you considerable stress because it requires too much of you. Your problem, Reyn, has to do with reacting to threats, to dangerous situations. It has to do with fear that you can't protect yourself. To stop that, you need to learn how to stay calm. How is any of what you are trying supposed to help?"

He stared at her. "What are you saying? That I should stop doing what he's asking of me?"

"No, no, I'm not saying that." She paused, brushing back loose strands of her gold-streaked hair. She glanced away, and her eyes had a distant, lost look to them. "You have to do what he tells you," she said finally. Then her eyes shifted back to find his. "Because if you don't, I'm not sure what will happen."

There was a long silence as he let that sink in. "You think I'm in danger, don't you?"

She nodded. "Maybe. Mostly because everyone who gets close to him is in danger. Even me."

"But he's your mentor. He won't hurt you."

She exhaled sharply. "I thought that was true once. I'm not so sure anymore." She took his hand in hers and squeezed it. "What I am sure of is that I will do anything I can to help you. But you have to be careful. You have to listen to me."

Arcannen rapped on the door sharply and then opened it, looking from one to the other. "What are you whispering about in there? Shouldn't you be in bed?"

Like they were children. Reyn shook his head. "We were just discussing ideas on how I can get better at bringing images to life. Lariana helped me before; I trust her."

Arcannen looked at her. No words were spoken, but something passed between them. The boy saw it clearly. An understanding, a shared insight, something—it was there. It made him wonder about what she had just told him. Was she really in any danger? Or was this all part of a game?

The sorcerer turned away, pulling the door closed again. "A few more minutes," he called over his shoulder.

The boy and the girl sat quietly again, facing each other, saying nothing. Lariana's hands still held his, squeezing and relaxing, over and over.

Be careful, she mouthed. *Promise me.*

He nodded. Then he leaned forward and kissed her lightly on the cheek, his lips close to her ear. *You be careful, too.*

Her hands squeezed his even harder and did not let go.

20

"BOY, WAKE UP!"

Hands were shaking him, bringing him out of the dream he was having. In the dream, he was with Lariana. They were flying over a countryside filled with flowers, the hues forming an intense pattern beneath where they stood at the bow of an airship. The colors were brilliant and lustrous, shimmering in the sunlight, an endless blanket covering the earth below. He was smiling as he looked at Lariana, and she was smiling back at him with such love, such desperate want, that he could barely believe how lucky he was.

"Reyn! Now! Get up! They're here!"

The dream vanished, and he opened his eyes, his vision blurry and dim. The room in which he had been sleeping was still mostly dark, lit only by a single candle in one corner. He sat up slowly on his sleeping mat and looked across the room to where Lariana, occupying the bed, was just waking, as well. The whole experience had a surreal feel to it.

"Who's here?" he asked.

"Who do you think?" Arcannen snapped, turning away, heading for the door. "Be quick!"

"What is he talking about?" Reyn muttered, blinking rapidly.

"Those men sent to kill us. They're here." Lariana was sitting on the edge of her bed in her nightdress, looking over at him. "Remember?"

He did, although he hadn't thought about it much in the days he had been training to master his use of the wishsong. "They're here?" he repeated, not quite awake yet.

"Get dressed," she told him, rising to snatch up her clothes before moving into a shadowed corner. She turned away from him and stripped off her sleeping garments.

He looked down self-consciously, although it didn't seem to bother her that he was in the same room. Turning away, he began pulling on his own clothes. *Those men sent to kill us.* What was he supposed to do? What did Arcannen expect of him?

He worried about it as he finished pulling on his boots and found a fully dressed Lariana standing in front of him, waiting. "Ready?"

To do what? But he didn't ask. Instead, he simply nodded, rose, and followed her from the bedroom to the central living quarters of their underground lair, where Arcannen was waiting for them.

"They were here last night, testing to discover if we were in residence, and apparently they decided that we were. They believed themselves quite clever, coming at us from the ocean side, thinking I would not bother putting up wards on that approach. So they tripped them, as I had intended they should, but they don't realize we know this."

He moved close to them, his eyes intense. "Now listen carefully. These are dangerous men, and they will not hesitate to kill any of us if they have the chance. I am quite certain they've killed before and more often than once. They know exactly how to carry out an assignment of this sort, and they are probably confident that we will not be able to stop them. But their confidence is misplaced. They are overmatched here. We will show them a quick finish."

"I don't want to hurt anyone!" Reyn blurted out in dismay. "You promised me!"

Arcannen took a moment to study him. "I know what I promised. And I know how to keep my promises. I will do what needs doing to rid us of these vermin. But remember, boy. Sometimes things don't work out as you intend. No matter how good your intentions, they aren't always enough. Promises can get you only so far. If one of these men gets past me, what are you going to do? Stand there and let him kill you? Or worse, kill me?"

He waited for Reyn's answer. The boy shook his head. "No, but I don't want it to come to that. If I don't stop hurting people now, I probably never will."

The sorcerer sighed. "How confident are you that you can control your magic? Is your confidence solid enough to tell me you can? No exceptions or excuses?"

"I can control it."

"Good. Then I have a plan. But it depends on you being able to make your magic work the way you did last night. Can I depend on you?"

Reyn nodded. "What sort of plan?"

"A simple one. Simple plans always work best. You will create images and bring them to life. A series of them, if you can manage it. You will point your creations against these intruders to distract them, and while they are busy fighting off shadows, I will dispatch them. You needn't do anything to help with that."

He turned to Lariana. "I want you to remain here, inside. This fight isn't for you. You would distract the boy, and he doesn't need that. What you can do is keep an eye on the rear entry, just in case one of them finds an opening and comes through behind us."

He handed her an arc flash, one of the newest of the new breed of handheld flash rips. She took it, studied it a moment, and looked back at him.

"Can you use it?" he asked. "Do you know how?"

She nodded. "But I think I should go with Reyn. He's used to me being there when he uses the wishsong magic."

"That may be true, but it is also true that you cannot *always* be there. Especially in situations like this when you would be at as much risk as he will. So you will remain here. Are we clear?"

"He's right," Reyn told her. "I would feel better knowing you are safely away from whatever's going to happen outside."

She gave him a look, but nodded wordlessly. He could tell she was upset and worried, but he didn't want her with him when he left with Arcannen. He looked back at the sorcerer. "Where are these men now?"

Arcannen tightened his cloak about his shoulders and gave him a wink. "Let's go find out."

They departed the room through the heavy protective door and stepped into the hallway that led to the outside of their safehold. Arcannen took the lead, moving swiftly and confidently. No trace of concern over what might happen was evident from his face. When they reached the outer door, he extinguished the smokeless lamps at the opening and turned to Reyn.

"I will leave this door unlocked. If things go wrong or become too dangerous for you to remain outside, come back through here. Throw the locks on this door and the one leading into my home. If I don't appear within the hour, take Lariana and go out through the rear door. Make your way south to the village of Corrin's Kirk. It's no more than five miles down the coast. Don't bother looking for me; I won't be coming."

"I'm not leaving you," Reyn said at once.

"You will if I tell you to, and I am." The sorcerer's face was carved in stone. "Don't argue with me; I am better able to make these decisions than you are. I don't think any of this will happen, but you need to be prepared if it does."

"Lariana won't leave you, either."

Arcannen smiled. "She will do what you ask of her, just as you will pretty much do what she asks of you. I see what's happening between the two of you. A blind man could see. So do what I say. Go, and take care of each other afterward."

Reyn shook his head. "I don't like it."

"You don't need to." Arcannen stepped over to the door, drawing the boy after him. "The weather warmed during the night, and the rains stopped. The mist is so thick you can barely see your hand in front of your face. I don't know what we will find out there. I don't know how many of these intruders there are or where we will encounter them. So it would be better to keep moving rather than staying in one place. We may become separated. I will try not to let that happen."

He paused. "Just remember. If you get in trouble and I can't reach you, don't panic. Use your wishsong. Do whatever you must to protect yourself. I don't like having to ask this, but life doesn't always give us the choices we would prefer."

The boy hesitated. "When this is over, will you continue to help me learn about the magic and not give up on me?"

"Give up on you?" Arcannen laughed softly. "I never had any intention of giving up on you. Never. No matter what happens, I will be there to see you through this."

He gripped the boy's arm and pulled him close. "Are you ready?"

Reyn nodded.

Arcannen raised the heavy crossbar and threw the locking bolts on the door leading out. A wall of heavy gray fog, thick and swirling, greeted them as they went through.

Elsewhere in the nearly impenetrable soup, Mallich was leading his hunters in their search of the ruins. He paid no attention to the wards that might be in place now, made no effort to hide their arrival. The plan was simple—find their quarry, corner it, and kill it. With the oketar doing the tracking and the crince given over to The Hammer's care, the outcome was a foregone conclusion. Arcannen, Mallich believed, would try to escape rather than stand and fight. That effort would fail because the animals would find him wherever he went, corner him, and bring him down. Even if they couldn't, the men would be there to finish the job. Simple enough.

Usurient wasn't so sure.

He trailed the others, doing what he had promised himself he would do—hanging back to let his companions manage the killing so he would be free to clean up the mess when things were over and done with. He was far less convinced than the others about how easy this would be or what their chance of success was. The others were confident in their strength and experience as predators, but the Red Slash Commander was equally convinced of Arcannen's uncanny ability to survive. He had seen it before, when the odds were far greater than now. The sorcerer had a gift for detecting traps and turning them back on those who set them. Usurient was not at all sure it would be any different here.

His sole source of comfort came from the weapon he had concealed beneath his Federation army jacket—a handheld flash rip rapid-fire that could bring down an entire squad of attackers in seconds. It was the newest development in the Federation efforts to expand their military capability. He had bargained for it a few years back—by which he meant he had used blackmail and threats against a weapons developer. Not very fair of him perhaps, but very effective when you wanted something as badly as he had wanted this weapon.

His eyes fixed for a time on the crince, watching as it slouched along on the far end of The Hammer's chain. The beast was incredibly ugly—a huge, misshapen animal possessed of a massive body and thick, heavy limbs. Its head hung so low to the ground it seemed to be dragging. It was not intelligent; its senses were not keen. But once it locked on the prey it was sent to find, there was no stopping it. A crince would go right through a wall of spears to get its jaws on a kill. Even if damaged. Even if dying. You could stop it by dismembering it or cutting off its head, but with an animal of this size and ferocity coming at you, who had time for that?

He pictured it with its jaws around Arcannen's smug face and found momentary pleasure in the image.

Bael Etris skittered up to him from one side—a teasing, taunting gesture—then darted away. He kept glancing at Usurient, an open promise of what he would like to do to him mirrored in his dark eyes. Usurient knew he would have to watch the other closely. If he gave the little vermin half a chance, he would find his throat slit. But he had dealt with men like Etris before, mindless killers with no discernible boundaries and no respect for authority. He knew how to keep them at bay while making use of them.

Which wouldn't be for all that long in this instance. Etris would be the first one he would dispose of when this was over.

Ahead, Mallich slowed. They were at the edge of the ruins now, close to where the real search would begin. The hunter stood waiting for the others, motioning them closer before speaking.

"We split up here. Two groups." His voice was a whisper. "Hammer with me, Etris with Usurient. The animals go with me. Hammer and I will come in from the land side; Bael and Dallen will go in from the coast. There's got to be ways in and out of whatever remains of the village, passageways carved into the rock. That's where the sorcerer will be. If he doesn't come out to meet us, we find one of those ways and go in after him. Mostly, we have to keep him in front of us. We don't want him to slip out and get around behind us."

"Or escape us altogether," Usurient added. "If he does, he will come hunting us like we hunt him."

"He's already hunting *you*, though, isn't he?" Bael Etris sneered.

Usurient glared at him. "Something you're going to put a stop to if you want to get paid."

"Oh, that's right. I'm supposed to save you. I wonder why that doesn't much interest me?"

Mallich gave him a look. "Enough. There will be a door hidden somewhere on the coast side. If you find it, go in. Kill everyone. Don't stop to think about it."

"Don't you worry." Etris was still looking at Usurient. "I know how to kill a man better than most."

"Let him go on his own," Usurient said suddenly. "I'll stay with you."

Mallich started to object, then thought better of it. He sighed wearily. "All right. You come with me and Hammer. Let's be quick about this. Remember. If Arcannen gets the upper hand, we won't live out the day."

They separated then, Bael Etris peeling off from the others and disappearing into the gloom. The other three stood watching for a minute, then Mallich beckoned. They started forward into the ruins, spreading out as they went. They kept one another in sight, although Usurient, on the far right, at times lost sight of The Hammer, on the far left. He kept Mallich in view; he was the one who mattered. The oketar roamed ahead, straining against their leashes, noses to the

ground, sniffing at rocks and debris. As hunters they were without
peer, but they were killers, too. The urge to engage and take down
prey was instinctive, and if there were living creatures anywhere
nearby, they would find them.

Usurient peered into the haze doubtfully. He couldn't see a thing.
It would have been better if they had gone in last night in the pouring
rain rather than risk an encounter in this fog. Maybe they should
have waited. But he knew that wasn't possible with these men. Waiting wasn't something they would tolerate. He picked his way through
the rocks cautiously, trying not to make any sound, grateful for the
roar of the ocean in the background, hiding everything in its white
noise.

Then, abruptly, something appeared in the gloom ahead of them.

As they left their shelter and stepped out into the mist, Arcannen
leaned close to Reyn. "Don't try to see in this fog. Try to hear. The
ocean doesn't muffle sound as much as it might seem."

Reyn nodded. It seemed to him that the ocean crashing against
the rocks drowned out everything, but he did his best to try to hear
through it. Arcannen was moving ahead, wrapped in his dark cloak,
head bent to the rubble. The boy followed, working hard at keeping
upright on the slippery rocks, watching his footing carefully so he
wouldn't fall. He was thinking hard about the images he would need
to create, the distraction he would need to cause. Perversely, he found
himself wishing he had never put himself in this position—even if it
had meant giving up his lessons in learning to control the magic. But
he couldn't have stood losing Lariana. She mattered too much to him.
She was the real reason he stayed with Arcannen. To keep her close,
he would have endured almost anything.

They had gone only a short distance when Arcannen abruptly
stopped. He hesitated a moment, apparently listening. Reyn listened
with him, but heard nothing.

Arcannen glanced back at him, gesturing to his head and then
his mouth. He was ready for the images the wishsong would provide. He gestured a second time. The intruders were just ahead. He

waited to be sure Reyn understood, held up a warding palm to tell him to remain where he was, and disappeared into the roiling mist.

Reyn watched him go, suddenly chilled to the bone. He was alone now; the sorcerer was no longer there to protect him. All he could do was obey the other's instructions. He formed an image in his mind of several men, a clutch of armed attackers, holding them carefully in place, waiting to see what would happen. As he had with the creature he created to frighten Arcannen earlier, he gave his creations more than visual characteristics; he made it possible for them to be smelled, tasted, heard. He gave the beasts tracking them a reason to think they were real beyond what their eyes would suggest. He found it easier today—more familiar, less challenging. He knew he was getting more proficient at using his magic. He built his protectors piece by piece and held them at the ready like guards at the gates of a city.

Then he waited.

And waited some more.

The images in his mind did not waver. Time slowed, then stopped.

Abruptly a nightmarish creature surged into view, a thing so terrible the boy almost fled. The four-legged beast was as big as a koden, all bristling hair and jagged teeth and claws, angry piggish eyes fixing on him, head lowered close to the ground as if it were too heavy for the creature to hold erect. A man appeared behind it, the beast connected to him by a chain gripped in his massive hands. The man was as huge and terrible as the beast, a mountain of muscle and bone, his features scarred and ridged and twisted.

They saw each other in the same instant, and Reyn only just managed to release his images and send them careening toward these monsters to intercept them. The images responded as he had hoped they would, moving swiftly and purposefully ahead, attackers that clearly threatened. The man slowed at once, but the beast roared in challenge and jerked hard at the chain. Reyn conjured and dispatched another three attackers, all of them spinning out into the mists like the ghosts they were. But it was hard to tell they weren't real with the haze swirling around them, and the beast seemed confused and angry.

The boy cast about in desperation. Where was Arcannen? He had created a distraction. Where was the sorcerer?

Abruptly, the big man released the chain, and the beast surged forward to attack the images. As they disintegrated under the force of its attack, it grew even more crazed, whipping this way and that in a futile effort to get its jaws around them as they surged past. It could see, smell, and taste them; why couldn't it touch them? Reyn sent two more, but he could feel his grip on things loosening. All he was doing was delaying the inevitable if Arcannen didn't appear.

Then two further beasts surged out of the mist—things that looked to be a crossbreed of several species, not so big and imposing as the first, but dangerous nevertheless. They attacked the images, as well, caught up in the maddened behavior of the larger creature, and quickly the trio became mired in a frenzy of snapping and tearing at empty air and phantoms.

A shadowy figure emerged from off to his left, less imposing than the giant and the dog, but clearly a threat. Reyn dropped to one knee, trying to think what to do. The man was coming for him, running now, knives in both hands.

In desperation, he invoked a fresh image, shadowy and faint like the others but still real in appearance, and sent it charging toward the three beasts. The animals were on it at once, but their efforts to bring it down failed as Reyn caused it to veer sharply away before they reached it. Fleeing, with the animals in pursuit, the image folded itself about the man with the knives, and the two merged and became one. The man slowed, confused, aware that something had happened, brushing at his face as if he had walked into a spiderweb. The merging was done so swiftly it would not have appeared real to humans; it would have seemed the trick it was. But to the beasts it was very real. Reacting instinctively and without hesitation, all three charged the image that had become the man and tore into it.

At the last moment, the man turned, realizing something was

wrong, hands lifting his knives defensively. Too late. The largest beast was on him so fast he had no time to react. He was brought down instantly, screaming as the terrible jaws closed about his face and ripped it off. Arms and legs thrashed futilely, blood spraying everywhere. Tossing aside what it had savaged, the beast began tearing at what remained, joined by its companions. In mere seconds the man was reduced to a lifeless husk.

Kneeling in the mist-slickened rubble, Reyn cringed in dismay. He hadn't meant for this to happen. He had only been trying to divert the attack. He had just reacted. Arcannen had said he would be there to help him, to prevent him from killing anyone. But the sorcerer had failed him.

Now the first man was coming for him, a huge battle-ax raised overhead. He was like a juggernaut bearing down on the boy— massive and unstoppable. Reyn scrambled to his feet to face the giant, trying to conjure an image to deflect the attack. But panic enveloped him, freezing him in place, stripping away all control, all reason. There was no image that would save him from this.

Where was Arcannen now?

He began backing away, trying to escape, knowing immediately that he wouldn't, that he was too slow. He cried out for Arcannen, knowing that this, too, was futile, that he couldn't hear him and wouldn't come . . .

Behind him the door to the passageway leading into Arcannen's lair opened, and Lariana appeared, a vision that seemed born of another conjuring. She advanced through the opening and braced herself, arms extended, her small flash rip pointing.

"Get down, Reyn," she called out to him.

He threw himself aside, the giant almost on top of him. Lariana's weapon made a snapping noise—quick and piercing—and he caught a glimpse of a strange fiery rope passing above him at tremendous speed. He heard the sound of an impact on flesh, and heard the giant grunt. When he looked, the huge man was down on his knees, his entire chest opened up as the flaming rope twisted around inside of him like a live creature.

The giant's eyes were glazed and staring as he pitched forward and lay still.

Reyn staggered up, and Lariana raced toward him. She flew into his arms and held him against her, and in that moment of gratitude and relief he knew with a certainty as sharp as a blade's edge that she would never let him go.

21

USURIENT WATCHED IT ALL HAPPEN FROM NOT twenty feet away, crouched within the convenient pile of rubble behind which he had dropped during the first few seconds of the encounter. He had not once given any thought to going to the aid of Mallich or The Hammer; his common sense told him that they were likely not going to come out on the winning end.

He shuddered now, remembering what he had just witnessed. The crince, freed from its chain, going after what appeared to be a ghost image that had attached itself to Mallich and led to his demise. He could still see the crince ripping its master to pieces, tearing at him until nothing recognizable was left. And then the oketar joining in on the frenzied feast, all of them becoming maddened and uncontrollable in a matter of seconds.

He glanced down at his hands. They were still shaking. He hadn't been able to stop them from doing so. That boy. What sort of magic did he possess? How had he managed to turn those savage animals against Mallich? How had he managed it so easily?

He picked up the flash rip from where he had dropped it and tightened his grip until his knuckles turned white, forcing his hands to be still. This wasn't over yet. He looked up to where the boy and the girl were still locked in an embrace, arms about each other, heads pressed close. The girl, he thought, was as dangerous as the boy, although her methods were more conventional. She carried a weapon even more advanced than his own, a prototype that was supposedly in no one's hands. Clearly this was not the case, and he found himself wondering how many others were out there that shouldn't be.

His gaze shifted momentarily to the inert form of The Hammer, sprawled face-forward in the rocks, lifeless. That girl had taken him down with two well-placed shots, either of which would have killed him. She was skilled with that weapon, and whatever she and the boy were to each other, they were a formidable pair.

Would they come looking for him? Not even knowing he was there, would they decide to mount a search just to see if they had missed anyone? He could face them, he supposed. He could kill one or even both of them perhaps. But did he want any part of such an encounter? What was the point?

It was Arcannen he had come to find, and the sorcerer hadn't made even the briefest appearance.

He watched the boy and the girl separate, moving apart but still holding hands, talking now, their voices too low to hear. In a moment they would be on the move. What was he going to do?

He watched the heavy fog momentarily enclose them in its folds. Now he could see the crince snarling at the oketar, driving them back as it dragged the remains of Mallich out of the rubble and into the rugged terrain inland, warning off its competitors. The oketar were snarling back, but even together they weren't a match for the crince, so they made no move to attack as it hauled its kill into the rocks and disappeared. After giving momentary consideration to the boy and the girl and deciding it wasn't worth the attempt, the oketar moved off as well.

Usurient had just about decided to stand up and shoot both the boy and the girl before either could respond and then have a look around for Arcannen when a door set deep within the back walls of the ruins swung open and the sorcerer walked out.

.   .   .

"Did you hear that?" Avelene asked Paxon, stopping short of the crest of the ridgeline fronting their approach route to the coast.

"It sounds like animals fighting," he said.

They had flown in during the early hours of the morning, departing Sterne before it was light and finding their way east by reading the stars. By then, the storm that had threatened early had blown south, taking clouds and wind and rain with it, leaving behind the beginnings of a warming trend that left the surface of the earth below covered in layers of brume.

Avelene had thought it might be best simply to fly into the ruins of Arbrox and confront whatever was happening there. But Paxon persuaded her that Druids would intimidate neither Arcannen nor those hunters sent by Usurient to stalk the sorcerer. They would simply be putting themselves in danger by announcing their presence. It would go better if they landed somewhere far enough away that they would not be seen and walk in from there. It might take a little longer, but it would gain them an element of surprise.

But now, concerned about the sounds they were hearing, they picked up their pace. Paxon's ears were sharp enough that he was certain he had heard screams as well as the guttural animal noises, which meant that some sort of attack was under way. The Highlander had his sword out, holding it before them protectively as he led the way. Nothing they encountered at this point was likely to be friendly.

The crest of the ridgeline elevated them to a view of a long, shallow depression in the terrain ahead marked by clusters of rocks and pockets of fog. They could just make out the ruins of Arbrox—broken walls and collapsed roofs, areas blackened by fire launchers and flash rips, a village destroyed almost beyond recognition. The growls of the animals had changed to something less clear, although the urgency was still there, and the screams had gone silent.

Something moved through the gloom, off in the distance, a huge figure lunging suddenly at something hidden from their view. In the next instant a pair of fiery projectiles struck it, and it fell to its knees and toppled forward.

Paxon and Avelene began running, scrambling down the rocky

slope in an effort to get to the scene. The sounds of their passage could not be heard over the roar of the ocean, but there was danger in coming in too quickly and being caught by surprise. Neither could be sure who was up ahead. So when they descended the rise, the Highlander slowed their pace and made a sweeping gesture toward the mist-shrouded lowlands ahead, reminding his companion to be wary of hidden dangers.

As they drew nearer the battle site, they saw two people clinging to each other within the ruins, vague figures in the gloom. The giant lay sprawled nearby, unmoving. The animals they had seen earlier, beasts the like of which neither had encountered before, were moving off, the largest of them dragging what appeared to be the remains of a man. Paxon motioned for Avelene to get behind him, but the Druid ignored the command and instead moved sideways to put a little distance between them. Everything ahead was locked inside a sea of gray mist that swirled in erratic circles and alternately concealed and then revealed the rocky terrain it covered.

They were within thirty yards or so when a door opened in the cliff face amid the ruins and Arcannen appeared. Paxon slowed involuntarily, a surge of excitement and exultation rushing through him. Avelene stopped, going into a crouch. The sorcerer, cowled and wrapped in his robes, a spectral look to his dark form, moved toward the embracing couple. The couple broke the embrace, and Paxon was shocked to see that one of the pair was the boy who had use of the wishsong, the one he had pursued unsuccessfully in Portlow.

The boy and his partner—a girl who looked to be no older than he was—had turned to face Arcannen when abruptly a man stood up from behind an outcropping of rocks to one side of them and fired a handheld flash rip at the sorcerer, half a dozen fiery charges slamming into the other. Arcannen simply flew apart, arms and legs flung wide, body disintegrating. An instant later, the attacker had dropped back into the rocks and out of sight.

But that wasn't the end of the strangeness. A second man now appeared—a lean, feral-looking creature armed with a long knife who surfaced from behind the ruins atop the cliffs and dropped down on the couple as they shrank from the carnage they had just witnessed. As the man attacked the couple with his blade extended, the boy flung out his hands in a warding gesture, his cry filled with despair, the sound emitting a burst of wishsong magic that sent this new threat flying. Instantly the girl bolted for cover, but when she looked back, the boy was still standing where she had left him, staring into space. She turned back, seized his arm, and pulled at him in desperation, but the boy didn't move. A moment later their attacker, recovering more swiftly than expected, launched himself at the girl, struck her a powerful blow, and knocked her to the ground, where she sprawled, unconscious. The boy still didn't move, and the man wrapped his arm about the other's neck and, using him as a shield, began backing toward the cliff face. The boy went without a struggle, almost as if he didn't realize what was happening.

Neither Paxon nor Avelene was quite sure who anybody was at this point. Given the likely possibility that the two attackers were part of the contingent sent to kill Arcannen, what did the boy and the girl have to do with anything? It felt odd that they should be here at all, especially the boy. Hadn't he seen enough of Arcannen in Portlow to stay clear of him?

Paxon glanced over at Avelene. She seemed undecided, staring at the scene below. "What do we do?" he whispered.

No response. Then she looked at him wordlessly and stood up. Together, they began walking toward the boy and his attacker.

It took only a moment for the man to see them. A knife appeared in his hand, and he pressed it to the boy's neck. "Where is he?" he screamed at them.

Both Paxon and Avelene slowed, confused. "Dead," the Druid answered. "They're all dead. Let the boy go."

The man looked around wildly, noting the giant's body and dismissing it. "Not them! The sorcerer! He's not dead! Are you blind? Where is he? You answer me! You want this one's throat cut, do you?"

He pressed the knife blade harder against the boy's throat, but the boy didn't even flinch. He just stared into space.

"Look down!" Paxon shouted at him. He pointed to the charred rocks and bits of tattered robe that lay almost at the man's feet. The man glanced at them and gave a shrill, wild laugh, as if this was the funniest thing he had ever seen.

Avelene kept moving forward, drawing Paxon with her. "Your fellows are all dead!" she called out. "You have nowhere to go. Let the boy go, and I will give you your freedom!"

The man spat at her. "You'll give me nothing. You'll do what I say or I'll kill him right in front of you! You stay where you are."

Avelene slowed, but not by much.

"How stupid are you, woman? You think the sorcerer dead? Just like that? Quick and simple, a flash rip does the job? Dead? He's got nine lives and then some! He's waiting us out—all of us—just to see who lives and who dies. Those that die quick are the lucky ones. But I'm not fooled because I see things you don't!"

Paxon experienced a flash of uncertainty. Was he right? Was Arcannen still alive? But if so, then who had the flash rip explosions torn apart?

He knew the answer before he finished asking himself the question. Magic. The sorcerer had used magic. It was an image the flash rip had destroyed.

He separated himself from Avelene by a few steps, searching for a way to disable their adversary. If he could get close enough, it should only take a moment to render him senseless. But it would be tricky, and he would get only one chance. He hesitated, glancing at Avelene. She was continuing her own advance, white fire flaring at her fingertips, tense resolve mirrored on her narrow features.

"Wait," she whispered to him.

The man continued backing away from them, working his way toward a gap in the ruins that would give him access to the coastline. "I'm not so stupid as these others, Arcannen!" he shouted at the ruins about him. "Not Bael Etris! I see you. You can't hide yourself from me, witchman!"

The mist was shifting in front of him with such frequency that he was disappearing into it every few seconds. Any attack would be semi-blind in these conditions. But Paxon knew they had to do something.

"You want this boy dead, Arcannen?" Bael Etris screamed suddenly. "Show yourself or he's meat on the—"

An explosion of smoke infused with a brilliant crimson light cut off the rest of what he intended to say, flooding the whole of the ruins surrounding Etris and the boy, completely enveloping both. At first, Paxon thought Avelene had caused it, but when he glanced over she was down on one knee, shielding her eyes from the glare. Throwing caution aside, knowing there was no time for it, he charged into the swirling miasma, the black blade of his sword alive with movement, its emerald light flaring in bright streaks against the crimson of the haze.

If he could just reach the boy . . . ·

But it was the girl he found instead. Blinded by the smoke and groping futilely for direction, she stumbled out of the gloom and collapsed at his feet. Kneeling beside her, one eye on his surroundings in case the next person to appear happened to be the one with the knife, he pulled her up and held her, whispering that she was all right, that she was safe.

She grasped at him in response, her words urgent, grateful. "Reyn, are you all right? I saw what happened to you! You used too much again, tried too hard! I warned you . . ." Then she stopped abruptly as she looked into Paxon's face. "No! Where is he? What . . . ?"

Abruptly she realized he wasn't the boy and pushed him away violently. She leapt to her feet in an effort to escape, but she wasn't strong enough to free herself from his quick hands, and he brought her down again with a rough yank.

"Whoa, hold on!" he said. "Not so fast. No running away until I find out what's going on."

She struggled for a moment and then gave up. To her credit, she didn't cry or whine. Instead, she faced him squarely. "You have to let me go! I have to find him! You don't understand what's happening!"

"I'll give you that last part," he replied, pulling her to her feet, one hand firmly clasped about her wrist. "So let's go have a look and see if we can change things. What's your name?"

She glared at him. Her delicate, beautiful features had turned hard and tight. "Lariana."

"Sharp eyes then, Lariana. Don't let us get caught by surprise."

They advanced cautiously, but no one else appeared until, after several long minutes, a crouching Avelene materialized almost on top of them. Her appearance was so sudden that Paxon barely managed to stay his sword arm from striking out at her.

"Calm down, Highlander!" she snapped at him, flinching away. Her narrow features took on an ironic look. "We're on the same side, remember?"

He exhaled in relief. "Can't see anything in this stuff."

"Why don't we get out of it then, give the winds a chance to blow it away? Who is this you have with you?"

"Lariana. She hasn't told me more than that, so far."

Wordlessly, the Druid led them away from the ruins and the mist and out onto the rocky flats where the air was still clear. Paxon glanced over his shoulder and was surprised to see that the crimson haze wasn't dissipating. It was hanging motionlessly above the rocky terrain, almost as if anchored in place, its weight enough that the sea winds couldn't budge it.

Avelene came close to Lariana, eyes fixing on her. "How do you come to be here?"

For a moment, it looked like the girl wouldn't answer. It seemed to Paxon as she hesitated that she was making up her mind about something. There was an air of desperation to her that issued in part, no doubt, from her concern for the boy. But he thought something more was at work, too. She was young and beautiful, and she was out in the middle of nowhere. That couldn't have happened by accident, so there was a story waiting to be told and she was trying to decide how to tell it.

Or at least how much of it she wanted to reveal.

"If I tell you, will you agree to help me look for Reyn?" she asked.

She was looking at Paxon, but he held his tongue. It wasn't his place to answer. "The boy?" Avelene asked. Lariana nodded, and the Druid shrugged. "Of course we will."

The girl took a quick breath. "I was brought here by Arcannen. He took me out of Rare Flowers, a school for young women in troubled circumstances, and brought me with him to this place. On the way, we picked up Reyn. This was no accident. Arcannen knew who he was. I was to help persuade Reyn to use his magic, to practice with it. He never told me why. Then these men came, trying to kill Arcannen. But he disappeared, and Reyn had to face them alone. I tried to help him, but then . . . well, you saw. The man with the knife knocked me down, and then that mist swallowed everything and the man disappeared and so did Reyn . . ."

"What was wrong with Reyn?" Paxon interrupted. "He didn't do anything to try to help himself. He seemed almost unconscious."

Lariana glanced at him and shrugged. "He must have been frightened. I don't know."

Paxon was reminded suddenly of how his sister had looked after she had first used the wishsong's magic and gone catatonic. The boy had worn a similar look, and he didn't think the cause was simply fear.

"Why did you help Arcannen?" Avelene demanded before Paxon could pursue the matter. "Don't you know who he is?"

The girl gave a sardonic smile. "I do now. At the time, I didn't care. He was going to get me out of Rare Flowers, and he said he would teach me to use magic if I helped him. That was reason enough for me to go with him. I knew what would happen if I didn't take the chance he was offering. No one else was going to do anything for me. Not anything I wanted them to do, anyway. I was on the verge of being thrown into the streets. They didn't like me at Rare Flowers. I was too difficult, they said."

"So this boy, Reyn, what kind of magic can he use?" Avelene pressed. "Have you seen him use it?"

Lariana shook her head. "I won't tell you anything else unless you help me find him. Or just let me go so I can find him on my own. I'm not afraid to do that."

Avelene smirked. "I guessing you're not afraid of much. But there's more to this than you know. We need you and Reyn to help us understand it. So you don't get to do anything on your own. We can search the ruins together, if you want."

This time Avelene didn't reenter the red haze as Paxon had chosen to do earlier, but conjured a spell that brought the wind about from the ocean and caused it to blow the scarlet mist out over the choppy waters and away. It took considerable effort to achieve this; the haze was stubbornly resistant to her efforts. But in the end it dissipated and was replaced by the familiar sea mists of earlier.

With the way forward more readily visible now, the trio plunged ahead, scrambling until they reached the spot where Reyn Frosch had last been seen. It took them only moments, and then they stood together casting about the empty terrain fruitlessly. Then Lariana spied the open door in the cliff face, a black, gaping hole in the rock, and she charged over with a sharp cry, heedless of any danger. Paxon and Avelene followed, and quickly they were down the hallway beyond and inside the sorcerer's lair.

Empty.

A swift search revealed that the rooms were deserted, and Lariana stood staring about the central living quarters in a furious attempt to understand. "Arcannen has him," she said finally.

"No," Avelene said at once. "Arcannen is dead. I saw the man with the flash rip send so many of those projectiles into him there was nothing left."

The sharp eyes fixed on her. "That's what he wants you to think. But he's alive. He's alive, and he's taken Reyn with him."

"And left you behind?" Paxon asked. "Odd."

"Not so odd. I was always expendable. Once he got what he wanted from me, once he used me to get to Reyn, to persuade him . . ." She trailed off. "I knew he would do something like this. I just hoped I would be able to keep Reyn close enough to prevent it . . ."

"But where's the man with the knife?" Avelene wanted to know.

"Dead," Lariana said at once.

"But what happened to him?"

The girl hesitated, shaking her head. "I don't know."

"We need to go back outside!" Paxon said suddenly. "Have another look around."

They departed the sorcerer's, going down the hallway and outside once more into the open air, where they began their search anew, eyes scanning the ruins through gloom and shifting mists.

"There!" Lariana exclaimed almost immediately, pointing upward.

Paxon and Avelene turned, eyes shifting. The Highlander heard his companion's sudden intake of breath.

A steel support rod jutted from the shattered walls of the buildings above where they stood. The body of Bael Etris hung from that rod, his lifeless husk pinned in place with enough force that the rod had passed completely through his body. His eyes were open and staring.

"So Arcannen is alive after all," Avelene murmured, looking at Lariana. "And you think he took Reyn with him?"

Lariana was nodding slowly. "Arcannen has him," she repeated. "But I know where they are."

22

REYN FROSCH ROSE FROM OUT OF A BLACK PIT, lifted by the rocking motion of the pallet on which he lay, summoned by the howling of a furious wind. He came from a long way down, a slow ascent back to wakefulness, his senses struggling to focus as his eyes blinked and his arms clutched protectively at his body. The world was gray, and there was a sense of not being anyplace he recognized or even anywhere solid but instead of being suspended in nothingness. He swallowed against the dryness in his throat, coughing hard as he did so, his body shaking.

"Hold on, hold on!" a voice muttered.

An aleskin was held to his lips and the pungent liquid slid between them and down his throat to loosen the tightness and waken him further. He drank greedily, hands lifting to clutch the skin so he could continue.

"There, that's enough," his benefactor announced, taking the skin away. "Let's sit you up. Then I have to get back to flying."

Hands pulled him from his slumped-over fetal position to one where he was sitting upright, and he found himself in a padded seat. Wind rushed against his exposed skin. He was flying in an airship below a sky thick with mist and gloom.

He fixed his gaze on the figure at the helm of the fast clipper.

Arcannen.

His memory came back in a rush. Slipping out from the sorcerer's underground lair into the ruins of Arbrox to face the men who had come to kill them. Searching the shifting haze until suddenly Arcannen was no longer there, and he was alone. Facing a giant with a huge beast on a chain, then another man with smaller beasts. Summoning the wishsong to create images and in the end to fool the beasts into attacking one of their handlers. Watching both men die—one by his hand, one by Lariana's . . .

Lariana!

"Where is she?" he demanded, his voice a rough croak, almost lost in the wind's rush. "What's happened to her?"

Arcannen glanced over his shoulder. "If you are referring to Lariana, I imagine she's with the Druid and her protector. She'll be all right."

"You left her?"

Reyn was incensed. He struggled to rise, to charge forward and take command of the controls, to turn this craft about and fly back to where she had been abandoned and rescue her. But without even looking at him, the sorcerer struck him hard across the face and shoved him back into his seat, where he collapsed once more.

"I went to a lot of trouble to save you. Kindly don't undo my efforts. Lariana will be fine. She knew this might happen. We talked about it long before now. Give her some credit for being able to take care of herself."

The blow still stung as Reyn shifted to a sitting position and rubbed his face. Blood dripped from his nose. He felt suddenly drained, robbed of strength and hope, despairing. "Why didn't you bring her with us?"

"That would have been difficult."

"You *would* say that, wouldn't you?"

"I say it because it is true. Think back. You were caught in a standoff with Bael Etris. He had a knife at your throat. He was clearly mad—raving and unpredictable. The Druid and her protector were too far away to do anything. You were frozen in place. So I used magic to create a smoke screen that hid all of you while I freed you and dispatched Etris. Lariana must have woken and stumbled away, probably in shock. I didn't know where she was. I could only save you. I did what I had to."

Reyn was not satisfied with his explanation. The sorcerer's calmness only served to make him angrier. He could explain all he wanted to but in the end the result was the same. He had left Lariana behind, something Reyn would never have done.

"You don't know what they will do to her," he said finally.

Arcannen chuckled. "Oh, you think they might hurt her, do you? Hardly. They want me. And quite possibly you, knowing you have magic. They don't care about her. They will try to discover where I am once they've figured out I didn't die in the attack. But she won't tell them. She's too clever for that. She'll lead them on a bit and then free herself and come find me. We worked it out a while back."

Reyn was confused. Worked it out? Arcannen couldn't have known how the confrontation with those hunters was going to turn out. He couldn't have known that the Druids would come searching for him in the ruins of Arbrox. So what was he talking about? Worked out what?

"Why didn't you stay close to me when we went out to face those men? Why did you disappear? Where were you?"

"Searching for you the entire time. Trying to reach you. I managed to get myself turned around in the mist. When the attack came, I was too late reaching you to make a difference. That was clever of you, though—using one of your images to turn those animals on Mallich. What a surprise that must have been! I always knew they'd kill him one day. Those beasts were too dangerous for the amount of trust he put in himself as their handler."

"Hunting animals?" Reyn asked. "I've never seen their like."

"Fighting animals. Killers. Used in sporting contests and on fugitive hunts. Dangerous beasts just standing still. Impossible to control if there's blood to be had. You saw for yourself."

"You should have warned me. You should have been there to help me. You promised."

Arcannen shrugged. "I told you I might not be available when you needed me and not to be overly dependent. You learned a valuable lesson today. And no harm done. Besides, Lariana was there when you needed help. Wasn't that enough?"

No, Reyn thought, it wasn't. He'd had to save his own life and been forced to kill someone yet again. And once again, he had gone catatonic in the process. So while there was no harm done to him physically, he'd suffered more than enough emotionally. Arcannen's explanation for why he had left him on his own felt weak. Lost in the mist? Turned around? He was seething as he puzzled it through.

"What did you do to the man with the knife?"

"Etris? As I said, I disposed of him. How I did it doesn't matter. Do you want something to eat? We still have a way to go."

Reyn rubbed his face again. The sting of the blow was beginning to diminish. "You had time to kill him, but not to save Lariana?"

There was a long silence. "Yes, Reyn. I had time to kill him but not save Lariana. If I had tried, we would all be in the hands of the Druids. Now do you think you can let go of your anger and stop whining about things you can't change?"

The boy lapsed into sullen silence, hardly appeased, barely able to restrain himself even now. What held him back was what the sorcerer had said about Lariana knowing what to do if they became separated. This bothered him in a way he couldn't explain. At the very least, it suggested she was privy to information that had been deliberately kept from him. She was the sorcerer's assistant, but he couldn't help wondering suddenly if she was something more. She certainly knew things he didn't, and she had demonstrated this on more than one occasion. He just hadn't thought much about it before now.

"Where are we going?" he asked.

"Now, there's the question you should have asked in the beginning." Arcannen flashed him a smile. "We're going to Sterne."

Reyn blinked. "Why are we going there?"

The sorcerer turned away. "To finish what we started."

· · ·

Paxon and Avelene were shepherding Lariana toward their airship—keeping her between them, still conscious of the possibility that she might attempt to flee. They had left their vessel moored out in the mists some distance back from the coast and the ruins of Arbrox, giving their Troll crew responsibility for keeping watch over it while they were away. They had taken time to bring Bael Etris down off the cliff face where he was hanging from that iron rod and bury him beneath a pile of heavy rocks. But the animals that had killed his companion were roaming around somewhere, and there was nothing they could do to prevent them from returning when they got hungry enough and digging up the dead man for food.

"Where are we going?" Avelene asked the girl for the second time, her patience clearly wearing thin. "We want to help you, but we won't if you don't tell us what you intend. Where are you taking us? How can you know where Arcannen is?"

Lariana's young features tightened. "You don't trust me?"

Avelene rolled her eyes. "Just tell me how you know where to find him."

Lariana shrugged. "It's simple enough. Arcannen wants revenge for what happened in Arbrox. He wants to get his hands on the Commander of the Red Slash. What did you say his name was? Usurient? He knew Usurient would send hunters to kill him, so he waited on them and dispatched them. If they failed in their efforts, he believed Usurient would bring the entire Red Slash to flush him out."

Paxon stared. "All of them? That's five hundred men and women. Why would he use a force that size?"

Lariana shrugged. "To demonstrate how powerful he is? To make certain that this time Arcannen doesn't escape him? It doesn't matter. All that's changed. Usurient won't come here now. Not after seeing you." She paused. "So Arcannen will go after him."

Avelene nodded. "To Sterne? Where the Red Slash is based?"

"Wouldn't you, if you were him?" Lariana looked off into the mists. Ahead, the Druid airship came into view. "He told me he could never forgive the massacre of the people at Arbrox. He was there; he saw it all happen. They killed every man, woman, and child in the village. They made no effort to take prisoners. Those were his friends. Arcannen is an odd man. A man with his own idea of what constitutes right and wrong. How others see him doesn't matter. He will do whatever he feels is necessary to balance the scales. To avenge the dead at Arbrox, he will hunt down those he holds responsible. Since Usurient thinks him dead, he won't be expecting him. So that's exactly where he will go. He is on his way to Sterne."

Paxon thought about it. Would Arcannen brave Usurient and the Red Slash in their own barracks? In the city where they had established their home base? There was a symmetry to doing so that would appeal to the sorcerer. They had destroyed his home; now he would destroy theirs. But how would he accomplish this?

"What does Reyn have to do with all this?" he asked Lariana.

"Arcannen says he wants to help Reyn. He says he knows all about his magic and understands how hard it is to have the use of something so dangerous. He calls it a wishsong; he claims it has a long history in Reyn's family. Reyn doesn't care about any of that; he just wants to find a way to stop hurting people. He doesn't always have control of the magic; sometimes he can't hold it back. When he gets angry or feels threatened it just breaks out of him. But he doesn't want that. He isn't like that."

Paxon found himself thinking again of Chrysallin. His sister had experienced the same phenomenon, the magic exploding out of her unexpectedly in a moment of extreme stress and panic. Like this boy. And he wondered anew if what he had witnessed back there in the ruins when the boy seemed to lose focus entirely was a form of the catatonia that had claimed Chrys.

Yet he hesitated to make the leap. Reyn Frosch had to be an Ohmsford; no one else possessed the wishsong powers. And given that there was only one Ohmsford still unaccounted for—his grandfather Railing's twin brother—Reyn must be descended from Redden. Meaning he and Chrys shared the same bloodline, of twin brothers, but each born to a different one. Nothing about their lives was the same, yet there had to be a link somewhere that explained why the magic would affect each in the same way. Yet the secret behind that link might be found not in their lives but in the history of the magic itself.

"Why would Arcannen take Reyn with him to Sterne?" Avelene was asking.

"I think he wants his help against Usurient. I think that is what he has wanted all along. Arcannen has been teaching him how to manage his magic. He's been doing this by having him practice with it. He has him create life-like images and then move them around. That's what he was doing back at Arbrox when he was threatened by those men and their animals." She hesitated. "But I'm not sure if he's doing what he says."

Paxon and Avelene exchanged a quick glance. "What do you mean?" the Druid asked.

Lariana sighed wearily. "Creating images is all he's had Reyn do since he found him. That seems to be all that matters to him. But I don't understand how it's helping Reyn with his problem. What he needs to learn is control, and I don't see how he's learning that."

"So you think maybe he wants to use Reyn for something bad, something that might harm him?"

The girl didn't respond. Avelene scuffed her boot against the rocky terrain and signaled ahead to the Trolls aboard the airship to prepare to get under way. The Trolls immediately began attaching the radian draws to the light sheaths and winching them into place. The diapson crystals were engaged by an unhooding of the parse tubes, and a rope ladder was dropped over the side to allow for boarding.

"That's what I think," Lariana answered finally. She pulled her travel cloak more tightly about her, hunching her shoulders. "He's not telling me everything, I know that much. Whatever he intends, I think he needs Reyn to make it happen. That's why he took him to Sterne."

Paxon thought about it. The wishsong was a powerful magic, capable of almost anything. It could easily be turned into a killing weapon if a magic wielder wanted to hurt others, if he was willing to go far enough.

Or, he amended, if the user lost control—as Reyn Frosch had been known to do. As Chrysallin had done.

But would he do so in this instance, facing the hardened soldiers of the Red Slash, men and women every bit as dangerous as he was, even without magic? Men and women against whom he, personally, held no grudge?

He glanced over at Avelene as they came up to the airship and began to climb aboard. She must be thinking about it, too, trying to decide what Arcannen intended to do with the boy. Whatever it was, they had to get to Sterne as quickly as possible and try to put a stop to it.

"Will you promise me something?" Lariana asked suddenly, turning to face them as they stood at the rope ladder. "I know I don't have any right, but I'll ask it anyway. Will you try not to hurt Reyn? Will you try to help him? Will you at least let me help? He doesn't have anybody but me. He seems strong because he has the wishsong, but he's afraid of the magic and what it can do. He's afraid to use it. I don't think he understands the game that's being played."

"We'll do what we can," Avelene replied, giving Paxon a sideways glance. "But if we're put in danger, we'll have to defend ourselves."

The girl nodded slowly. "I know this. I understand. But Reyn is very young. He's been on his own for a long time, but he doesn't understand the world that well. He can be misled. He can be made to do things he doesn't intend to do. If you can help him . . ."

"You talk as if you're older than he is, and I doubt you are. What are you? Sixteen? You barely know this boy, yet you worry for him as if he were . . ." She trailed off abruptly. "You love him, don't you?"

Lariana hesitated. "Yes." She said it in a way that dared them to contradict her. "More to the point, he loves me. He trusts me. He depends on me. I can't abandon him. I won't. That's why I'm asking for your help. We both need it."

Paxon went up the rope ladder, thinking about what she had just said. Something was wrong. Her admission sounded reasonable, but the fact that she had been recruited by Arcannen to help teach the boy control of the magic was troubling. Where exactly did her loyalties lie? If her chances in this world rested with the sorcerer, then why would she risk so much for the boy? Was she really in love with Reyn Frosch? She came from a place where young girls were bought and sold for very specific reasons, but never to act independently of their master's wishes. Yet she seemed to be saying that this was what was happening here.

He could not help thinking that in his experience everyone who came in contact with Arcannen ended up damaged in some way. It made him wonder about Lariana.

And about Reyn Frosch.

The boy remained quiet for a time, thinking through what Arcannen had said. They were on their way to Sterne to find Usurient and the Red Slash. *To finish what we started.* But what exactly was that? They hadn't actually started anything, had they? Usurient had sent those men to kill him—and likely all those with him—but had failed. It had cost them their lives. So now he intended to carry the fight to Usurient in Sterne. How would he do that? What did he intend?

He wanted to ask but at the same time he didn't. He was afraid of the answer. He was frightened of what Arcannen wanted him to do. He had been promised he would be taught different uses for his magic while learning how to master its unstable power. He had been taught virtually nothing beyond how to create images of fighting men. He had been promised he would not be asked to hurt anyone when they were back in the ruins of Arbrox, but that hadn't worked out at all. Why was there any reason to think things would be different this time?

He wished Lariana were there. He wished he could talk with her. She would find them, Arcannen had said.

"How is Lariana supposed to find us?" he asked the other, finally breaking the silence.

Arcannen glanced back. "I told her earlier what to do. She knows where we are going and what I intend. Once she gets free of the Druids, she will come looking. We won't be hard to find. Her part in this is too important for her to fail."

"What part? What do you mean?"

"Lariana is my student. She works for me. She does what I tell her to do, and she is very good at it. She knows what's needed. Stop worrying."

Reyn felt his heart sink. It was the truth, wasn't it? Lariana wasn't his. She was Arcannen's, and the sorcerer was using her to persuade him. All along she had known so much about what was going to happen, about how to train him, about what he was supposed to do. She had guided him every step of the way. She had kissed him. Kissed him! She had made him feel good about himself for the first time in a long time. She was very clever and she had taken advantage of him.

He looked down at the planking of the deck at his feet and felt his heart break. He was a fool.

"What is it exactly that you intend?" he asked, no longer able to stop himself from doing so. What was the point in pretending he wasn't going to try? Fool or not, he could not abandon his hopes for Lariana and himself, for the possibility that he was mistaken.

"Well, in my experience, when someone tries to kill you and fails, they will probably try again. I'm not keen on that happening. Best I kill them first, don't you think?"

"Usurient, you mean?"

"Yes, Dallen Usurient. Especially. He thinks me dead. He fled thinking he had killed me, and there is no one to tell him otherwise. We have plenty of time to reach him before he discovers the truth. We have time to set a trap and spring it."

Reyn looked up. "We?"

"Yes. You're to help me. It's part of your debt to me for my aid in training you to control your magic. You *can* control it better than before, can't you? You *have* been doing your exercises as Lariana instructed? Everything has gone just as it should?"

He did not want to give anything away. "Yes."

"Then we have no problem, do we?"

"I don't know. Why do I have to help at all? Can't you do whatever you intend to Usurient without me? If you think you can catch him by surprise anyway—"

"No, no, no," the other interrupted quickly. "Killing Usurient is only part of it. You still don't understand, do you?"

He glanced back at Reyn and held his gaze. "Well, do you?"

The boy shook his head. "I guess not."

"Then pay attention. We're not going to stop with Usurient, boy. He's only one of many responsible for what happened at Arbrox. We're going to destroy the entire Red Slash command."

23

THE DRUID AIRSHIP SLIPPED OUT OF THE NIGHT with its diapson-powered running lights dark and its Troll crew at the ready, descending into Sterne like a ghost. The public airfield lay below, empty of movement, its vessels moored and secured, its lights still on for late arrivals but their pilots and crews asleep save the night watch. Stripped of their black robes and reduced to ordinary garb, Paxon and Avelene stood at the bow with the girl Lariana and watched the earth rise to meet them.

The plan was simple. They had chosen the public airfield to avoid alerting Usurient and the Red Slash to their presence. They had shed their Druid robes to allow them to move about the city unnoticed. Once disembarked, Lariana could lead them to Arcannen. She would not be required to reveal herself to him while doing so. Instead, Avelene and Paxon would subdue him and free Reyn Frosch, and then all of them would depart for Paranor aboard the airship.

None of them really believed things would work out that way, although each thought so for a different reason. Paxon and Avelene had discussed at length how to overcome the sorcerer while flying in from the coast, but it always came back to the same thing—the element of surprise. Ostensibly, Avelene possessed the training and skill with magic that would allow her to render Arcannen at least temporarily unconscious—although she had never made practical use of either in a dangerous situation, so Paxon was doubtful. His own belief was that Arcannen would never be taken down by anything but brute force, so he was expecting to have to use his blade to achieve what was needed. Even then, there was no reason to think the sorcerer would still be alive at the end. Or even that Paxon himself would. Avelene, on the other hand, was confident in her abilities. Enough so that she had already told him that in a direct confrontation with Arcannen, her magic would prove superior.

What Lariana thought was a mystery. She wasn't saying much beyond asking that she be given a chance to save the boy.

"He doesn't know what he's doing," she kept insisting. "He's being led around by the nose. He thinks Arcannen is going to train him to control the magic. But what Arcannen is going to do is train Reyn to obey him. I can see it in the way he's acting with Reyn, how he's manipulating him, twisting his thinking. I have to get to him and let him know."

Paxon wasn't sure what Lariana did or didn't have to do, but he was pretty sure by now that she was keeping something from them. Maybe she believed what she was telling them. Maybe she actually thought she was right about Arcannen and Reyn Frosch. But there was a secrecy about her that kept him wondering exactly where her loyalties lay. Whatever happened in the hours ahead, he was going to keep a close eye on her.

"You will let him go when I have him safely back again, won't you?" she asked at one point. "You'll let us both go? You won't lock us up or give us over to the Federation?"

She said it just as they were preparing to climb down the rope ladder and set out into the city. She sounded so poignant that it gave the Highlander pause. But Avelene was quick to remind her why they were there in the first place.

"We are Druids, Lariana. We have a mission to fulfill. Our obligation is to the larger population of the Four Lands. Surely you can see that Reyn is a danger not only to himself but also to others. He has to find a way to control his magic. Arcannen is not the one to teach him.

We are. At Paranor, we can help him. He can receive the training he needs. Real training, not something like what he's been getting. You can come, too, if you wish. Your visit will last only as long as it takes Reyn to master the skills he needs. Then you are both free to go wherever you wish."

She spoke the right words. She made the situation as clear as she could. But Paxon saw the look of doubt in Lariana's eyes, saw the reticence reflected on her features, and understood at once what concerned her about Avelene's words. However you looked at it, she and the boy would become prisoners anew. The boy, at least, would not be allowed to leave Paranor until it was deemed safe to let him do so. That could take months. It could take years. It might never happen.

She turned away from them without comment, climbing quickly down the ladder to avoid their eyes. But Paxon had already seen all he needed to see to know what she was thinking.

They departed the airfield without passing by the manager's office, leaving it to the Trolls to sort out the arrangements for their stay, moving off into the darkness that wrapped the outskirts of the city, silent shadows fading from view.

"Where is it that we're going?" Avelene whispered after they had left the airship behind.

Lariana turned. "It's not far from here. He's hiding in the cellars of the old Federation army barracks out by the bluffs. He thought that would be the last place anyone would look for him, and there are several ways in and out of the cellars if anyone should come looking."

"It doesn't sound as if it's going to be easy to trap him there," Paxon observed.

But Lariana shook her head. "There are three ways in or out. We can lock down two of them from the outside before we go in. Then it's up to you."

The city lay off to the right now, their path taking them along its eastern borders toward their destination. Neither Paxon nor Avelene knew anything about the abandoned barracks, so they were watchful as they neared the low, squat buildings that appeared all at once as they topped a rise and started toward a chain-link fence. There were no lights in the windows of the buildings; the entire complex was dark and empty looking. The grounds were littered with debris and overgrown with scrub; there was no sign of life.

When they spied the gates, Paxon moved into the lead, his black sword drawn and ready. But no one appeared, no sounds or movement drew their attention, and they reached the fence gates without incident.

Even so, Paxon experienced a twinge of uneasiness. He looked down at the huge lock on the gate holding a heavy chain in place. "We'll have to break it."

Avelene moved him out of the way, placed her hands on the lock, squeezed firmly while whispering something the Highlander couldn't hear, and the lock opened.

She arched an eyebrow at him. "There's a trick to it. You have to speak softly."

Pulling the chain free from where it bound the gates together, she pushed the right side open before stepping back. "Lead the way," she said.

Paxon moved Lariana up beside him. "Show us the doors we need to secure." He lifted a cautionary finger. "And careful you don't give us away."

She gave him a cold look and started ahead. They bypassed the main entrance and worked their way around the building to a side door with a heavy iron bar, and she locked it down. She did the same with a second door. After that, she was ready to turn back, but Paxon insisted they investigate the entire outside of the complex. In case, he said, she might have missed a way in or out.

But they found nothing else in their search and arrived back at the main entrance. "Won't there be wards in place?" Avelene wanted to know.

Lariana shrugged. "Can't you find out? You have magic, don't you?"

Ignoring the taunt, Avelene spent several long minutes testing the entry. She used words and hands both, murmuring as she touched and rubbed the smooth surfaces, creating small streaks of blue light that burrowed through seams in the metal parts and disappeared inside. Her absorption in the effort was complete, and at one point her eyes were closed and she was holding herself completely still. It made Paxon wonder what was required of you even to know that creating magic was something you might be able to do.

When she was finished, she stepped back. "No wards seem to have been laid. I don't think it's even locked."

"That doesn't sound right," Paxon observed with a questioning glance at Lariana.

"The wards will be laid farther in," she said. "Traps, too. He never does anything the obvious way. Besides, he couldn't come and go easily if the passageways were protected by magic. And he couldn't abide that. He wants to be able to flee quickly if he needs to, not be slowed by having to spend time taking down wards and avoiding traps."

Paxon nodded slowly. "You seem to know him well."

"I've had time to study him." She hugged herself as if the idea of it made her uncomfortable. "I understand how he thinks."

"Let's just go in," Avelene declared, yanking down on the iron handle. The door released and swung inward soundlessly. She looked at them, her lavender eyes bright. "There. That wasn't so difficult."

Maybe not, Paxon admitted wordlessly, but he was still uneasy. As they moved into the darkness, Avelene took the lead, using a pale white werelight balanced on the tips of her fingers to illuminate their way. The entrance led to a long, narrow corridor that branched in several directions. Without hesitating, the girl chose the one that continued straight ahead, and they followed it past numerous rooms, most with their doors closed, but a few left open to reveal dark, windowless spaces. The corridor branched again and then again. They were in a maze, and Paxon quickly realized how easily they could become lost.

Finally, they reached a large open space that spread away into the darkness. A high ceiling rose into shadow, and the walls were stripped and windowless. Furniture had been piled against the walls so that the center of the room was left bare and empty.

Lariana started ahead once more, but Paxon took hold of her arm and pulled her around to face him. "Wait a minute," he said, his instincts suddenly on edge.

"What is it?" Avelene hissed.

The Highlander shook his head. "I don't know. Something."

Lariana freed her arm from his grip. He glanced at her questioningly, but she said nothing, just glared at him. "Avelene," he said. "Can you detect anything?"

The Druid placed her werelight on his fingertips, a cool flameless glow that tingled slightly but otherwise left no impression. He held it up for her as she began making small gestures that caused the air to stir and fresh light to appear and then illuminate the dark corners of the box-like chamber. The blue streaks reappeared, weaving their way along the surface of the walls and across the ceiling. She continued her search for a few minutes more and then shook her head.

"There is *something*, but I can't tell what it is. Or even *where* it is. Complex magic of an unfamiliar form—very sophisticated. But it doesn't seem threatening. I don't detect any edges or teeth to it."

Lariana stepped forward. "We're wasting time. If he's here, he'll be just ahead." She pointed. "Come on, I'll show you."

She started across the room before either Paxon or Avelene could prevent it, her determined stride carrying her quickly beyond their reach. When she was perhaps fifteen feet ahead, still illuminated by the glow of the werelight, she turned.

"You should have listened to me," she called over her shoulder. "Now you have to trust me, like it or not."

Then abruptly the floor opened up beneath her, and she disappeared.

In a building deep in the heart of the city, Arcannen sat hunched over a small table, writing on a piece of paper. A smokeless lamp burned away the shadows that threatened to close in on him, the edges of its light reaching to where Reyn Frosch sat watching from across the room.

They had arrived in Sterne earlier that evening, and Arcannen had brought him straight here. But then the sorcerer had gone out again, explaining as he left that he had important preparations to make for Lariana's arrival. On his return, several hours later, he had gone right to work on the invitation. It appeared to Reyn that they were inside a complex of living spaces, but it was hard to be certain because no one else seemed to be around. Their new quarters were spare, but adequate—a central living space, a room with two beds, and a few other pieces of furniture.

"What are you doing?" the boy asked finally.

"Extending an invitation," the other answered. He didn't look up. "Are you hungry?"

Already impatient and agitated over what was happening—even without knowing for certain what that was—Reyn had become increasingly unhappy as the minutes dragged by.

"I don't need to eat," he snapped. "I need to know what's going on. I need to know what's happened to Lariana. Are you going to tell me any of this?"

"Soon. Why don't you get some sleep? This might take a while."

"What might take a while? What are we doing?"

Arcannen looked up now. "Waiting on Lariana. Didn't I already tell you that? Didn't I say she would be coming to join us later? Well, later isn't here yet. Try exercising a modicum of patience. You're tired and you're not thinking straight. Get some sleep."

Reyn slouched in his chair. "I'm not tired."

"Just unhappy. A condition entirely of your own making. My regrets." The sorcerer went back to writing. "Do what you choose. But stop complaining."

The boy waited a few minutes, then he rose and walked over to the small pantry area and looked in the cold box. It contained cheese, bread, and a handful of dates that still looked edible, along with a container of ale. He found a plate and a glass in the cupboard. He still wasn't hungry, but it was something to do. Carrying his meal with him, he returned to his chair, sat down again, and began to eat.

More than once he had considered trying to leave. *Escape,* he corrected himself, since by now he considered himself as much a prisoner as anything else. Arcannen was determined to avenge himself against Usurient and the Red Slash, and use Reyn to help him. Nothing the boy said to prevent his involvement seemed to help. The sorcerer's plan, whatever it was, remained a mystery—and his own role equally so. Even Lariana's purpose was shrouded in hints and suggestions of deceit and trickery. He could not shake his suspicion that she was leading him on. He could not help thinking her commitment was not to him, no matter what she said; it was to Arcannen. He even wondered if they were lovers, and that possibility cut at him with a knife's edge. The idea of it was unimaginable, but it nagged at him nevertheless. Their relationship was clearly more than what either was telling him, and his relationship with both was clearly something less.

Across the room, the sorcerer had written out and thrown away three drafts of his mysterious invitation, dissatisfied with each effort. *Too many words,* the boy had heard him mumble earlier. Now he was at work on a fourth draft, his head bent to the task. Reyn wondered again what he was doing. It seemed to absorb him, his attention given over to it completely. Perhaps now was the time to work his way over to the door and simply slip out.

But that sort of thinking was not just foolish; it was dangerous. Lariana had warned him about going against Arcannen in even the smallest way, and while he might be questioning much of what she had told him, he was pretty sure of this.

Finally, the sorcerer finished a draft that satisfied him, and he lifted his head, leaned back in his chair, and stretched. "There. That will do. Now let's get some sleep. We might have a few hours."

Reyn grimaced, feeling petulant. "I'm not sleepy."

"You weren't hungry, either. But suit yourself. Just don't try to leave the room."

The sorcerer rose, walked into the bedroom, and lay down on one of the beds. Reyn watched him roll over until his back was turned and then listened as his snores began. He was asleep. This was the boy's chance. Just get up, walk over to the door, and leave. No hesitation, no sounds.

You could do it, he told himself. *You know you could.*

Yet something told him he couldn't. Arcannen wouldn't have left anything to chance. There would be wards or warnings that any such attempt would trip. As tempting as the opportunity might be, he knew he should pass it up.

He slouched in the chair, his mind working, his doubts and fears roiling in dark waves, and wished he had never started any of this. He should have found another way, back when he was still in Portlow and there was a chance. Now he was trapped, not only by the sorcerer's expectations and demands, but also by his attraction to Lariana. Even knowing she might not feel toward him as he had hoped, even believing it was all a game.

He was still worrying it like a dog would a bone when he fell asleep.

And found it waiting for him when a hand rested on his shoulder and shook him awake. "Reyn."

Lariana.

He opened his eyes to find her bending over him, her smile heartbreaking, the sound of his name on her lips so welcome it brought tears to his eyes.

She started to kiss him, but then Arcannen appeared, his dark shadow sliding into the light as he came up behind her to rest his hands on her shoulders, causing all the boy's doubts and fears to return in a rush so that he shied away from her touch.

"What word?" the sorcerer asked, eyes only for her.

"It went as expected," she answered, glancing back at Reyn, sensing his reluctance, her expression suddenly uncertain. "They wanted me to lead them to you, so I let them think I was. I followed your instructions, disappeared when the magic allowed it, and left them to find their way out. What happens now?"

"You go out again." He walked over to the table. Picking up the invitation he had taken such pains to compose, he brought it over, folded it twice, and gave it to her. "Take it to the Command Center at the Red Slash compound and present it. Don't linger, don't give them a chance to detain you. Now, go."

And with a final look at Reyn, her expression unreadable, she was out the door and gone.

Dallen Usurient was sitting alone in his office, trying to make sense of what had happened earlier on the coast of the Tiderace, attempting to put all the seemingly disconnected pieces together in a recognizable form. He had thought to sleep long ago, his escape from the ruins of Arbrox and flight back to Sterne having worn down what remained of his strength. His hands had finally stopped shaking, and the images he had carried back with him of the fates of his companions—the ones that had twisted and torn at his sanity for hours—had finally subsided.

But he was hardly whole. Nothing had turned out as expected save for one thing—Arcannen was dead. He knew the sorcerer was dead. He had killed him, had shot him to pieces with a handheld flash rip when he had finally appeared out of hiding and exposed himself. But the deaths of Mallich and The Hammer were terrible nightmares that would haunt him forever, and he could assume that Bael Etris had met a similar fate—though he would not take it for granted, not for a second.

But the boy and the girl—who were they? What sort of power did the boy possess that he could turn those animals against their handlers so effortlessly? Where had he come from? And the Druids! How had they found their way to Arbrox? Had they been tracking him all along, somehow alerted to where he was going and what he intended? Or had they learned of Arcannen's whereabouts through another source? Had they seen and recognized him before he had managed to get clear of them?

He stood up and paced the room for a few moments, trying to still the thoughts that roiled through his brain, sharp daggers that pricked and cut at his confidence. What did he do now? He had to deal with matters as they were, and he wasn't at all sure how to do that.

But Arcannen—Arcannen was dead. He clung to that as he would a lifeline, drawing on what comfort it offered him. The worst was past with the sorcerer dead. Whatever else threatened, that much at least was behind him.

He sat down again at his worktable and began considering choices for how he would handle his affairs from now on. Deny all involvement in whatever was discovered at Arbrox. After all, those who knew the truth were dead. Arrange to have the bodies discovered and file a report with the Federation Army High Command that did not implicate him. Track down Bael Etris, if he was still alive, and quietly put an end to him. Pretend that he knew nothing . . .

A knock sounded at his door. He jumped, instantly enraged. "What is it?" he screamed.

His aide entered, his face terrified, holding a folded sheet of paper. "A street boy just delivered this. I was told you would want to see it right away. Said it was a matter of life and death."

Usurient rose. "Give it to me." He snatched the paper away and motioned his aide out of the room. When the man was gone and his door closed again, he opened the paper slowly and read:

ARBROX IS HERE
Sunrise
Horn of Honor

That was all. But that was enough. Usurient read it again and again, trying to make it mean something other than what it clearly did. No amount of twisting or turning of its words could change the essential truth of it.

Arcannen was alive.

And Arcannen was summoning him.

He looked down and found that his hands were shaking once more.

24

R EYN FROSCH WAS STILL STRUGGLING WITH THE mix of emotions generated by Lariana's abrupt reappearance and even more abrupt departure; everything had happened so quickly, there was no time to sort it out. Then Arcannen said, "How would you like to have the answers to all those questions you've been asking?"

It caught the boy by surprise; he hadn't expected any answers at all until the girl returned and wouldn't have been surprised if Arcannen had continued to put it off even then.

But Arcannen led him over to the table on which he had composed his mysterious invitation and sat him down. Taking a seat across from him, the sorcerer leaned forward. "We are done with games, boy. We are done with practice. What happens next is a real test of your abilities. Can you stretch your magic in a way you haven't tried and master it in the process? We're going to find out tonight."

Reyn felt his throat tighten. *Tonight?* "What do you mean? What's going to happen?"

The sorcerer cocked his head slightly. "You've done well enough with images, but your magic has so much more potential. Let me tell you a little about its history. Once you understand what is possible, you might be better able to accept what I intend for you to do."

He leaned back again, his gaze drifting off into the shadows of the room. "Lariana's worked so hard with you. Tell me. Do you like her? It appears that you do. A great deal, in fact. Isn't that so, Reyn?"

"I like her a lot," the boy answered. There was no point in pretending otherwise. Surely Arcannen knew as much. "But you already know that, don't you."

He made it a statement of fact rather than a question. Arcannen laughed. "I do. And I'm happy for you. But let's leave that subject for later discussion. The wishsong, then. The wishsong appeared centuries ago, an aberration created by Wil Ohmsford's wrongful use of the Elfstones. It first manifested itself in his children. We've discussed this. What matters is that the sister, Brin, could make use of his gift in almost any way she chose. With it, she could change the world around her, altering the look and feel and behavior of other living things. She could literally bring a seedling to bloom or cause that very same bloom to wither."

Arcannen paused. "Do you see what I am saying? She had the power of life and death at her command. What she could do to flowers, she could also do to humans and animals. There were no limits to her abilities. I think it likely there are no limits to yours, either."

Reyn shook his head. "I don't want that kind of power."

"But you already have it! You've already exercised it, willingly or not. You've shown you can impact people by using your magic. You've caused people to die! Even if you didn't intend it, you can't deny the fact. You command power enough to cause people to explode at the sound of your voice. If you chose to, you could cause them to wither like flowers. You need to accept this, and then you need to find a way to control it. Because sooner or later, it's going to break free again. If you recognize how it works, you have a better chance of being able to manage it. And not through manipulating images, but through contact with actual people, working through your difficulties by discovering how they can be managed."

The boy just stared at him for a moment, trying to take in what he was saying. "You're talking about experimenting on people? Testing my magic on them?"

"That's it exactly. That's how you learn. Fortunately, we have the right subjects for you to test yourself against. Men and women who believe in testing themselves against others, although mostly against those who can't fight back. Imagine their surprise when they come up against you."

"The Red Slash." He shook his head vehemently. "I won't do it."

"Oh, I think you will."

"You promised me I wouldn't have to kill anyone! You gave me your word!" Reyn felt a surge of desperation wash through him. "Did you lie to me about everything?"

Arcannen looked offended. "I lied to you about nothing. I've tried to help you. I've tried to teach you what having your magic requires of you. I'm still trying. We just need to advance your methods beyond make-believe."

"But you promised! You said I wouldn't have to kill anyone!"

"Did I say anything about you killing anyone? Are you listening to me or not? What I said was that you learn how to manage your magic through contact with real people, not through projecting images. I'm not asking you to hurt anyone."

Reyn shook his head. "That was what you said the last time. Look what happened there! These are trained soldiers; they'll have experience I don't! They won't let me do anything to them. They'll get behind me or slip past me, and then they'll kill me or I'll have to kill them! They'll come for me and you won't be there!"

He was practically hysterical. He could feel his control over himself slipping; he was on the verge of crying, already shouting in dismay. He was beginning to shake. But Arcannen reached out, took him firmly by the shoulders, and held him fast.

"You won't have to kill anyone—and I won't let anyone harm you. I will be right there with you, standing at your side the whole time. We won't be fighting our way through mist and darkness. We won't have to deal with rabid beasts and wild-eyed predators of the sorts we encountered before. The Red Slash and Dallen Usurient are soldiers. They'll come at us like soldiers, and we will treat them as such. But they must be made to face the consequences of their willful and egregious transgressions, Reyn. They can't be allowed to get away with murdering an entire village of innocent people. We're agreed on this, aren't we?"

The boy nodded reluctantly. "We're not agreed on how it should happen, though."

"Listen to me." He held a finger in front of Reyn's nose. "You won't have to hurt anyone. I promise you. I told you I wouldn't ask that of you. What happened in Arbrox was unavoidable—an accident, an unfortunate turn of events. But that won't be the case here. I will make sure of it. You just have to do what you're told. Just this one last time. Then, maybe you'll want to apprentice with me when this is finished—you and Lariana! Why not? I can teach you both about magic. I can train you."

There was nothing at this point that Reyn Frosch wanted less, but he kept his thoughts to himself.

Arcannen seemed to sense the boy's reluctance. His mood turned dark again. "Don't mistake the reality of our situation, boy. Don't think your troubles will be over even after you've mastered your magic. The Druids will still be looking for you. The Federation will still try to hunt you down. You'll always be a danger in their eyes, no matter how you change what happens with your gift. You frighten them. You are an aberration, and they want you gone. They've never stopped hunting me, so don't expect that it will be any different with you."

Reyn nodded slowly, mostly to show he understood, because he wasn't at all convinced his situation was the same as Arcannen's.

"Will you do as I tell you, then?" the other asked.

"You haven't told me what it is you want me to do yet."

"No, I haven't, have I?" He gave a weary sigh. "But, really, I shouldn't have to tell you. Not after what I've done for you. Not after all the help I've given you. It should be enough that I simply ask the favor." He paused, his gaze hard and fixed. "So why don't you just tell me you will do what I ask, and then I will tell you what it is."

Reyn stared, confused. "Just tell you I'll do it? Without knowing what it is?"

Arcannen nodded. "Yes, that's it exactly. Demonstrate a little gratitude for once. Show a little faith. Go on."

And if I don't? he almost said. But something in the other's look stopped him. "All right. I will do what you tell me."

"Now, that wasn't so painful, was it?" The sorcerer gave him a look. "You make everything so hard, even when things should be easy."

He shook his head in a remonstrative gesture. "Lean forward."

Reyn did so, stretching out over the table to meet the sorcerer halfway. As he did so, Arcannen placed an arm across his shoulders as he might have a child's. And as if someone else might hear, he began whispering in the boy's ear, revealing in detail exactly what was going to happen and what part Reyn was to play. As the whispered words filled his ears, the boy felt his horror grow by leaps and bounds, and he shuddered inwardly, fighting not to pull away in repulsion.

When Arcannen had finished, his smile was much wider and so frightening that the boy flinched at the sight of it. "Appalled, are we?" the other asked softly. "Hesitant, now that we've heard what's intended?"

Reyn couldn't make himself answer. He just stared at the sorcerer wordlessly.

"That's why obedience is so important. That's why I asked for your commitment first. That's why I insisted you give it. So you wouldn't be tempted to refuse me later." He paused. "You're not thinking of refusing me now, are you?"

Reyn shook his head, aware that any other answer would be a mistake. "No, I'm not refusing."

Arcannen nodded. "That's good. That's very good. But if you should be tempted at any point to change your mind, think carefully before you do. You wouldn't like what would happen if you crossed me."

He rose, came around the table, and gave Reyn a clap on the back. "I have to go, make some preparations. I want you to rest and be ready for when it's time. Dawn approaches. Think about what you need to do and how you will do it. Think about whatever mental preparations you should make. I need you to be strong for me when it's time. I need you to be able to make your magic work."

He crossed to the door and stopped, looking back. Reyn was still staring straight ahead and did not turn. "One last thing. About what I just said? If you should decide to disobey me, I will gut Lariana from neck to navel right in front of you."

Then he was out the door and gone.

Deep within the abandoned Federation army barracks, Paxon and Avelene were examining the floor through which Lariana had disappeared. They kept crisscrossing the stonework, searching for the bolt-hole they knew must be there, but try as they might they could not find a trapdoor or even a hint of whatever magic had served to provide her with an escape.

Finally, after long minutes had passed and nothing had been gained, Avelene called a halt. "That's enough. We're not going to find anything. Lariana's gone. Whatever magic was used to aid her, it's sophisticated beyond anything I've seen. This has to be the sorcerer's work."

"So the girl was lying to us all along," Paxon observed bitterly. "She's Arcannen's creature."

Avelene was looking around, distracted. "I think we can retrace our steps out of here if we can remember all the twists and turns. We should get started." She turned away, moving toward the door through which they had entered. "I don't think you should jump to conclusions about Lariana."

Paxon hurried to catch up, his anger hot and roiling within him. "What do you mean?"

"I'm just not sure what game she's playing yet. Maybe she's Arcannen's cat's-paw, but maybe she's got something else in mind. It's in the way she acts and talks, going back and forth, always straddling the fence. I can't quite make up my mind."

Paxon snorted. "Well, I can. Her loyalties lie in one place and one place only. With her own best interests. She'd turn on anyone if the opportunity presented itself."

"Maybe" was all Avelene said.

They left the room and passed down the corridor that had brought

them in and then down several more before finally reaching the doors
that would allow them to exit the building.

Doors that this time around were firmly barred.

Paxon slammed the palm of his hand against the metal in frustration. "We should have known. The plan was to delay us any way they
could."

"But not try to kill us," Avelene observed. "Interesting. That doesn't
seem like Arcannen."

Paxon stopped pounding and stared at the doors. "No, it doesn't.
What do you think?"

The lavender eyes fixed on him. "I think it is the same as before.
He *wants* us to try to break free."

"Another trap."

"I would not want to chance it."

The Highlander exhaled sharply. "What do we do?"

The Druid shook her head. "Find another way out."

"One of the other doors?"

She gave him a look. "I don't think so. I wouldn't trust them, either."

Paxon found himself wondering what the point of all this was.
Why had Lariana gone to the trouble of leading them into this complex? Couldn't she have found a way to lose them in the city without
going through all this? She was quick and smart; she could have gotten free at some point. Why pretend she was leading them to Arcannen? It just further convinced him that she was firmly allied with the
sorcerer and using Reyn for her own purposes.

Which would be Arcannen's purposes. Which would mean killing
Dallen Usurient. But she had insisted she was trying to help Reyn and
prevent him from having to kill anyone else. Was she lying or was
something else going on?

"We're missing something," he said suddenly.

Avelene gave him a look. "I'm listening."

"Why does Arcannen need the boy to help him kill Usurient?
Why can't he just do it by himself?"

"Maybe he has some special form of retribution in mind that requires the boy's help. Nothing too ordinary would suffice for someone like him."

"He still wouldn't need Reyn Frosch for that. What if we've been looking at this the wrong way? What if you're right about that special form of retribution but wrong about its target?"

The young woman stared at him. "What does that mean?"

"Well, think of it like this. If Arcannen doesn't need him to kill Usurient, maybe he needs him for something more complicated. What if Arcannen intends to kill not only Usurient but all the soldiers of the Red Slash? After all, the entire company carried out the massacre at Arbrox. Wouldn't Arcannen see them as equally responsible for what happened? Would he really confine his revenge to just Usurient?"

"So you think he needs the boy to help him because he's going after more than just one man? But how much help can he be, even with the aid of the wishsong's magic?"

"I don't know. I just have a feeling about this. He has to need Reyn or he wouldn't bother keeping him close. He found him and took him along and trained him. He's used Lariana to help him with all this. I think whatever he's got planned involves destroying the Red Slash entirely."

She thought about it for a moment. "Sounds to me like you're whistling in the dark. But on the off chance you might be right, we'll need to act quickly. He knows we'll find a way out of here soon enough, and he won't want us interfering with his plans."

"Will we? Find a way out of here?"

"Come with me. I have a thought or two myself. We're going back inside that room."

They retraced their steps through the complex to the chamber where Lariana had disappeared—Avelene in the lead, guiding them with use of her werelight—making their way back to the place they had last seen the girl. The werelight glimmered brightly against the shadows as the Druid held it up and peered around the room.

"We were looking at this wrong, too," she said suddenly. "Over here."

She led Paxon to a corner of the chamber, where a section of wall had cracked open just enough to reveal that it was a hidden door. "Ah," he said.

"We were fixated on what we thought we saw, which was Lariana dropping through a floor. But that was an illusion created out of magic. Arcannen left it in place here, and Lariana triggered it and then slipped out this door while we were distracted."

"So she knew it was there. She had to."

Avelene nodded. "She knew."

They eased through the doorway into a narrow tunnel that wound through several twists and turns before ending at a section of wall that Avelene quickly determined was there to provide concealment for another hidden door. She tested the portal for traps using Druid magic, found none, and, bracing herself, pushed on it until it opened outward into the night.

Paxon breathed in the fresh air, looking up at a clouded sky. "Very smart of you."

She pulled a face. "It took me entirely too long to see the obvious. You're the one who's sharp. I think you're right about what Arcannen intends. But I also think you're wrong about Lariana."

"Why do you keep saying that?"

"Call it instinct. There's something more complex at work in that girl than what we're seeing."

He shook his head. "What do we do now?"

She gave him a shove away from the building. "Haven't you learned anything, Paxon? Wherever we find the Red Slash, that's where we find the sorcerer. Let's hurry."

When the door to their quarters opened again, Reyn was expecting Arcannen's return. But it was Lariana who entered, and instantly Arcannen's final words came back to him with razor-edged clarity.

I will gut Lariana from neck to navel right in front of you.

But was that threat real or another ploy to gain his compliance? He stiffened as she turned to him, still suspicious in spite of his fears for her, still wary of the truth behind her role in what was happening to him. She saw the expression on his face and glanced around.

"Where is he?"

"He went out. He didn't tell me where he was going."

She gave him a hard look. "What's wrong? And don't try to tell me it's nothing. I know you well enough by now."

"Maybe it's me who doesn't know you."

She folded her arms. "Maybe you should tell me what you mean by that."

When he looked at her, even now when he knew what she might be, he was so unnerved that he had to look away again quickly. "I'm finding out some things I didn't know about you. Arcannen told me on the trip back. He said you and he . . ."

He stopped, unable to finish, not even really sure where he was going. What he wanted to say and what he was afraid might be true were getting all mixed up, and everything was coming out wrong.

She pursed her lips. "He and I what? Better finish that sentence, Reyn. Let's hear all of it."

With an effort, the boy pulled himself and his thoughts together. "It wasn't so much what he said as what he hinted at. That you and he . . . might be more than teacher and student. That your relationship might be something else. But it's not really that, either. It's how you seem to know so much that I don't. He tells you more than he tells me. You had a plan for finding us after we left you with the Druids. You and he had worked it out ahead of time. No one told me. I was worried sick about leaving you. I know he's told you other things, too. About his plans for Usurient. About what he intends for me."

She waited on him, saying nothing.

"It just feels like you're closer to him than you are to me, and I can't stand it! I was so certain about us in the beginning. I thought you and I would be . . . would have a chance at . . ." He trailed off. "You kissed me like it meant something! Like I meant something. I've stayed because of that, even when I thought I ought to go. I couldn't bear leaving you!"

He took a deep breath. "Just tell me if I'm wrong about all of this. Tell me if I'm being foolish."

She nodded slowly. "Well, you are definitely being foolish. But not in a bad way." She came over and sat next to him. "You liked it when we kissed, didn't you?"

"You know I did."

"Then you should know I did, too. That was real. That meant something to me, too."

Her perfect features crinkled momentarily, as if disrupted by an unpleasant thought. "In the beginning, when Arcannen came to Rare Flowers, I would have done anything to persuade him to take me away. It was important to me that I leave before I was thrown out. Before I was back on the streets. Before I was forced to do things I didn't want to do. I would have given myself to him, if he asked. I offered, in fact. But he wasn't interested. He isn't interested now. Arcannen sees people as pieces on a chessboard to be moved about as he thinks fit. He uses them to accomplish his ends. He doesn't bond with them. He doesn't feel love or desire or even friendship. People are there to serve his purposes. That's all. It's true of everyone, including you and me. So you can stop worrying about the nature of my relationship with him. It's not all that different from yours."

Reyn nodded. "But he suggested . . ."

"Yes, yes!" She made an impatient gesture. "He does nothing but suggest! He's so good at manipulation. Much better than I am, and I'm very good. I've had to be. He brought me with him to Arbrox because I know how to get people to do what I want. No, stay quiet. Just listen. Don't judge until you hear me out. He wanted you to fall in love with me so you would do what he wanted. So you would stay with him. So I did what I was told. I made you fall in love. At first, it didn't matter to me that you did. It was just something I had to do. But, gradually, it did matter. Now it matters so much I can't stand another minute of knowing what I am doing to you. Everything's turned around. It's all different!"

She seized his shoulders. "Look at me! Do hear me? Do you understand what I am telling you?"

He took a deep breath, his eyes fixed on hers. "I think so."

"Say it, then."

"You're in love with me."

"I'm in love with you. So now it's your turn. Do you still love me?"

He nodded. "I don't think it could be any other way."

"All right, then. I'll tell you the rest of it. Yes, I knew things you didn't. Arcannen confided in me but not about anything that really mattered in the long run. I didn't know what he was going to do with you in Arbrox. I didn't know how he was planning to use you. I did what he told me, but I didn't know. Do you still love me?"

"I do," he said firmly.

She leaned forward and kissed him hard on the mouth. She held the kiss for a long time, letting him feel the passion behind it.

"We have to get away from him," she said, breaking away. "We can't let this go on. He will use you to kill Usurient, but it won't stop there. He will continue to use you afterward. If not in the same way, then in some other equally abhorrent manner. Your magic is valuable to him; he wants it for his own!"

"I know." Reyn felt the world rush back in, the loss of her lips against his almost unbearable. "But it's much worse than you think. He intends to destroy the entire Red Slash brigade, all five hundred of them. Usurient is just the head; he wants the body as well. He told me so while you were gone." Reyn hesitated. "He also told me that if I didn't do what he wanted when it was time, he would kill you right in front of me."

She went white. "You see what I mean? He doesn't care any more about me than anyone else. I'm here to serve a purpose. He will use me in whatever way he can. He will do whatever it takes to make me fulfill his purpose."

"If we try to escape him now, he will hunt us down and kill us." Reyn kept his voice steady and his eyes locked on hers. "You know that, don't you?"

"It doesn't mean we can't try. It doesn't change what we have to do."

"I know. But I'm afraid. Afraid for you. Do you really love me?"

"I love you enough that I want to spend my life with you. Enough that I will give it up for you if I have to."

He smiled, the first smile he had allowed himself. "And I love you enough that I will find a way to permit the one and prevent the other."

He pulled her to him, and his arms went around her slender waist. "I won't let you go," he whispered. "No matter what, I won't."

25

THE BOY AND THE GIRL WERE STILL LOCKED IN their embrace when the door opened and Arcannen walked in. He gave them a momentary glance and continued on into the tiny kitchen area, where he began rummaging around for something to eat. "I hope this helps your preparations," he said.

Reyn did not reply, pulling back from Lariana, immediately intimidated. The girl just smiled. "Of course it helps. It's called motivation."

Arcannen shrugged, putting together some cheese and bread before carrying his meal over to the little table and beginning to eat. "You delivered my invitation?"

"Directly to his personal aide."

"Who didn't know who you were?"

"Who barely got a look at me. I was wrapped up and my face was dirt-smudged and covered. I was a street kid so far as he could tell."

The sorcerer nodded. "Then we're ready. Do you want something to eat before we go? Either of you?"

Neither spoke. Reyn was looking down, trying to find a way to keep his courage up. He was scared out of his wits, knowing what was coming, what he was expected to do. He hadn't discussed the specifics with Lariana, but Arcannen had made it plain enough. Reyn was to be responsible for rendering the Red Slash vulnerable to whatever form of rough justice the sorcerer had decided to mete out.

He was also certain that he wanted no part of it. But trying to get away with Lariana at this point was impossible. Arcannen would not let him out of his sight from here on in; they only had a few hours until dawn, when the confrontation would occur, and he would stay close to them. But even if Reyn had thought to challenge the other, he knew he lacked the confidence to use his magic against him. It wasn't that he didn't want to. It was his reluctance to engage in a life-and-death battle with the sorcerer. It was his fear that at some point he would falter, his distaste for what he was attempting strong enough to cause him to hold back, and against an opponent like Arcannen any hesitation would almost certainly be fatal.

He wished he were made of stronger stuff. But his only use of magic against others had been fueled by threats to his own life, which had caused an instinctive lashing out in self-protection. Any attack on Arcannen at this point would not be like that. It would have to be an aggressive, deliberate strike, and as such it was not something he was convinced he could manage to sustain.

Besides which, he was not at all sure he was the other man's equal, even with the wishsong to aid him. Arcannen was more experienced and likely better able. And he would be putting Lariana at risk, as well. Better, he believed, to bide his time and wait for the right opportunity. He would recognize it when he saw it. He just needed to be patient.

Even knowing, as he did, that time was running out.

Even knowing he had no idea what sort of opportunity he needed.

"Maybe you should eat something," Lariana whispered to him, echoing Arcannen's suggestion.

But he wasn't hungry and didn't think he could keep anything down even if he tried. It was taking everything he had just to hold himself together long enough to try to get through what lay ahead. His mind was working madly, his thoughts running rampant, as he fought to stay calm enough to think about what he might do if he was given even the smallest chance to stop what was going to happen.

Whatever he did, saving Lariana was his main concern. Setting her free from the sorcerer's domination had to be the end result of anything he might try.

I love you enough that I will give up my life for you, she had said to him.

She would, too. He knew she would. And he would do the same for her, if that was what it took to save her.

Arcannen rose and came over to where they were sitting, dragging over a chair to join them. He sat down heavily, but his lean face was wreathed in a smile. "Time to examine the larger picture, children," he declared.

The boy and the girl exchanged an uncertain glance. "Oh, don't worry," he continued. "It isn't anything you probably haven't already considered. I just need to reaffirm for you what the purpose of today's exercise with the Red Slash will mean in the days to come."

He leaned forward, resting his elbows on his knees, assuming a decidedly vulture-like look when hunched over in his dark robes. "Word will travel quickly before the day is out. It will reach every city, hamlet, and village in the Four Lands. The mighty Red Slash, pride of the Federation army, has been destroyed! Not by another army or even a smaller force. But by two men, each a powerful wielder of magic, each a determined antagonist to those who would prefer magic banned throughout the world and see those who practiced it brought to their knees. The message will be clear. You come after us—those rare few of us with the skills and talent to use magic—at your peril. You lack the grit and the experience and the means to harm us. Hunting us down will only bring an end to your lives, not to ours."

"If we live out the day," Lariana interrupted. "There is every chance we won't, given what you intend to try doing."

"Ah, but you don't actually *know* what I intend, do you? The fact is, the odds are so completely in our favor that I see no real obstacle to our success. I have kept the details from both of you so that you wouldn't have to think on them until it is time. I leave nothing to chance. I take no unnecessary risks."

He paused. "Assuming that Reyn can indeed control his magic as both of you have led me to believe, we will be successful. And you can do that, can't you?"

He spoke directly to Reyn, who looked at the floor, saw his chance for saying otherwise slip away from him like a shadow before light, and nodded. "I will do what is needed."

"There!" Arcannen sat back. "The amount of magic required is extreme, but not beyond your capabilities, and the whole plan should take no more than a handful of minutes. We will work as a team, you and I. We will feed off each other's energy. But the best is what will come later. Because this doesn't end here. No, this is where it begins!"

As Lariana warned, the boy thought. *Of course it begins here. Of course it will continue. And it won't end until I am dead, killed one way or another. Which will not be at a time of my choosing. All the choices will be made by him.*

The sorcerer was already talking again. "Your training will begin in earnest after this. I will take you on as my apprentice and show you all the wonderful things you can do with your gift. Lariana will be my helper and your companion. We will be a family, the three of us—one bonded not by blood, but by common purpose."

"To what end?" the girl pressed. "You have a larger goal in mind, do you not?"

"I do. I would finish another matter long left in limbo. I would gain control of the Druid order and see it become the force it was always intended to be. It is an accomplishment that I almost realized once before. This time, when I pick up the loose threads, I will see it to a successful conclusion. I will see the Druids placed under my leadership or I will see them destroyed."

"I don't want any part of this!" Reyn blurted out, unable to stay silent any longer. "I don't care anything about the Druids!"

Arcannen nodded patiently. "Of course you don't. Right now you don't. But that will change. You will come to see them for what they are—rapacious, controlling, self-centered, and dictatorial. They want all the magic for themselves, all that exists or might one day exist, and they will do what they need to do to gain possession of it. There will be no consideration given for you or me or anyone who is not a part of their precious order. What care they for the likes of us? You've seen how they are already. They almost killed you back in Portlow. They've hunted you ever since. Look at Lariana! She was fortunate to be able to escape them before they could hurt her! If we hadn't made plans for that eventuality, they might be using their dark arts against her right this moment!"

His eyes shifted. "Isn't this so, Lariana?"

She nodded slowly. "I was fortunate to be able to slip away from them when they weren't paying close attention."

"Because you knew, as I did, that they would have used you against Reyn!" he snapped triumphantly.

At one time, Reyn Frosch might have believed this. But not now. Not given what he had come to realize about Arcannen. Whatever their intentions, the Druids had done nothing to threaten or harm Lariana in any way. She hadn't said much about the details of her journey back to Sterne with them, but he was convinced it wasn't anything like what Arcannen was suggesting.

"How soon do we leave?" he asked abruptly.

The sorcerer gave him a sharp look and then stood. "Why not right now? Come, children. Let's make history!"

And together, they left their hiding place and went out into the night.

Paxon and Avelene approached the Red Slash barracks cautiously, noting from some distance away the activity taking place. It was early morning now, less than two hours before sunrise, and normal people were sound asleep in their beds. Not so these soldiers. The entire compound was brightly lit and alive with sound and movement. Shouts and cries and a rolling out of weapons and gear signaled ongoing preparations for a major mobilization. The Druid and the Highlander watched what was happening from the rise on which they stood, looking down over the buildings and parade yards where the men and women of the company hauled and loaded and fell into their perfect formations, one by one.

"What do we do now?" Paxon asked Avelene.

She pursed her lips. "We go in. We find Usurient and talk to him." She gave him a glance. "Don't worry. We aren't the reason for all this. We don't have anything to fear."

He wasn't so sure, thinking back on the encounter at Arbrox. But there was no way to reach the Red Slash Commander other than by walking through the compound gates. A conversation of some sort was necessary, if only to give warning that he and his soldiers were in danger.

"We could just wait and watch," he said slowly, musing on it. "We could shadow him and find out what he's about. It should become clear soon enough."

"Wait too long and we risk losing Arcannen yet again." She shook her head. "I think we need to speak with the commander before he does anything precipitous."

Paxon shrugged. It wasn't his place to make this decision, and his purpose in being here was to protect Avelene. He would do what that required.

They left the rise and proceeded to the front gates, which stood open waiting to disgorge the soldiers and their equipment. It was an awful lot of personnel and armament for an encounter with one man, a boy, and a girl, Paxon thought. Either Dallen Usurient knew more about the magic capabilities of the three than Paxon, or this was about something else entirely. Whatever the case, it felt like there was an element of real fear involved. The air was thick with the taste and smell of it; the frenetic behavior of the soldiers testified to its presence.

Scared men were dangerous men, Paxon thought as they reached the gates. Avelene had better watch herself.

Guards stepped forward to intercept them, weapons raised. "The compound is closed to outsiders. Turn around," one said.

Avelene ignored the command, stepping forward to confront him. "Tell Commander Usurient the Druid and her companion from Arbrox are here to speak with him. Tell him we have information he needs."

The guards looked uncertainly at each other. "Do it," she snapped, her tone flat and hard.

One left immediately, hurrying away. The other stood where he was, blocking their way and looking decidedly self-conscious about it. Avelene held her ground, standing right in front of him, refusing to give way. Long minutes passed, and finally the first guard returned, his face stricken.

"Come this way," he said when he was still ten feet away from them, almost as if he was afraid to come closer.

He turned away at once, not bothering to look back to see if they were following him. Paxon and Avelene glanced at each other and set off in pursuit, surprised at a reaction that seemed equal parts fear and revulsion. These were hardened soldiers, not inexperienced boys, and time in the Federation army usually gave them an advantage over whoever or whatever they might come up against. So it was a surprise to both the Druid and the Highlander that the soldiers they had just encountered should seem so intimidated.

"Watch yourself," Paxon whispered to Avelene at one point.

He was uneasy about this entire business, but more so now because of the reaction of the soldiers. As they made their way through the mobilized compound, he kept shifting his gaze, taking everything in, looking for any suggestion of a potential threat. But everyone seemed so caught up in their efforts to organize whatever effort was under way that almost no one even bothered to glance at them.

When they reached a large building at the center of the compound, the guard opened a door leading in and stood waiting for them to enter. Once they were inside, he closed the door behind them.

"What is it you want?" a disembodied voice demanded. "Haven't you caused enough trouble?"

Dallen Usurient walked out of the shadows at the rear of the room to face them. His visage was clouded by displeasure and frustration, clearly annoyed to have to deal with what he saw as just another distraction.

"You seem to have recovered from your experience at Arbrox," Avelene observed. "I assume you know how much danger you're in?"

The Red Slash Commander made a dismissive gesture. "None at

all. I have to inconvenience myself with this sorcerer and his grandiose plans for my demise, but that won't require much effort. Unless you've come to pick up where you left off in Arbrox, I don't have to worry and we have nothing further to talk about."

"You tried to kill us back there," Paxon pointed out.

"I didn't know who you were!" Usurient's voice was shrill. "I saw what Arcannen did to my companions and I panicked. I should never have gone along on that trek in the first place. But I thought I might be able to help. Or at least keep the men I sent from making fools of themselves. I was wrong. Is there anything else we need to discuss? I have a lot to do to get ready for sunrise."

"What happens at sunrise?" Avelene asked.

He looked at her in surprise. "You don't know? I thought that was why you were here." He fumbled in his pocket and produced a crumpled piece of paper. "He sent me this earlier tonight."

He passed the paper to the Druid. She took it, unfolded it, and read its few words before passing it to Paxon. "Where is this Horn of Honor?" she asked. "What is it?"

"It's a monument to fallen soldiers that sits in the Federation burial grounds, out on the bluff above the city."

"Have you secured it?"

"The moment I received this note. What difference does it make to you? You're not invited to the party."

Avelene shook her head. "You should let this invitation go unanswered. You should step aside and let Paxon and me handle it. We're better equipped to deal with Arcannen."

"Step aside? For one man? I should have taken the Red Slash back to Arbrox and squashed him like a bug in the first place! I wasted my time on those hunters. Now get out of here!"

Avelene never moved. "Do you know what he intends? Because we do. He intends to wipe your Red Slash off the map."

Usurient stared at her. "That's ridiculous."

"He has a boy with him who has command of a very powerful magic called the wishsong. He can affect anything if he decides to use it. We think Arcannen holds you responsible for the deaths at Arbrox, and he intends to avenge those who died by eliminating their killers."

"Soldiers, not killers," he corrected her. "And what he intends and what he can accomplish are two entirely different things. He is an enemy of the Federation, and I have been charged with bringing him to the proper authorities to answer for his crimes. Or, if he decides to make a fight of it, to be sure he doesn't ever do so again."

"I repeat," Avelene said, "let us take care of this. If he thought you had any chance of stopping him—even with your entire command backing you—he would never have come here and offered you this challenge. He is very dangerous. Much more so than you think. We have faced and fought him twice now, Paxon and I. So let us use our skills and experience to stop him. Don't risk your soldiers."

The Red Slash Commander hesitated, and Paxon could tell he was bothered by what she said. He had enough experience with the sorcerer to know that Arcannen was nobody's fool and not given to rash behavior. He would have a plan. But then his demeanor changed, his anger resurfacing to sweep aside all other emotions and bury every consideration but one—putting an end to his enemy once and for all.

"Tell you what. You go back to mixing potions and sacrificing lizards and I will go back to soldiering." His eyes were suddenly empty and dangerous. "Now get out of here. I don't want you underfoot when things become unpleasant."

Avelene straightened; her slender form was rigid as she glanced at Paxon. Then she looked back at Usurient. "You are making a mistake, Commander."

"Yes, well, it's my mistake to make and answer for. I'm prepared to do both. But you're not going to be satisfied with my answer, are you? You're not going to accept it." He shook his head. "Wait here."

He walked to the door and called out. Seconds later an entire squad of soldiers had crowded into the room, all of them carrying weapons, all of these weapons pointed at Paxon and Avelene. The Highlander gave no thought to drawing his sword. It was pointless to think of fighting where there was nothing to be gained by doing so.

"Take them to the guardhouse and lock them inside," Usurient

ordered. "Relieve this one"—he pointed to Paxon—"of his blade before you do. If they try to escape, stop them. An hour after sunrise,
you may release them."

He gave them a critical look. "I don't trust you. Or Druids in general, for that matter. You constantly interfere in things that don't concern you. You might try to interfere in this. You have that look about
you. So, yes, I've changed my mind about letting you leave. I need to
be assured that you won't get underfoot. And, yes—before you question it—I can do this. You may have diplomatic immunity from our
beloved Prime Minister—as I suspect you do—but it doesn't extend
to this base and my command. Here, there is only one law, and it's
mine. Now good-bye."

They took Paxon's sword, and then he and Avelene were escorted
back outside on a short walk to a solid stone-and-iron structure that
could hardly be mistaken for anything but a prison. They were led
inside and placed in one of the cells, a cramped space empty of everything but a cot and a chamber pot. A heavily barred window let in
light through a two-foot-square hole. The soldiers backed out carefully, closing the heavy iron door behind them and sliding the crossbar into place.

In the ensuing silence, the Druid and the Highlander faced each
other.

"They don't really think they can keep us in here, do they?" Paxon
asked.

Avelene gave him a look. "Who knows what they think? What
they think doesn't matter. Only what we think matters."

"Well, I think we can walk out of here anytime we want," he said.

"But that isn't the trick, is it?"

"No? Then what is?"

"The trick is to leave without them knowing it."

He nodded. "That stands to reason. Unfortunately, I don't happen
to know that trick."

She gave him a wink. "I do."

.   .   .

The Horn of Honor was a huge stone monolith engraved with the names of those soldiers stationed in Sterne who had perished committing particularly memorable acts while in service to the Federation army. The memorial stood at the far end of a broad plateau that overlooked the city proper and the broad sweep of the Prowl River directly below. The plateau itself served as the resting place for all of Sterne's Federation soldiers, whether or not their names were engraved on the Horn, if at some point they had been stationed in the city. All were memorialized by small squares of white marble that bore their names and beneath which their cremated remains were preserved in tiny boxes.

This night, the plateau was filled with members of the Red Slash. They stood in loose formation all across the bluff, gathered by squads and brigades, filling the open spaces between the stone markers, surrounding the Horn on all sides. The entire command was present, save for those few left behind to maintain a presence within the barracks.

At their front, standing just apart and facing toward the head of the roadway that led upward to the bluff, was Dallen Usurient, resplendent in his scarlet dress uniform, his posture erect and rigid, his hands clasped behind his back to conceal the handheld flash rip he was hiding within the sleeve of his great coat. He wanted to appear unafraid at the prospect of a confrontation with Arcannen while at the same time remaining prepared for it. By now word of what they were doing and on whom they were waiting had spread through the ranks. A few, perhaps more, would be frightened, if only by the rumors they had heard. So he must do what he could to keep his soldiers calm; he must set a good example.

He glanced around briefly, taking in the spectacle of the entire Red Slash standing ready to fight. They bore weapons of every sort— blades and crossbows, spears and darts, flash rips and rail slings— strapped and sheathed or drawn and held ready, a formidable challenge to any enemy. They provided a spellbinding sight, a tableau worthy of an elite fighting unit. Torches burned at the perimeter of the burial ground, their uneven spray of firelight casting shadows in all directions, layering the landscape with intricate patterns. The faces of his soldiers glowed red and yellow; some were colored almost brown by the flames. It gave them an otherworldly look, an alien appearance that brought a shiver to his spine.

Where are you now, Arcannen Rai? How will you react to this when you come face-to-face with it?

He was anxious to find out, eager for the first time since he had received the other's note, confident that whatever the sorcerer sought to do by arranging this confrontation would end badly for its instigator. This would be no Arbrox. This would not be a repeat of what had happened to Mallich and his men. No amount of games and tricks would fool this many experienced men and women into reacting foolishly. No type of magic would cause them to turn and run.

No, it would end here. It would end with Arcannen's long-overdue death and the slow disintegration of his corpse after it had been hung from the city walls.

He was looking forward to it. He was anxious to watch it happen.

He started at sudden movement on the roadway before him. Shadows appeared. Three figures, faceless black forms, emerged from the night. The firelight illuminated them with its inquisitive flicker as they approached and revealed their features.

Dallen Usurient smiled.

Arcannen Rai was here.

26

REYN FROSCH WAS FEELING THE FIRST TWINGES OF fear as he climbed the road leading to the bluff where a blaze of torchlight lit up the whole of the sky in an eerie orange-and-yellow glow. At first, it was difficult to determine what was happening, the light flickering and dancing across its black backdrop, erasing the softer glow of moon and stars and revealing in garish color the wisps of cloud that hung overhead in the windless air like strange elongated birds. It was only when he came closer to the end of his journey that he could discern the light's source, and then glimpse the heads and spear points of the Red Slash soldiers revealed in a sea of shifting shadows like sea creatures risen from the deep.

"You remember what you are to do?" Arcannen whispered out of the side of his mouth.

The boy nodded, unable to speak.

"You can do this, can't you? You can be strong enough when it's needed?"

Again, his nod.

Although Lariana was walking next to him, she did not reach to take his hand when he silently willed her to do so. He felt overwhelmed by what waited, even before being able to take its exact measure. But when he saw the whole of it—five hundred soldiers crowded together across the heights, their faces lit by the torchlight in strange colors and their weapons on fire with the reflection of the flames—he felt all the strength go out of him and his courage turn to water.

"What a glorious sight!" the sorcerer whispered.

Reyn wanted to turn around immediately. What chance did they stand against so many? The soldiers seemed to be everywhere, these men and women of the Red Slash. They filled the burial ground with their dark presence. This was suicide. Yet he kept walking, kept his feet moving, knowing there was no choice but to go forward. Any deviation now would doom both Lariana and himself. Neither would survive Arcannen's wrath. They had been clearly seen by now, the eyes of the hundreds turned on them, and he could imagine the affront—the disdain!—these men and women felt at this foolish challenge. Three against hundreds! It was a fool's chance. It was ridiculous. The outcome was a foregone conclusion.

Yet Arcannen seemed not the least disturbed. If Reyn did as he was told, the sorcerer insisted, all would be settled before the sun had fully risen. Already, the boy could see glimmerings of first light in the distance, beyond the bluff and the firelight, illuminating the ragged outline of the mountains east. He closed his eyes momentarily against what he was feeling, the prospect of his fate a dark shadow descending upon him like the sky falling.

He knew what he was expected to do. Arcannen had explained it to him as they walked, his voice kept low and soft so that only the two of them could hear. Lariana was not permitted to listen in, and Reyn had been given no chance to confide in her. His part in this effort was crucial, the requirements of his magic's use enormous. But Arcannen assured him that such use had been made before, and that his heritage of the magic made him equal to the task.

"You are no less able than those who came before you. You are no less endowed with their power. Use it as I have told you. Bind these creatures and hold them fast; do not waver in your strength, do not give thought to what you witness afterward. Do this, and your future is assured."

By which he meant that although Reyn would live, his life hence-forth would belong to his mentor. What he was not saying was that the boy would never be free of the legacy he would forge by his magic's dark use; he would be a killer of men and women, forever bound to a history he would write in blood and death this night. He and Lariana would have each other, but only on Arcannen's terms and only until their usefulness was at an end. Then they would be cast aside, broken and hollowed out, emptied of everything good and decent.

He would not stand for it, he told himself, enraged. He would not allow it to happen.

Yet here he was, atop the bluff, walking toward the man in the scarlet dress uniform. The Commander of the Red Slash struck a dominant pose as he watched them approach, his expressionless face revealing nothing. But his eyes spoke for him. There was no kindness in those eyes, no hint of pity or forgiveness, no trace of compassion. He would let them come until they were close enough to be danger-ous, and then he would crush them as a man's foot would a scattering of ants.

"Begin," Arcannen whispered suddenly.

Without stopping to think about it, Reyn summoned the wish-song, his voice soft and unsteady in its modulation as he brought his magic to life. He did not attempt to employ it yet; he had been in-structed to wait on that. Instead, he was to cause it to build within him. He was to gather and hold it at the ready, and, when directed to do so, to employ it against these men and women in the way Arcan-nen had instructed.

But already he was having trouble. His efforts were forced and his willingness to act was compromised. The magic spread through his body in jagged lurches, an uneven and uncomfortable presence. He pushed ahead, but he could tell it was a broken, fragmented sum-moning and would likely fail him when it mattered.

"Dallen Usurient!" Arcannen called out to the man in scarlet.

"You should never have come!" replied the other.

"You should never have murdered the people in Arbrox! If you had shown even the least compassion, I would not be here."

"And yet here you are, and you will shortly be the worse for it!"

Arcannen stopped, the boy and the girl at his side. They were perhaps fifty feet away from Usurient, and there were soldiers spread out on either side of them now, all watching closely, their weapons held ready. They would have been told not to act except on command, Usurient confident in their strength and certain of their readiness to act when it was necessary. Arcannen had told the boy he could depend on this.

"It is his pride in his soldiers that will lead him to his death," the sorcerer had said. "His fall will be of his own doing."

Reyn continued to build his magic, feeling it spread through him from toes to fingertips until the aura of its still-inaudible sound cloaked him with its vibration. Still, he struggled with holding it together, with smoothing it out and keeping it pure. Still, he fought to ready it for the use he had been told to make of it.

And still, it neither responded nor felt quite as it should.

"If he were to strike us down the moment he saw us, he could save himself," Arcannen had said to the boy. "But he will not do that. First, he will demonstrate his superiority—to himself and his soldiers and us. He will command the stage as an actor in this play before he brings down the curtain. He will revel in his sense of power. He is obsessed with his need to reassure himself that he remains supreme and that I am vulnerable to him. He will want to make that evident before he acts. Watch closely."

Now, with the light cast by the torches just beginning to fade along the edges as the sunrise slowly brightened in the east and chased a reluctant night's darkness westward, Dallen Usurient brought out the handheld flash rip he had been hiding behind his back and pointed it at the sorcerer.

"You are a fool, Arcannen, to believe you could harm me here. Did you truly expect I would come alone? You have overstepped yourself this time. You have thrown caution to the winds of chance and hope, and neither has the power to save you."

"Do you think so?" Arcannen sounded interested. "Is that really true?"

"I think that and much more. What you thought you could accomplish by coming to me like this . . ."

Lariana stepped closer to Reyn. She reached over and took his hand in her own. Immediately Reyn felt the wishsong grow stronger within him. Just her touch was enough to steady him, to fuel his confidence and dispel his hesitation. His doubts and fears faded; his certainty in himself blossomed in the space of a heartbeat.

"I love you," she whispered.

" . . . with no other protection than this boy and girl, no weapons save a magic that has limits even for you . . ."

"Now!" Arcannen breathed at the boy.

Reyn released his magic in a rush, allowing it to spread outward in all directions from where the three stood clustered together at the forefront of the Red Slash command—an expulsion of barely audible sound that passed through the air like the gentle brush of a morning breeze and filled the empty spaces between the soldiers before enfolding them and sliding into their ears like whispers, acting on their bodies in ways of which they were not immediately aware.

" . . . remains a mystery to me, one that I expect I will never unravel, even after you are dead and gone and become no more than a fading memory . . ."

He stopped talking abruptly and his expression changed, revealing that he had sensed finally that something was terribly wrong. His voice faltered, his words turning guttural and vague and the hand that gripped the flash rip slowly lowering to his side.

All across the burial grounds and to the edges of the bluff, an eerie silence descended.

Avelene burned away the locking bar on their cell door and pushed it open. The halls within the blockhouse stood empty and silent, the darkness so complete that almost nothing of either one of them was visible to the other. She took the Highlander's arm and led him to the building door, his guide through the deep gloom. While he could see nothing, he could hear well enough, and there was a noticeable decrease in the sounds of movements and voices without.

Holding him by his shoulders, Avelene moved him to one side of the door and placed in his hand the hilt of his sword, which she had somehow managed to retrieve. *Just in case,* she whispered, her lips placed next to his ear. His eyes had begun to adjust, and he could see the slow, rhythmic movement of her hands, barely visible in the darkness, sliding over the closed door. When she was finished, nothing had changed. The door remained closed; the lock was still intact. He waited for her explanation, but she said nothing. Instead, she brushed him up one side and down the other, bringing together handfuls of air and dust, her movements suggesting that she was covering them from view.

She bent close again. "Walk with me. Say nothing, do nothing but maintain a steady pace. Watch me and only me. No one will notice you."

He wanted to ask how that could be and what difference it would make while they were trapped in this building. But he knew better than to challenge her. He knew he should simply trust. She waited for his response, and he gave it with a nod.

Taking his hand firmly in hers, she walked him to the ironbound door and through it as if it weren't there.

Just like that, he was back outside, the night air cool against his skin, the sky filled with stars and moonlight. Guards stood on either side of the prison door, and he blinked to be certain he wasn't imagining what had just happened. He had passed through a solid door, making an escape that no one had noticed.

Avelene led him through the camp, still holding his hand, avoiding contact with or proximity to anyone. The garrison had been reduced to a handful of soldiers, most of whom were engaged in cleaning up debris or carting off excess stores and arms. Guards at the prison and at the gates leading in were the only ones not occupied by these more mundane tasks. The bulk of the Red Slash was gone, marched out by Usurient to engage in a confrontation with Arcannen and his young charges. They would converge on the Horn of Honor, a place neither the Druid nor the Highlander knew how to find but which they believed must be somewhere close to the city proper. A burial ground for the fallen of the Federation army, Usurient had said. On a bluff overlooking the city.

They passed through the gates that had brought them in, and not once were they challenged. When they were outside and far enough away that they could no longer be seen, Avelene released Paxon's hand. As she did so, she disappeared momentarily and then reappeared as before.

"Nice trick," he said.

She nodded. "It involves displacement of air and light, which mostly are what allow eyes to determine what's there and what's not. In this instance, we were always half a step ahead of where we could be seen, allowing us to appear invisible."

Paxon looked around, searching for some indication of the way they should go. As he did so, she grabbed him and pointed.

Off to their left and high above the city, the sky was on fire, the flames visible even from where they stood.

"They'll be there," she said. "We'd better hurry if we expect to do any good."

He stepped in front of her suddenly. "One minute. Let's talk about this. What is it you think we can do if we mix in this? Stand up to Usurient and his Red Slash? Stop Arcannen from carrying out whatever plan he's made? What?"

"I don't know, Paxon!" she snapped, a flash of anger surfacing. "I just know we should do something besides stand around here!"

"We are in agreement about that." He kept his voice calm. "But we should have an objective before we blunder into the middle of a confrontation between people who want each other dead. There are too many of them, Avelene. We should agree now on our purpose in putting ourselves at risk."

She hesitated. "You want to help the boy, don't you?"

"I think that makes the most sense. He is the one worth saving."

"And not the girl?"

"As I understand it, the mission of the Druids is to find and recover wild magic in whatever form it takes. That would describe the boy."

"All right," she said. "The boy. But the girl, too, if we can."

"Not Arcannen?"

She kept her face deliberately expressionless. "Let the sorcerer and the Red Slash have their way with each other."

They set out at a fast trot, initially following the road they had turned onto coming out of the barracks, then angling this way and that along other roads and pathways that at last brought them to the base of the bluff. From there they were able to discover the solitary road that wound up to the plateau. Long minutes had passed by then, and they were both winded. They slowed by unspoken agreement to a fast walk, not wanting to run blindly into whatever waited. From atop the bluff, they could hear voices. Halfway up the road by now, they pressed ahead.

"Please agree to let me take the lead when we get there," Paxon whispered to her.

She glanced at him, frowning. "Why should I do that?"

"Because I am supposed to be your protector. I can't protect you from behind when the danger lies ahead."

"I am better able to protect us than you are. Or is this about what happened in Portlow with Arcannen?"

"This is not about the past."

"You still think I am not yet healed, that I can't be trusted."

He could barely mask his frustration with her. "I don't think that. I just want to do my job. But it's true," he added, "that I faced Arcannen and fought him to a standstill. Let me use what I learned from that."

She didn't say anything for a moment, then she gave a reluctant nod. "All right. You take the lead. No promises that I'll let you keep it, though."

He had to settle for that. He knew she wouldn't give him anything more. Whatever she claimed, she was looking to settle accounts with Arcannen. If the chance presented itself, she would take it. But she was dangerously overconfident, and that could easily lead to recklessness. He would have to watch out for her.

And the boy and the girl.

And perhaps even himself, if time allowed.

The voices atop the bluff had gone suddenly still. A deep, pervasive silence had fallen. Paxon and Avelene slowed automatically, suddenly wary of what might be happening.

Then everything exploded into violence and horror, and it seemed in that instant as if the whole world had gone mad.

Reyn Frosch stood motionless atop the plateau, facing out toward the hundreds of Red Slash soldiers who had suddenly lost all control over their muscle function. The wishsong magic had robbed them of their ability to move, severing the lines of communication between their brains and their bodies, turning them into living statues. The boy could feel the magic working, the vibrations that signaled its presence audible above the crackle of the torch flames burning along the perimeter of the Red Slash ranks. He could see the astonishment, anger, and fear reflected in the eyes of their commander and those men and women standing closest to him, and he experienced within himself a strange mix of elation and revulsion.

What he had done felt both satisfying and at the same time horrific, and his conflicting emotions warred within him.

Arcannen strode forward imperiously, coming to a stop directly in front of Usurient and peering into his helpless eyes. "What was that you were saying?" the sorcerer whispered. "That nothing can save me? That I am a fool?"

He reached into his robes and brought out a skinning knife. "What should I do with you?" he continued softly. "What sort of punishment should I visit on someone who destroys an entire village? Who kills innocent, helpless people? Should I skin you alive?"

He lifted the blade in front of the man's frantic eyes and ran its edge smoothly down the bridge of his nose, splitting it open. "How does that feel?" he asked, dipping his finger into the other man's blood and wiping it on his lips. "Sting a little bit, does it?"

Usurient was screaming, but no sound came from his paralyzed throat. Reyn felt sick. Watching Arcannen torture the helpless man was causing him to recoil from his own efforts, and already he could feel his control slipping.

"Stop this, Arcannen!" he heard Lariana hiss. "Reyn can't maintain his hold over the magic forever!"

She was genuinely angry, and it caused the sorcerer to turn. "Careful, Lariana," he cautioned. "It could just as easily be you on the receiving end instead of this pathetic creature."

But he put away the knife and stepped back. "Still, she's right, Dallen. Time slips away. You and I must say good-bye."

He stretched out his arm toward one of the torches, and a solitary brand flew from its iron stanchion into his hand. He held it before the other man teasingly and then touched its flames to his clothes and set him afire.

The flames engulfed Dallen Usurient immediately. They should not have burned with such fury, but Arcannen had used his magic to apply an accelerant. The Red Slash Commander lit up like a stack of dry kindling, his entire body engulfed by crackling flames. Reyn had a glimpse of the man's horrified face as he struggled in vain to break free of the killing fire; then he disappeared into the conflagration and was consumed.

Without giving his victim even the briefest backward glance, Arcannen walked out into the burial ground amid the remainder of the Red Slash soldiers and looked around. "In the time you have left, remember this!" he shouted at them. "You brought this on yourselves!"

His arms lifted and the sleeves of his robes fell away. Reyn watched the sorcerer's hands weave and gesture. Almost instantly flames leapt from the torches to land on the uniforms of the immobilized men and women. Like Usurient, they caught fire instantly, the flames spreading swiftly over their bodies to consume them.

Down through the ranks Arcannen strode, waving right and left as he passed by his victims, his gestures drawing streaks of flame to one soldier after another. A dozen, several dozen, a hundred, and then so many that it was impossible to count them, these human torches filled the bluff top. Fueled by flesh-and-blood tinder, the flames spread, creating a blaze of light that soon banished the shadows entirely. The sorcerer danced and whirled and laughed as he continued to wreak his vengeance, and all around him Red Slash soldiers died.

It took him no time at all to kill them, and Reyn could feel the weight of his participation in the carnage bearing down on him, crushing his spirit and his hopes, destroying his self-respect and his belief in himself as an essentially good person, rendering him as small and pitiful and dark as the man he was assisting in this atrocity. Making him an accomplice in murder, a wretch he had never thought to become. His voice faltered, and he could feel the magic begin to fail.

Lariana was next to him, grabbing at him, pulling him away. "That's enough! Stop it! We have to get out of here! Reyn, stop!"

He did not think he could. The magic was clinging to him in spite of his growing reluctance to hold on to it. It refused to let go, as if it were fighting to draw his breath from him. He might not have been able to free himself at all but for the sudden emergence of two figures— wraiths come up the road from the city—that materialized abruptly out of shadows and smoke. They staggered a bit as they encountered the full force of the wishsong's power, but the Druid threw up her defensive shield immediately, driving it back, keeping it at bay. With the magic already weakening as Reyn fought to respond to Lariana's urging, they passed through its field and advanced toward the boy and girl unimpeded.

"Reyn Frosch!" the Druid called out to him. "Wait!"

But Reyn had no intention of waiting. Although drained by his efforts, he seized Lariana's hand and bolted for safety, racing into the midst of the burning soldiers. *Escape!* It was all he could think about. He would not break free of Arcannen only to fall into the hands of the Druids. But what escape was there for him? What escape for Lariana? Escape to where? This hunt to find and make use of him would never end. Escape, as both he and Lariana had feared all along, was possible only in death.

And suddenly he knew what he had to do.

"Arcannen!" he screamed. On hearing him call out, Lariana wheeled back in astonishment. He ignored her. "Arcannen, help us!"

But the sorcerer was already aware of what was happening. The soldiers who had been frozen in place so completely only seconds earlier were able now to move again. Most bolted for safety, but a few of the more determined ones turned their weapons on him. Had a larger number of them responded, the result might have been different. But only a handful acted, and the sorcerer's magic was sufficient to deflect the arrows and spears and blue-tinged bolts of power emitted by the diapson-fueled weapons. When they saw that their efforts were having no effect, the soldiers fell back immediately. Arcannen ignored them, swirling green fire cradled in both hands as he strode toward Paxon and Avelene.

Paxon stepped forward to meet him, the Sword of Leah drawn and ready, its own magic surfacing, snakes writhing in the dark metal. Still several dozen yards away, Arcannen struck out, the green fire flung from his hands, expanding into much larger globes that slammed into the black blade and shattered in jagged shards. The resultant explosions were unexpectedly powerful, and Paxon was flung backward, staggered by first one blow and then the second.

Instantly Avelene rushed forward to take his place, hands coming up, her Druid magic springing to life.

No! Paxon thought at once.

But she never hesitated, responding to the inexorable urges that drove her to engage this man she both hated and feared, and she blocked his assault, throwing off the green fire and absorbing the force of his strikes. She kept her defenses firm, advancing on him with relentless purpose as he launched a third and then a fourth assault. Paxon was on his feet again, staggering up, still stunned from the force of the blows that had struck him, still woozy from their impact. His vision and his footing unsteady, he went forward anyway. He had to reach Avelene.

On the far side of the bluff, unexpected movement drew his eye. Two figures flew across the flats through the ranks of burning Red Slash. The boy and the girl were outlined clearly against the light. Paxon stared. What were they doing? They were headed for the edge of the bluff, a dead end!

Other pairs of eyes watched their flight as well, a handful belonging to those soldiers who had given up attacking Arcannen and were searching still for a way to get clear of the carnage. But on catching sight of the boy and the girl and recognizing them instantly as allies of the sorcerer, they remembered what the boy had done to them and reacted instinctively. Weapons came up, heavy flash rips and rail slings lifting and pointing, and for an instant time froze.

Then all the weapons discharged at once. The deadly missiles sped toward their targets, and the boy and the girl went down in a rain of jagged metal and diapson fire, struggled momentarily to rise before they were struck again, and, with their arms reaching out to each other, they collapsed and lay still.

Both Avelene and Arcannen had been distracted by the attack. Both had watched as the boy and the girl died. But it was the sorcerer who recovered quickest from the shock. Wheeling back toward the Druid, he lashed out at her with swift and certain accuracy, the green fire of his magic dispatched in a fiery streak that dropped her like a stone.

Paxon charged forward, horrified and enraged by what the sorcerer had done, determined that this time he would put an end to him. But Arcannen had already shifted his attention to the Highlander, throwing up a screen of fire and sending globe after globe of flaming magic streaking toward him. Paxon knocked aside the attacks, one after the other, his sword blade flashing in the torchlight. He smashed Arcannen's blows, scattering their fiery shards, pushing ahead even though he was all but blinded by the explosions and smoke. He could feel the force of the other's assault weakening, and he rushed forward until he reached the place where Arcannen had been standing only moments earlier . . .

Only to find him gone.

He wheeled about instantly, searching through the haze of ash and debris. *No,* he told himself in frenzied disbelief. *He can't have escaped! I can't have let that happen!* He swept aside curtains of smoke with his sword and pushed farther out onto the bluff. Then he slowed in dismay. All around him, human torches were collapsing into piles of charred flesh and bones. He covered his nose and mouth with his hand. The stench was horrific; he was standing in a slaughterhouse.

In the end he was forced to accept that he was standing there alone.

Sick at heart and fearing the worst, he hurried back to where Avelene lay sprawled on the ground. He knelt beside her, bending close, trying not to look at the ruin of her chest, trying not to see what was unavoidable. He saw her eyes follow his and heard the rough whisper of her voice.

"Should have . . . listened to you."

"I'm getting you off this bluff and down into the city," he said quickly, reaching down and lifting her into his arms, hearing her gasp with pain as he did so. "We'll find a healer for you."

"No," she whispered, her mouth close to his ear as he cradled her head against his shoulder, moving as quickly as he could toward the road leading down. "My . . . fault. Took my eyes off . . ."

She said something more, but he couldn't understand her. He was almost running now, ignoring the weight in his arms, putting aside all thoughts for himself. The soldiers who had survived the carnage on the bluff had disappeared. There was no one to stop him.

"Avelene?" he whispered. "Stay with me."

She might have responded. He couldn't be sure. He thought she was still breathing. He could feel her breath against his cheek.

And then he couldn't, and by the time he had reached the base of the bluff she was gone.

27

ONTHS PASSED. SUMMER DRIFTED INTO AU-
tumn, and the weather turned cold more quickly
than was normal, the year's end still weeks away
when the skies darkened and the first snows fell. There were yet flowers in many parts of the Four Lands, and they were hard-pressed to
survive the heavy white coating that layered them, though some
managed to struggle on.

In the Westland, deep within the Sarandanon, the farms that dotted
the Elven breadbasket that stretched from the Rill Song west to the
foothills of the Breakline were closing up shop for the year. Crops were
in, fields were turned over to wait for the next planting, animals brought
in, and equipment stowed. Families began planning visits to friends
and relatives while the weather would still allow for it, hasty outings
organized and carried out, one eye on the horizon all the while.

For those who had been putting off visits to the healer in the tiny
hamlet of Backing Fell, a fresh urgency surfaced. Their medical needs
had not seemed particularly pressing before now, being mostly of the
nagging sort, and thoughts of doing anything about them had been
pushed to the side. But with that first snow a fresh attitude surfaced,
and most chose to act while they could to prevent their various conditions and symptoms from blossoming into larger problems when

the snows would prove too difficult an obstacle to overcome and win-
ter might tie them down on their homesteads until spring.

Besides, they genuinely liked the young healer and his wife, even
if they weren't Elves, and barely grown at that, so young they might
have been the children of their patients. In most situations, the healer
might have been dismissed as not yet ready to carry out the demands
of his profession, still in need of further education. What could a
Southlander know of healing and Elves, after all? But these suspicions
were abandoned almost at once. After the first few brave souls visited
and returned with stories of his gentleness and skillful ways, others
quickly took advantage to make their visits, too, and the doubts disappeared.

It was rare to have a healer in such a small community, in any case.
There had been none at all for so long. But the boy healer seemed not
to care about the size of the community or the number of patients it
provided for his practice. He seemed disinterested in larger cities and
more populous regions. This was where he belonged, he insisted
when asked about his choice. This was where he felt most at home.

And that young wife! Now, there was a catch. So lovely, like a
china doll, her features perfect, her skin so pale and unblemished, her
smile warm and she so willing to share it with everyone. She aided
him in his practice, and then took time to bake breads and churn
cream and knit scarves and bonnets for children and old people—all
of it done without charge. She would go out in all kinds of weather to
sit with the sick and injured. She would deliver medicines rather than
have those who needed them make the trip in to where her husband
did his work.

They were a welcome addition to this farming community, to this
scattering of families and neighbors, to the lives of the people of this
vast and empty cropland where helping hands were often the life-
blood needed for survival. This young couple understood. Ask anyone, and they would tell you so.

Two days after the first snowfall, the initial white covering melted
enough to allow for easy passage by foot or wagon or on horseback,
the healing center was packed with fresh patients anticipating more

bad weather all too soon. The young healer was working his way through the complaints and ailments of his patients with good humor and steady hands. Their problems were never challenging in ways he could not fathom or for which he could not find a reasonable solution. He was good at his craft, though how he had perfected it over such a short period of time was something he was careful to keep to himself.

He worked steadily so that he could satisfy all of his patients' needs by day's end and had just finished servicing the last when the door opened and a tall Highlander dressed all in black walked through.

For a second, the young healer did not recognize him. But when he did, he froze where he was, gone cold all through. "How did you find me?"

Paxon Leah shrugged. "It was convincing myself it was worth the effort that took time."

Reyn Frosch moved over and sat down heavily on one of the waiting chairs, clearly shaken. "Is Arcannen still alive?"

Paxon took a seat across from him. "So far as I know. He disappeared again after he finished destroying the Red Slash."

The boy immediately looked uncomfortable. "I don't use magic like that anymore. I never will again. So if you've come to me about that . . ."

"No, I've not come about that."

"What, then? What do you want with me?"

Paxon shrugged. His eyes were tired and his face worn. All the life looked drained out of him. "The woman I was with that last night on the bluff? The Druid? She died there. Arcannen killed her. I was supposed to protect her, and I couldn't manage it. I was the Ard Rhys's Blade, and I couldn't save her. At the time, I thought you and Lariana were dead, too. But something about the way it happened bothered me. To satisfy my curiosity I went back to the bluff to look for your bodies, and there was no sign of them. There should have been something, but there wasn't."

Reyn clasped his hands in front of him. "So you got permission from the Druids to come looking for us?"

"You don't understand. I didn't do this for the Druids. I did this for myself. I wanted to believe that something good had come out of that night. That the terrible destruction I witnessed had a happy ending for someone. It didn't for Avelene, and it didn't for me. It didn't for those men and women of the Red Slash or for Usurient, either."

He leaned forward, suddenly animated. "But what if you and Lariana were still alive? What if you and she had gotten clear and found the life she said you both wanted? If you had, I could take some small measure of satisfaction just in knowing. That's why I came looking for you."

The young healer stared. "What did you tell the Druids when you left to find us?"

"I didn't tell them anything. I asked for time away and they gave it to me. I'm not sure I will go back. I'm not sure I can stay with them after what happened. Avelene's death haunts me. And there was another Druid I was close to who died before her. I may have had enough. I may need to find a different life, something that doesn't involve people dying. I explained this to the Ard Rhys. He wanted to take my sword from me but I wouldn't let him. I told him it belonged to me. In the end he agreed to let me keep it. Of course, he thinks my keeping it will bring me back to Paranor. And he may be right."

They were silent a moment, avoiding each other's eyes. "Do you still use the sword?" Reyn asked finally.

Paxon shook his head, eyes downcast. "I haven't had to. I haven't been in a situation where it was necessary. I would prefer not to have to use it again for the rest of my life." He looked up. "You seem to have been able to do that with the wishsong."

"Not entirely. I use it in my healing practice. But using it that way helps people."

"Then you should keep doing so. I can't say that's true for me."

Reyn looked down again. "You don't think Arcannen might have followed you?"

"No one followed me."

"But he might still be searching for us."

"I don't think so. He doesn't know about the absence of your remains. He fled immediately after. Now he's a hunted man. Everyone in the Four Lands and the entire Druid order is looking for him. He hasn't time to go chasing ghosts."

"Ghosts." Reyn smiled again. "How strange to think of Lariana and me like that, but I guess it's what we are. Ghosts reborn to another life."

At that moment, the door to the healing center opened and Lariana walked through. She was as striking as ever, even dressed in common clothes that were stained and worn. As soon as she caught sight of Paxon, she stopped. "You!"

Paxon held up his hands in a placating gesture. "I'm not here to cause trouble. I came for something else entirely. Reyn can explain it to you."

Which the other did, taking great pains to be certain that all the rough spots were smoothed over and the concerns and fears put to rest. Paxon didn't miss the way he deferred to her as he did so, how solicitous he seemed, as if perhaps his dependence on her exceeded normal boundaries. He supposed it was the result of what Reyn had gone through, but it bothered him nevertheless. It took time and patience for the healer to complete his explanation, but in the end Lariana simply nodded her acceptance and sat down next to him, taking his hands in hers.

But when she looked over at Paxon, her eyes were cold and hard. "Then we won't be seeing you again after this, will we?"

She was every bit as beautiful now as the first time he had seen her, but her protective attitude toward the healer seemed almost dangerous. There was a determination mirrored on her face and evident in her voice that reflected more clearly than words the way she felt about him. The two had made a life for themselves in this remote section of the Westland—a life she had clearly imagined from the beginning and likely had brought to pass in large part through sheer force of will once they escaped Arcannen.

"No, you won't be seeing me again," he affirmed. "It's sufficient for me to know you survived and have a life devoted to helping others."

"It was Lariana who suggested I take up healing," Reyn was quick to point out. "She wanted me to find a constructive way to use my magic. I found that I could, that the magic had a good side to it. I knew I could never go back to singing in taverns and the like. Not with Arcannen and the Druids still out there. I can do more good with it this way in any case, curing sickness, mending bones, giving life back to those who are in danger of losing it . . ."

He trailed off, looking over at his wife for what Paxon believed was approval. "It helps make up for the ways in which I used it before. It gives something back of what I took away."

They were quiet for a moment, all of them, lost in their separate thoughts. Lariana continued to clasp Reyn's hands in her own. He, in turn, leaned against her, head lowered.

Like a puppy, Paxon thought. Like his need for her was so overwhelming, so unabashedly desperate, that he constantly required reaffirmation that she was still there.

He was suddenly troubled by the urgency of it, by the depth of Reyn's dependence on her. In this relationship, she was clearly the dominant party.

He glanced out the window, noted the approaching dark, and rose abruptly. "I have to go. I have another visit to make and a long way to travel to make it. If I learn anything you need to know about Arcannen, I will get word to you."

Reyn and Lariana stood up with him. "You could spend the night," she said quietly. "You could have dinner with us."

"I think it's best that I go." He was suddenly uncomfortable; her attempt at hospitality felt insincere. "I'm happy for you. I'm glad you found a way to start over. This life seems right for you."

"You'll find something, too," Reyn said quickly, as if suddenly wanting to give the Highlander some small reassurance.

"I imagine so." Paxon Leah managed a smile, but it was an effort for him to do so. He didn't believe what he was saying. He didn't think he would ever find the sort of happiness they had found, whatever its true nature. He didn't even think he would ever find any real peace of mind.

The Highlander nodded in farewell and went out the door into the growing dark. He did not look back.

. . .

Reyn Frosch watched him go, his arm still around Lariana, his thoughts tinged with sadness.

"I feel sorry for him," he whispered.

Lariana's gaze was steady and cool. "Don't."

"No?"

She shook her head slowly. "You have to make the best of the life you are given. He hasn't learned that yet. So, no."

"All right. It was just a comment."

"I want you to forget about him. I want you to think about us. This life is ours, not his. He won't be coming back."

"Well, I don't *want* him to come back."

She leaned in and kissed him hard on the mouth. "Listen to me. You and I have our own life to live, our own path to follow. We made this life out of hopes and dreams we shared. The past and those who lived it don't belong. Let them go."

He smiled and nodded. "As long as I have you."

Her eyes found his. "You will always have me. Always."

She would make him feel even more certain of it that night when she told him she was carrying his child.

Paxon Leah returned to the Sprint he had left at the edge of Backing Fell when he had walked out to the healing center. It was the one he had built for himself years ago when he was still living in Wayford and running shipping for a living, knowing nothing of the magic of the Sword of Leah. He had left his airship behind when he went to live and train with the Druids. But after leaving the order he had gone home to retrieve it and begin his search for Reyn and Lariana.

He had been lucky, really, to find them. He had started with nothing but his hope that they had survived. He had considered asking the Druids to use the scrye waters to discover if he was right but had decided against it. Doing so would necessarily have required that he reveal what he was looking for, and he didn't want to do that.

So he had resorted to intuition, common sense, and five months of flying to places he thought they might go to hide. He talked to hundreds of people, investigated dozens of dead ends, listened to his heart, and constantly reminded himself how much this could end up meaning to him. He was beaten down and despairing of his life and its purpose. All the hopes he had harbored when becoming the Ard Rhys's Blade lay shattered beneath the Horn of Honor on those burial grounds. He kept telling himself that it would make a difference if something good could come out of all the carnage Arcannen had created. It would matter if the boy and the girl had found a happy ending.

He had gotten lucky, of course. An old man in a village not far from Backing Fell, in a chance encounter at a tavern on a deeply silent and frosty night, had sat across from him as he told his story and recognized his description of the girl. A young couple, he said, recently come to a nearby village—she as beautiful as a new snowfall, he newly a healer of special skills. They could be the ones the Highlander was looking for.

And so they were. But now that he had found them, he found himself wondering exactly what it was he had found. Not the fairy-tale ending he had wanted. Theirs was a complex and personal relationship that he was not meant to understand. Certainly, it did not feel as warm and wonderful as he had hoped. There was an undercurrent of dominance and subjection that had left him feeling chilled and disappointed. It had not brought him the satisfaction he had sought. Instead, he was adrift again, his long search ended, its particular purpose fulfilled, but his peace of mind not yet found and the rest of his life a story still unwritten.

Oddly, it was the nature of his disappointment that gave him fresh direction. It was the conclusion to one search that had revealed to him that he must undertake another. One more visit was needed to complete what he had come to perceive as not so much a quest to learn how the lives of Reyn Frosch and Lariana had turned out as a journey of self-discovery.

He flew east again for a few hours, not wanting to linger in Backing Fell, even though he was immensely tired, knowing that his presence would only make Reyn and Lariana more uncomfortable than they already were. Better to press on to another place so they could begin the process of consigning him to a back corner of their lives once more. Better they should start to forget him again as soon as possible.

He set down on the easternmost edge of the Sarandanon, where he slept the night inside his vessel, a blanket pulled around him, the sky above him bright with moon and stars. Before he slept, he thought of Chrysallin, still back at Paranor in the care of the Druids, and wondered what he was going to do about her. Before he had left, he had told her that he was going away, that he was taking time to go on a personal quest.

"What sort of quest?" she had asked at once. "This is because of Avelene, isn't it?"

She was always so smart. "Because of Avelene and Starks and the way I feel about myself just now. Will you be all right?"

She had given him that familiar look, the one that suggested he ought to know better than to ask such a question. "I think I might be more all right than you are. Why are you doing this, Paxon? Can't you find what you need here? Like I did?"

"It's not the same with me as it was with you, Chrys. Paranor became a sanctuary for you. For me, it was supposed to supply a direction. But now I wonder if perhaps I've taken a wrong turn. I have to find that out."

"But how will you do that? Where will you go to find the answer?"

"I'll go where I have to, I guess." He had embraced her and kissed her forehead. "Don't worry. I won't forget about you."

She had grabbed him by his arms and held him away from her. "I am stronger than I was before I came here. You know that. Just be careful for yourself. Try to remember that your friends did not die because of you."

He had been uncertain about his decision then and he was uncertain about it now. Chrysallin had inherited the wishsong, and she would find out, sooner or later. Aphenglow Elessedil had insisted it would happen, and he was no longer inclined to dispute her conclusions. Something would cause it to surface—a trauma, a memory, or simply chance. But something. She would need to be ready for it when it happened, and he had come to believe that meant telling her the truth about her inheritance of its magic.

In part, this had happened through research he had undertaken on his return from Arishaig. Avelene had done much of the work already, but now he felt he needed to do some as well. With Keratrix to help him gain access, he had begun studying the Druid Histories, searching for links with the past that might tell him something of how the wishsong had evolved.

What he had found had given him the first clues about what might be true, but he was still puzzling it through, still considering the possibilities.

Whatever happened as a result of his wanderings, he knew he would have to return to Paranor long enough do something about his sister. He couldn't just leave her with the order. If the magic manifested itself anew, they might never let her leave. They might choose to try to turn her to their own purposes. Perhaps they might genuinely believe it was the best thing for her. But they would be fully aware, too, of how much it would help them to have a user of such powerful magic as a member of the order.

It was an unpleasant conclusion, but an inescapable one.

When morning came, with dawn a misty gray light and a harsh cold wind blowing out of the north suggesting the firm possibility of further snow on the horizon, he set out anew. He flew from the Westland into the Tirfing, the grasslands still green and fresh below him but the air bitter with heavy clouds rolling in, and then he continued through the remainder of the day to the Borderlands before turning south.

By nightfall, he had reached the city of Wayford and landed his vessel at the public airfield. As he climbed out of the pilot box he found himself searching for Grehling Cara, but a man he didn't know was taking the night watch this evening. It was just as well, Paxon told himself as he gave his Sprint over to the other's care. He still wasn't sure about what he was doing, and he didn't want to have to talk about it with anyone.

He walked off the airfield and into the city proper. It was early still, the taverns and eating establishments doing a brisk business and the pleasure houses just opening their doors. People moved in knots through the crowded streets, maneuvering for position as carts, carriages, and riders on horses all pushed their way through to wherever they were going. Laughter and shouts rang out from every quarter, and there was an air of joyful expectation in their sounds.

Paxon took it all in, but kept his purpose fixed and his pace steady as he passed on. Eventually, he moved into a district of shops and food stalls, and then he was on the street he had come to find. Everything was very quiet and still; there were few people, and the windows of the shops were dark and shuttered. As he walked up the street, his pace slowed. He was preparing himself for what he would find, for how he would be received. He had hopes, but no expectations. Expectations now would only make his disappointment sharper. He knew how things might have gone. He understood that time and chance both might have passed him by.

When he reached her door, he hesitated. He stood there for several minutes, trying to decide whether to turn around and walk away. It was still possible to do so. It might be better, in fact. In spite of what he had come to do, in spite of the distance he had traveled to do it, it might be the wiser choice.

He lifted his hand to the iron knocker and then dropped it, filled with indecision.

What am I doing?

Then, abruptly, the door opened, and Leofur Rai stood there looking at him.

He waited for her to say something, but she just stared, arms folded across her breasts. She looked the same—brilliant green eyes, honey-colored hair with silver streaks, intense no-nonsense gaze.

"I . . . couldn't decide about this," he said finally.

She faced him in silence, waiting.

He straightened. "I came here because I had to see you. I had to tell you how wrong I've been. I'm about as unhappy as I could possibly be, and I know it's due in no small part to having stayed away from you. I should have come before now. I thought to do so countless times—more times than I care to think about—but the longer I waited, the harder it got and finally I couldn't make myself do it."

She still did not speak, but she nodded.

"Something bad happened. Something so terrible that it caused me to consider leaving the Druid order. It made me rethink everything. Maybe I should have done so sooner—I don't know. I've been looking for answers, but I haven't found them yet. I've been on a sort of identity quest. I know I'm not making sense; I can't seem to find the words. The point is, it led me here. It opened my eyes. I know now I will never be happy without you. I will never be complete. I realize that. And I know it's probably too late for us, but I had to come say it all anyway. I owed you that much. And I had to find out. About us. Because I'm hoping there's still a chance we can be together."

He paused, the pain of his emotions sharp in his chest. "Leofur, I love you. I think I always have. I know I always will."

She watched him a moment longer. Then she unfolded her arms and reached for his hand and squeezed it. "Maybe you better come inside, Paxon," she said, her face expressionless. "We might need a little time to work this out."

His hopes came to life, the glow in his heart warm and bright as he stepped through her door.

Terry Brooks is the *New York Times* bestselling author of more than thirty books, including the Dark Legacy of Shannara adventures *Wards of Faerie, Bloodfire Quest,* and *Witch Wraith;* the Legends of Shannara novels *Bearers of the Black Staff* and *The Measure of the Magic;* the Genesis of Shannara trilogy: *Armageddon's Children, The Elves of Cintra,* and *The Gypsy Morph; The Sword of Shannara;* the Voyage of the *Jerle Shannara* trilogy: *Ilse Witch, Antrax,* and *Morgawr;* the High Druid of Shannara trilogy: *Jarka Ruus, Tanequil,* and *Straken;* the nonfiction book *Sometimes the Magic Works: Lessons from a Writing Life;* and the novel based upon the screenplay and story by George Lucas, *Star Wars*: Episode I *The Phantom Menace.* His novels *Running with the Demon* and *A Knight of the Word* were selected by the *Rocky Mountain News* as two of the best science fiction/fantasy novels of the twentieth century. The author was a practicing attorney for many years but now writes full-time. He lives with his wife, Judine, in the Pacific Northwest.

www.shannara.com

www.terrybrooks.net

Find out more about Terry Brooks and other Orbit authors by signing up for the free monthly newsletter at www.orbitbooks.net.

ABOUT THE TYPE

This book was set in Minion, a 1990 Adobe Originals typeface by Robert Slimbach (b. 1956). Minion is inspired by classical, old-style typefaces of the late Renaissance, a period of elegant, beautiful, and highly readable type designs. Created primarily for text setting, Minion combines the aesthetic and functional qualities that make text type highly readable with the versatility of digital technology.

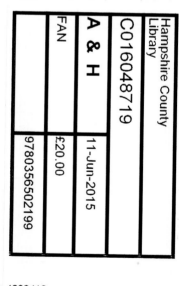

SHANNARA
the
FOUR LANDS

SOUTHLAND

WESTLAND

HOAR FLATS

KERRSHALT TERRITO

Breakline Mts.

The Fangs

Breakline Mts.

Kensrow Mts.

Worl Run

Basin Draw

Halys Cut

Syioned

Streleheim Plains

Arborlon

Emberen

Valley of Rhenn

Sarandanon Valley

Drey Wood

Matted Brakes

Pykon

Grimpen Ward

Whistle Ridge

Spires Reach

Shroudslip

Hollows

GRASSLANDS
OF THE
TIRFING

CALLAHO

Korn

Rock Spur Mts.

Irrybis Mts.

Bakrabru

Myrian Lake

Wing Hove

WEEKS

ARTWORK BY